Once Again A Bride

JANE ASHFORD

sourcebooks
casablanca

Published by Sourcebooks Casablanca, an imprint of Sourcebooks, Inc.
P.O. Box 4410, Naperville, Illinois 60567-4410
(630) 961-3900
FAX: (630) 961-2168
www.sourcebooks.com

Printed and bound in the United States of America
RRD 10 9 8 7 6 5 4 3 2

One

CHARLOTTE RUTHERFORD WYLDE CLOSED HER EYES and enjoyed the sensation of the brush moving rhythmically through her long hair. Lucy had been her maid since she was eleven years old and was well aware that her mistress's lacerated feelings needed soothing. The whole household was aware, no doubt, but only Lucy cared. The rest of the servants had a hundred subtle, unprovable ways of intensifying the laceration. It had become a kind of sport for them, Charlotte believed, growing more daring as the months passed without reprimand, denied with a practiced blankness that made her doubly a fool.

Lucy stopped brushing and began to braid Charlotte's hair for the night. Charlotte opened her eyes and faced up to the dressing table mirror. Candlelight gleamed on the creamy lace of her nightdress, just visible under the heavy dressing gown that protected her from drafts. Her bedchamber was cold despite the fire on this bitter March night. Every room in this tall, narrow London house was cold. Cold in so many different ways.

She ought to be changed utterly by these months,

Charlotte thought. But the mirror showed her hair of the same coppery gold, eyes the same hazel—though without any hint of the sparkle that had once been called alluring. Her familiar oval face, straight nose, and full lips had been judged pretty a scant year, and a lifetime, ago. She was perhaps too thin, now that each meal was an ordeal. There were dark smudges under her eyes, and they looked hopelessly back at her like those of a trapped animal. She remembered suddenly a squirrel she had found one long-ago winter—frozen during a terrible cold snap that had turned the countryside hard and bitter. It had lain on its side in the snow, its legs poised as if running from icy death.

"There you are, Miss Charlotte." Lucy put a comforting hand on her shoulder. When they were alone, she always used the old familiar form of address. It was a futile but comforting pretense. "Can I get you anything…?"

"No, thank you, Lucy." Charlotte tried to put a world of gratitude into her tone as she repeated, "Thank you."

"You should get into bed. I warmed the sheets."

"I will. In a moment. You go on to bed yourself."

"Are you sure I can't…?"

"I'm all right."

Neither of them believed it. Lucy pressed her lips together on some reply, then sketched a curtsy and turned to go. Slender, yet solid as a rock, her familiar figure was such a comfort that Charlotte almost called her back. But Lucy deserved her sleep. She shouldn't be deprived just because Charlotte expected none.

The door opened and closed. The candles guttered

and steadied. Charlotte sat on, rehearsing thoughts and plans she had already gone over a hundred times. There must be something she could do, some approach she could discover to make things—if not right, at least better. Not hopeless, not unendurable.

Her father—her dear, scattered, and now departed father—had done his best. She had to believe that. Tears came as she thought of him; when he died six months ago, he'd no longer remembered who she was. The brutal erosion of his mind, his most prized possession, had been complete.

It had happened so quickly. Yes, he'd always been distracted, so deep in his scholarly work that practicalities escaped him. But in his library, reading and writing, corresponding with other historians, he'd never lost or mistaken the smallest detail. Until two years ago, when the insidious slide began—unnoticed, dismissed, denied until undeniable. Then he had set all his fading faculties on getting her "safely" married. That one idea had obsessed and sustained him as all else slipped away. Perforce, he'd looked among his own few friends and acquaintances for a groom. Why, why had he chosen Henry Wylde?

In her grief and fear, Charlotte had put up no protest. She'd even been excited by the thought of moving from her isolated country home to the city, with all its diversions and amusements. And so, at age eighteen, she'd been married to a man almost thirty years older. Had she imagined it would be some sort of eccentric fairy tale? How silly and ignorant had she been? She couldn't remember now.

It wasn't all stupidity; unequal matches need not

be disastrous. She had observed a few older husbands who treated their young wives with every appearance of delight and appreciation. Not quite so much older, perhaps. But... from the day after the wedding, Henry had treated her like a troublesome pupil foisted upon his household for the express purpose of irritating him. He criticized everything she did. Just this morning, at breakfast, he had accused her of forgetting his precise instructions on how to brew his tea. She had *not* forgotten, not one single fussy step; she had carefully counted out the minutes in her head—easily done because Henry allowed no conversation at breakfast. He always brought a book. She was sure she had timed it exactly right, and still he railed at her for ten minutes, in front of the housemaid. She had ended up with the knot in her stomach and lump in her throat that were her constant companions now. The food lost all appeal.

If her husband did talk to her, it was most often about Tiberius or Hadrian or some other ancient. He spent his money—quite a lot of money, she suspected, and most of it hers—and all his affection on his collections. The lower floor of the house was like a museum, filled with cases of Roman coins and artifacts, shelves of books about Rome. For Henry, these things were important, and she, emphatically, was not.

After nearly a year of marriage, Charlotte still felt like a schoolgirl. It might have been different if there were a chance of children, but her husband seemed wholly uninterested in the process of getting them. And by this time, the thought of any physical contact with him repelled Charlotte so completely that she didn't know what she would do if he suddenly changed his mind.

She stared into the mirror, watching the golden candle flames dance, feeling the drafts caress the back of her neck, seeing her life stretch out for decades in this intolerable way. It had become quite clear that it would drive her mad. And so, she had made her plan. Henry avoided her during the day, and she could not speak to him at meals, with the prying eyes of servants all around them. After dinner, he went to his club and stayed until she had gone to bed. So she would not go to bed. She would stay up and confront him, no matter how late. She would insist on changes.

She had tried waiting warm under the bedclothes but had failed to stay awake for two nights. Last night, she'd fallen asleep in the armchair and missed her opportunity. Tonight, she would sit up straight on the dressing table stool with no possibility of slumber. She rose and set the door ajar, ignoring the increased draft this created. She could see the head of the stairs from here; he could not get by her. She would thrash it out tonight, no matter what insults he flung at her. The memory of that cold, dispassionate voice reciting her seemingly endless list of faults made her shiver, but she would not give up.

The candles fluttered and burned down faster. Charlotte waited, jerking upright whenever she started to nod off. Once, she nearly fell off the backless stool. But she endured, hour after hour, into the deeps of the night. She replaced the stubs of the candles. She added coals to the fire, piled on another heavy shawl against the chill. She rubbed her hands together to warm them, gritted her teeth, and held on until light showed in the crevices of the draperies and birds began to twitter outside. Another day had dawned, and Henry Wylde had not come home. Her husband had spent the night elsewhere.

Pulling her shawls closer, Charlotte contemplated this stupefying fact. The man she saw as made of ice had a secret life? He kept a mistress? He drank himself into insensibility and collapsed at his club? He haunted the gaming hells with feverish wagers? Impossible to picture any of these things. But she had never waited up so long before. She had no idea what he did with his nights.

Chilled to the bone, she rose, shut the bedroom door, and crawled into her cold bed. She needed to get warm; she needed to decide if she could use this new information to change the bitter circumstances of her life. Perhaps Henry was not completely without feelings, as she had thought. Her eyelids drooped. Perhaps there was hope.

❧

Lucy Bowman tested the temperature of a flatiron she'd set heating on the hearth. It hissed obligingly. Satisfied, she carried it to a small cloth-draped table in the corner of the kitchen and applied it to the frill of a cambric gown. She was good at fine ironing, and she liked being good at things. She also liked—these days—doing her work in the hours when most of the staff was elsewhere. This early, the cook and scullery maid had just begun to prepare breakfast. Barely out of bed, and sullen with it, they didn't speak. Not that there ever was much conversation in this house—and none of it the easy back-and-forth of the servants' hall in Hampshire.

The Rutherford manor had been a very heaven compared to this place. Everyone below stairs got along; they'd gone together to church fetes and dances and formed up a kind of family. For certain, the old housekeeper had been a second mother to her. When Lucy'd arrived, sent into service at twelve to save her parents a mouth to feed, Mrs. Beckham had welcomed her and looked after her. She'd been the first person ever to tell Lucy that she was smart and capable and had a chance to make something of herself. Thinking of her, and of that household, comforted and hurt at the same time.

Lucy eased the iron around an embroidered placket, enjoying the crisp scent of starched cloth rising in the steam. She'd made a place for herself in Hampshire, starting in the laundry and working her way up, learning all she could as fast as she could, with kindly training. She'd been so proud to be chosen as Miss Charlotte's lady's maid eight years ago. Mrs. Beckham had told her straight out, in front of the others, how well she'd done, called her an example for the younger staff. It had warmed her right down to her toes to see them smiling at her, glad for her advancement.

And now it was all gone. The house sold, the people she'd known retired or scattered to other positions, and none of them much for letters. Well, she wasn't either, as far as that went. But she couldn't even pretend she'd be back in that house, in the country, one day.

Not that she'd ever leave Miss Charlotte alone

in this terrible place. Lucy put her head down and maneuvered the iron around a double frill.

Mr. Hines tromped in, heavy-eyed and growling for tea. A head on him, no doubt, from swilling his way through another evening. Cook's husband, who called himself the butler, was really just a man of all work. Lucy had seen a proper butler, and that he was not. What he was was a raw-boned, tight-mouthed package of sheer meanness. Lucy stayed well out of his way. It was no wonder Cook was short-tempered, shackled to a bear like him. As for the young women on the staff who might have been her friends, both the scullery maid and the housemaid were slow-witted and spiritless. If you tried to talk to them—which she didn't, not anymore—they mostly stared like they didn't understand plain English. And if that wasn't enough, the valet Holcombe took every chance to put a sneaky hand where it didn't belong. Him, she outright despised. Every word he said to her was obviously supposed to mean something different. The ones she understood were disgusting. She'd spent some of her own wages on a bolt for her bedroom door because of him. Couldn't ask Miss Charlotte for the money because she didn't need another worry, did she?

The iron had cooled. She exchanged it for another that had been heating near the coals and deftly pressed the scalloped sleeve of a morning dress. The rising warmth on her face was welcome, though the kitchen was the most tolerable room in this cold house. She had to pile on blankets until she felt like a clothes press to sleep warm.

The scullery maid brushed past her on the way to

the pantry. "Mort o' trouble for a gown no one'll see," she said.

Lucy ignored her. Any remark the staff made to her was carping, about her work or her mistress, though they'd eased up on that when they saw they weren't going to cause any trouble. But they baited and humiliated Miss Charlotte something terrible. It still shocked Lucy after all this time. She couldn't quite give up expecting *him*—she refused to name the master of this house—to step in and stop them. But he was a pure devil; he seemed to enjoy it. Lucy liked to understand a problem and find a solution for it if she any way could, but there was nothing to be done about this pure disaster of a marriage.

Holcombe surged into the kitchen. He'd be after early morning tea for *him,* and nothing in the world more important, in his book. Lucy turned her back and concentrated on her ironing. "Have you seen Mr. Henry?" he asked. "Hines?"

"Why would I?" was the sullen reply from the man sitting at the kitchen table.

Holcombe stood frowning for a moment, then hurried out—without any tea. Which was strange, and interesting. Lucy eyed the others. They showed no signs of curiosity. As far as she'd been able to tell over the months, they didn't have any.

The scent of porridge wafted from the hearth, and Lucy's stomach growled. Mrs. Hines could make a decent porridge, at least. She wasn't good at much else. On the other hand, *he* ordered such bland dishes that it was hardly worth any bother.

Holcombe popped back in. "Hines, come with

me," he said. The cook's husband grumbled but pushed up from his chair and obeyed. This was one of the things that showed Hines wasn't a real butler. He snapped to when the valet spoke in that particular tone and did as he was told. The two men left the kitchen, and they didn't come back.

Something was up, Lucy thought. *He* next to worshipped his routines, threw a fit if any little detail was altered. Despite months of grinding frustration, she felt a shred of hope. Any difference had to be for the better, didn't it? She took her finished ironing and headed upstairs to see what she could see before waking her mistress.

❧

When Lucy pulled back the curtains, Charlotte swam slowly up from her belated sleep. Her memory sputtered and cleared. She sat up. "You should have told me, Lucy."

"Told you what, Miss Charlotte?"

"That Henry spends nights away from home. The knowledge could hardly hurt my feelings at this point."

"Away…?"

"Come, Lucy, the household knows these things."

"They don't talk to me." Was this it then? *He* hadn't come home last night?

"I know they haven't befriended you, but there must be gossip…"

"Never, miss. I don't know what you're talking about." Lucy opened the wardrobe and surveyed the row of gowns. "Except… Mr. Holcombe's in a right taking this morning."

Charlotte threw back the covers. "I'll dress at once and see him."

"You know he don't like to be…"

"I don't care." And she didn't. Not a whit. Holcombe might be the most insolent of all the servants, but Charlotte was finished with being cowed.

She hurried Lucy through their morning routine. She would demand that Holcombe appear, and if he refused, she would hunt him down wherever he lurked and force him to tell her the truth. Chin up, eyes steely, Charlotte marched out of her bedchamber and down the hall. In what passed for a drawing room in this house, she jerked the bellpull. Minutes ticked by; no one answered the summons. Charlotte rang again, then gave it up and started for the stairs.

A heavy knock fell on the front door; it sounded as if someone were striking it with a stick. Charlotte looked over the banister. The knock came again, echoing through the house. Who could be calling at this hour?

The housemaid hurried out and began to undo the bolts. Charlotte heard the swinging door at the back of the hall and knew that other servants were behind her. The front door swung open.

"Miss," said a deep voice from the stoop. "Is there a gen'lmun at home pr'haps?"

Charlotte hurried down the stairs.

"Who wants to know?" demanded Holcombe, surging out of the back hall.

"It's the watch," replied the deep voice. "Are you…?"

Charlotte moved faster. "I am the mistress of this house," she said, more for Holcombe's benefit than the visitor's. "My husband is apparently not at home." A glance at Holcombe showed him pale and anxious, completely unlike the snake who delighted in taunting her. Charlotte turned her attention to the burly individual on her doorstep. Bearded, in a long stuff coat and fingerless gloves, he looked like any of the men who patrolled the streets of London. His staff was tall beside him.

"Ma'am," he said, shifting uneasily from foot to foot. "Er…"

"Is there a problem?"

The man held out a visiting card, which seemed so incongruous that Charlotte just stared at it. "I wonder if you might recognize that, ma'am?"

She took the small pasteboard square and read it. "This is my husband's card."

"Ah." The watchman didn't seem surprised. "Might you want to sit down, ma'am?"

"Just tell us what has happened!" exclaimed Holcombe, typically ignoring her authority, her very existence.

"Yes, please tell us," Charlotte agreed.

The man on the step stood straighter. "Regret to inform you, ma'am, that there has been an… incident. A gent'lmun was found earlier this morning. His purse was missing, but he had a card case in his waistcoat pocket. That there card was inside it."

"But… what happened? Is he hurt? Where have you taken…?"

"Sorry, ma'am." The visitor grimaced, looking as if he wished very much to be elsewhere. "Regret to tell you, the gent'lmun is dead. Footpads, looks like. Caught him as he was…"

"Dead?" Somehow, Lucy was at Charlotte's elbow, supporting her. "But how... are you sure? I cannot believe..."

The man shuffled his feet. "Somebody must come and identify him for sartain, ma'am. Mebbe a...?"

"I shall go!" interrupted Holcombe. He glared at Charlotte, at the watchman, at the other servants. No one argued with him. The watchman looked relieved.

They all stood in stunned silence as Holcombe ran for his coat and departed with the watch. Charlotte never remembered afterward how she got back up to the drawing room, only that she was sitting there when Lucy entered some indeterminate time later and said, "It's him. He's dead."

Charlotte half rose. "Holcombe is...?"

"He's back with the news. Right cut up, he is." Lucy's lip curled.

"Henry is dead?" She couldn't help repeating it.

"Seems he is, Miss Charlotte. Happens more often than we had any notion, Holcombe says. Streets aren't half safe, after dark. London!" Lucy knew that many people saw the city as thrilling, with every sort of goods and amusement on offer. She hated the filth and the noise—wheels clattering, people shouting at you to buy this or that from the moment you stepped into the street. Strangers shoving past if you walked too slow. She had discounted Holcombe's horror stories, however. He enjoyed scaring the scullery maid out of the few wits she possessed with tales of hapless servants who wandered into the wrong part of town and never came out. Lucy had refused to show any fear just to irk him. Now it seemed he was right, after all.

Charlotte sank back onto the sofa. She hadn't wanted this, not anything like this. She'd longed for change, but she'd never wished…

"Can I get you something? Tea? You haven't eaten a crumb."

"I couldn't."

"You have to eat."

"Not now."

Lucy bowed her head at the tension in her voice. "Shall I sit with you?"

"No. No, I'd like to be alone for a while."

Lucy hesitated, then bobbed a curtsy and went out. Charlotte folded her hands tightly together, pressed her elbows to her sides. This wasn't change; this was life violently turned upside down. This was the fabric of daily existence ripped right in two.

She hadn't ever loved Henry. She had tried to like him, almost thought she did, before he made that impossible. In these last months, she hadn't hated him, had she? No, she hadn't gone that far. She had wished, over and over, that he had never entered her life. But she hadn't wished him dead. Yesterday, at about this time, he had been haranguing her about his tea, and now he was removed from the face of the earth. How could this be?

Two

Sir Alexander Wylde rode into the stable yard behind his town house feeling, as usual, that a morning ride in London was the definition of constriction. Small landscapes, slow gaits, and the tedious interruption of acknowledging acquaintances who also chose to ride early. It was almost, almost, worse than no ride at all.

Leaving his horse with the groom, he entered through the back door. He had taken only two steps along the corridor when he heard a crash in the upper regions, followed by pounding footsteps and inarticulate cries, and then a thump, as if some largish piece of furniture had toppled over. Another man might have started in alarm or run toward the stairs, but Alec merely frowned and walked a little faster. His main emotion was disappointment; Lizzy had promised.

He had to climb two flights to discover the source of the uproar. On the way he passed a housemaid with an apron full of broken china; she avoided his gaze. Frances Cole stood outside Anne's bedchamber wringing her hands.

The moment she saw him, she began to wail. "The

creature is filthy and vicious. It is absolutely out of the question. This is too much, Alec! She has gone too far!" The latter phrase had become something of a refrain in the last few months, since Lizzy's third governess had decamped. "I will not go in there," Frances added half hysterically.

Frances, a cousin of Alec's mother, had had the main charge of Anne and Lizzy since their mother died soon after Lizzy's birth, an arrangement that seemed to be rapidly breaking down.

Alec opened the bedchamber door and stepped inside. For some reason, Frances pushed the panels closed practically on his heels. He discovered his sixteen-year-old sister Anne lying in her bed, still pale but no longer so frighteningly listless. In fact, there was a bit of the old sparkle in her green eyes. He had brought his whole household up to town this spring because of Anne, who had coughed her way into increasing weakness through the winter. Nothing seemed to help, and he had finally bundled her into a carriage filled with blankets and furs and hot bricks to consult an eminent Harley Street physician. Just yesterday they had gotten the very good news that it was not consumption, a dread that had been hovering over them all for weeks. He suspected that relief was partly behind this latest ruckus, whatever it was. "Where is…?"

Lizzy popped up from behind the bed. "I got her to cheer Anne up," she declared self-righteously.

"I'm all right, Alec," Anne said at the same time.

With the ease of long practice, Alec went to the heart of the matter. "Her?"

From beneath the bed came a sound remarkably

like a growl. Alec looked at Lizzy. It was a bitter-sweet irony that his thirteen-year-old sister so closely resembled their mother, as her birth had caused Lady Wylde's final illness. Alec, Anne, and their brother Richard took after their tall, lean father, with wheat-colored hair and green eyes. Lizzy was shorter, already rounder, with their mother's brunette coloring and deep blue eyes. He suspected she was going to be breathtakingly lovely when she got her full growth, and the thought of her eventual entry into society—when he dared think of it—terrified him.

There was no putting it off any longer. Alec knelt and peered under the bed. At first, he saw nothing. Then he became aware of a pair of yellow eyes glowing in the farthest, darkest corner. A gamy smell reached his nostrils. Gradually, the shape in the shadows revealed itself as a cat, a large cat. A sinking sensation, based on more than a decade's experience, settled over him. "Where did you find it?"

"In the back garden, near the gate," replied Lizzy.

An alley cat. Alec could not imagine how his sister had gotten this animal into the house and up the stairs. No doubt the crashes he'd heard were involved. He checked her for bites and scratches, and saw none.

"We have no pets at all here in town," Lizzy pointed out. "Anne misses them so much."

Alec looked at Anne. She was trying not to smile, well aware of her big brother's descent into Lizzy's toils. "Does Anne indeed?" Of course it was Lizzy who missed them. "Animals belong in the country."

"Lots of people have dogs in town. I've seen them. Fashionable people."

They had small fluffy lapdogs, Alec thought; yappy, annoying, but not creatures spawned in the gutter. "If Anne would like a kitten…" It sounded weak, and he knew it. But Anne's smiles were so rare these days.

"But she has no home. She's hungry; you can feel all her ribs!"

A pleasure Alec hoped never to experience. "Lizzy, it's a practically wild animal. Who knows what sort of…?"

"I know she smells a bit," Lizzy interrupted. "Well, who wouldn't, being out in the street like that? I'm going to give her a bath."

"You most certainly are not! She'll tear you to pieces."

"No, she won't. Here, look." Lizzy disappeared behind the bed. Alec stood and watched her, kneeling, hold out a hand and make a soft, low sound. There was a pause, and then the cat half emerged from under the counterpane. It was a calico, dirty, skinny, with a torn ear, but it pushed its head under his little sister's hand for stroking. "See?" Lizzy gave him the angelic smile that all too often got her her way.

Alec took a step toward them. The cat drew back and growled like some much larger creature.

"She just has to get used to you. Don't you, Callie? I've named her Callie, for calico, you see."

Anne laughed—at the name or perhaps at Alec's looming defeat. It hardly mattered; it had been far too long since he'd heard her laugh. Alec stepped back and wondered which of the two footmen could be recruited to help Lizzy bathe a feral feline. It would have to be Ethan. Ethan had time and again proved himself up to anything. Alec would sacrifice his leather driving gloves to the enterprise. "All right," he conceded. "Just as long as…"

Lizzy leapt up and flew to hug him. "You are the very best brother in the world!" Anne laughed again, her eyes dancing when he smiled at her. Alec became aware of a painful tightness in the center of his chest— hope. Then Anne's laugh turned to a hacking cough, and his spirits sank once again.

Though Alec's university days had been cut short by his father's death, when all the responsibilities of family and property had devolved upon him, those tasks had not seemed onerous until this winter. He had left Anne and Lizzy to Frances; kept an occasional eye on his brother Richard, currently cutting a carefree swath at Oxford; and managed the estates without undue effort. He was well trained for the role that had always been his future and had found ample time to establish himself in town during the Season and enjoy the many pleasures available to a man of wealth and station. For four years, all had run smoothly; then Anne's illness descended, upset his routines, and showed him where his real priorities lay. Nothing came before his family.

Anne got her cough under control. "I'm all right," she insisted, only too aware of her siblings' worries.

"If that animal makes you worse…"

Lizzy's deep blue eyes filled with tears. Despair showed in every line of her face and body. "If Callie makes Anne sick, of course she cannot stay."

"It isn't the cat," Anne said, so weary she was angry with them both. "I was coughing long before she arrived."

Lizzy brightened. "Once she's clean, she can sit on your bed and keep you company, as I do."

"Bring her along then." Alec could see the fatigue. Over the last few months, it had become horribly familiar and frighteningly obdurate. They needed to leave and let Anne rest. He ushered Lizzy out—her arms overflowing with cat. Frances had disappeared, a new habit of hers. As he went ahead to inform Ethan the footman of his fate, the only bright spot he could see was the certainty that, like all cats, this one would undoubtedly object to a bath. With any luck, it would run away. And he would not be hunting it through the London streets, no matter how much Lizzy cajoled.

Cravenly, Alec snatched bread and sausages from the breakfast room and retreated to his study, safely distant from cat bathing mayhem and the reproaches of Frances Cole, or of the housekeeper who had known him since he was three years old. He had every excuse; his desk was piled with pleas from his Derbyshire tenants for reassurance and assistance.

Many had expected the state of the country to improve with the end of the long war against Napoleon, but not those who saw the new textile machinery putting more and more people out of work and watched rising food prices threaten Englishmen— Englishmen!—with starvation. Alec's jaw tightened. Not on his land. He could not, like some landowners he knew, ignore such distress.

As he took a letter from the top of the pile, Alec had to restrain a sigh. Perhaps he should find someone to help with the cascade of correspondence. Lately, there seemed no end to the tasks that must be done, the decisions that could not wait. There were men—he knew them—who would toss this stack of paper into the fire and go in search of their own amusement without a thought of consequences. Alec opened the first letter and began to read.

He'd gotten through half the pile and begun to think of luncheon when Ethan knocked and entered the room. "There is a person to see you, sir."

Alec observed a long scratch on the footman's right cheek. "A person?"

"A matter of business, he says." Before Alec could respond, he added, "Your gloves... I'm sorry, sir, but..."

Alec held up a hand. "I never expected to see them again, Ethan."

The young footman looked relieved. "Er, the animal? Well, it's clean." He looked dubious. "Seems quite... fond of Miss Elizabeth."

Alec decided he didn't really want to know any more about the cat. "All right, bring this person in."

Ethan returned with a small, elderly man whose stance and somber dress proclaimed solicitor or man of business. For some reason, he wore his hat and greatcoat, as if still in the street. Beside the tall broad-shouldered footman, he looked tiny. "Mr. Seaton," Ethan announced, and closed the door.

The wizened man surged into the room. "I fear I bring you shocking news, Sir Alexander." He shook his head, thin lips turned down. "Shocking."

Alec came to his feet. "My brother?"

The snap of the words startled his visitor into taking a step back. "No, no, I know nothing of your brother. It is your uncle."

"Lord Earnton?" Even as he said it, Alec knew that

his aunt would send someone he knew to impart any significant news.

Seaton drew himself up. "Sir Alexander, I regret to tell you that your uncle, Henry Wylde, has been killed by footpads. In the very streets of London. Another outrageous example of the degradation of the lower classes. I blame the government…"

"Uncle Henry?" It felt odd even to call him that. For as long as Alec could remember, his father's youngest brother had been practically a recluse. He never appeared at family gatherings or showed the least interest in any of his relations. Alec's only real memory of him was nearly twenty years old—of a red-faced, cursing man who threatened him with a caning when he touched some dusty artifact in a case. He sank back into his chair. "Killed?"

"Murdered, sir, as he walked home from his club. I don't know what this country is coming to when a gentleman cannot even…"

"And you have brought me word of this," Alec interrupted.

"Naturally."

"As a family member. I see. Thank you."

The grizzled man stared at him. "As the executor of Mr. Wylde's will."

"I?"

Seaton pulled a thick document from his coat pocket. "He said you were the best of his idio… er… relations."

In other circumstances, Alec might have been amused, but he was too much astonished. "I barely knew the man."

Seaton nodded. "He mentioned that he was not in

close touch with his family. Nonetheless, he wished these final matters to be handled by kin."

And he had to choose me, Alec thought, but did not say. "Please sit down, Mr. Seaton."

The man did so, placing the document on the edge of the desk. "As you know, Mr. Wylde was a... unique individual. And I must say his will is... eccentric."

How could it be otherwise? Alec thought. He waited for the bad news that he was somehow sure was coming.

"The provision it makes for his wife is not what one would..."

"Wife? He wasn't married."

"Indeed he was, sir. Recently, in the last year."

Alec tried to imagine the sort of woman who would marry his Uncle Henry—stout, pug-faced, sour, desperate, were the attributes that came to mind. He shook his head. "Eccentric in what way, exactly?"

"It might be better if you read the document yourself, sir."

"I am asking you to summarize it for me." His tone was meant to intimidate, and it did. Seaton looked quite cowed as he rose and scuttled toward the door. "Mr. Seaton!"

The small man gave a bow that was more like a flinch as he reached for the doorknob. "I have done my duty, Sir Alexander. Mr. Wylde was a most... difficult client."

"And you are pleased to wash your hands of his affairs?"

The man's expression was answer enough. He slipped out of the study; Alec strode after him. "Mr. Seaton!"

His visitor made for the front door. He had nearly reached it when the cat streaked out of the back hall, skidded on the marble floor with a rattle of claws, and careened toward the study. Alec hastily shut the door. Thwarted, the animal glared at him, spun, and sank its teeth into Ethan's ankle.

"Callie!" called Lizzy's voice from the rear premises.

With the look of a man escaping a madhouse, Seaton rushed out. Pain in every line of his handsome face, Ethan bent to extricate himself. Alec's sister appeared through the swinging door at the back of the hall. "Callie, no!"

The cat loosed the footman.

"She is still a little angry with Ethan, I'm afraid," said Lizzy, hurrying forward. Seeing her brother's expression she added, "And a new place is so frightening at first, you know. Cats must learn their territory before they..."

"Her territory does not include the lower floors," Alec said. "If you cannot keep this animal under control..."

Callie rolled onto her back, splayed her paws, and gazed at Lizzy with adoring yellow eyes. It was the finest impersonation of innocence Alec had ever seen, and netted him a look of deep reproach from his little sister. "Upstairs," he insisted.

Pushing out her lower lip as if bending to the whims of a tyrant, Lizzy scooped up the cat and started up the steps. Callie watched Alec and Ethan from over her shoulder. It was difficult not to interpret her expression as triumphant. Spots of blood spread on Ethan's white stocking. "Get someone to see to that," Alec told him. "And Ethan?"

"Yes, sir?"

"If that cat bites you again, you have my permission to kick it."

"Yes, sir. Thank you, sir."

Sir Alexander returned to the study, and Ethan allowed himself a grin. He hadn't really minded bathing the cat, or blamed it for objecting. It—she, Callie—was only being true to her nature. And washing a writhing alley cat was actually better fun than arranging china and silver in proper table settings or opening the door to visitors, or any of his London duties, really. The "treat" of coming up to London was not a treat to him. He wished his mother had not pulled her strings to get him sent. Oh, he was good at his job and most likely would have been included this year. But others in the household had dearly wanted to come. A shame not to let them. His father would be just as angry when he got back home.

Ethan moved toward the back stairs and winced. That cat had a good set of fangs on her. She'd bit deep. The laundress would give him a rare tongue-lashing about the stained stocking, though it was hardly his fault this time. He went down to the basement and, limping more than was strictly necessary, into the kitchen. There, he found an ample audience for his afflicted ankle. "Miss Lizzy's new cat," he said, exhibiting the bloodied fabric.

The cook, housekeeper, kitchen maid, and second footman needed no further explanation; they'd heard all about the latest addition to the household. Witnessed her yowls from the scullery, too. "Bit me right in front of a caller," Ethan added. "Sir Alexander, too."

"That animal bit Sir Alexander?" Sparks practically shot from Mrs. Wright's eyes. The housekeeper did not tolerate such breaches in her rule.

"Lord have mercy," said Cook.

"No, bit *me* in front of Sir Alexander." Ethan put on a pathetic expression. "Need a bit of nursing, I do."

The kitchen maid, a likely lass, stepped forward.

"I'll take care of it, Sally," said Mrs. Wright. "No doubt you have work to do. And if you don't, I'm certain I can find…"

"Sally could hold my hand while you patch me up," Ethan teased.

The housekeeper, who had known him since he was two years old, gave him a look. "You may have grown up tall and handsome, but you're not as charming as you think, Ethan Trask."

"Yes I am." He gave them the smile that had melted female hearts since he was fifteen. Well, fourteen if he counted Alice Ackerly, which he certainly did.

It swayed them, and made his fellow footman James grin in appreciation. "Away with your devilment," said Mrs. Wright. She shooed him toward the door. "Come along. I'll bind it up. And find you a new pair of stockings, I suppose. Or…" She paused in the doorway. "You kept the one that wasn't ripped in your fool 'cricket match'?"

"Yes, ma'am," replied Ethan quickly. Some things were best glossed over.

"Good. Fetch it then, and we'll make up a pair."

"All the way to the top of the house on my wounded leg?" he moaned.

The housekeeper snorted. "And count yourself lucky I don't make you learn to knit. Stockings don't grow on trees, you know."

Twenty minutes later, Ethan was bandaged and

back in the kitchen, where luncheon trays were being readied. Sir Alexander had chosen to go out. As he carried a tray up to Miss Cole's sitting room, Ethan wondered how this spring in London would turn out. Miss Anne's illness had turned the household topsy-turvy. With her sister gone all pale and tired, Miss Lizzy was jumpy as... as her new cat. And Miss Cole, who used to be steady as a rock—Ethan remembered this—twitched and squeaked if you came on her unawares. Which you couldn't help doing, because she was lost in a fog half the time, and what with the apologizing and worrying she'd have palpitations like his gran... well, he was just glad it wasn't his problem. Sir Alexander would figure things out; he always did. Bit of a brooder, but smart as a trained ferret.

Ethan's family had been intertwined with the Wyldes for generations, in one capacity or another. The same age as Richard Wylde, Ethan had shared some games—and played some pranks—with the younger brother in their early years. Alexander, already off at school, was just an older boy—more serious and distant than his brother. But as time passed, Ethan grew to admire the current master of the house. He accepted service with grace and gratitude. More importantly, he managed the estates with an eye to the hundreds of people who depended on the land for their livelihood. He acknowledged their work and listened to their concerns, as many landowners did not. Ethan wouldn't have cared to have that responsibility himself. He liked to feel he could kick over the traces at any moment, and no one the worse for it. And that's the way it was, no matter what his father said.

He knocked on the sitting room door and waited until a vague voice told him to enter. Frances Cole sat on the small sofa, no fancywork in her hands, no book or newspaper. She looked at him as if she didn't remember who he was. "Luncheon, ma'am." He set the tray on the table by the window. "Nice pot of tea for you as well."

"Oh… yes. Thank you."

Yes indeed, he was very glad it was Sir Alexander's problem, Ethan thought as he eased out of the room. He had plenty to do thinking of himself, and no taste at all for complications.

Three

"ALL THE SERVANTS ARE LOOKING FOR NEW POSITIONS?" Charlotte asked Lucy.

Her maid nodded. "After the way they treated you? They know you won't be keeping them on. Good riddance, I say."

After Lucy went out, Charlotte wondered what choices she would have. She had brought a good bit of money to her marriage, and inherited more when her father died. But it had all fallen under her husband's control, and Henry had added lavishly to his collections during the time she lived in this house. Some of the items looked quite expensive. They could be sold, she supposed; there would be records. She could discover how to do that.

She fingered the folds of the mourning gown she had worn for her father, and only just put off. Black didn't become her, but Henry's nephew would expect it. The nephew she hadn't known he had, who was due to visit her in a very few minutes. Henry had never mentioned his family; she'd assumed he didn't have one. It was bizarre how little she knew about

Henry, personally. But he treated any question like an insult—became abrupt, sneering, critical. Of course she had stopped asking. Charlotte's chin came up. She was sorry for what had happened to him, but she wasn't going to miss him—not one little bit. If this nephew of his expected a great show of grief, he would be disappointed.

The bell rang. She heard the door, footsteps on the stair, and then Lucy ushered in the caller, and Charlotte's spirits sank. He looked like Henry—tall, lean, regular features, and sharp green eyes. His hair was wheaten rather than silver, but the relationship was only too obvious. His face was not set in the harsh, intimidating lines that Henry's had exhibited, but he was much younger, after all. Time would no doubt limn them.

"Sir Alexander Wylde," Lucy announced. He looked as if he didn't approve of her country accent, or the fact that she dropped his hat and coat and gloves on the sofa.

Charlotte rose. Mr. Seaton had warned her that her visitor was a baronet and must be treated with all due respect. "Hello," was all she could manage.

He stared at her. "*You* are Mrs. Henry Wylde?" He spoke as if he didn't believe it.

Charlotte heard clear echoes of Henry's constant disapproval. She wanted to burst into tears; she wanted to snap at him; she wanted to throw him out of her house. With difficulty, she controlled herself and said, "Yes." She sat back down. "Thank you, Lucy," she added as her one ally turned to go.

Sir Alexander took the chair opposite her without

invitation. "I beg your pardon, but we had no idea...
how the dev... how did you come to be married to
my uncle?"

"In the usual way." Charlotte sat very straight. She
kept her chin high, trying to show that she would
not be intimidated. "I was told you have charge of
his will?"

He looked around the room, evaluating and
disdaining, Charlotte thought. "Have you no family
to lend you support in these... trying circumstances?"

Clearly, he thought she was a nobody who had
latched onto his uncle. "My father, George Rutherford,
died last summer at his estate in Hampshire. I have no
other family. He told me that he had he seen to all
the necessary legal matters when I married. I brought
a substantial dowry..." *Stop babbling*, she told herself.

Her visitor's expression was odd. It almost looked
like pity, if such an emotion had been possible from
a connection of Henry's. Charlotte braced herself for
bad news. Was there anything left in the world but
bad news?

Had her father's mind been up to legalities? She had
so wanted to rely on him, to believe he was still the
man who had cared for her so kindly all her life.

"I see." The two words were heavy with fore-
boding. "My uncle's will is... unusual."

He looked as if he wished she didn't exist. Well,
Charlotte wished he didn't. Her hands closed into fists
in her lap.

"It mandates that this house is to become a museum
for his collections." The man spoke quickly, as if to get
it over with. "Scholars and other... qualified visitors are

to be admitted on request. You are permitted to remain as long as you oversee these visits, learning as you can about the objects and imparting this knowledge. There is, apparently, a catalog. If any item is sold, all his assets, including the house, revert to the British Museum."

"What?"

"There is sufficient income from investments to maintain a… small household. Not perhaps on the scale…"

Charlotte was speechless with outrage.

"I took the time to go over the document with my solicitor before visiting you, and—"

"Took the time? How very *kind* of you."

"—his opinion was that the will would stand up in court, I fear. If you had been married for a longer time…"

"I brought him eight thousand pounds!" Charlotte burst out. "Along with what my father left me. Are you telling me he spent it all on his wretched 'collections'?"

"I cannot say for sure…"

"He did." She clasped her hands so tight they hurt. "He married me for the money, of course he did; why did I not see it? Why did my father not…?" Her voice broke, and she despised herself for it.

"Mrs. Wylde…"

"Do not call me that! Do not ever call me that!" She should have known. There were so many things she should have known. Why had she let herself be moved about like a chess piece? Why hadn't she *thought*?

"If I can assist…"

"Apparently you cannot." No one was going to tell her what to do again, ever, Charlotte vowed. She would never again be taken by surprise in this horrible way. "Just give me…"

The drawing room door flew open, and Holcombe strode in, brazen as ever. Lucy trailed him, making helpless gestures. "I want to know what I have inherited," he said.

Rage brought Charlotte to her feet. She wanted to shout at him, at everyone. She wanted to sweep them aside like sparrows. It took every ounce of willpower to keep her voice even. "What is left to the servants?"

"Who is…?" began Sir Alexander. He paused, took in her expression and Lucy's, looked at Holcombe. He stood up. "There are no bequests to the servants in my uncle's will."

"Nonsense! He promised me…"

"You heard Sir Alexander!"

The valet ignored her, addressed the visitor. "You can't tell me it all goes to this whey-faced chit of a girl? Mister Henry would never have done such a thing." Lucy looked as if she might hit him.

"You are dismissed, Holcombe," Charlotte said through gritted teeth. "Pack your things and leave this house immediately."

Holcombe glared at her. "As if any of us would work for you. I told Mister Henry you were a mistake. From the moment I saw…"

"Silence!" Sir Alexander's voice was like a whiplash. "How dare you speak to Mrs. Wylde in this fashion?" Everyone stared; it was as if a different man had entered the room—a hard-faced, dangerous man.

"She's nothing but a…"

"You heard what she said. You are dismissed. You have twenty minutes to vacate this house."

Holcombe gaped at him.

"And should anything besides your personal possessions turn up missing when you've gone, you will find yourself before a magistrate before you can draw a breath."

Holcombe looked almost frightened. It seemed he might speak, but he thought better of it, raising a defensive shoulder and positively slinking from the room. Lucy waited a moment, her eyes bright, then followed.

Charlotte was trembling. For so many months she had longed to see Holcombe set down, to have someone besides Lucy acknowledge his insolence. And now this stranger had demolished the man with a few words. It was overwhelming. No one in her life had ever stood up for her so fiercely. A wave of heat washed her skin; she was exultant and tearful and ashamed all at once.

"That was...?"

"H-henry's valet."

"His valet?" Her visitor appeared astonished. "You know, you cannot let servants overstep..."

Rage came flooding back. "Cannot? How am I to stop them when the master of the house encourages them to persecute...?" Charlotte bit off the word, battered by her conflicting emotions. He had intervened, but of course he didn't really understand. How could he? And why would he want to? She couldn't bear to expose the humiliations of her life to this... this Wylde. "Are there... documents I must have?"

Sir Alexander drew papers from an inner pocket. "Will you be employing Mr. Seaton?"

"No!" She wanted nothing to do with anyone

associated with Henry. She practically tore the pages from his hand.

"Then I would recommend Harold Wycliffe. He is the solicitor who reviewed the will for me. His card is there with the…"

"All right!" She moved toward the door. "I need to think."

"Of course." He retrieved his coat and hat. "If I can be of any…"

"Lucy will show you out." She hoped. He was probably thinking that her household was in complete disarray. And he would be right.

Sir Alexander bowed and passed through the drawing room door. "Please do not hesitate…" She shut it in his face. She couldn't help it.

❧

Now there was a proper gentleman, Lucy thought as she closed the front door behind their visitor. Silently, she went over his speech to Holcombe yet again in her mind. She'd been desperate for someone to squash that slimy bug for months and months, and this Sir Alexander had done it so thoroughly. The look on Holcombe's face when he was threatened with a magistrate! Lucy hugged the memory to her. His defeat was so long overdue. It did her heart good. Maybe there was some hope for better things, after all.

Suddenly, the strain of the past months descended on Lucy in one headlong rush. She had to put a hand to the wall to keep from sinking right down onto the floor. The carping, the frustration, the helplessness; it had been the worst year of her life, and no mistake.

She swayed, and the movement flickered in the mirror on the opposite wall. There she was, reflected, a slender young woman in a dark gown and white apron. Lucy was always too busy checking Miss Charlotte's hair or the drape of her gown to study herself in a mirror, but now she leaned forward and took stock. She'd never been pretty like her mistress, which wasn't such bad news. A pretty maid had a load of extra troubles in this world. Her face looked even sharper than it used to, though, her chin more pointed. The gardener's boy back home had claimed she looked like a fox, which was a rare compliment coming from him. She wondered what had become of Tom. He was good with plants, so he'd probably found another post.

The troubles that had burdened both her and her mistress hadn't taken all her curves. Lucy turned a little to reveal them in the mirror. Her brown hair wasn't as glossy as before, maybe, or her cheeks as rosy. She raised a hand to her cheek; her dad had always said she had good strong hands, like him. A person could do right well with good strong hands, he'd claimed. She liked using them, too, liked to work, liked learning tasks that she could do well.

She moved closer to the mirror. Her eyes were still a plain, steady blue. The lines of strain around them were new. She looked worried, even though she wasn't particularly worrying just now.

Life had been weighing on her a sight more than she could let herself admit, she realized. She didn't mind being relied on—was proud to be. But Miss Charlotte had needed—still needed—more help than she could possibly give. She didn't know enough or have the power to change things.

But this unexpected nephew, now. He did. He was a nobleman. His clothes spoke of wealth. His manner—the way he said "silence" and instantly cowed Holcombe—showed he was well accustomed to giving orders and having them obeyed. He would know important people and understand the law.

He'd left a card, Lucy thought, stepping back from the mirror. If Miss Charlotte didn't put it away somewhere safe, she would make sure she did. She wanted to know how to get hold of Sir Alexander Wylde. He was just the ticket.

❦

Alec strode through the March drizzle, wondering if there was any hope of finding a cab in this out-of-the-way neighborhood. He supposed he would pay now for sparing his horses a cold wait.

Nothing about the visit had gone as he expected. His uncle's wife—he could hardly think of the girl in those terms—had turned out to be the antithesis of his pug-faced vision. Quite pretty, with her gold-copper hair and deep hazel eyes, her trim figure evident even in that stuffy black gown. No pretensions to fashion; that, at least, was as anticipated, but appealing despite her dowdiness.

Why in God's name had she married Henry Wylde? He'd thought first of penury; yet, if she was to be believed, his uncle had coveted *her* money. Social advancement seemed equally unlikely. She was clearly well bred and hadn't appeared stupid; she could not have imagined that his uncle moved in exalted social circles. The thought of affection, of his dour uncle courting, was preposterous. There must be something wrong with her that was not immediately apparent.

He spotted a hackney discharging a passenger ahead and waved down the driver. There was clearly something very wrong with her household. The behavior of his uncle's valet was beyond anything. Even Uncle Henry would have sent the man packing, surely. And the place had felt almost... abandoned, which was ridiculous. What had the fellow said, though? That none of the servants would work for her? That had to be an idle threat, born of his obvious animosity.

He gave his address to the cabby and climbed in. He had done his duty and would continue to do so, though she didn't seem to want his help. It was a relief, really; he had far too much to do already. Wycliffe would manage bank accounts and all the other necessary arrangements. But, bouncing over the cobblestones, he found that Charlotte Wylde lingered in his mind. Her youth—could she be even twenty?—the impression he had gained of a forlorn yet resolute spirit.

He had expected, been braced for, a weeping female falling on his chest and demanding his attentions and aid. Of course he was delighted that no such thing had happened. Of course he was completely and only relieved.

He felt even more so when Frances pounced on him in his study bare moments after he reached home, saying, "You are not actually going to let Lizzy keep that cat?"

"What has it done now?" Alec sighed.

"That is not the point! If you keep indulging Lizzy, she will never learn to control herself."

"She's been worried about Anne…"

"We have all been worried about Anne! But that does not give us license to ride roughshod over others' sensibilities."

Alec refrained from saying that it seemed to have given Frances such license. The familiar calm, equable Frances had not been much in evidence lately. As she glared at him, waiting for a reply, he suddenly noticed a resemblance to Lizzy in the lines of her face. Of course Frances had the dark hair and deep blue eyes of his mother's side of the family, he knew that.

But the contrast between the two had always been more striking than any similarity—Frances thoughtful and reserved; Lizzy in constant motion and high flights.

Frances had the rounded shape of the maternal line, too, though it felt odd to notice. She was indelibly associated with his father in his mind, a parental figure. He'd thought of her as old, but she wasn't more than, what, early forties? Right now, she looked older, tired and harried and thoroughly irritated. "The cat is on probation," Alec answered at last. "It is to be confined to the schoolroom and Lizzy's bedchamber."

"Oh, very likely."

Sarcasm, from Frances? This, also, was new. "Lizzy promised me that…"

"Lizzy promised? And how often has she kept a promise?"

"I think you're being a bit harsh. Lizzy does not break her word."

"Except when she cannot *help* it, because, you see, some circumstance *forced* her to do... whatever it is."

Frances's echo of Lizzy's voice was spot on. Alec almost made the mistake of smiling. "So, as usual, you will give me no support?" Frances added. "You will leave the discipline to me, and disappear into your far more *important* concerns than your sisters' conduct or future."

This was so unfair, and so unlike her, that Alec had to say, "Frances, what is the matter? All winter you have been..." He tried to find a word that would not offend.

"I? You are going to blame *me*?"

"It's not a matter of blame. I only wondered if there was something..."

"Oh, why do I bother? No one ever listens to me!" Frances whirled and stormed from the room in finest Lizzy fashion, leaving Alec bewildered and rather concerned. Was Frances ill? Had something serious happened, and no one told him? He stood beside his desk, wondering if he should go after her, and finally admitting that he did not wish to. He sat down, eyed the piles of correspondence on his desk. Was the perilous state of the country more important than his sisters' conduct and future? Of course not. Not... precisely. But... that was an unfair comparison. He'd done nothing wrong, Alec thought resentfully. Frances had always managed the household without visible effort. She hadn't appeared to want advice from him. It was unjust to accuse him of neglect. He would tell her so—at some appropriate point, when things settled down. As they would; of course they would. No question.

Alec reached for a letter from the pile with an incongruous sense of relief.

Four

CHARLOTTE WATCHED THE CANDLELIGHT WAVER ON the pages of her book and listened to the silence. Propped up in bed with plenty of pillows, her bedchamber warmed by a bright fire, she should have been quite contented. No one would be criticizing the amount of coal she had used, or sneering at her choice of reading material. Tomorrow, no one would insult her in her own home, or look at her as if they wished she did not exist. But still, she found the emptiness oppressive. The narrow town house wasn't large; she'd grown up in a sprawling place far bigger. Yet its four stories were meant to contain many more than one young woman and her maid. The rapid departure of the other servants had left too much space behind. It opened around her and kept her awake deep into the night, with too much time to consider her mistakes. How had she let her life come to this? Why had she not protested?

Her thoughts strayed back to her recent meeting with the solicitor Harold Wycliffe. That choice, at least, seemed wise. She'd been wary of Sir Alexander's recommendation, but Wycliffe had proved to be a pleasant, middle-aged man, thoroughly sensible and competent, and so she had invited him to look over and organize all of Henry's papers. His explanations were clear and sympathetic, if depressing. She would have a small income, enough to maintain the house and hire a few servants; enough, perhaps, to salvage some sort of life from the ruins of her fortune. But ruined it definitely was. Her legacy had been poured into the shelves and cases that crowded the first floor of the house like millstones around her neck. Henry had spent it so fast it was dizzying.

It also was maddening. And then to have to face vultures such as Mr. Ronald Herriton, a fat, blustering antiquities dealer, who had called insisting that Henry had meant for him to have his entire collection. He'd offered Charlotte what he called a "very good price," a figure she knew could not approach what Henry had spent. And he had refused to believe that Charlotte was unable to sell him anything—this, when she would have liked nothing better than to be rid of every musty old bit. She and Lucy together had just barely gotten him out of the house.

Her only comfort in the chaos was Wycliffe's parting remark. "There is nothing in the will, you know, that requires you to *announce* the creation of a museum."

It had taken her a moment. "I must keep all his glass cases and bookshelves and pedestals as they are, but if no one is told…?"

Wycliffe had had a gleam in his brown eyes.

"No one will know to visit," she added slowly.

He had departed with a smile, and Charlotte's spirits had lifted for hours, until she realized that this did not answer the larger question of what her life was to be now. Henry had socialized only at his club. They'd never entertained; she had no friends in London. She could invite old chums from Hampshire, she supposed, but most were married and busy with their new families. And the thought of any of them entering this cold museum of a dwelling made her flush. She could so easily imagine their astonished glances, their hushed pity.

Could she not have fought harder against Henry's scathing sarcasm, the servants' sly mockery? Even better, could she not have refused to marry him at all? What was wrong with her?

A vivid memory from the months before her marriage arose. She had come upon her father in his cherished library. But instead of reading or making notes, he was turning slowly in the center of the room, his face an alien mask of bewilderment. "Where is the Symposium?" he said.

From their years together, she understood what he meant. "Plato is there, Papa, with all your Greek books." She pointed to a rank of shelves.

His dark eyes had flickered, lit. "Elinor. Are you back so soon, my dear?" he responded.

Elinor, Charlotte's mother, had been dead for ten years, and Charlotte did not at all resemble her portraits. "Father?" she'd replied in a shaken voice.

For a terrifying instant, he had gazed at her with an absolute lack of recognition. It was as if she faced a stranger in her beloved father's image. Then he'd recovered, laughed, insisted it was the sort of momentary lapse that might happen to anyone. But it wasn't. And it wasn't the first. Charlotte had felt the rock of her existence turning to sand. She'd been in shock when he insisted she marry, she thought, and his insistence had so reminded her of the man who had held and guided her whole life. She'd had to see him as right. Tears clogged her throat. He hadn't been right. He'd been dying.

Something thumped downstairs. Charlotte swallowed, frowned, and dismissed it as the settling of an empty house. She was almost used to being startled by how different it sounded uninhabited. The noise came again—not a creak—much more substantial. Probably nothing, she told herself, and didn't believe it. Heart pounding, she slipped from her bed, picked up a candlestick, and opened the door a crack. She heard rustling, a distinct footstep. Someone was downstairs. Lucy?

She tiptoed across the hall and opened Lucy's door. She had moved her maid downstairs for company. Lucy curled peacefully in sleep, but the wash of candlelight woke her. "Wha...?"

"Shhh. There's someone below," Charlotte whispered.

Lucy threw back her covers, and they stood together at the head of the stairs, straining their ears. Another soft bump; if Charlotte had been asleep, it would likely have gone unnoticed. Bug-eyed, Lucy wrapped her arms around herself.

The candlestick wavered; hot wax dripped onto the lace at Charlotte's cuff. She was just as frightened as Lucy looked, but something within her refused to be intimidated any longer. She drew in a deep breath and spoke as loud as she could. "Jonathan, I believe there is someone downstairs. Go and see."

Lucy goggled at her.

Charlotte swallowed and spoke again, pitching her voice as low and gruff as she could. "Yes, ma'am. Right away." She stomped heavily on the hall floor, trying to sound large and dangerous.

There was a crash downstairs and a flurry of footsteps. Then all was silent. Charlotte went still, listening with every fiber of her being.

"Miss…?"

"Shh." All senses on high alert, pulse still hammering, she let the minutes tick by. "I think they've gone," she concluded at last.

"Oh, miss! When you spoke…" Lucy sagged against the wall. "Jonathan?" Her laugh had a ragged edge. "Was it the footman from home you were thinking of?"

Home would always be Hampshire. Charlotte nodded.

"I wish he was here! What are we going to…?"

"Right now, we are going into my bedchamber and locking the door. In the morning we will consult Mr. Wycliffe." Charlotte tried to keep her voice steady, but it shook.

Lucy heard the tremor and automatically tried to think of some comfort as she followed her mistress into the room and watched her turn the key. Lucy had known Charlotte Rutherford since she was seven years old—a sweet child, the sort the whole household had cosseted when her mother died. It had been so hard to see her sad. It was not long after that tragedy that Lucy had become her personal maid. At just five years older, she had often felt like a big sister, and had many times consoled and advised like one. At this moment, however, she found no comforting words to speak. The creeping sounds below had thoroughly unnerved her.

Miss Charlotte put the candle on the nightstand and climbed back into bed. At her gesture, Lucy joined her in the big four-poster. "Can we leave the candle burning?" she ventured.

"Absolutely."

Lucy appreciated her crisp tone and her resolute look. She'd been brave as a lion tonight, speaking right up and scaring off the burglar. More like her old self, the mistress of the Hampshire house, a grown woman, not a forlorn little girl. As they settled on the wide feather mattress and her pulse slowed, Lucy hoped Miss Charlotte might have a plan. She'd spent all that time with her father, learning historical things and who knew what else. Her head was chock-full of ideas, and surely some of them must come in handy now. Lucy curled up under the coverlet and tried to relax.

Mr. Rutherford had been an odd duck. Lucy knew he'd loved his wife and daughter, but sometimes it was hard to see. He'd go off into his library and just... forget about everything and everybody else— dinner, appointments, outings, birthdays. He'd caused a load of disappointments he never even noticed. If somebody—Miss Charlotte, say, when she was small—complained, he truly didn't understand at first. The promise, or whatever it was, had just slipped away, no unkindness meant. And the worst of it was, when he was put in mind of it again, he was crushed. He took it so hard that you felt miles worse for having mentioned it. It got so the household just ignored his forgetfulness right along with him. It was easier.

Which hadn't served Miss Charlotte well with her poor excuse for a husband, Lucy thought. If she'd complained... but no. *He* wouldn't have listened; he'd just have made life even more dreary, though Lord knows how it could have been. The trouble with husbands was you were stuck with them, with the law all on their side, as she understood it. Lucy sighed and turned over, careful not to wake Miss Charlotte, whose breathing had evened out into sleep. At least he hadn't been a lecher. Lucy didn't know what she would have done if he'd laid his dry old fingers on her charge. The very idea made her shudder.

The minutes ticked past, and Lucy lay awake in the silence. Tonight's disturbance had unsettled her, but these days, if she woke in the middle of the night, she found it hard to go back to sleep. All her life, she'd shared a room, first with her sisters and then with another maid; she didn't like falling asleep and waking alone. Houses were meant to be full of people. Of course, empty was better than full of nasty people like Holcombe—wasn't it? Lucy realized she wasn't sure. Maybe any people were better than this awful emptiness. They had to get in new staff soon as may be.

Lucy wasn't completely clear on the state of their finances. She knew they couldn't go back to Hampshire. The estate was sold and gone. She thought there was money to hire some new servants, but how did you do that in this huge dirty city? At home, families knew each other, and vouched for you. Her grandmother had been a friend of Mr. Rutherford's cook, and had recommended her for a position. Everybody knew Gran would skin her if she misbehaved. Back home, you understood who you could trust and who was likely to let you down.

Did people in London even have families? Well, they must, o' course. But how did you find them? Who could you ask if there were good people looking for posts? She had no idea, and she didn't think Miss Charlotte did either. Maybe London servants were all like the lot who'd left. Why, the very robbers who'd crept about downstairs could apply, and they'd never be the wiser.

Lucy had a moment of sheer fear. What were they going to do? Then she remembered. They were going to see Mr. Wycliffe tomorrow, and she'd bet money that he would tell Sir Alexander what had happened. If he didn't, she would—somehow. Between the two men, they'd know what to do and, more importantly, how to do it. With that thought, Lucy settled into sleep more happily than she had for quite a while.

❧

At first light, they went downstairs together. Lucy carried a heavy candlestick like a club. They found one display case pried open, with an empty space where some object had been taken. A piece of pottery lay on the floor, but not broken. The flimsy lock on the French doors leading to the tiny back garden had been forced.

Having no one to send, they took a cab to Wycliffe's office themselves.

And so it was that Alec found himself facing Charlotte in her drawing room little more than a week after their first meeting. He'd been called away from some particularly urgent letters—dire even—about conditions in Derbyshire; a sense of emergency, of looming disaster, gripped his consciousness. And now there was this. "The house is empty but for you and your maid?" he said again. He couldn't believe it. The girl looked flustered and anxious and hardly older than his sister Anne. She was, apparently, incapable of managing a household.

"I will be hiring servants." She made an impatient gesture. "Mr. Wycliffe and I could have dealt with this matter. I don't know why he bothered you…"

"He was obliged to tell me as executor of my uncle's will. And how would you have done that, exactly?"

"What?"

"How do you intend to 'deal with' a burglary?"

"I… I…"

Of course she had no idea. Very few people, in Alec's experience, were capable of decisive, intelligent action. "This is a serious matter."

"I know that! I am the one who was here, and might have been murdered in my bed!"

And so, people substituted emotional outbursts for clear reasoning. The ploy was all too familiar to Alec. "You will come and stay with my sisters."

"No, I won't."

"You propose to remain here alone?" He could see in her face that she didn't want to; she was sensible in that, at least. He waited for her to suggest a plausible alternative. She merely sulked. "I brought my carriage. Have your maid pack up your things. I will speak to Wycliffe." She started to protest, clenched her fists, then her jaw. Her visible struggle was oddly affecting. Torn, she was perhaps trying to be sensible. What had she said at their first encounter? Alec had a vague impression that she'd had more than her share of difficulties lately. But he had no time.

"What is *your* plan?" she blurted out as he turned away.

"I shall place a couple of men in the house to watch over it, and to catch the thief if he returns. They will put in a much more effective lock, of course. And I shall notify the watch and the magistrate…"

"I would have done that! Notifying, I mean."

Alec waited. She said no more. "Pack your things," he repeated, and went downstairs to consult with Wycliffe about hiring an investigator to look into this incident.

An hour later, he was relieved to find Charlotte and her maid with filled valises, ready to depart. Checking another task off his list, his mind returned to the letters on his desk and the seemingly inevitable tragedy unfolding in the countryside. As they drove from his uncle's utterly unfashionable neighborhood to more familiar districts, Alec didn't notice the looks exchanged by his two passengers, or the deepening anxiety in Charlotte's hazel eyes.

Five

STEPPING DOWN FROM THE CARRIAGE BEFORE A TOWN house that made Henry's—hers—look pinched and mean, Charlotte was acutely conscious of her appearance. In Hampshire she'd had only the dressmaker who sewed for her mother, with very outmoded ideas of fashion. She'd turned to her for mourning gowns when her father died, partly out of foolish sentiment, she supposed, but mostly because Henry had been so beastly about anything she needed. She had no doubt that her clothes would be despised in such a modish house. Sir Alexander obviously despised her already. Not that she cared. Straightening her spine, she stepped up from the pavement. It was just that she had been mocked and belittled for so long she really didn't think she could bear any more. As they passed through the front door, held for them by a smart young footman, she was near tears.

Something small and mottled black hurtled down the beautiful curving stair, trailing shreds of white. Footsteps pounded above. A housemaid emerged on the landing, followed by a superior manservant who roused unwelcome memories of Holcombe. "That... that creature is possessed by the devil!" the manservant exclaimed.

The black thing turned out to be a large calico cat. It crouched in the back corner of the hall guarding what looked like the mangled remains of a neckcloth.

"It *attacked* me as I came up the back stairs," the man added. He held up a bleeding hand. "It was lying in wait! Six freshly pressed neckcloths spoiled and one"—he pointed a shaking finger at the cat—"destroyed."

The footman took a reluctant step toward the cat. A pretty brunette girl of perhaps twelve came running down the steps. "Lizzy!" said Sir Alexander. Charlotte waited for her to cringe at the annoyance in his voice, but the girl merely disentangled the cat and scooped it up into her arms. The animal's ferocity vanished at her touch. It lolled in the girl's arms. "I told you that beast was to be confined..."

"Frances left the schoolroom door open. I told her not to."

A tall, aristocratic-looking woman with the same dark hair had joined the servants above. "Alec. I cannot... I simply cannot..." The sentence trailed off as if she couldn't even define what she was not able to do. She walked slowly down the stairs. She had the upright posture of a grand dame.

Sir Alexander sighed, and Charlotte turned to examine him. His lean face showed impatience, perplexity, resignation—but none of the cold anger Charlotte had expected. The girl—Lizzy, apparently, arms overflowing with cat—turned to her. "Hello," she said brightly.

"Frances, Lizzy, this is Mrs. Wylde," Sir Alexander said. "I told…"

"You are not to call me that!" It burst out, unthinking, and caused a startled pause. Charlotte flushed with embarrassment. Yet she couldn't bear to hear that name over and over again. "My name is Charlotte."

"Shall I call you Aunt Charlotte?" said the girl, and giggled. "You don't look at all like an aunt, I must say."

She didn't sound mocking, just amused. But the really interesting thing was her brother. Charlotte kept waiting for the sarcastic scold, the threats of punishment. Instead, when the manservant had said the cat was possessed, she had almost thought his lips twitched. But that couldn't be.

"This is my incorrigible sister Elizabeth," he continued.

"Lizzy," the girl interjected.

"And our cousin, Frances Cole."

"Such a way to greet a visitor," the older woman murmured. She pressed a handkerchief to her lips.

"Welcome to the Wylde household."

Now he sounded… not sarcastic exactly, but exceedingly dry. Charlotte felt as if she'd taken a step in the dark and found the floor several inches lower than anticipated. "Thank you, Sir Alexander," was all she could find to say.

"Oh, you can't call him that," said Lizzy. "It sounds so odd. Come upstairs. I'll show you your room, and you must meet Anne." She peeked around Charlotte. "Who are you?"

"Lucy, miss." She bobbed a curtsy.

"Hello, Lucy. I'll introduce you to my maid, Susan.

You'll like her." She turned and started up the stairs. When Charlotte and Lucy hesitated, she repeated, "Come on then."

Charlotte couldn't quite believe that no one would object, but no one did. She walked upstairs at Lizzy's side, Lucy trailing behind them. The cat gave a soft hiss. "Please don't be offended," the girl said. "She does that with everyone. She's still getting accustomed to the house, you see." On the landing, the servants backed as far away from the cat as they could.

"Accustomed to...?" Charlotte thought the cat was rather getting the house accustomed to her. Or perhaps subjugated was the better word.

"She's just come. I found her outside the garden gate. Frances says she has the manners of a street urchin." Lizzy grinned, and Charlotte found herself grinning back. They started up a second flight of stairs.

"I had a cat when I was small," Charlotte offered. "He slept by the fire and sat on my lap."

"Callie is a more independent sort."

"I can see that."

"I know she is untrained. She just needs a little more time. Here is Anne's room." Reaching around the cat, Lizzy opened a door. "Anne, here is Aunt Charlotte!" she announced, and giggled.

She led the way into a pretty bedchamber, hung with floral chintz and warm from a large fire. The soft colors made Charlotte think of her old home. A girl who seemed a few years younger than Charlotte lay in the big four-poster. Her wheaten hair and green eyes made her kinship to Sir Alexander obvious. Her skin was far paler, however, and the form under the coverlet looked very thin. "Hello." She coughed on the word, and kept coughing.

"Anne has been ill, but she is *much* better now," said Lizzy, as if it had to be true.

"Yes, I am," declared Anne, and gasped. Her midsection quivered as she struggled to control the coughing.

Charlotte knew it wasn't true. She'd heard that sort of cough most winters through her childhood.

"I see you've met Callie," Anne added. "What did she do now, Lizzy? I heard shouting."

"She chewed up one of Alec's neckcloths. Ames was so angry, he said she is possessed by the devil." She smiled, revealing a fetching set of dimples.

"Oh, Lizzy." Her tone was rather like Sir Alexander's. It mystified Charlotte, who had no brothers or sisters. They didn't seem to excuse Lizzy; they weren't precisely angry. Was it worry?

"It is only a neckcloth, and Ames is always so stiff and proper."

"That does not excuse Callie. You promised to keep her up here…"

"And so I shall, if people will not leave the doors open everywhere." Lizzy turned away from her sister's skeptical gaze. "I'm taking Aunt Charlotte to her room."

"It seems odd to call you aunt," Anne said with a tired smile.

"Just Charlotte would suit me." She hesitated, but she had to speak. "You know… my father was troubled by a cough almost every winter. There is an herbal mixture that helped him be rid of it."

Anne looked surprised, then interested. "Really?"

"We must get some right away!" exclaimed Lizzy.

"I would be happy to try it," her sister agreed. She coughed again. "This is so very tiresome." For a moment, her face looked pinched and worn. "Tell Alec the name; he will send someone out to ransack London."

Charlotte nodded and followed Lizzy back to the hall, then along it to an equally pretty bedchamber papered and hung in blue. "This is yours," Lizzy said. She went over and rang the bell. The cat squirmed, and she tightened her grip. "I need to take Callie back to the schoolroom. She wants to get down."

"I can see that she does."

"And I don't want her getting loose again… just now."

"Very wise."

"Susan will be right up." Lizzy turned to Lucy. "She can show you…" The cat writhed, nearly escaping her arms. "I must go." Lizzy ran.

"Seems a funny sort of house," said Lucy.

"Doesn't it?" Charlotte agreed.

Once Lucy had been taken under Susan's wing and gone off to explore her own quarters, Charlotte shed her cloak and bonnet and sat in the armchair by the fire. Everything in this room was lovely—the veined marble hearth, the blue wallpaper subtly striped with cream, the silver candlesticks and Dresden figurine on the mantle. The crackle of the fire soothed in a chamber without drafts; the air was scented with potpourri. She felt her senses open and expand. Her room in Hampshire had been rather like this. She had made her own potpourri, from her mother's recipe. She had gathered beautiful things around her. Over these past months, it had been easier—imperative—to be shut down, to feel less, and then less still. Now her being stirred, eager to come back to life. And why not?

Charlotte's hand closed on air. She would not be hemmed in any longer. She was free now—to savor, to expand, to make her own decisions. Nothing could make her return to the cramped, stunted life that Henry had forced upon her. Nothing would.

❧

On their way to the top floor, Lucy and Susan passed a housemaid carrying a stack of clean laundry. Her dark blue dress and white apron were neat as a pin, and she gave Lucy a cheerful smile when Susan introduced her. She didn't stop her work to gossip, however, which raised the household in Lucy's estimation. When she found her bag already in the cozy chamber she'd been allotted at the top of the house, her opinion rose further. But still she had to say, "Odd sort of pet for a young lady."

Susan laughed. Stocky, blond, and talkative, she had an infectious laugh. "Miss Lizzy took that cat in off the street, and a right argy-bargy it's been, I can tell you."

"I wonder she was allowed." Lucy did more than wonder, after months in a house where it seemed nothing was allowed. She'd been braced for an explosion of masculine wrath in the entry hall and was surprised when it didn't come.

"Miss Lizzy has a way of getting what she wants. That child can wheedle the birds from the trees. Do you want to unpack? Or come along down and meet everyone?"

"I'll come." Lucy had had more than her fill of solitude.

As was proper, Susan took her first to the house-keeper. In the tall, correct, cordial Mrs. Wright, Lucy recognized the sort of authority and experience she'd admired in the senior staff of the Rutherford house. Cook had it, too, in a more approachable way. She was plying the bitten manservant, who turned out to be the master's valet, Ames, with tea and cake at the kitchen table. The sticking plaster on his hand seemed no hindrance to his appetite, though Ames moaned artistically now and then round a mouthful. From the amused glances exchanged, Lucy gathered that he had a taste for drama. When he held out his cup for a refill, his tragic expression set the kitchen maid—Agnes, Lucy reminded herself—giggling. She didn't stop chopping carrots, though.

Something deep inside Lucy eased. The rich scent of simmering broth filled the air. The fire crackled in the hearth. The whitewashed walls and brick floor were spotless. The Wylde servants chatted easily with each other, clearly on good terms. She was settled with her own cup and plate during a round of welcomes. Another part of her relaxed, and then another. This was how it was meant to be. Every detail showed the rhythms of a well-run household, and to her that meant safety, respect, companionship, and a sense of possibility.

She'd been horridly alone even before all Miss Charlotte's servants left, she understood now. No one in that house had given her credit for her skills, or advice about her difficulties, or a laugh to lighten a hard day. They hadn't offered those things to each other, either. Bleak; it had been purely bleak. Back in a place full of life and energy, she knew she never wanted to be in such a situation again.

The footman who'd been at the front door earlier came in—Ethan, they named him. He crossed his arms and leaned against the wall, listening with a lazy smile and exhibiting his fine broad-shouldered figure. Lucy ignored him. She knew his type—the kind they warned you about—full of himself, with his well-turned leg and handsome face. Expecting every female he met to fall at his feet, and most likely deep as a puddle. Footmen were hired more for looks than brains. One of his sort—the servant of a visitor in Hampshire—had broken the heart of Lucy's best friend, and nearly cost her her place. Lucy wasn't about to be taken in.

That jet-black hair and those warm brown eyes did draw the eye, though, much as she wanted to deny it. Lucy found hers straying, and he managed to catch her gaze. "The cat bit me too," he told her, raising one shapely leg in a smooth white stocking that showed no sign of a bite. Then he smiled at her. It was a flat-out beautiful smile. Lucy felt it all the way to her toes, felt her own lips automatically start to curve in response. She looked away.

"And haven't you made the most of it," Cook replied.

"A bit more gravy, Mrs. Wright, I'm wounded. Best have James lift the keg, Agnes—my leg, you know."

"You scamp."

It was said with affection, and everyone laughed, Ethan included. It seemed he was well liked. But that didn't mean he could be trusted, Lucy told herself.

She wouldn't make that mistake. Hadn't she just spent months watching the misery menfolk could bring to your life?

∽

Ethan watched the new girl refusing to laugh. He saw a small female with a sharp chin, glossy brown hair, and wary blue eyes. Unless he was mistaken, a very neat figure lurked under her countrified gown. And he wasn't ever mistaken about that sort of thing. Her gaze shifted from person to person, observing carefully, and clearly not trusting things to be as they seemed, which was interesting. Ethan was a dedicated observer himself. You learned a lot by being quiet and watching, particularly in the place he loved most in all the world—the forest. For him, in fact, observing was the only way to learn. Reading was no good. Little black marks on a page never penetrated his thick skull. Unlike his brother Sam, who loved figuring so much he got the parson to teach him "mathematics." Now apprenticed to the estate steward, Sam was likely to make a big success of himself. You'd think that would be enough for their dad, but no...

The point was: Ethan got new skills by watching them done. Watching had taught him all kinds of things that people didn't even know he knew.

Agnes said something that made Lucy really smile, and Ethan straightened. She lit up like a Christmas tree when she smiled. Ethan hadn't thought she was pretty, but when her face filled with life and light, she was something better. She was a dazzler. And he'd bet she didn't even know it. She didn't strike him as one of those girls who posed in front of mirrors and tried out their charms.

It was an irresistible combination. A vastly appealing girl he hadn't known all his life, who was also nothing like the pert London misses he'd encountered, who put him right off. He tried to catch her eye again, but she wasn't having any. Hah, a challenge; he purely loved a challenge.

❧

When he was in town, Alec read his newspaper over breakfast. Even this year, with his sisters along, he'd had no qualms about maintaining that habit. Anne was the only other early riser in the family, and her illness kept her abed. But he'd barely begun the following morning when their houseguest appeared. She paused in the doorway as if startled. "Good morning…" he began, and stopped. This name business was awkward. He couldn't use her first name. But he'd been forbidden to call her Mrs. Wylde, which admittedly felt strange on the tongue. Perhaps she felt the same; she murmured something unintelligible, eyes on her feet. "I trust you slept well?"

"Yes, thank you."

Why was she hovering half out of the room? "The tea is still hot, I believe. If you would care to ring for a fresh…"

"No, no."

She practically scuttled into the breakfast room, quickly helped herself from the dishes on the sideboard, and slipped into the chair farthest from him. Alec wondered if something had frightened her in the night.

"Please continue with your newspaper," she said. The teapot wavered a little in her hand. "I did not mean to interrupt."

It finally occurred to him that his Uncle Henry had been a bear at the breakfast table. He couldn't imagine anything more likely. She wasn't accusing him of a wish to be rude. He watched her add milk to her tea. This girl's association with his irascible relative still seemed like a wild tale that couldn't be true. Alec ate a bit of ham, spread butter on a piece of toast. When he judged that she'd had time to settle, he said, "I understand you know of a possible remedy for Anne's cough?"

Again, she started. "How did you...?"

"Lizzy told her maid Susan, who mentioned it to the housekeeper, who immediately informed me. If you wish to keep secrets, do not tell my little sister."

"It wasn't a..."

"Of course." Was there no way to put this girl at ease? "The remedy?"

"It is an herbal mixture. A doctor in Bath recommended it when my father was visiting there, and we ordered it at once. It was very helpful to him."

"In curing his cough?" She nodded. "Tell me the name, and I will send out for a supply."

Finally, she smiled a little. "Anne said you would have London ransacked for it."

"Of course." Now she looked startled again, and he couldn't fathom why. It seemed she was odd. Of course, she would have to be, to have married Henry Wylde.

Silence fell over the table. Alec missed Anne more than ever. Even when they didn't talk, their morning silences were companionable, not stiff and empty like this one. He examined Charlotte Wylde. She hunched over her plate, head down, eyes on her breakfast. She wore a shapeless black thing that he thought he'd seen before. Her coppery hair was pulled up too tight. She was pale, the very definition of subdued.

Alec was suddenly reminded of a thoroughbred he'd come across in a neighbor's stable, a roan with exquisite lines and a lovely delicacy of movement. The minute they approached, the mare had shied and cowered, backing as far away from them as she could and shivering at any touch. It was obvious she'd been mistreated, even ruined. Alec had bought her on the spot, paying the man's exorbitant price because he could barely speak through his fury. It had taken long patient months to convince that mare that her high spirits were permissible, even welcome, and his opinion of that particular neighbor was forever changed.

Alec caught himself. He was being ridiculous—probably offensive—comparing the girl to a horse. She looked up, caught him watching her, and dropped her eyes. Her cheeks reddened, and he felt his do the same as he looked away.

"What is going on at my house?" she blurted out, as if she must say something, however random.

Alec found he had to clear his throat. "As planned, I have two stout men stationed there. They will take it in turn to watch for intruders. Wycliffe is making a report to the authorities, at this moment, probably."

"But you can't just leave these men there forever. Where am I to…?"

"Exactly. That is why I think it best that we

engage an investigator. You have heard of the Bow Street Runners?"

"No."

"It is an organization that hunts down criminals, with a good record of success."

"Engage…?" She frowned. "For pay?" When he nodded, she added, "Are they very expensive?"

"They are well worth the money, I understand."

"But where is it to come from?"

"This is certainly a proper use of my uncle's estate…"

"Further reducing what I am left with. I should have some say in the decision."

"There is no reasonable alternative." Her head was up now; back straight, her eyes glittered with emotion. It was an attractive change, even if she had no idea what she was talking about.

"That's not true. The… the burglar might come back, and be caught by your 'men.'"

"Highly unlikely."

"You can't be so sure of…"

"We are faced here with an extremely serious situation," Alec pointed out. "First, my uncle is killed, and then his house is broken into. Surely, you would not wish to live there continually wondering if you are in danger?"

"No! Of course not. That's not what I…"

"The Runners know the criminal underworld. You do not. I do not. Turning the matter over to them is the only sensible choice."

She glared at him, cheeks glowing, her pale complexion positively transformed by their exchange. She had no argument, of course, because there wasn't one. His plan was the only sensible course of action. Satisfied that he had convinced her, Alec rose. "If you will excuse me, I have a good deal of work to get through this morning."

She merely shrugged, but Alec didn't hold it against her. He knew it was difficult to be bested in a dispute. Lizzy would have tossed a slice of toast in his face.

❧

She could have said "Work?" in a sarcastic, disbelieving tone, Charlotte fumed. She hadn't thought of it until he was gone. With obvious wealth and a house full of servants, what could he know about real work? Of course, dictating to everyone around him probably took a great deal of time. It must be such a burden to always know better! He had talked to her as if she were a child or a fool.

The worst of it was—an investigator was a good idea. If she'd known about such people, she would have hired one herself. She was perfectly capable of doing that.

Charlotte sighed and sat back in her chair. She could have; she would have. But she had to admit it was pleasant not to need to make the arrangements, to have the matter decisively and intelligently handled by someone else. Whenever she thought back to the stealthy footsteps in the night, she couldn't help but tremble. A weakness, no doubt, which just made her angrier.

She turned back to her breakfast. Her eggs were cold, but she could go to the sideboard and replace them if she wished to. The tea was delicious—better than she'd brewed for Henry, she supposed! There were sausages and crisp toast and homemade marmalade—all of it much nicer than the meals she and Lucy had been scraping together. It was a very comfortable house. The servants seemed cheerful, and the sisters happy, aside from Anne's illness. It reminded her of home. She closed her hands on her napkin. The past was past; she must stop being melancholy and get on with life.

No one else had appeared by the time Charlotte finished breakfast. Returning to the front hall, she wasn't sure what to do with herself. She didn't feel like sitting in her bedchamber. She had no duties. In the flurry of packing, she'd forgotten to put in her sewing or her book. Tentatively, she began to explore. She discovered the dining room, a formal parlor, and a butler's pantry before coming upon the library at the back of the house. Going in, closing the door behind her, she felt suddenly much more at ease. The room was smaller than her father's library, but also much tidier. Shelves covered every bit of wall not needed for the door, fireplace, and two windows; the books on them looked handled, not merely decorative. The bright fire and comfortable chairs showed that the room was often used. She trailed her fingers along a row of bindings, chose a book, and curled into an armchair to read. Contentment settled over her like a warm blanket. For the first time in days, weeks, Charlotte relaxed.

Sleet spattered the windows; the fire popped. She drifted a thousand miles away on an account of travel in the wilds of Turkey and was aware of nothing

nearer until a female voice said, "There you are."
Charlotte started, dropped the book, and came to her
feet. The older woman she had barely met yesterday
stood in the doorway. "Forgive me for startling you.
You must enjoy reading, Mrs...."

"Charlotte. Please."

She inclined her head. "And I am Frances."

She looked far more composed this morning, her
dark hair fashionably dressed, her lilac gown immaculate. Charlotte envied her air of refinement and grace.
"I love to read, yes."

"I suppose Henry has... had a great many books."

"Not really. He collected other things, and the
volumes he had were too rare to be touched."

Frances looked surprised, and Charlotte immediately wished she hadn't answered so honestly. She had
held things pent up for so long, now they just came
tumbling out. She couldn't seem to stop it.

"Come up to the drawing room. We've had no
opportunity to get acquainted."

Following the lady of the house up the stairs and
into an elegant room hung with green brocade,
Charlotte was again aware of her stuffy black gown,
her unusual situation. What must Frances Cole think
of her?

"I hope you found your room comfortable?"

"Perfectly." Charlotte sat on the delicate sofa beside
her. "Thank you so much for allowing me to visit
without warning in this..."

Frances waved this aside. "We're delighted to
have you."

She said it; she smiled; but Charlotte didn't believe

her. "I hope not to put you to any trouble. I would be glad to…"

"Oh, trouble." Frances gestured again, and Charlotte glimpsed something beneath her polished demeanor. Was it weariness? Anxiety? She wasn't sure. "*You* are no trouble at all."

The emphasis suggested that others were more troubling. Charlotte didn't know what to reply.

"It is a relief to have another woman in the house," Frances added. "It has always been just me, you know, ever since Elizabeth died."

"Eliz…"

"My cousin Elizabeth—the children's mother."

"Ah, yes." Frances gazed across the room as if looking into another time. Charlotte wondered if she had forgotten who she was talking to.

"The family chose me, you know, to help out when she died. Well, there I was—no money and I hadn't found a match in the two seasons Papa could afford. Living at home; twenty-nine years old. Clearly an old maid. I had to go; there was no choice. And then, of course, James…" She blinked and seemed to return from wherever her thoughts had taken her. "I beg your pardon. I… I had meant to ask if there was anything else you needed?"

"Nothing at all," Charlotte assured her. She felt an impulse to say more—but what? The door burst open, and Lizzy danced in.

Frances's expression tightened. "Lizzy, you are supposed to be doing your schoolwork."

"I've finished."

"All of it?"

"Every bit."

Frances's smile was strained. "She stays ahead of me on all points." The bell rang downstairs. "Who could be… where is the cat?"

"I shut Callie in the schoolroom, as ordered." Lizzy pouted.

"Good." Frances turned back to Charlotte. "I am not at home to callers this morning, but best to be…"

An imperious voice penetrated from the stairs. "Nonsense, of course she will receive *me*."

"Drat!" exclaimed Lizzy, and bolted from the room.

She was replaced by a nervous young footman, not the one Charlotte had seen yesterday. A woman somewhat older than Frances and a younger man who might have been her son were right on his heels. "Er, Lady Isabella Danforth and Mr. Edward Danforth," he said.

"Oh dear," breathed Frances, not quite inaudibly, as she stood up.

Six

"Was that Elizabeth running down the corridor? Really, Frances, she's become a positive hoyden," said the newcomer. She raised her brows at the footman. "Are you going to take our things, young man?"

Charlotte had thought the Wylde ladies' clothes very fine, but as the footman hurried to divest the callers of a beautiful fur-trimmed pelisse and a many-caped overcoat, she knew herself to be in the presence of true high fashion, such as she'd seen only in magazine illustrations. The woman's deep green morning gown was intricately and exquisitely cut, its high neck and long sleeves severely elegant and very flattering to her small wiry frame. The younger man's pale pantaloons and dark blue coat fit him perfectly; his neckcloth and mirror-bright boots proclaimed a Pink of the *ton*. They also had a distinct air about them—she couldn't define it exactly—confidence perhaps.

Lady Isabella Danforth's sandy hair and green eyes suggested she was related to the Wyldes. Her companion, on the other hand, had coal-black hair and blue eyes, and a narrower, more delicate face, with the advantage of thick, dark lashes. He was one of the handsomest men Charlotte had ever seen. Noticing her gaze, he smiled at her.

"Hello, Bella," said Frances as the footman went out. "Charlotte, this is Alec's aunt—Henry's sister—and her son, Edward Danforth. Bella, this is Mrs. Charlotte Wylde."

The caller turned avid eyes on Charlotte, surveying her from head to foot, as if committing every detail of her appearance to memory. "It is true then? Henry was secretly married? We only just heard."

"It wasn't a secret," said Charlotte, flushing under her scrutiny.

"But he didn't tell anyone." Lady Isabella looked from her to Frances. "Unless… you and Alec knew?"

Frances shook her head.

"How very odd." Lady Isabella's sharp gaze shifted back to Charlotte. "Quite a… romance."

Charlotte grimaced at the revolting thought and saw that the visitors noticed.

"Edward saw Henry quite often at his club, you know. I can't conceive why he didn't mention you."

"Because all he cared about was spending my money on his wretched collection." Charlotte flushed. She'd done it again, blurted out her thoughts like a gauche schoolgirl. Had a year of misery obliterated all her social skills?

"Really? My dear, how dreadful for you. Are we going to sit down, Frances?"

Their hostess's cheek reddened. "Of course." She gestured at the sofa and sat. The others followed suit.

"If only I had known," Lady Isabella continued.

"I could have introduced you into society, shown you the way to go on, you know." She smiled at Charlotte, then looked away. Charlotte had the feeling that her ugly black gown positively hurt the visitor's eyes. "Poor Henry was quite… eccentric, of course. I don't believe he ever accepted an invitation, but not even to tell his family that he had married!"

"He never talked of anything but some chunk of pottery or bit of parchment he'd gotten his hands on," said Edward Danforth. His voice, low and melodious, matched his appearance. "Not once, in all the times I ran into him in the clubroom."

Charlotte nodded feelingly. She and Edward Danforth exchanged a knowing glance, which held long enough for Charlotte to feel a flutter of warmth.

Lady Isabella shrugged. "Ah, well, Henry was secretive even as a child. I remember once—he must have been about five, because it was the year James left for school—little things began to go missing around the house. Trinkets, mostly, but then one of Mama's diamond earrings disappeared. It was such an uproar—the house turned upside down, the servants being questioned, one of the housemaids nearly taken before a magistrate. And then all the things were discovered in a box hidden in Henry's bedchamber. He was furious when they were taken away."

"He didn't care that the housemaid…?" began Frances.

"Not a whit." Lady Isabella made an airy gesture.

Charlotte had no trouble believing it. Things had meant far more to Henry than people.

The young footman returned with a tray, setting

it on a low table in front of Frances. "Will you have some tea?" she asked.

Edward shook his head, but his mother nodded. "Charlotte... may I call you Charlotte? We are family, after all."

"Please."

"We met the strangest man when we called at Henry's house. Quite... rough-hewn. He would scarcely speak to us; it was difficult even to discover that you were visiting here."

"He is keeping watch over the house. Someone broke in during the night and stole one of Henry's... artifacts."

"No!" Lady Isabella put a hand to her cheek. "While you were at home?"

"Yes. It was very frightening."

"Terrifying, I should think." She took a cup from Frances and sipped.

"You should get rid of the whole lot," Edward put in. "Sell it as fast as you can."

"I should like nothing better, but I cannot. Henry's will made the collection into a museum. If anything is sold, even one object, the entire estate goes to the British Museum, including the house."

Lady Isabella drew herself up so abruptly she almost spilled her tea. "That is outrageous!"

Charlotte was touched by the older woman's visible anger. "But perfectly legal, I'm told."

"You poor thing. And so you are left all alone."

"Hardly alone, as she is quite welcome here," said a voice from the doorway. Sir Alexander walked in and took up a station by the fireplace. "Hello, Aunt Bella. Edward."

"Alec, dear," replied Lady Isabella. Her son merely nodded.

Charlotte heard the lack of enthusiasm in both their voices, and wondered at it. The atmosphere in the room seemed to tighten.

"You do know that rumors are flying all over town," she added, almost as if it were Sir Alexander's fault. "First Henry's murder—murder, unthinkable! And now I hear there has been a robbery as well. In our own family! We can only be thankful that the Season hasn't really started."

"Indeed."

"What do you intend to do?"

Charlotte expected him to explain about the Bow Street Runner and the investigation, but he merely repeated, "Do?" in the tone she herself found uniquely irritating.

"To stop the talk, of course. The Wyldes have practically become a scandal. You should hear all the tiresome jokes being made on the name."

"I'm sure I have, Aunt, at one time or another."

"Of course he has," Edward said to his mother.

Charlotte couldn't help but compare his soothing manner to Sir Alexander's rigidity. The cousins seemed to be opposites in many ways.

A small movement caught her eye. One of the double doors leading to the corridor shifted a bit, but no one entered. A moment later a small dark shape was pushed through the opening. Charlotte glimpsed a white hand helping it along. The door closed. The cat Callie skittered across the floor and disappeared under the table holding the tea tray.

"What was…?" began Lady Isabella. A paw flashed out and snagged the fringe on one of the armchairs. "It's some sort of animal!"

"Just a cat, I think, Mother." Edward sounded amused.

"Oh, for God's sake." Sir Alexander bent, reached under the table, grabbed, and missed. Callie erupted from the other side, raced across the room, and clawed her way up one of the brocade curtains. She hung there, well above all their heads, glaring. Edward laughed.

Lady Isabella, on the other hand, went rigid, as if the incident had been designed to offend her. "A little joke of Elizabeth's no doubt. I have told you and told you to send her to school."

"So you have," said Sir Alexander through gritted teeth.

"Well, you must admit that I am right! She is completely out of hand. I am sorry, Frances. I don't mean to criticize your disciplinary methods, but really you…"

"Enough." Sir Alexander strode to the bellpull and yanked it. "As you say, you have made your opinion quite clear on many occasions, Aunt." A footman arrived in a rush, not the one from before. "Our guests are leaving, Ethan. Fetch their things."

Lady Isabella stood, her green eyes flashing much like Sir Alexander's. "This is the way you treat me? And you wonder that I…?"

"On the contrary, I don't wonder at all. Allow me to see you out." He herded his aunt toward the door. Edward followed with easy grace and an amused glance for Charlotte as he exited.

Lady Isabella's voice drifted back from the stairs. "Do not expect me to help you…"

"I expect nothing," Sir Alexander replied.

Frances rested her forehead in her hand. Charlotte considered trying to coax the cat down off the drapery, but decided that stillness was the best choice at the moment.

"She practically forced her way in," said Frances when Sir Alexander stood in the doorway once more. "There was nothing I could do." Callie hissed from above.

The master of the house turned back to the corridor and shouted, "Lizzy!" There was no doubt he was heard all the way to the top stories.

"It's rather like Bedlam here, isn't it?" popped out of Charlotte's mouth.

Sir Alexander turned on her. "It is nothing of the kind!"

Lizzy rushed in, the ribbon sash of her gown dragging behind her, blue eyes sparkling. "Is she gone? I got rid of her, didn't I?"

Sir Alexander stalked to the far corner of the room, seized a straight-backed chair, and carried it to the window where the cat perched. "Come here!" he said to his sister. It was the voice Charlotte had heard when he spoke to Holcombe, and Lizzy rushed to obey. He climbed onto the chair, heedless of his boots on the satin seat—the slender legs creaked a little—and without hesitation grasped Callie by the nape of her neck. For an instant, the cat relaxed. Sir Alexander plucked her from the curtain and thrust her down to Lizzy, who caught her in her arms. "Take that animal away and do not let me see it again."

"What? Ever?"

"Do not test me just now, Lizzy! Do as I say!" He stepped down from the chair.

The girl goggled at him. "But, Alec, it was only…"

"Now!"

Lizzy looked scared. Clutching the cat, she ran out. Her feet pounded on the stair to the upper floors. Sir Alexander stood still, his back to the room, his fists closed; then, without another word, he strode from the room, his tread audible on the lower staircase. The room seemed curiously empty when he was gone.

Frances Cole dropped back onto the sofa and burst into tears.

As Charlotte went over to sit beside the weeping woman, it occurred to her that Sir Alexander Wylde thought he was in control of his household, his universe, but he wasn't, not in the least. She patted Frances's shoulder. Maybe he had been; his manner was certainly that of a man used to getting his way. But something was unraveling now. The threads were escaping from him, snapping like the warp of a broken loom. She only hoped she was present when he finally realized this.

"I b-beg your pardon," Frances said on a gasp. "Please forgive me for this… this… I don't know what's come over me. What you must think of all of us!"

Not knowing what else to do, Charlotte patted her shoulder again. "Nothing bad. Not at all."

The reassurance simply made Frances cry harder. "I believe Lizzy would *love* school," she sobbed. "A good one, I mean. All those other girls to be friends with and… and m-match her high spirits. But she refuses even to c-consider leaving home."

"She wishes to be with her family, I suppose." Charlotte could certainly understand that.

"And this winter! It has been so difficult, nursing Anne... so worrisome. Lizzy *needs* a governess. She h-hasn't enough to do, but she keeps chasing them off with her p-pranks. She n-never knew her mother, you know. I have done the best I can, but..." Tears overcame her.

"I'm sure you've done very well," was all Charlotte could think to offer.

"James... their father was such a b-bulwark. To have him die so young! But he *would* go out in the w-worst weather. Sometimes I think he cared more about his wretched tenants than..." She gulped back the rest of this sentence.

"When did he die?" Charlotte wondered.

"F-four years ago. Things had been more trying since then, but only... Then when Anne could not shake off her cough..."

Frances sniffed, and Charlotte concluded that Anne's father had died of a lung complaint. "It must have been frightening," she said.

"H-horribly." The older woman drew in a breath and visibly struggled for control. She pulled a handkerchief from a pocket in her gown. "What you must think of me!"

"I think you have been under a great strain."

"Yes." Frances sniffed, dabbed her eyes, then blew her nose. She nodded, as if unable to help emphasizing the fact to herself, but she did not meet Charlotte's eyes. "I am feeling so *old*," she added forlornly.

"You know," Charlotte began, a thought forming.

"I had a very good governess myself, as well as lessons with my father, and I enjoyed my studies. Particularly geography; I love maps. Perhaps I could spend some time with Lizzy, tell her what I remember."

"Would you do that?" exclaimed Frances.

"I'd be happy to."

"But... why?" Frances could not seem to imagine anyone wishing to take charge of Lizzy.

"I would be glad to have something to do," Charlotte told her. She had felt singularly useless over the last year. "To repay you for your kindness in taking me in."

"But you are not obliged to..."

"I know. It would be a pleasure."

"Then of course I accept." Frances clutched her hand like a lifeline. Charlotte would have felt flattered if she hadn't suspected that any offer to amuse Lizzy would have been met with equal gratitude. How had one young girl reduced this cultured woman to such a state?

And so, a short while later, Charlotte went in search of Lizzy. She found the schoolroom without difficulty, a large comfortable chamber at the top of the house with dormer windows looking out over London rooftops. The fire was burning low, however, and there was no Lizzy and no cat. A moment's thought sent her back down to Anne's room, where she was cheerfully admitted. Lizzy hunched in an armchair by the hearth; a soft growl came from under the bed. Charlotte also noticed a bottle of the herbal mixture on a small table at Anne's bedside. The ransacking had yielded quick success.

"Alec is really angry," Lizzy said. "I've never seen him so angry." It had the sound of a much-repeated litany.

"He'll get over it," Anne replied, as if she had said this quite often as well.

"He's going to put Callie back out in the street," the younger girl said.

"I don't think he will, Lizzy." Anne looked at Charlotte, shook her head very slightly.

"He hates her!"

"He doesn't. He just... You know you should not have put her in the drawing room. You promised..."

"It was only to chase off Aunt Bella! I thought Alec would be glad. He doesn't like her."

"That is not precisely true, Lizzy." Anne glanced at Charlotte again. "They have had some disagreements, but that does not mean that he..."

"And she is always trying to get me sent away," Lizzy muttered. "I won't go. No one can make me."

The girl looked so anxious that Charlotte decided just to plunge in. "I was thinking, Lizzy, my... a friend of mine used to tell me wonderful stories about all the countries on the globe. My father did, too. I thought you might like to hear some of them."

Her attempt at subtlety failed. "Lessons?" Lizzy made the word sound dire.

"How interesting," said Anne. "May I come and hear, when I am better?"

Lizzy sat up straighter, surprised. "You don't have to do lessons anymore." She turned to Charlotte. "Anne is almost seventeen. Our aunt is to bring her out next year."

"Lady Isabella?"

"Oh no," said Lizzy. "Aunt Amelia, our mama's sister. She is married to an earl!" She waited for Charlotte to be impressed, and Charlotte tried to look duly awed. "Mama named us for queens, you know. She was descended from… some Tudor or other. Not the one with all the wives!"

"Lizzy demonstrates her deep knowledge of history," teased Anne.

"Oh, bother history. It's deadly dull." Lizzy pretended to yawn.

"Even with all the wives?" Charlotte wondered, and got a small smile. "So Lady Isabella is your father's sister?" She remembered this but couldn't quite contain her curiosity about the tension in the drawing room.

Lizzy nodded. "Alec *doesn't* like her. She did something bad about my grandfather's will."

"Lizzy," said Anne.

"Well, she did. Though I don't know precisely what." Clearly, the girl would have liked to know. "There's no reason not to tell Charlotte. She's our aunt, too." Her mood seemed to be recovering rapidly.

"Shall we go and look at the globe in the schoolroom?" Charlotte suggested. "It seemed a very fine one."

Briefly, Lizzy pouted. "Oh, all right. But I'm bringing Callie!"

"I'm sure she is fascinated by geography. Cats are extremely territorial."

Lizzy giggled.

❧

Walking into the kitchen with some things for the laundress, Lucy Bowman was transfixed by the sight of Ethan applying a cloth to his bare ankle. His white stocking lay crumpled on the floor beside his chair, exposing his leg to the knee.

He grinned when he saw her. "Cat bite turned a bit nasty," he said. "Cook made me a poultice."

Lucy removed her gaze from his leg. Of course he could have applied the remedy in his own room, as was proper, but he had to draw attention to himself and show his fine limb to all the world. What sort of man got bitten by a cat anyhow? The sort who kicked cats. Lucy ignored him, left the laundry in its basket, and went over to the worktable by the hearth. Cook and Agnes were deep in luncheon preparations. "Is there an apothecary shop nearby?" she asked. "Miss Charlotte was wanting some rosewater."

"You should ask Jennings," said the cook. "She knows where to get the best of that sort of thing."

Lucy had been introduced to Miss Cole's very superior dresser at the servant's dinner table, and was deeply in awe of her. "Oh, I wouldn't want to bother her."

"There's one two streets over," said Ethan. "I've fetched plenty of things from there for the family."

Lucy didn't look at him. "Thank you."

Cook scooped up a dollop of icing and began to frost the cake before her. Lucy's mouth watered at the look of it. "So she went right up the curtain?" It sounded like a question the cook had asked before, and enjoyed hearing the answer.

"Dangling there like a Christmas ornament," Ethan replied. "Hissing and spitting over everyone's head."

"The cat?" Lucy couldn't help asking. Tales of

Callie's adventures had become a staple of the servants' hall. "Was that the shouting earlier?"

"Sir Alexander was that angry," Agnes answered. She seemed to relish the thought. "Now Susan says Miss Lizzy's afraid he'll throw the cat out of the house. And so he should. She's like a wild beast, she is."

"Ah, now, she's mostly afraid, I expect," said Ethan. "Likely people haven't given her much reason to trust them, out there in the street."

Surprised at this level of understanding, Lucy turned to him. He was putting his stocking back on. She blushed and turned away again. "I'll just run over to the apothecary then. Won't be a minute, if anybody's looking for me."

"I'll go with you." Ethan stood. He was so tall.

"There's no need for you to…"

"You shouldn't be out all alone in a strange part of town," the cook declared. And that was that.

Once they'd fetched coats and hats and set off, Lucy had to admit it was nice to have an escort. On previous errands in the city, she had sometimes attracted unwanted attention; once, she'd been quite frightened. And no one to tell about it, of course; only Miss Charlotte, who had far too many worries already. Now she could observe the bustle of the street with interest instead of wariness.

"From the country, are you?" asked Ethan.

Lucy's gaze fell to her feet. He might as well just say that she was gaping like a hayseed. "What if I am?"

"Ah, good for you. I'm country bred myself."

"You are?" He looked so at home, walking along the city street, fine in his rich livery. But his nod seemed heartfelt. "I grew up in Hampshire. We lived there until last year when Miss Charlotte got married."

"To Mr. Henry Wylde. Seems that was a bit odd, eh?"

Lucy put up her chin. She wouldn't be gossiping about Miss Charlotte to anybody.

"I'm a Derbyshire man, myself. It's my first time in London, as well. 'Course I'd heard a good deal about it from my family."

"They'd been before?"

"Aye, with the old master as died a few years back. My dad's head of the stables up at the estate. Ma was a nursery maid there before they married. Granddad used to be head gardener, before his joints got so bad."

Lucy had heard of these families with generations of service. They were a kind of gentry below stairs. She was just a farm laborer's daughter. The contrast kept her silent until they reached the shop.

Her business was quickly managed. Ethan joked with the apothecary's assistant like an old friend, somehow bringing her into it until she felt like she knew him, too. When the parcel was made up, Ethan took it; then he opened the door for her. Lucy reminded herself to think nothing of it. She had no doubt he treated every female to his easy charm.

As they left the shop a heavy cart trundled by, barely missing their toes, the driver cursing at the top of his lungs. Ethan pulled her back into the doorway, holding on just a bit longer than strictly necessary. Before Lucy could object, a loud thump suggested the reason for the driver's rage, and when they edged around the cart, they saw that it had collided with a sweeper's barrow. Manure lay scattered over the cobblestones and the pavement opposite like a smelly carpet. The boy clutched his broom and cowered under the driver's tongue-lashing. "Give over," shouted Ethan in a voice that easily carried over the din.

The burly driver turned to glare at him. Standing in the cart, he towered over them.

"You hit *him*," Ethan said.

"He was right in the bleedin' way, warn't he? Halfwit!"

The sweeper sniveled and wiped his nose with a dirty sleeve.

"And now he has all his work to do over again. Let him be." Ethan showed no sign of fear under the driver's scowl. He met it steadily, and after a moment the man growled another curse and slapped the reins of his huge team. The horses leaned in, and the cart slowly moved off. Ethan stepped over to the sweeper, nimbly avoiding the clumps of manure.

The boy ducked his head as if he expected a blow. Ethan pulled a small coin from his pocket and held it out. Wide-eyed, hardly daring to believe, the young sweeper took it and made it disappear into his ragged coat. "The big wagons can't turn easily, you know," Ethan told him. "You should take care when you see one of them coming." Mouth hanging open, the boy nodded.

Ethan picked his way back to Lucy and led her around the mess as they headed toward the house. "I hate this great dirty place!" he exclaimed.

Lucy had a lump in her throat, moved by what he'd done. Nobody paid any attention to the boys who swept the streets. "All the noise and shoving," she agreed.

"What sort of job is that for a lad?" he continued as if he hadn't heard her. "Mucking out a stable is one thing. Doesn't take you all day. And afterward, you can go out into the air. Maybe exercise the horses." He was moving so fast that Lucy had to trot to keep up. "I can't wait to be home again," Ethan declared fiercely.

Lucy would have agreed with this, too, and just as fervently, if she'd had a country home to return to. Reminded that London was likely her fate, she said only, "Slow down, can't you?"

Seven

THREE DAYS LATER ALEC KNOCKED AT ANNE'S
bedchamber door just before noon. Invited in, he
was startled to find her dressed and sitting in the
armchair by the fire with a book. "What are you
doing out of bed?"

"I'm feeling so much better the doctor said I could
sit up today."

"Are you sure that's wise?"

"Well, I am not to run up and down the stairs. But
I've been sleeping wonderfully. No coughing. And I
feel stronger. He said Charlotte's potion is a wonder,
and he intends to recommend it to his other patients."

Alec hardly dared believe it, but Anne did look
better. Some color had returned to her cheeks. She no
longer had that frightening languid air, as if the least
effort was beyond her.

"I like her."

"Who?"

"Charlotte, silly!"

"Oh, yes." He took the chair on the other side
of the hearth and continued his scrutiny of his sister.

He'd been worried about her for so many weeks; it was difficult to trust the improvement.

"She has actually gotten Lizzy interested in maps and exotic places on the globe. Lizzy has decided to become an intrepid explorer. I warn you, she wishes to purchase a sword stick."

"What?"

Anne gave him a look. "You are not listening to me."

"Yes, I am. Lizzy… *Lizzy* is learning geography?"

"Charlotte has been teaching her."

"She needn't do that. She is a guest here."

"They both seem to be enjoying it."

"Really?" He couldn't picture his boisterous sister enjoying any type of study. "I'm still in Lizzy's bad books, I suppose?"

Anne shrugged. "Until you release the cat from 'prison.'"

"The storeroom is not…"

"I was teasing, Alec. You're not really going to get rid of Callie, are you?"

He grimaced. "Anyone would think I'd threatened to drown the animal. I wager it would actually be happier if I sent it down to the country. If you could see the reproachful looks I get if I happen to pass the kitchen."

"I heard that Callie managed to ingratiate herself with Cook. I can't imagine how."

"She caught a mouse in the scullery. And presented it to Mrs. Dunne with due ceremony. Devious creature. She has the instincts of a Russian diplomat. She's turning the whole household against me."

Anne laughed. "But Alec, you'll let her out eventually?"

"If Lizzy promises… Oh, what am I saying? Lizzy will promise, and then she will 'forget' or imagine that some situation *requires* that she break her word." Frances had been right about that much. Alec felt a rising sense of unease. He had never had to oversee his willful little sister here in town, where she was surrounded by strangers and pitfalls she knew nothing about. And Anne, whom he'd always trusted to prevent Lizzy's most distempered freaks, was in no condition to do so.

"She doesn't mean…" Anne began.

He had to move; he really could not sit still any longer. "Do *not* overdo and exhaust yourself," he said over his shoulder. He shut the door upon the concern in her face, and tried to do the same with his own. In fact, he knew just how to divert his mind from his own problems. He went to his study and immersed himself in correspondence.

By luncheon, the mood had passed, and when Charlotte answered his summons at three o'clock, Alec had recovered his equanimity. "The Bow Street Runner is due, and he has asked that you be present," he told her as she entered the study. For some reason, she frowned. "If you do not wish to speak to him…"

"Of course I wish to speak to him," she answered snappishly.

Alec wondered if trying to teach Lizzy was irritating her nerves. A knock on the study door put the thought from his mind, however. Ethan opened it and said, "Your caller, sir." He ushered the fellow in and closed the door behind him.

Alec faced an odd little man, unremarkable in every

way. Mid-sized, with mouse brown hair, gray-blue eyes, and forgettable features, he wore a long gray coat that would pass unnoticed in most parts of London. Not outside this house, perhaps, but in a wide variety of other neighborhoods. "Good afternoon, Mr...?" Why hadn't Ethan announced the fellow's name? Or taken his coat, for that matter?

"Jem Hanks, sir, lady." As if in answer to Alec's thought, he added. "I don't tell me name to just anyone, ye ken."

The words came with a darting observant glance—sharp, evaluative, some might have said impudent. It was strange. The Runner came from the servant class, but he was nothing like a servant. He was, in fact, unique in Alec's experience.

He pulled a notepad and stubby pencil from his coat pocket. "I talked to Mr. Wycliffe a time or two already. And looked about a bit. I had a few questions for the lady."

"Of course," said Charlotte. She sat on the small sofa under the window. Alec returned to his desk chair. "Do sit down, Mr..."

"I prefer to stand, thankee, sir. Now this gent as called on you, Ronald Herriton, what can you tell me about him, ma'am?"

Charlotte sat straighter, hands folded before her. "Well, he said he was an antiquities dealer, and he wished to purchase my husband's entire collection. On the spot. For what he called a very good price. He evidently expected me to take his word for the value. As if I wouldn't have the sense to consult several experts about such a sale. He also claimed that Henry had promised him the opportunity to buy after his death. Clearly a lie, considering Henry's will. He was loud and unpleasant. My maid and I had a good deal of trouble getting rid of him." She paused, thinking. "He is very fat."

A corner of Jem Hanks' lips twitched. "That he is. Did you tell him that you en't allowed to sell, 'cause of the will?"

"No, I didn't wish to reveal anything to him, or talk to him any longer than I had to. He…" Her shoulders shifted. "There was something… unsettling about him."

"Was there now?" The Runner's sharp gaze flicked up from his notebook and down again. He wrote something on the page. "I looked through your husband's papers at Mr. Wycliffe's office. There's a pile of letters about this or that pot or coin or statue. Were you acquainted with any of the writers?"

"No. Well, except…" She stopped.

"Yes, ma'am?" The Runner's pencil was poised.

"My father," Charlotte continued in a low voice. "They corresponded for several years about ancient Rome. But my father died six months ago."

"Very sorry to hear that, ma'am." Jem Hanks waited a moment, then said, "So the others…?"

She shook her head. "On the very rare occasions when my husband had visitors—always to look at his collection—I was not… invited."

Alec wondered if his uncle had actually been off his head. The more he learned about his life, the less he thought of his reclusive relative.

"Too bad. I would like to find those gen'lmen."

"Have you talked to Holcombe? I would say, of the household, he knew Henry best. I don't imagine that my husband... confided in him." The idea was unimaginable. "But Holcombe liked to poke his nose into everything."

"Who's this Holcombe?" Hanks leaned forward like a hound on the scent.

"My uncle's former valet," Alec replied. He was feeling rather left out of the conversation. "He was dismissed right after my uncle's death."

"And no one told me?"

"I thought you had received a list of the servants from Wycliffe."

"He missed one, seemingly. First name?" The Runner's pencil hovered over the page.

"Uh..." Charlotte looked blank, then chagrined. "I have no idea."

The pencil drooped. "No matter. I'll find 'im."

"So what have you discovered so far?" Alec asked. "Have you anything to report?"

"It's early days yet, sir. But one thing I know. Twarn't your common garden-variety criminal as broke into the house. How would they know about this 'collection,' fer one thing? And it en't the type of stuff they can sell easy, is it? Old coins and papers and the like. Second thing I know—there's no word on the street about the job."

"That's why you're wondering about Henry's fellow collectors?" said Charlotte. Most astutely, Alec thought. "But surely none of them would..."

Jem Hanks shrugged. "By what I'm hearin' some folk are close to daft about this old jun... these 'antiquities.' Go to just about any length to get their hands on 'em."

"It's true there is a great rivalry amongst collectors," Charlotte said thoughtfully. "Henry used to positively gloat when he beat someone out on a purchase."

"Yes, ma'am. And if they've heard they can't be buyin' these perticular ones…"

"They might try to steal them?"

"Send someone to do it, more like." Hanks nodded to himself. "There's just the one thing…"

"What?" said Charlotte and Alec at the same moment.

"Well, some as I've talked to say this Henry Wylde was fooled and cheated a good deal. Paid too much for poor stuff or fakes. So…"

"It needed only that!" Charlotte exclaimed. "He didn't just spend my money, he wasted it." She pounded the arm of the sofa with a closed fist. Jem Hanks watched her with an interest that Alec found unsettling.

"Have you any other questions?" Alec said.

"Only one, sir." He turned to Charlotte. "Is there anyone your husband mentioned in perticular? Friend, enemy, person he envied? Anybody at all that I should concentrate on, like?"

Charlotte frowned, took her time. But in the end, she shook her head. "Not that I remember. Henry talked mostly about *things*, you know—things and their history—not people. He didn't much like people."

"Ha." Jem Hanks closed his small notebook. "Well, I'd best get back to it. More than likely I'll have other questions as matters develop. You let me know if anything comes to mind. Anything at all. Don't matter if it's small. Thankee, ma'am, sir." He nodded, turned, and slipped out of the room without waiting for a response.

Silence descended. Charlotte frowned at the carpet. No doubt she was unsettled by the encounter.

"An odd sort of man, Mr. Hanks. But he seemed to know his business," she said.

"He came highly recommended," replied Alec. She rose, took a step toward the door, stopped. What was this awkwardness that rose between them, Alec wondered? First the breakfast table, and now here. He generally found conversation untaxing; he was known among his friends for smoothing over sticky encounters. But something about this young woman paralyzed his skills. And yet he didn't want her to go.

"You have a great many letters," Charlotte observed.

"Estate business."

"Do you have many estates? My father never received so much correspondence."

"It's the times."

"The…?"

"The current state of the country."

"What do you mean?" She grimaced. "I'm horribly ignorant. Henry didn't take any newspapers, as my father used to do, and he refused to let me subscribe to the circulating library."

"What the deuce was wrong with the man?" burst from Alec.

"Just selfishness, I think." Her expression was sad now rather than outraged. "Complete and utter selfishness. Tell me about things in the country."

Unlike his sisters and brother—or Frances, who actually seemed to blame their tenants for his father's death—she seemed sincerely interested. "You've heard of the new textile machinery?"

"Some. Where I grew up it was all agricultural."

"Well, machinery is changing the world, and for the worse, right now, for many families. People on my land, or in nearby villages, who used to sell what they wove on their home looms have been put out of business by cheaper goods from the factories."

Charlotte nodded. She didn't appear bored.

"Some leave their homes to work in the mills, but those jobs are backbreaking, and still don't pay a living wage. So either way, they starve."

"Couldn't they just... do other things?"

"Such as?"

"I... I don't know. Grow more food?"

Alec sighed. He was all too familiar with the futility of explaining this problem to members of his own class. "Most of them were already growing all they could. A few go into service or join the army. But this is a massive change. And by and large, there are no other things for them to do."

"Can't they be offered assistance, to find new...?"

Alec's bitterness overcame him. "Our government feels that protest equals treason, and we should hang those who object to these conditions."

"Surely not!"

It was always the same, Alec thought. Now she would recall that she had urgent business elsewhere. A cup of tea, perhaps, or a thrilling novel. He waited, but Charlotte merely gazed at him as if waiting for a solution to the intractable. "You like to read?"

She looked startled. "Yes."

"You're fond of Lord Byron, perhaps?"

"I have read some of his…"

"But not, I imagine, his work about the plight of the weavers, and the fact that the government is, yes, hanging young Englishmen for attacking the new machinery. Frame breakers they call them." Alec shuffled through the papers on his desk. "Here."

Charlotte came to join him. She leaned over the page and read aloud:

Some folks for certain have thought it was shocking,
When Famine appeals and when Poverty groans,
That Life should be valued at less than a stocking,
And breaking of frames lead to breaking of bones.
If it should prove so, I trust, by this token,
(And who will refuse to partake in the hope?)
That the frames of the fools may be first to be broken,
Who, when asked for a remedy, send down a rope.

She turned to look at him, her coppery eyes intense with feeling. "But what can be done to help them?"

Those eyes were very close, and the anxious sympathy he saw in her face was such a relief and a revelation. No one close to him had been moved by the emergency he felt rising around him every day. No one seemed to want to hear or understand, while Alec felt the world was teetering on the brink with so few—so very few—people straining to save it.

He was suddenly aware that their shoulders were touching. Hers was warm against his coat sleeve. Under the dowdy black stuff of her gown was a slender, rounded body. She was lovely, he thought.

He hadn't quite realized. It had taken the touch of her warm and ardent spirit. Such a small shift would put his arms around her; a mere bend of his head would set his lips on hers.

Shocked, he stepped back. This young woman was living under his roof and his protection, in company with his sisters. "I'm doing all I can for my own people in Derbyshire." It came out rather stiffly.

"That's what these letters are about?"

"Yes." He didn't mean to be dismissive, but her nearness was deeply unsettling.

"There are so many. Do you need help? Perhaps I could…"

"I believe I have matters well in hand," Alec lied.

Charlotte drew back at the undeniable snub. "I mustn't keep you from your work then."

"Thank you."

She turned and strode out with a rustle of skirts. Alec sank into his desk chair and grappled with his entirely inappropriate impulses. Charlotte Wylde was alone—without family or any other protector—and under his authority as executor. She was extraordinarily appealing. She was recently bereaved, though how she could be mourning his reprehensible uncle he could not… She sometimes seemed even younger than her age—nineteen, he had discovered in his uncle's papers… Of course, she was not a total innocent. She was a widow not a deb… one of his most agreeable liaisons had been with a widow. An utterly different case!

They were barely acquainted. She had entered so readily into his concerns… the quick sympathy in her eyes… for the workers, not for him. She was his aunt, for God's sake! He snorted. This was maddening and pointless. The best thing would be to banish all thought of her from his mind. Alec returned to the letters awaiting his attention, and struggled for some time to follow his own excellent advice.

∽∾

Ethan watched the houseguest storm up the stairs and wondered what had happened in the study to make her angry. Not likely to be Sir Alexander; he was never impolite. Must have been the visitor. There was a strange little man—refused to give his name, glared at Ethan like he was a thief when he tried to take his coat. They'd never had a caller like him before.

Ethan was suddenly reminded of Harry Saunders. Everybody back home knew Harry was a poacher, though nobody could prove it. He had the same half-furtive, half-sly, and insolent air about him as the man just gone. Harry was a sneak, always popping up where least expected and slipping a few rabbits or even a deer out from under the noses of the gamekeepers. He enjoyed it, too; wouldn't trade the poaching for honest work despite some run-ins with the magistrates. The visitor was like that, only on the other side seemingly. Somebody—Mrs. Wright, maybe?—had said he hunted down criminals for pay.

Ethan tried to imagine tracking quarry through the wilds of London instead of the forest. You'd have to know where to search, where to lie in wait, but he couldn't picture such places. He didn't even want to—surely they'd be dark, filthy, and treacherous. He couldn't shake the conviction that city dwellers were meaner and more crooked than country people. Look at some of the footmen he'd met from other households; all they seemed to think of was how to extract larger tips for tasks they were supposed to do anyway, and then wasting their money on drink and tailors and other useless trash.

Ethan wondered if her mistress's bad mood would help him out with Lucy. He hadn't made much progress there. She still avoided him, though he'd been as charming as he knew how to be. Now and then, he fancied he caught a gleam in her eye that said she wasn't immune. But as long as she kept away from him, nothing could follow from that. And it was becoming more and more important to him that something did follow. Maybe he'd just go and tell her that her "Miss Charlotte" was upset. She'd want to know. It was part of the job to keep track of the moods of the gentry. Sometimes—mealtimes, for instance—you even had to listen at doors to get a jump on their requests.

Before he could go looking for Lucy, though, Miss Cole came down the stairs, a small envelope in her hand. "Ethan, would you take this note to Lady Earnton's house?" she asked.

"Yes, ma'am. Right away." He wondered why she hadn't rung for him to fetch the note. But Miss Cole had been flighty and unlike herself for quite a time now.

Nodding her thanks, she went back upstairs. Ethan fetched his coat and gloves and told Mrs. Wright where he was off to. It was a cold, raw March afternoon, the sun already slanting down, but Ethan didn't mind. An errand was a chance to move. Delivering notes and packages and escorting the young ladies about was the best part of his job here in town. Nothing to compare to his long rambles in the woods during his time off at home; but for all he didn't like London, there was always something to see. He spent far too much time kicking up his heels in the front hall, or setting tables, serving meals, then clearing off the tables again. Ethan liked to accomplish things, and none of that felt like an accomplishment.

He walked fast. He knew the way to Sir Alexander's aunt's grand place; he'd been there several times before and could be quick. He'd take the chance and look in on his grandparents on the way home. They were visiting his Aunt Liv, and her house wasn't far out of the way. Aunt Liv was one family member who liked London; after being up to town a few years as a house-maid for the Wyldes, she'd married a local grocer and stayed on living here. No one would be the wiser if he spent a quarter hour or so at her house.

His grandad always had good advice, and he could talk to him about his plan for the future and how to get on with it. Everything was in place. Old Elkins was more than ready to give up his place and move to his daughter's farm in Cornwall. The joint ache this past winter had like to done him in. He'd taught Ethan most all he knew. There was just the last step, the trickiest one, of asking. That and dealing with his dad's disappointment. The second part was what kept him quiet when everything else pushed him to act.

Eight

"I THINK WE SHOULD MAKE CALLIE HER OWN PLACE here in the schoolroom," Charlotte said. "The dormer would be perfect."

Lizzy eyed the nook doubtfully. Anne, almost fully recovered now except for regaining lost weight, smiled from a chair by the hearth.

"We can clear it out and make it perfect for her. I'm sure she'd calm down if she had a refuge like that."

The calico cat, crouched under the other armchair, made no comment. Since being released from the storeroom, she had been even more wary of everyone but Lizzy. "Not like a pen," said that young lady now.

"Not at all. Very cozy. She can come and go as she likes—around the room."

"It's not fair that she must stay shut in here."

"You are allowed to take her to your bedchamber…" began Anne.

"You know, I think Callie might prefer it," Charlotte put in. Arguing with Lizzy was always a mistake; she had the cunning and tenacity of a barrister. "Cats need to know every bit of their territories, you know. But this house is too large for Callie to explore, full of unknown corners. I think it makes her uneasy." That was one way to describe swarming up a curtain and spitting on her host, Charlotte thought.

"How do you know so much about cats?"

"I like to read."

Lizzy made a face at her. They had had this discussion. "Oh, all right," the girl said.

Under Anne's amused gaze, Charlotte and Lizzy cleared out the small bookcase and other bits and pieces that had collected in the dormer. They created a nest from old blankets and a hidey-hole from an upturned hatbox. Lizzy moved the cat's food and water dishes closer. "Callie can watch the pigeons from the window ledge," Charlotte pointed out.

When they were finished, Lizzy coaxed her pet from under the chair and carried her to the dormer, plopping down on the blankets with Callie on her lap. "This is your place," she told her. The cat curled in her lap. "She likes it," Lizzy pronounced.

Relieved, Charlotte sat in the abandoned chair, her ankles now safe from lashing claws. Anne smiled warmly at her, and Charlotte thought, not for the first time, how agreeable it was to have female companionship. The days had been passing so pleasantly. She had grown very fond of Anne and Lizzy; Frances seemed much more at ease and welcoming. Lucy was happy too, making friends among the staff, greatly admiring its efficiency. The whole household was a delight—well, except for its master.

Alec had gone distant—and mainly absent. Or perhaps this had always been his habit, disrupted by her arrival. Mostly, he was shut in his study, not to be disturbed, or out at his club or... somewhere. Somewhere not lacking in female companionship of a wholly different sort, she suspected. Charlotte and the girls most often ate dinner without him in one of the small parlors rather than the dining room. The meals were lively and enjoyable, but she sometimes missed...

However, Alec obviously found her uninteresting, as well as useless. Why had she offered to help with the pile of correspondence that grew every day on his desk? He'd made it clear he judged her quite incapable, the sort of ignorant chit who simpered over Byron and wasted his precious time. She certainly wouldn't bother him again.

"Tell us a story from the globe," Lizzy urged.

Much better not to think of him at all, Charlotte told herself, and searched her mind for one of her father's tales about far-flung places and exotic peoples. Briefly, her throat grew tight; so many times, she had sat with him just as Lizzy did now, begging for stories. Holding quite a different cat, however, she recalled with smile. "You remember Captain Cook?"

"He sailed all around the Pacific Ocean," Lizzy answered.

"Very good. Well, when he first arrived at New Zealand in... 1769, I believe it was, he had great difficulties with the Maori tribesmen." Watching Anne and Lizzy grow attentive, then engrossed, Charlotte felt contentment spread through her. She had always wished for sisters, and it was almost as if she had them now.

❧

Lucy crouched by the kitchen hearth, keeping a close eye on the curling iron she was warming over the coals. It was tricky getting the heat just right—hot enough to curl hair well and properly, but never so hot as to singe it. She'd heard awful stories of maids who burnt off the little ringlets ladies liked to wear dangling by their ears. She could so easily imagine the bits of shriveled hair in a row on the dressing table—and the smell! Miss Charlotte would never give her the sack over such a mistake; she'd understand. That made it even more important to get things right.

"I have found that the iron should be touchable," said a voice from above. "If it burns the fingers badly, it will do the same to hair."

Lucy scrambled up to face Miss Cole's high-toned dresser. Jennings's fabled experience and assurance still overawed her. She couldn't help dropping a curtsy. It was received with a slight smile.

"You are doing hair now?"

She would not be tongue-tied and awkward like a country bumpkin, Lucy told herself. "No, ma'am. I was just going to practice, like, on Agnes." The kitchen maid giggled over the pile of potatoes she was peeling.

"Ah." Under Jennings's calm, evaluative gaze, Agnes's smile faded. "Commendable." Even the housekeeper sometimes deferred to Jennings, who was rumored to be the highest paid of all the staff. She hardly even looked like a servant. Her gowns might be in dark colors, which you would expect to fade into the background, but they were beautifully cut and draped. Lucy had heard that the dresser sold her mistress's castoffs, a perk of her position, and made her own wardrobe. Tall and thin, with a bony face, Jennings kept her hair drawn back in a tight bun and was somehow more elegant for that. "Come along," she said to Lucy. Behind her back, Agnes crossed her eyes and stuck out her tongue, but Lucy didn't feel the slightest urge to laugh.

Agnes's eyes bugged when Jennings turned and caught her. "Remove the curling iron from the fire," the older woman said. Agnes jumped to obey.

Lucy followed Jennings up to the chamber she occupied, next to Miss Cole's dressing room. She had her own little sitting area in a corner, and Lucy was waved to a chair. "I understand you have a deft hand with a flatiron."

Lucy flushed with pleasure. "I've tried to get it right."

"You like your work?"

"Yes, ma'am."

"You don't mind being a servant?"

"Mind...?" Lucy wasn't sure what she meant.

"Some see it as demeaning, you know. My own sister works from dawn to dark on her husband's farm—exhausting, dirty work and barely feeding them these days—and still thinks herself better than I."

"Farm labor is dreadful hard." Lucy remembered the constant toil from her childhood. Her father rose every day stiff and aching and went to his bed tired out.

"So it is. I, on the other hand, am not tied to a scrap of played-out land. I have a valued profession, for which I'm very well paid. If I find I'm not valued, I can leave whenever I like and find a better place. I am not a slave."

Lucy wondered why Jennings was telling her this. It

was interesting, but it made her a little uncomfortable. "No, ma'am. Of course not."

"Not everyone is in my position, of course. I've made sure to acquire the right skills."

Lucy knew it was true. Fine ladies, duchesses even, fought to hire the best dressers. They stole them from each other and gave them all sorts of privileges to keep them happy.

"The more you know, the more independence you have. I've noticed that you like learning things, Lucy."

Lucy nodded. "That I do."

"I'm glad you have some ambition. I hate to see a girl with skill waste herself."

Was liking to learn the same as ambition? Lucy wasn't sure.

"In time, you might get a post such as mine here in London, at the highest levels."

Lucy didn't dare tell her that she longed to go back to country. She was sure Jennings wouldn't approve.

"Do you have any schooling?"

Lucy nodded proudly. "My mother made sure we all went to the village school every day we could. I can read and write and do some figuring." She nodded again for emphasis. "I don't get cheated in the market."

"That's good." Jennings showed one of her thin smiles. "I would be happy to teach you what a superior dresser needs to know, if you like."

"Oh, yes, ma'am." Lucy was thrilled at the thought. She had no doubt of one thing—the more you could do, the better off you were likely to be in this world.

Jennings bowed her head magisterially. "I believe learning should be passed along, to give as we have been given to, and in helping others advance themselves. When they deserve it."

Ignoring the touch of steel in Jennings's voice, Lucy said, "Thank you, ma'am. Thank you very much."

"Is she going to tell Cook I was cheeky?" muttered Agnes when Lucy returned to the kitchen for the curling iron. Clearly this had been worrying her ever since Lucy left.

"Who?" Ethan lifted a luncheon tray ready to go upstairs.

"Jennings. I…" Agnes showed him the face she'd made earlier.

Ethan laughed.

"I don't think she will," Lucy assured her. Jennings's mind had seemed to be on other things.

"Do her good to loosen up a bit." Giving Lucy one of the smiles that sizzled right through her, Ethan went out.

❧

After luncheon, Frances Cole invited Charlotte to join her in the drawing room. Lizzy and Anne exchanged speaking glances and disappeared up the stairs, but Charlotte was happy to accept. As she'd discovered on her third day in the house, Frances was engaged in a mammoth embroidery project—a wall hanging for the Wyldes' Derbyshire home—and always looking for additional hands. The sisters saw it as a penance, but Charlotte enjoyed short doses of fancy work. She and Frances had already spent several pleasant hours in this way, and they had shown Charlotte another side of the older woman. Embroidering, Frances was relaxed and happy, full of stories about her childhood doing needlework with her mother.

She had narrated several such anecdotes, and Charlotte was just finishing a rose petal when Frances said, "I wrote to my cousin Amelia Earnton to tell her that Anne will be able to join the dancing class she has arranged after all. I'm so glad. I feared she would be too ill."

After a moment, Charlotte remembered the name. This was the aunt married to an earl. "Dancing class?"

"It's often done. They've gathered a group of young people who will be making their bow to society next year."

"To teach them to dance?"

Frances smiled. In this peaceful mood, she seemed almost another person. "If they need it, but more to introduce them to each other, so they have some acquaintances when they are thrown into the whirl of their first London Season."

"That is a very good idea." How she would have loved to have a readymade circle of friends in town, Charlotte thought.

Frances set a complex knot stitch. "Amelia will be taking over supervision of Anne more and more, of course. I suppose I shall hardly see her at this time next year." She sighed. "It will be just Lizzy and me left. Lizzy will not like that."

"I don't think she will…"

"Oh, don't misunderstand me. We are quite fond of each other—despite what I may say in the heat of the moment." Frances smiled again. "But Lizzy requires so much activity! She really should go to school."

"Perhaps she will reconsider once Anne is busy elsewhere."

"Perhaps." Frances didn't sound as if she believed it. They sewed in silence for a while. "In a few years they will all be off to lives of their own. Alec will marry, naturally, and I shall not be needed in his household."

Remembering stories she had heard of the ill treatment of poor relations, Charlotte grew concerned. "You would not be turned out?"

"Oh no. Alec would never do that. And in any case James, his father, left me a tidy sum in his will. I am quite independent. It just seems that my… work… the work I was given to do fourteen years ago is nearly over. It's odd to think of."

"You have been a very busy person."

"Too busy sometimes," Frances laughed. "But I am less and less so. I used to help James a good deal with the estate work, but Alec prefers to handle it himself."

Charlotte was well aware of that!

"Richard is at Oxford; Anne is nearly out." She shook her head.

"What would you most *like* to do?"

"What?"

"It is a subject I have been thinking and thinking about myself. For some reason, I never considered it much before. But we need to, don't we? If we don't, who will?"

"Will…?"

"Think about what we want—ourselves, separate from what others may need or plan."

"Ah." Frances said nothing more for such a long time that Charlotte wondered if she had overstepped her bounds. At last, however, she spoke very quietly, eyes on her sewing. "There was a time when I thought... hoped, perhaps, that James... He was twenty years older, of course. But I was about the age of his wife—my cousin Elizabeth. It seemed no impediment. However, he did not... there was never any approach to..." She stopped, pulled dark green threads through the cloth several times, then added, "He talked to me quite frankly, you know, trusted me. We were good friends, and I believe I was a comfort to him in many ways. And I had the children; I loved... love the children as if they were my own. I had less than many women have, but also more than a great many." She glanced briefly at Charlotte, then dropped her gaze to the needlework again.

"Since he's been gone, I feel just a little... lost. Everything is so different."

Moved, Charlotte leaned forward and put a hand on one of hers. She had no words to offer. Frances's story made her feel young and inexperienced. But she could show how much she sympathized.

Frances gave her a warm smile. She turned her hand up and squeezed Charlotte's. "It has been so short a time, but you feel like one of the family," she said.

Charlotte's eyes pricked with tears. Nothing she could have said would have been more welcome than this. Frances patted her hand and went back to her needle. The moment passed; the conversation retreated to more general subjects. But Charlotte would hold it close in her heart ever after.

With a quick knock on the drawing room door, Ethan came in. He presented a silver tray holding a visiting card. Frances picked it up. "Edward?"

"Mr. Danforth is below, Madame."

"Oh. Well… I don't… I suppose he should come up."

What was it about the Danforths, Charlotte wondered? Frances didn't seem to dislike them; it was more as if they confused her so much that she didn't know what to do.

Alec's cousin strolled into the room looking more handsome than ever in a many-caped driving coat—the essence of a fashionable man about town. "Afternoon, ladies." He smiled at Charlotte. "We finally got a warmer day in this blasted icy spring, and I dared pull out my curricle." He made it sound like an adventure. "Care to take a drive… Aunt?" His blue eyes glinted with humor at the ridiculous title.

"Now?" said Charlotte, then berated herself for sounding childish.

• "Well, if you are not particularly occupied." Edward looked at the vast piece of embroidery as if he pitied her.

"I don't know whether…" Frances began. At an amused glance from Edward, she trailed off into silence.

She didn't need anyone's permission, Charlotte thought. A burst of excitement went through her at the idea, and at the prospect of glimpsing some of London society at last. She had dreamed of it on leaving home, and been so bitterly disappointed. She slipped from under the embroidery canvas. "I'll get my things."

In her bedchamber, however, she nearly balked. All

she had to wear was the cloak she'd gotten when she attained her full height at sixteen. It was dark green, not black, and utterly utilitarian. Her bonnet was black, but hopelessly outmoded; even her gloves were unfashionable. Edward Danforth would take one look at her and withdraw his invitation, ashamed to be seen with such a dowd. Charlotte peered into the mirror in despair, and then, with an effort, threw it off. He would not dare to be so rude. She would grasp her chance at a real outing, think what he would.

In fact, he did not show by the flicker of an eyelid any condemnation of her dreadful ensemble. He handed her into the kind of shining equipage she'd only seen from afar, laid a rug over her knees, and raised a finger to his groom, who left the horses' heads and swung up behind. "A turn through the park?" he said, and Charlotte smiled up at him.

It wasn't far. She admired Edward's driving skill as they negotiated some narrow turns on the way. Their swift passage in the open carriage, feet above the street, was thrilling. Everything seemed different from up here.

The lanes of Hyde Park were sparsely populated; Charlotte put it down to the chilly temperatures until she remembered that morning was the fashionable time for riding. Had Edward planned it this way? He nodded to a few passersby but didn't stop. "Not much going on in town as yet, though people are trickling back."

By "people," he meant the *ton*, Charlotte understood. There were, of course, hordes of unfashionable people all over the streets of London. "The Season hasn't started," she replied, trying to sound knowl-edgeable. He smiled at her, and Charlotte felt as if her ignorance was perfectly transparent, and yet somehow charming. She flushed.

"No. But the bad weather has spoiled the hunting, which will bring everyone back in short order. Do you hunt?"

Charlotte merely shook her head.

"What *do* you do, auntie?"

The glimmer in his eyes made it a joke, but she still smarted at this reminder of her lamentable history. "Please don't call me that."

"Your wish is my command, Mrs...."

"Not that either!"

Edward laughed. "What am I to call you then?" Her flush deepened; she could not ask a young man she barely knew—and such a very attractive one—to use her first name. "How about 'ma'am'?" he suggested. "Bit of a regal touch, dash of deference. That's the ticket."

"You're making fun, but..."

"Not at all, ma'am. Perfectly serious."

She couldn't resist his smile, the glint in his blue eyes—and the fact that she had no alternative. She didn't want to hear anyone call her "Mrs. Wylde" ever again. "Oh, very well."

"Yes, ma'am; thank you, ma'am." Before the jest could turn annoying, he added, "They say this art exhibit 'round the corner will be all the rage once the Season gets under way. Care to take a peek?"

Charlotte gathered the scraps of her dignity. "That sounds pleasant."

With the good sense not to repeat the word "ma'am," Edward turned his team toward the park gates. Their destination was not quite around the corner, but it was nearby. He pulled up before an imposing redbrick building and handed the reins to his groom. "Walk them, Sam," he said as he jumped down and offered Charlotte a hand.

Inside, the walls of large rooms were crowded with pictures right up to the ceiling. Here and there, people wandered; most seemed more interested in each other than in the artworks. Charlotte examined a portrait of a fat man in full court dress and wondered what in the world to say about it. It seemed very ugly to her.

"My dears, hello, hello!" trilled a voice, and she turned to find Edward's mother bearing down on them. "How lovely to see you again." Lady Isabella enveloped Charlotte in a quick embrace, scented by violets, then took her arm. Her fur-trimmed cloak, with matching hat and muff, made Charlotte's look like a candidate for the ragbag. "I couldn't induce Edward to come to this exhibit. Now I see what is required—more attractive company than his mother." She laughed and pulled Charlotte along. Arm in arm they strolled through the rooms, Edward trailing behind.

"That landscape is pretty," Charlotte ventured, feeling that she must express some opinion if this exhibit was so important.

"There's Cecily Harcourt," was Lady Isabella's reply. "She still looks rather plump, doesn't she? She delivered Seton's child only a month ago. They say her husband hasn't the least idea that the boy isn't his. I suppose Cecily is quite adroit with her... timing."

Charlotte glanced at the woman in question, then away. She tried not to look shocked. It was the first time anyone had treated her as a married woman, not a girl who must be sheltered from scandalous gossip.

"Isn't that Helen Trent?" Lady Isabella went on. "I'm surprised she dares show her face in town with all those gambling debts unpaid. Three thousand pounds or more, I heard. I know she can't be blackballed from the clubs the way a gentleman can, but you'd think she'd be ashamed."

"She's barred from all the decent gaming houses," Edward put in.

"Really?" Lady Isabella relished the tidbit. "What will she do, I wonder? They say she cannot live without cards or dice."

"Find another 'patron,' I expect," answered Edward carelessly.

His mother's laugh trilled out. "She's hardly the beauty she once was, darling. I don't think any rich man will be lured in to cover her sort of losses." Seeing Charlotte's expression, she added, "Poor Helen generally loses."

"No head for it at all," Edward agreed. "If she can't get anyone to frank her, it'll have to be the moneylenders."

"Edward, shame on you! What a shocking idea." In fact, his mother appeared to find it delicious. "Let's sit. Looking at art is so tiring."

She hadn't actually looked at any, Charlotte thought. But she was happy to sit on one of the cushioned benches. This glance under the shiny surface of society had left her a bit dazed.

"Dear Charlotte." Lady Isabella's gloved hand

patted one of hers. "I am so glad to have this opportunity. Ever since we met I've wanted to talk to you about Henry's will. It is just so very unfair to you."

Charlotte had to nod. Whenever she focused on her true situation—which she did as little as possible—she was stung by the injustice of it all. It was much more pleasant not to think about it.

"I feel for you because the same thing happened to me."

"Really?"

Edward had drifted away. He stood, hands behind his back, gazing at a huge historical painting of Lot's wife turning to a pillar of salt.

"When my father died," Lady Isabella explained. "He left me next to nothing. Henry as well. Everything went to James." Seeing Charlotte's frown, she took it to be confusion. "Our elder brother; Alec's father, you know. It was outrageous. I took the matter to court."

Charlotte remembered a vague mention of something like this. "To challenge the will?"

"Yes, indeed. I was the one who stayed at home to care for Mama, you know. It always falls to the daughter, does it not? James and Henry were off to school, town, wherever they liked. Do you know I was thirty-one before I broke away to marry? Can you imagine?" Her laugh was less musical this time.

Charlotte didn't know what to say. Lady Isabella seemed to expect a response. "Your suit in court was successful?"

Lady Isabella looked away, her thin shoulders stiff. "Well… no. Except, I made my point, you see. I told them all exactly what I thought."

Which accounted for her reception at Sir Alexander's house, Charlotte concluded. "I'm told that Henry's will is quite legal. He was free to do as he pleased with the house and estate; I have no grounds to dispute it."

"Of course they tell you that." Lady Isabella leaned forward. "Those who benefit will always discourage…"

"The thing is… I beg your pardon, Lady Isabella, but it seems to me that *no one* benefits from Henry's will. Unless you count being allowed to live in that house…" Which she did not. In her mind, the will was a mirror of Henry Wylde's character—slyly spiteful. She didn't want to think of him, still less spend months grappling with legalities. "I don't wish to go to court."

The older woman leaned tensely toward her for another moment, then sat back. "Well, of course it's your choice, my dear." She rose. "Shall we see some other paintings?"

They walked into a further room and found Edward there. He looked bored. Lady Isabella barely glanced at the pictures before moving on. It was impossible to take in so much at one time, Charlotte thought. There must be at least fifty paintings in every room. By the time they had made the circuit of the building, colors and images were blurred together in her mind.

"Very striking," Lady Isabella said as they returned to the entrance. "Don't you think, Charlotte?"

"Uh, yes. It was lovely to have an outing." That was certainly true. She smiled at both the Danforths.

"Poor dear. I should be delighted to take you about London this Season, but… please don't be offended…"

Charlotte had no doubt what was coming. "I need some decent clothes!"

Lady Isabella cocked her head in agreement. "Of course, with blacks... your wedding clothes are much smarter, I imagine?"

Charlotte hesitated, then decided to throw herself on Lady Isabella's mercy. Wardrobe was clearly her area of expertise. "I... my father thought I should have my trousseau made in London. The marriage... came about rather quickly, and... my seamstress in Hampshire..." Charlotte fingered the folds of her old-fashioned cloak. "Then, when I got here, Henry would not allow me to spend..."

"My dear, say no more. Men have no notion of these things."

Henry had known very well, Charlotte thought. He'd wanted every penny for his own purchases.

"My own dressmaker is a genius with the needle and very quick as well. I would be happy to recommend you to her."

A sternly suppressed longing surged up in Charlotte and crashed. "I don't want a wardrobe full of black gowns." It was excruciating, not to mention hypocritical, that she had to appear to mourn Henry.

"Well, yes. Hmm. Such a brief marriage, and really unknown, after all. There can scarcely be gossip... Henry was not exactly a member of society. No, I don't think black is necessary. You cannot wear bright colors, of course." Lady Isabella surveyed her. "That dark green becomes you, and perhaps a bronze—yes, that would be very striking for evening."

Charlotte knew that some people expected mourning

dress for months and months. The idea was hateful. Rebellion rose in her. She would *not* wear widow's weeds for Henry Wylde; she did not care who objected. "I should like to see a bit of society."

"Of course you would, dear."

"I hate black!"

Lady Isabella considered her. "It is very becoming on some, but with your coloring…"

"I won't buy it!"

"Very wise."

"But you think I could attend… that is, you would be willing to…"

"Evening parties would be acceptable. Not balls, I'm afraid."

It was more than she'd dared hope for. Charlotte determined to write Wycliffe immediately and ask about drawing funds from the estate. Surely something could be spared.

And so, a surprisingly few days later, she stood before the mirror in her bedchamber in the first truly modish gown she'd ever owned. Lady Isabella's dressmaker had been a marvel. She'd altered two gowns she had on hand to fit Charlotte, in particular a midnight blue—nearly black—velvet evening dress more beautiful than any garment she'd ever worn. And two more were being sewn especially for her. The woman had given her a special price as a friend of a longtime customer.

"Ooh, Miss Charlotte," said Lucy, adjusting a flounce of the lavender morning gown trimmed with bunches of purple ribbon. "That's gorgeous, that is!"

Charlotte was almost tearful at the vision in the

mirror. She hoped she wasn't vain or frivolous. It had just been so long since she had anything so pretty.

"I was thinking, miss." Lucy hesitated.

"What?" Charlotte turned to admire the fall of the skirt in back.

"Jennings, Miss Cole's dresser, has ever so much experience. She's up on everything to do with fashion. I was thinking I might ask her to do your hair once, to show me, like." As if afraid of objections, Lucy rushed on. "She's been very kind to me, says I have a dab hand with an iron. If I saw her doing it, then I'd get the knack."

"That's a wonderful idea, Lucy. If you think she really would."

"I do, miss. She's offered to help me learn."

"Then please ask her."

Lucy beamed.

Nine

EXACTLY HOW, ALEC WONDERED, HAD HE ENDED UP at the theater in this box full of females, about to be subjected to an evening of Edmund Kean? He vastly preferred comedies; he despised Kean and the set who raved over his stage frenzies. A year ago, or the year before that, he would have been engaged in some wholly different, much more... palatable form of amusement. With a very different sort of female.

Had it been Lizzy, dying to see a play? No, it was Anne, he remembered. He'd overheard her wistful comment about reading dramas but never actually seeing one performed. It was simply assumed, when he mentioned purchasing tickets, that Lizzy and Frances, and Charlotte, would come. Lizzy had been so excited; impossible to disappoint her. Even Frances had been pleased, and Charlotte... He'd been avoiding Charlotte, yet here she was beside him, stunning in a dark velvet gown. She'd undergone a transformation since he'd last looked, moving from winsomely pretty to riveting. Whenever he turned his head, he was mesmerized by the coppery golden glimmer of her hair, her sparkling eyes, smooth white arms, the curves under the soft folds of…

As if reading his mind, Lizzy said, "Doesn't Charlotte look splendid? Have you even noticed her new gown? Jennings did her hair specially."

It took Alec a moment to find his voice. "Very nice."

"Very nice," Lizzy mocked. "What a sourpuss you've been lately, Alec. Always gone off somewhere, never taking the time to…"

"It's quite a good crowd for so early in the year, isn't it?" interrupted Anne, ever the peacemaker. She leaned over the rail of the box, taking in the scene; there were roses in her cheeks again, for which Alec felt a surge of gratitude. It would be good for her to get a taste of London society, with her come-out just a year away. He hadn't thought of that before. There was so much that he'd never expected to think about.

"The lady in that box across the way seems to know you, Alec," said his youngest sister with a giggle.

"Lizzy," Frances admonished.

"Well, it can't be any of the rest of us. And she keeps looking over here and smiling and playing with her fan."

Alec followed her gaze, and recognized the sophisticated young matron who had considerably enlivened his last stay in London. The depth of her décolletage brought back steamy memories. Her dazzling smile when he nodded politely signaled a clear willingness to add to them whenever he chose.

"Is she on your list?" Lizzy asked.

"Be quiet, Lizzy." How had he failed to consider that this outing would bring together two unrelated parts of his life? Which were definitely to remain unrelated.

"Alec intends to make an arranged marriage," Lizzy proceeded to tell Charlotte. "He is very cynical and does not believe in love matches."

"How could anyone, after watching our grandparents continually rip at each other? Father knew what he was doing, choosing a partner on a rational basis."

His entire party stared at him, openmouthed. Anne seemed about to speak, then said nothing. Frances looked deeply shocked, but she could scarcely be more shocked than Alec himself. He couldn't believe the words that had escaped his mouth. He was well accustomed to his sisters' teasing; he'd never lost control in such... to expose his family's most private... in front of... His face burned with humiliation. Why couldn't Lizzy curb her tongue? Why could she not learn some discipline? "If you cannot behave with more propriety, Lizzy, I shall take you home immediately."

"But all I..."

"Did was make spectacle of us for all to see."

"How did I do that? That's not fair!"

Lizzy gazed at him with huge, hurt eyes. Anne looked distressed, Frances uneasy. In his awareness that Lizzy had a point, he didn't dare glance at Charlotte. Blessedly, before the silence grew unbearable, the curtain rose, and the performance began.

Kean ranged across the boards as Hamlet. Some poet had said that his acting was like reading Shakespeare by flashes of lightning. And why would you want to do that, Alec wondered? He ignored the play and struggled to recover his equilibrium. What was wrong with him? He did not lose his temper. He did not criticize his family. He did not, and he would not, and that was the end of it. So… why…?

Not even looking at the stage, he told himself he was tired and worried. The times were so bad that the country was a tinderbox awaiting a spark. Not his own tenants, perhaps, but he'd heard from some of them about others—unspecified others—who were threatening violence. If they carried their grievances into action, the government would crush them, and what would become of his own people in that case? Might he rush home to find a line of gibbets across his green fields? What could he do—what more could he do—to make certain that never happened?

Servitors entered the box with lemonade and ices, and Alec came back to himself to discover it was already the first interval. He had ordered refreshments to be served here, to avoid the crush in the lobby. Lizzy greeted them with vociferous delight. "What I don't understand is," she said as she dug in to an ice, "why isn't Hamlet king? His father was the king."

"His uncle took over," replied Charlotte.

"But what reason did he give? Wouldn't all the people in…?"

"Denmark," Anne prompted.

"Yes. Wouldn't they expect Hamlet to become the king? Everyone knows the Prince Regent will become king, and he has lots of uncles. Doesn't he?"

"He certainly does," replied Alec drily. And a bigger set of gamblers and lechers and incompetents could hardly be imagined.

"Claudius usurped the throne," said Anne, savoring the verb.

"But how? With an army?" Lizzy wondered.

"With… um… persuasion and intrigue," Charlotte offered, with admirable ingenuity, Alec thought.

Lizzy contemplated this as she finished her ice and reached for another. "Why didn't he kill Hamlet then? In the history books people are always trying to make me read, they do that when they u… usurp." She wrinkled her nose at their surprised expressions. "I *have* read some of them!"

"I expect he thought Hamlet's mother wouldn't like it," Frances put in.

"Oh, yes. He wanted to get on her good side, because he wanted to marry her." Lizzy nodded wisely.

Alec found he was smiling.

"She seems rather stupid, doesn't she?" Lizzy looked from face to face. "I mean, she can't understand why Hamlet is upset. But he didn't get to be king. Why wouldn't he be upset?"

"Very true," said Alec. Lizzy shot him a glance, saw his smile, and returned it. Alec felt his chest lighten with relief. He didn't enjoy being at odds with his sister.

"So, Hamlet thinks that his uncle killed his father. He knows his uncle married his mother and took away his kingdom?"

The rest of the party nodded, enjoyment of Lizzy's commentary evident in all their faces.

"But he isn't doing anything about it?"

"He's thinking about what he should do," said Anne.

Lizzy cocked her head. "He seems a bit damp, doesn't he? Compared to King Arthur and his knights, or the princes in fairy tales? They're always righting wrongs and fighting injustice. Hamlet just keeps *talking*."

"Well done, Lizzy. You've hit on the characteristic he is most famous for," Alec told her.

There was general laughter. Seeing Frances throw back her head and indulge in a hearty laugh, Alec was abruptly struck by the memory of a picnic, ten years or more ago. He'd been home from school, so it must have been during the summer holidays. Frances, his father, his brother, and sisters had all been there, around a bright blanket on the shore of the stream that ran through the estate. The picture was vivid in his mind—green grass and paler willows, splashes of wildflowers, the sound of water in the background and his family's laughter close by. But mostly he remembered the feeling of contentment that had enveloped him that afternoon, for the first time in a long while, perhaps since his mother's death. And he had known somehow, even at fourteen, that it came as a gift from Frances Cole. She didn't laugh enough these days. He needed to see about that.

"What do *you* think Hamlet should do?" Charlotte was asking Lizzy when he came back to himself.

Lizzy's dark blue eyes narrowed. She scraped the last of her second ice from the dish. "Challenge his uncle to a duel. They could fight each other for the kingdom."

"Not a bad idea, actually," Alec said. He would have preferred it over what was to come.

Lizzy looked around. "Is that what he does?"

"You'll have to wait and see," Anne told her.

Lizzy wrinkled her nose at her sister. "Well, next time I would rather see a comedy."

"I couldn't agree more," Alec told her. "What do you think of the play, Anne? Is seeing better than reading?"

"Of course. Although Mr. Kean is…"

Alec waited.

"He seems awfully…" Anne searched for a word, "…excitable."

Alec burst out laughing again, wholly in sympathy with his sisters. Charlotte was laughing, too. Their eyes caught and held, and Alec found he couldn't look away from the warmth of those coppery depths. He wanted to… rise and… or reach out a hand. Anne leaned over to speak to her; Charlotte turned away. Alec kept gazing at her until the curtain rose, and Edmund Kean came railing and frothing onto the stage.

❧

Ethan looked around the servants' hall of Sir Alexander Wylde's town house, at a circle of lamp-lit faces. With the family out for the evening, all the staff were present except Thomas, the coachman, and Jennings. As usual, she'd claimed she had tasks to do in her room. She put herself above the rest of them, Ethan thought, even the housekeeper, which was laying it on a bit thick.

Mrs. Wright knitted and kept a benign eye on the younger staff. Cook and Agnes were hulling chestnuts, some of which they'd roast in the fire later on. Ethan hefted his mug of mulled cider and let his gaze linger on Lucy. She was smiling; she looked happy. It was the first time Ethan had seen her so at ease. He liked seeing it; she'd been that anxious when she first arrived. Tonight, she was the picture of contentment, and a lovely picture it was.

"Oh, Ethan was crazed about animals when he was a lad," said Susan. "You'd only to tell him of a downed bird or a wounded hedgehog, and there he'd be. Eight years old, and he had a little kit with bandages and all."

Ethan gave her a lazy grin. The young lady's maid was practically a sister to him. They'd played together as toddlers and grown up on the estate side by side.

"Most of 'em died, o' course," Susan added. "And what a to-do we had then. You stopped doing the funerals after a while, though, Ethan. Why was that?"

"I started to wonder if I'd done them a service, keeping them hanging on, like. I figured out that some of them died 'cause they could never live in a cage." It had taught him a lot about the way nature worked.

"Our Ethan's quite the fee-losopher," James said.

Ethan poked his fellow footman in the ribs, and they tussled briefly. He didn't really mind the teasing. He knew the others liked him, as he did them.

"Let him be now," said Mrs. Wright. "Our Ethan's an easygoing lad, but there are limits."

And there it was. They didn't go too far, and next they'd be twitting James about his finicky ways with boot polish, or Agnes about her weakness for sweets and the lengths she'd go for a bit of cake. Nobody was mean with it.

Ethan caught a flash of black in the corner of his eye. If it was a rat, Cook would... but, no. It was Callie edging along the wall. Was the cat trying to escape the house where she was increasingly confined? A creature like her was used to wandering of a night. However, she was probably used to kicks and thrown stones, too. Not likely to be missing those. Callie settled by the fire with her paws tucked underneath her; she noticed Ethan's gaze and looked away. Maybe she was just lonely, upstairs on her own.

Ethan thought no more about it until a few minutes later, when a lightning paw flashed over the edge of the table, snagged the bit of cheese remaining on James's plate, and disappeared. Talking, James groped about the plate, then looked down, puzzled, at the empty dish.

Ethan bit back a laugh and an urge to peek under the table. Callie was a slick little thief, and no mistake. And why shouldn't she be? Her skills had kept her alive out there in the street. He looked up and caught Lucy's blue eyes dancing. She'd seen it, too. He raised his brows. Should they turn the cat in? Lucy smiled at him, a free and easy smile that hit him amidships and just about stopped his heart. What was it about this particular lass? He'd known prettier; he'd known livelier. But somehow Lucy Bowman made every other girl he'd met fade from his mind. For the gift of that smile, Callie would go free, Ethan thought.

James decided he'd eaten the cheese after all. "I don't know what's going to come of it," he said. "Folk I know are near to starving. No joke, their young ones are hungry more days than not."

Mrs. Wright shook her head. "The hardship's something terrible in the country."

"And I've heard from my brother that there's some want to take steps," James added. "They're sick of waiting for help that don't arrive and a government that don't listen. Right back home, this is."

"You should tell Sir Alexander if there's talk of violence," admonished Mrs. Wright.

James's jaw hardened. Ethan knew he'd never risk getting his friends in trouble.

"He's doing his best to make things right," the housekeeper went on. "He has a fund for those in need, and all." But James was clearly not convinced.

"Everybody said things would be better when the Frenchies were beat," put in Agnes. "We'd been fighting those devils since 'afore I was born. Why en't it better with the war over?"

Nobody knew. Though James faithfully read the newspapers that came into the house, and Mrs. Wright corresponded with a number of people in Derbyshire, the problem was too knotty even for their collective wisdom.

A pan rattled, then fell with a great clatter in the scullery. A streak of black hurtled across the kitchen and out toward the stairs. "Drat that animal," said Cook. "She can't be hungry. I sent up a pile of scraps not two hours ago."

"I reckon she can't forget *being* hungry," said Ethan. He rose. "I'll go and make sure she's back in Miss Lizzy's room."

It took awhile to corner Callie. Once he had, and returned her to her place with only two or three scratches to show for it, Ethan got an idea. He lingered in the back hall, waiting for Lucy to come up from the kitchen, praying she'd be alone when she did.

His luck was in. Some while later, she appeared on the stairs, alone. He pretended to be just returning from his errand. "She's a handful, that cat," he said.

"Did she bite you again?"

"No, we've reached a better understanding." As

Lucy started past him, he added, "It's a fine night." He hoped it wasn't too cold, anyway. "Care to step out for a breath of air?"

"I need to…"

"Lovely moon out there." Lucy gave him a look, and Ethan acknowledged it hadn't been his smoothest approach. "Where's your favorite place to see the moon?" he added before she could leave.

That made her pause and think. "In the gardens, back in Hampshire, there was a whole patch of white roses. I was out there once when they was blooming, and the moon was full. It was right beautiful." Her voice had gone softer.

"Mine's the forest." Ethan edged her toward the back door, and she went. They turned right and walked into the small garden behind the house. "'Course, the forest is pretty much my favorite place for anything."

"Like, the woods, you mean?" Lucy wondered.

"'Woods' says small to me," Ethan answered. "The Wyldes keep a good bit of land in trees, for timber mostly. And it's good for some of the steeper bits, keeps the soil down. You get deep in that forest, and it's… a different world."

"Different how?"

Moonlight poured over the neat flower beds as Ethan struggled to put it into words. "The light's all green, coming through the leaves, and the air like to… smells green. Sounds are softer, some of 'em, or sharper. Crack of a twig can seem like a gunshot. And there's no sign of another person, anyplace; you might be the first ever to step in that particular spot."

Lucy stared up at him as if she hadn't really seen him before. "Don't you worry about getting lost?"

"You could; it's that big. But old Elkins taught me how to find my way about."

"Elkins?"

"He's the forester. He trained me. That's what I mean to do—take his place now he's ready to leave it." The words just slipped out of him. He'd never told another soul about his plan for the future. But once started with Lucy, he couldn't seem to stop. "Forester gets a cottage of his own, out at the edge of the trees. It's all I've wanted—to look after a piece of land, and maybe a family, someday." Ethan had never cared for possessions; he wasn't like his sister, always longing for new things. "My dad's going to see it as a step down for the family. He already thinks I'm feckless, and this'll properly enrage him." Why was he telling Lucy? It seemed he had to, that she had to hear it.

"Your dad doesn't know what you mean to do?"

"Nobody knows. I haven't told anybody... else." What if she talked about it, Ethan thought? "Appreciate it if you wouldn't mention it."

Lucy stared up at him with parted lips. Was she amazed, or just bewildered? Ethan couldn't tell. All he knew was—the world had fallen away. He couldn't see anything but her face, silvered by moonlight, familiar and strange, wildly appealing. He stepped closer, reached for her. He bent his head to take those lips for his own.

She tasted of cider and cinnamon. Her body was supple and yielding under his hands. Ethan pulled her close, and closer as her mouth softened under his. Desire and response flashed between them and set him afire. He pushed the kiss, wanting more.

Lucy stiffened, struggled, pushed away from him, and backed up. She raised a hand to her trembling mouth. "I almost believed you weren't..." She sounded near tears. "I reckon you're right pleased with yourself now. You can brag to your friends that you got round me after all. Another conquest to add to your long list."

"It isn't like that, Lucy. I'd never..."

She turned and ran.

Now he'd done it. Ethan cursed himself for a fool. He'd behaved like the bad sort she thought he was. And no way to make her believe that kiss had been different from any other in his life, that he flat out hadn't been able to resist her. Worse, they'd both be in big trouble if anyone found out what had happened tonight.

Moving much more slowly, Ethan made his way back inside. He'd have to go back to the kitchen, joke about the cat, pretend he was carefree and heedless and hadn't a thought of Lucy Bowman in his head. It was going to be damned hard. But he'd do it. He'd do just about anything to protect Lucy, he realized.

❧

Alec's anticipation of the second interval was dashed from the beginning when Edward Danforth stepped through the curtains at the back of their box. "Mama sent me over with salutations," he said with a graceful bow. "She's holding court, of course." He indicated a box to the left, where Alec discovered his Aunt

Bella entertaining several older gentlemen. She must have been fashionably late. He hadn't seen her come in. Politeness required that Alec bow. She gave him a little wave that seemed to epitomize everything he disliked about this branch of his family—their unshakable air of superiority, their careless amusement at those who could not match their social ease, their taste for malicious gossip. But most of all it was his aunt's impervious self-regard; her baseless lawsuit had outraged the whole family. Yet she sat there as if she'd done nothing wrong; indeed, he knew she maintained she was in the right, despite the unequivocal verdict of the law courts.

Edward leaned over the back of Charlotte's chair. "Are you enjoying the play? Ravished by Kean's genius?" Alec wanted to dismiss his cousin as a posturing coxcomb. Only, he wasn't. Three years older, he had always outstripped Alec in the social graces.

"We are finding him a little… excessive," Charlotte replied, smiling up at Edward. Alec became conscious of a desire to toss his cousin over the rail into the pit.

"Do not let anyone hear you say so!" Edward pretended shock. "He is all the rage, ma'am, I assure you." They exchanged a twinkling look. What did he mean by calling her "ma'am"? It was ridiculous, though Charlotte appeared to be enjoying it.

"Hamlet is becoming rather annoying," offered Lizzy.

Edward gave her a lazy smile, but otherwise ignored her. "Kean's death scene is much admired," he told Charlotte. "Perhaps that will sway you."

"Does he die?" said Lizzy. "I shouldn't be glad, I suppose…"

"You're looking very pretty, cousin," Edward said to Anne. "Next year, you'll have a broad acquaintance and more interesting supplicants in your box than a mere relation."

Anne flushed and returned a shy smile.

"Don't let us keep you from your friends, *cousin*," Alec couldn't help saying. "I know you find family gatherings tedious."

"Less so every day," Edward responded, sharing out a smile between Anne and Charlotte. "Indeed, I think I must pay far more attention to my family... obligations."

He said the last word as if it meant something quite different. Yet there was nothing one could object to in the sentiment. He'd been a slippery creature since he was eight years old, Alec recollected. "The play is about to start up again," he said. He didn't care whether it was true. He just wanted Edward gone.

The latter met his eyes, laughing at him. "A few more minutes, cuz. Pray don't turn me out."

There was no answer to that, and he knew it. Alec was forced to watch him flirt expertly with Charlotte and Anne for ten long minutes before the interval finally ended. And by then even Lizzy looked charmed. It was Edward's gift—without a doubt—easy charm. Alec had never envied it quite so much as tonight, and he refused to ask himself why this should be so.

The play wound up to its gory conclusion. Alec held cloaks and recovered gloves as his charges chattered about the cascade of deaths and, in Lizzy's case, how Hamlet might have avoided his serial mistakes. As they waited in the press of patrons searching for their carriages, he noticed that Frances looked tired. "Let us walk a little," he suggested. "I told Thomas to wait down this way."

Thus, they found the carriage much sooner than otherwise, though no one seemed to notice his forethought. Lizzy had turned the conversation to Edward Danforth. "It will be a great help to you next year, Anne," she said. "He can present you to all his fashionable gentleman friends."

"His set is not suitable for Anne," Alec couldn't help replying.

"Why?"

"Never mind, Lizzy. Just be assured that I know what is best for Anne and for you."

"That sounded very like your Uncle Henry," Charlotte commented.

"Nonsense!" The insult left him rigid with anger. And the snap of the word rang loud inside the carriage. The resulting silence lasted all the way home.

Ten

THE FOLLOWING THURSDAY, CHARLOTTE TRIPPED
down the stairs of the Wylde town house to find Lady
Isabella waiting for her in the drawing room, making
desultory conversation with Frances Cole. Charlotte
suspected that she had come in from her carriage
because she wanted to check Charlotte's appearance,
and smarten her up if necessary, before shepherding
her into society. For the first time in more than a year,
however, Charlotte was feeling confident. Frances's
high-toned dresser had not only taught Lucy to do her
hair in a becoming new way, but she had also directed
them to shops and markets where everything from hats
to slippers could be bought on the cheap. Charlotte
had used a small amount of money to great effect, so
that even though she had on the same velvet gown
she'd worn to the play, she was pleased with the result.
She was also very grateful for the warmth of the April
evening. It allowed her to carry a new shawl rather
than the embarrassment of her tired old cloak.

Lady Isabella, in a floating gown of sea green satin
that matched her eyes, surveyed her from top to toe.

She gestured. Obedient, Charlotte turned in a circle. She felt thoroughly evaluated, from the knot of silver ribbons in her hair to the new evening slippers on her feet, and briefly, her nervousness returned.

"Very nice," said Lady Isabella finally. She sounded a bit surprised, and Charlotte couldn't blame her. Her dreadful blacks had probably given the impression that she had no fashion sense at all.

"You look lovely," added Frances, who had stood aside for the examination.

Charlotte gave her a broad smile, knowing that Frances wished her well despite whatever frictions existed with Lady Isabella. "Will we be late?" Charlotte worried as they went out to the carriage.

"My dear, only nobodies turn up before nine."

The invitation had said eight; left to herself, Charlotte would have arrived with the nobodies. Of course, she was a nobody, she reflected. But being of little importance in society's scheme of things had its advantages. It was one reason she could ignore the conventions of mourning dress. Too, she didn't expect to be much noticed tonight; she would keep to the sidelines and learn about how to go on at a first-rank *ton* party.

Their destination proved to be a huge house in Grosvenor Square. The buzz of conversation rose and rose as they climbed the stairs—exhilarating and intimidating. The atmosphere positively crackled. It was just as she had dreamed when she first knew she would be living in London. It was gaiety and color and life—all the things she had been missing because of Henry.

Lady Isabella greeted the formidable woman at the top of stairs, and they exchanged uneffusive smiles. She murmured a name, which Charlotte missed, then said, "And this is my sister-in-law, Mrs. Charlotte Wylde."

The name jarred. She'd somehow forgotten that she must be presented in that way, but there was no help for it. She bobbed a curtsy under the hostess's raised brows—whether at her youth or her existence or some other cause, Charlotte didn't know. "Very pleased to meet you."

Passing that first hurdle, they moved into a spacious reception room full of chattering people, servants gliding through the crowd with trays of goblets filled with golden champagne. This was to be a musical evening, no dancing. Not that Charlotte cared. It was all just as she had imagined—the rainbow of silks and satins, the glitter of jewels, the rise and fall of sophisticated talk. She followed Lady Isabella into the press, watching her nod right and left as they passed acquaintances, envying her sure knowledge of this new geography.

She seemed to have a clear destination in mind, and did not stop to speak to anyone. Her goal turned out to be two ladies of around her own age and equally fashionable, posted in a corner, scanning the room. They greeted her with airy kisses and murmurs of, "Bella, dear. You look stunning."

She returned the compliments and introduced her friends to Charlotte as Mrs. Reverton and Mrs. Prine, not making it clear which was which. Both had crimped brown hair, solid figures under their modish ensembles, and the eyes of raptors. They scanned Charlotte like canny shoppers considering a purchase, and immediately turned their attention back to the party.

"I declare, if Sara Lewis continues to damp her gowns in that shameless way she'll catch a chill and expire one day soon," said either Mrs. Reverton or Mrs. Prine.

Following their gaze, Charlotte observed a young woman whose gauzy pink gown clung to her like a second skin, revealing a surprising lack of… anything underneath.

"She imagines it will bring young Thornton up to scratch," replied either Mrs. Prine or Mrs. Reverton. "A peek at the goods, so to speak." She tittered. "Look at him, practically drooling on her."

Her companion nodded, and Charlotte gave up trying to differentiate them. There was a gawky young man bent over the girl in pink. He was nearly a foot taller and so thin he looked like a scarecrow in evening dress. He also looked as if he could scarcely believe she was smiling at him.

"She underestimates his mother," Lady Isabella commented.

"Don't they always?" The three exchanged knowing looks. "How often does a girl without money or connections have any wits?"

"Very rarely." Lady Isabella's tone was bone dry. "Oh, my, there's Teddy Symmes."

The others gave small gasps. "No, where?"

"Over there, near the garden doors."

Their heads swiveled. "He has the cheek to appear in public?"

"There weren't any charges filed," Lady Isabella pointed out.

"But, my dear, everyone knows. Caught with his footman! How can he show his face?" They stared at a stocky man near the French doors as if he were a bizarre zoo animal. Charlotte almost asked what was so shocking about being in the company of one's servant, but decided not to reveal her ignorance. She didn't want that battery of eagle eyes turned on her.

The three women's conversation continued in this vein. They had forgotten all about Charlotte, seemingly, and she learned much more than she wanted to know about a number of people in the crowd. She began to wish that the musical part of the evening would begin, so that they could turn their attention to something else. It took her another half hour to understand that the quartet playing on the small balcony *was* the promised entertainment. An occasional run of notes threaded through the din of conversation, never enough to decide what they were actually playing.

She grew just a little weary of standing in one place. Lady Isabella was clearly too occupied to introduce her to some lively young people, as she had promised. Edward did not seem to be present, as she had thought he would be, and she didn't know anyone except the Danforths. One couldn't just speak to people without an introduction, even if she'd had the nerve. Of course, she was enjoying herself immensely; she took care to show it with a bright smile. She sipped from a glass of champagne. It made her cheeks even hotter in the rising heat of the room, and then she was left with the empty glass and no servant in sight.

"May I take that for you?"

Charlotte started, turned, and found Sir Alexander Wylde at her side. Surprise made her blurt the first thing that came into her head. "How did you find me?"

"I had my own invitation for this evening."

Charlotte's cheeks grew hotter still. Of course he didn't inquire where she was and follow her to this gathering. Why would he? He belonged to the *ton*, belonged at this party, whereas she was here on sufferance.

He looked very elegant in evening dress, with an air, a way of holding himself, that was quite different from his manner at home. Charlotte was reminded, suddenly, of the moment when he had rescued her from Holcombe in one slashing sentence.

He drew her a little away from Lady Isabella and her friends. They were so deep in their dissection of some hapless deb that they didn't notice. He took her empty glass and somehow made it go away. People passing nodded cordial greetings, and he acknowledged them. "You are enjoying yourself?"

"Of course."

He bent closer. "What?"

Like Lady Isabella and her friends, he seemed to know how to pitch his voice to be heard above the cacophony. Charlotte felt she was practically shouting when she repeated, "Of course."

"Good."

The single word, his expression, made her feel defensive for some reason. "It is a lovely party, is it not? Very interesting to see a bit of society." She was aware of a stubborn set to her chin, but she didn't care. His green eyes met hers with what looked like sympathy, but she must be mistaken. There was no reason for that.

"Has Aunt Bella been helpful, told you something of the *ton*?"

"Oh, yes." Charlotte prayed he wouldn't ask for examples.

One corner of his mouth curved up, as if he heard much more than she'd said, but he merely turned toward the crowd. "You see the fellow by the entrance, the one with the striped waistcoat?"

Charlotte's heart sank. Did people in London society talk nothing but scandal? She looked and had no trouble picking out the man he meant. The stripes were inches wide, and of a truly startling yellow and green.

"Percy Gerard, a prime example of the dandy set," he added. "Padded coat, you see, and rather a lot of... ornamentation."

The young man seemed in danger of choking on his massive neckcloth. His coat was so pinched in and padded out that he looked rather like a frog, one with a gleaming array of fobs and chains across its stomach.

"Quite a few Pinks of the *ton* here tonight," Sir Alexander pointed out, without of course actually pointing. Now that she knew what to look for, Charlotte discovered a liberal sprinkling of similar, extreme ensembles in the crowd. "Most of their attention goes into their tailoring. And outdoing one another in setting new fashions."

"What is that... instrument Mr. Gerard is holding?" He was surveying his fellow guests through a sort of lens on a stick.

"Quizzing glass. Meant to make you wonder if you

have a smut on your nose or an outmoded gown. But I've always suspected the fellow can't see two yards without it."

Charlotte laughed. Sir Alexander's comments felt different from Lady Isabella's spiteful snipes; this was more like a road map for unfamiliar territory.

"Now, Lord Wraxton there is an altogether different type."

Charlotte followed his subtle nod and discovered a tall, saturnine gentleman leaning against the wall. His coat was plain and dark, his waistcoat and neckcloth austere.

"One of our leading Corinthians," Sir Alexander said: "His set goes in for athletics, boxing, hard riding, and expert driving, an ostentatious lack of excess. Chancy tempers, too. Wraxton is famous for his crushing set-downs."

"Of whom?" said Charlotte, fascinated.

"Just about anyone who crosses his path."

"So, they're rather alike then—dandies and... Corinthians."

He raised his eyebrows. "How so?"

"They both have an inflated opinion of themselves."

He laughed. "And what are you, Sir Alexander?"

He looked startled. "I? I... hope I am simply a gentleman." He went on before Charlotte could reply. "You can spot young ladies in their first or second seasons by their..."

"Age, surely," she interrupted, wanting to show that she had good sense, at least.

"Not necessarily. A young woman may be married..." He paused briefly at this near approach to her own unfortunate situation. "The debs wear simpler gowns, no satin or velvet, plain jewelry and not much of it."

"I wouldn't have expected you to notice fabrics," Charlotte joked, to cover the brief awkwardness.

"A man on the town must learn to recognize the difference."

"Between...?" For a moment she was confused. "Ah. Married and unmarried young women," she concluded. The married ones had far more freedom and far more... possibilities, if they chose to see it that way. If she hadn't already known that, Lady Isabella's conversation would have made it perfectly clear.

"Indeed. The debs come with dragons, which..."

"Dragons?"

Sir Alexander looked down at her and seemed to recall himself. He reddened. "Got carried away, picking apart a situation. Anne says it's one of my besetting sins."

"But what do you mean, dragons?"

"Mother, duennas, chaperones," he muttered quickly. "The hovering tribe who makes certain the debs don't get into trouble."

"Unlike the young married women, who can get into as much trouble as they wish?"

"No. I didn't mean... Nothing of the kind!"

She couldn't resist. "So, you gentlemen need these clues to sort out who you can get into trouble with?"

Sir Alexander glowered at her. "You have no idea what you're talking about."

It was true; she didn't—precisely. But she wanted to. And it turned out to be such fun teasing him.

There was a heady freedom in the knowledge that she didn't have a host of critics watching, eager to tell her how to behave. She was so very tired of being told what to do. "I suppose the dragons would be the ladies in the chairs," she said to divert him. Gilt chairs lined the walls, nearly all occupied by older women. They looked as if they were chatting, but Charlotte had noticed that their sharp eyes swept the room like lighthouses above rocky shoals.

He gave one brief nod. "You have misunderstood me if you think…"

Charlotte felt a hand brush her arm. In the next moment, it was drawn into Edward Danforth's. "Hullo, cuz," he said to Sir Alexander. "I believe this young lady is promised to me." His tone made it a jest, almost. "Said I'd make her known to a few friends of mine," he added carelessly.

Sir Alexander looked thunderous as Edward pulled Charlotte away. "Wasn't that rather rude?" she said. It had been rather exciting as well.

"Cousins, no need to stand on ceremony," he replied.

Which was nonsense, but Charlotte let it go. "You are very late to the party."

"On the contrary, I am precisely on time." He gave her a smile to melt hearts.

"Fashionably late?"

"Timed to a nicety." He laughed at himself, and she had to laugh with him. "Come and meet my friends."

"You might have invited Sir Alexander."

"And share your attention? Never." With a speaking glance, Edward put his free hand over his heart.

Charlotte felt a small flutter in the region of her

own. This was flirting. It was like the champagne; it bubbled.

"Cousin Alec is so very *worthy,* you see," Edward added. "Sterling fellow, of course, but he tends to put a damper on things."

Charlotte didn't know how to answer. His tone made her uncomfortable, though she'd had similar thoughts. Sir Alexander Wylde could be gruff and dismissive and vastly infuriating. He'd been quite pleasant tonight, though, made her feel so much more at home in this buzzing room.

"Here we are." They'd reached the far corner of another large reception room, opening at the left of the first. A group of young people had rearranged gilt chairs into a loose circle near the doors to the garden, open for the air. A table that looked like it had come from outside sat in the middle, and two young men were setting food on it.

"George and William raided the supper room," one of the women told Edward. "Had to overpower a footman guard. But you know George can't go two hours without eating."

"Here now, you were the one claimed you were perishing from hunger," the stockier of the two men replied.

"Attention all, this is Charlotte Wylde," said Edward.

"The one who was married to your fusty old uncle?" asked the same woman. Charlotte flushed. She hadn't realized that Edward had talked about her.

"The very one." No one seemed to think anything of it. Edward began to point. No one seemed to mind that either. "And this motley crew is George and

Celia Elliott, William and Margaret Billings, Richard Taylor-Smythe, Sally... er..."

"Beaton," supplied Margaret, the woman who had spoken first.

"Right. And..."

"Lydia Trent," said Celia.

"Very pleased to meet you," said Charlotte, frantically trying to imprint the names on her memory, attached to the right faces. Edward stepped away, and she nearly panicked. But he was back in a moment with another chair. The circle shifted, opened, and he offered her a place in it with a flourish. She sat down, still reviewing the names in her mind.

The stockier man—George, brown hair and round face—gestured at the tabletop. The second man—William, thin, black hair—had taken a chair on the far side of the circle. "We have lobster patties, some promising Stilton, some sort of filled pastry, lemon tarts," George announced.

"My angel," put in the plumpish blond woman. Celia, Charlotte reminded herself, who seemed to be George's wife rather than a sister or some other relation.

"Would I return to you without lemon tarts, my darling?" George teased.

Definitely wife.

A handsome dark young man, with two champagne bottles under each arm, joined them. "Ah, here's the last of us," Edward said.

"And the best of us," the newcomer responded, to a hail of catcalls.

"Tony Farnsworth," Edward finished.

"Fall to, fall to," declared George. "Descend like

the ravening hordes. I can get more. No mere footman keeps me from sustenance." He popped a lobster patty into his mouth. "Umm, not bad." Celia Elliott took two lemon tarts. The rest of the group reached for whatever tidbit tempted them. Tony opened the champagne; someone found Charlotte a glass.

Most of the group had obviously known each other for years. At least, all the men had, Charlotte concluded. They teased each other mercilessly, with references to school and previous Seasons that they all found hilarious. She decided that Margaret had merely married into this melee, while Celia *might* be Richard Taylor-Smythe's sister. After a while, Edward shifted into the seat next to Charlotte and gave her a running commentary, which he seemed to think explained their arcane jokes. It didn't really, but she didn't care. The laughter was exhilarating, and she seemed to have been effortlessly accepted as part of the group.

At one point, a frowning older woman came by and extracted Lydia Trent, leading her away like an erring child. Everyone seemed to find this hilarious. Charlotte's glass never emptied, somehow, no matter how often she sipped. The food was exotic and delicious. This was the kind of evening she'd imagined, Charlotte thought, years ago in Hampshire, stuck miles from any sort of true society. Here were people with a sense of fun, ready to enjoy themselves and happy to welcome others with the same bent. She grew giddy with the sheer joy of it. She laughed along with them at the jokes she didn't understand and joined the numerous toasts that Tony proposed. He seemed to have a penchant for toasts.

Much later, driving home, very correctly, with Lady Isabella, she found it hard not to giggle at everything she said. Fortunately, her hostess was preoccupied by some juicy anecdotes she had picked up during the evening. She dropped Charlotte at the Wylde house without lengthy farewells, departing as soon as she saw the front door open.

Charlotte danced in and stopped dead when she discovered that Sir Alexander was the doorkeeper. "Where's Ethan? Or the other one—what's 'is name? James. That's it. Same as your father." She giggled.

"I sent them to bed. It's very late."

"So late it's gone to early," she agreed. This had been a phrase of her father's. "You're playing footman?" She giggled again.

"I take it you had a pleasant evening?"

"Wonderful!" Arms outstretched, she spun. "If only there'd been dancing. Can't dance, though. Must mourn for Henry. Stupid!" She twirled faster, loving the way her velvet skirt belled around her, feeling her shawl slip, and letting it. The floor seemed to tilt suddenly; she missed her footing.

Sir Alexander caught her, held her effortlessly upright. She gazed up at him. "You're frowning. Why frown so fierce?"

She swayed, and his arms tightened. They felt very right around her. Somehow her arms moved of their own accord. Her hands slid over his broad shoulders and laced behind his neck. The evening had been a mere taste of life and happiness. She wanted more.

"You're... drunk." Sir Alexander sounded strange.

"Not used to champagne," Charlotte admitted.

She giggled yet again. "It's lovely, though. All those bubbles." Moved by hope or impulse or desire, she stood on tiptoes, tugged him down, and kissed him.

It was sheer lunatic experiment at first. She wanted to know what it was like—a proper kiss, and a kiss from this particular man. Her only previous such experience had been with an awkward young man at a country assembly, and it had not gone very well. Charlotte knew there must be more to it, the way people spoke of passionate embraces.

Before she could think any more, Sir Alexander jerked her tight against him and took control of the enterprise with a demand and heat that melted her bones. No, she'd never been kissed before, hadn't understood the meaning of the word. His mouth educated her, and she rushed to learn with every fiber of her body. This was lightning; this was glory.

Then it was over. He pushed her away, balanced her at a distance with a hand on each shoulder. Bereft, she reached for him. He let her go completely and stepped back. Charlotte swayed a little, mainly from disappointment.

"Can you get to your room without help?" He sounded furious. "Or must I ring for a servant?"

"Of course I can! I am not… drunk."

"You're giving a fine imitation of it then."

Charlotte's buoyant mood collapsed at his critical tone. He'd begun to sound like his uncle again. "Don't you ever have fun? Just forget about everything and… and… revel in the moment? You're so…"

"Unwilling to speak with you in this condition," he interrupted.

"The condition of enjoying myself?" she taunted.

"I hope you enjoy tomorrow's headache as much!" He turned on his heel and walked away, heading toward his study despite the hour. The door closed with a censorious snap behind him. Charlotte gathered her skirts and marched up the stairs, refusing to accept the possibility that they were tilting, just a little, now and then.

After a few minutes, Ethan eased through the swinging door at the back of the hall, walked quietly to the front door and shot the bolts. He hadn't meant to spy; he'd only stayed up, despite the master's permission to retire, to be sure everyone was safely home and the house locked up. It was his duty, after all, and if the place was wide open in the morning—as it might have been left seeing Sir Alexander's current mood—they'd look to him for the reason. And so he'd seen what he shouldn't have, and quite a surprise it'd been, too. For the master as well, if he was any judge— though hardly an unpleasant one. No harm in a kiss, o' course, as he would tell Lucy if she ever spoke to him again. Even a kiss like *that*. That had looked like a scorcher, for sure, and who would have thought it? Their guest was a widow lady, he reminded himself. Lucy might call her Miss Charlotte, but she was really Mrs. Wylde, and it seemed she knew what she was doing when it came to kisses. Whew!

House secured, Ethan moved quietly to the back stairs and made his way up. At the first landing, he heard footsteps above him. It had to be Lucy, her mistress safely abed. He went faster and caught up to her in the narrow attic corridor that housed the servants' quarters. "Lucy," he whispered, very conscious of people sleeping on either side of the hall.

Lucy gasped and whirled, one hand clutched to her chest.

"Didn't mean to scare you," he murmured hurriedly. "I've been locking up." Lucy merely backed toward her room. "Wait. Just talk to me for a…"

"Leave me be," Lucy hissed.

"I've told you I meant no offense."

"Doesn't matter what you meant, or what you mean now, I'm having none of it."

"Shh." Ethan glanced at the rows of closed doors.

"You're a vain, lecherous rogue, and you can just stay away from me," said Lucy between clenched teeth.

"I'm no such thing. Lucy, it was just a kiss."

"Something that don't mean nothing," she replied fiercely. "Something you do all the time. I know it." Her mouth trembled.

She looked so forlorn. Ethan wanted nothing more than to take her in his arms and assure her that it had meant something. But this wasn't the time or place. His hands curled into fists; there never was a time or place. That was the damnable thing.

"I'm not like that," Lucy continued. "I don't go about…" Her voice shook. "What Miss Charlotte would think of me if she ever heard what I done."

She didn't need to regret it quite as much as that, Ethan thought. He'd be damned if she hadn't enjoyed it at the time. "Your 'Miss Charlotte' would understand better than you think, seemingly. She was just kissing Sir Alexander in the front hall."

Lucy gaped at him. "That's a dreadful lie."

"Full as she could hold of champagne, too. That's not the kind of goings-on we're used to in this house." The look on Lucy's face immediately made him sorry he'd said it.

"Is someone out there?" James's voice came through the door panels. "Ethan?" Bed springs creaked.

With a whisk of skirts, Lucy hurried down the hall and disappeared into the room she shared with Susan. Seething with frustration, Ethan went into his own.

James was sitting up in bed. "Were you talking to somebody?" he asked sleepily.

"Who would I be talking to at this hour? Go back to sleep." Blearily, James obeyed. But it was quite a time before Ethan was able to do the same.

Eleven

ALEC FOUND THE BREAKFAST ROOM BLESSEDLY EMPTY when he entered it the following morning. He gathered whatever came to hand, took a pot of tea, and shut himself in his study before that could change. All night, through fitful sleep and restless dreams, his thoughts had been full of Charlotte. Her lips, the feel of her body against his, the brightness of her coppery eyes dimming as he pushed her away. Memories of her drowned his senses and wreaked havoc in his mind. They lingered now, despite anything he could do.

Alec had always seen himself as a sensible son of his sensible father. Of course he had "fun"—Charlotte's accusation still stung. But he knew where to draw the line; he prized stability, reasonable action. Now, he'd begun to fear that his grandfather's blood ran strong in his veins as well—his grandfather who'd succumbed to "love" and poisoned the inner sanctuary of his family for decades. At the moment, Alec felt just as reckless, as helpless, as the forebear he'd always—despised? pitied?—because his life had been overturned by a slender girl who'd thrown herself at him like a…

No, it hadn't been like that. She had fallen into his arms as naturally as… in his house, with his sisters sleeping upstairs, he'd almost swept her up and carried her to his bed. Unthinkable. He wished her gone, or better yet, never met. He wanted so much to see her that he had to resist going to her chamber. When Edward had snatched her away at the evening party, he'd been enraged. He didn't know what to do. He knew only that this felt dangerous, and he hated it.

Alec forced himself to work, and as he read tale after tale of distress in the letters on his desk, his own problems began to recede. Whole families were starving; he couldn't even imagine what it would be like to watch one's children wasting away from hunger. Or, perhaps he could, just a bit. Anne's illness had driven him nearly mad with helplessness. If it hadn't been conquered finally, thanks to Charlotte… He was thinking of her again.

He gritted his teeth and opened a report from his steward, Hobbs, who administered a relief fund Alec had established for tenants on his estates. That idea had worked well. The only difficulty was that they were receiving appeals from more and more people who were not tenants. Alec had agreed to respond to those in neighboring villages, but word of the fund had spread further. Requests were coming from all over the county and beyond, far more than Alec could fulfill even if he bankrupted himself. Frustrated, angry, he sat amid the piles of paper and nearly despaired. He would force himself to make another round of visits, urging fellow landholders to help their own people. Some treated him like a beggar, some like a fool for "wasting" his income. Some actually laughed at him. Not that he went to see those sorts more than once.

There was a soft knock, and the door opened to reveal Frances, crisp in a blue morning gown. "May I interrupt you a moment, Alec?"

He remembered that he had meant to speak to her. Another thing swept from his mind by his enchanting houseguest. "Is anything wrong?" he asked, hoping that she knew the question covered past circumstances as well as present.

"Not wrong, really. It is just that Charlotte has given me a great deal to think about." Her tone was distracted, as if she were only half here.

"Charlotte?" Could he never escape the girl? He met her at every turn.

"Yes. She's a very thoughtful girl."

Alec compared this judgment with the twirling siren he'd encountered last night and found no connection.

"Is that house you own near Butterley still vacant? The little manor with the fine gardens?"

"The...?" Alec gathered his wits. "I believe so. I've heard nothing of a tenant from Hobbs."

"Ah. What would you think if I should want it?" Frances cocked her head and smiled at him.

"Want what? The house? What for?"

"Well, to live in. Not at once of course, but eventually. When I leave."

"Leave?" Alec felt as if he'd gotten so far behind in this conversation that he would never catch up. "Leave... us?"

Frances looked at him with benevolent impatience. "Children do grow up, Alec. You will not need me forever."

"But… you… we…"

A tap on the door announced Ethan. "That Mr. Hanks is here again, sir," said the footman.

Frances turned with an airy wave. "This can wait. There's no hurry, obviously." She went out in a rustle of cambric. Alec sat at his desk, stunned by the revolution in his household arrangements that she had implied.

"Sir?" said Ethan after a while.

"What? Oh, the Runner. Send him in, I suppose." The man looked just the same—gray and forgettable with the shaded eyes of a hawk. "You have something to report?"

"Not exactly a report. I wanted to talk to you, like."

"You have more questions for Mrs. Wylde?"

"In a manner of speaking. After a bit, mebbe."

Something about the way he said those words puzzled Alec. "Sit down. Tell me what's on your mind."

"Yes, sir." Hanks took one of the chairs on the other side of the desk, brooded briefly, then spoke. "Here it 'tis. I en't much of a believer in coincidence. So it's always stuck in my craw, so to speak, that this Henry Wylde is killed, and then his house is robbed, if you take my meaning?"

"You think these things are connected." It seemed obvious once he said it.

"Well, here's a man with mighty regular habits, no incidents reported. And then, of a sudden, two crimes committed."

"So you think someone killed him because of his

collections?" Alec paused. "You mentioned the last time you were here that my uncle was foolish about his antiquities purchases. Perhaps there was a dispute with someone who cheated him?"

"Good thought, sir." Hanks nodded his approval. "I en't found any such thing, however. And I believe I've talked to near everyone he bought from."

"Ah." Alec's momentary view of himself as a brilliant investigator receded.

"Here's the thing." Hanks hesitated.

"Yes?"

"Well, sir, your common footpad is no killer. He hits 'em, takes when he can get, and runs. Mebbe now and then he hits too hard, accidental, like. But this weren't like that. Mr. Wylde's head was beat right in." Ignoring Alec's wince, he added, "Murder is mostly personal."

Chilled, Alec said, "Just tell me what you came to say."

"I talked to that feller Holcombe."

"A malicious man and, I suspect, a liar."

"Yes, sir," Hanks agreed. "I talked to the other servants as well. Tracked 'em down around the city. And what I learned, reading between the lines and making allowances, you understand, was that Mrs. Wylde was made downright miserable in that house. Just about tormented, I would say. Mebbe enough to… snap."

Alec thought of things Charlotte had said, that he knew, about her former situation.

"She had every reason in the world to wish her husband…"

"Stop." Alec struggled with his temper and a sudden fear. "You cannot be about to accuse a young woman of quality of murdering her husband?"

"Not herself, sir, no. She was seen at home that night. But hiring it done p'raps. And I en't saying for sure…"

"Ridiculous! Outrageous!"

Hanks didn't quail in the face of his anger. "In such a case, the wife expects to inherit, see, but your uncle's will put a damper on that, and so…"

Neither man had heard the study door open.

"You're asking me to believe that Charlotte Wylde hired a murderer, and then a thief…?"

"Well, I 'spect it would be the same man, sir. And I en't saying fer…"

"What?" asked a quavering voice. Alec looked up to find Charlotte in the doorway, staring at him as if she couldn't have heard correctly. "What?" she said again.

"Ma'am," offered Jem Hanks. He didn't look at all embarrassed. He simply watched her with his raptor's gaze.

Alec, on the other hand, flushed scarlet. "It is an insane theory…"

"They told me the Runner was here. I came down to help. You are accusing me…?" Hand on the doorknob, she swayed a little. Her face was ashen. "Hiring…? You think that I would…?"

"Of course not."

She didn't seem to hear him; she was staring at Hanks. "How would I hire…? Henry gave me no money."

"Hypothetically, a… person might promise payment from the inheritance. And then when there weren't none to speak of…"

Charlotte clutched the doorknob like a lifeline. "A 'person' might, I suppose. I did not."

Hanks continued to watch her. Alec suddenly

wondered if he had come here to do just that. He looked from one to the other, shaken to the core by the last night and morning. An insidious inner voice suggested that he had taken a stranger into his home, where his young sisters lived. He had accepted everything she said without question. He actually knew nothing of her background, beyond her assertions. Of course these accusations were idiotic. There was no question of murder. Only misunderstanding and a creeping doubt… and encroaching chaos. "I think it would be best…"

"Do not say that to me!" Charlotte shrieked. "Don't you dare! My father 'thought it best' to marry me off to a cold, cruel man. My husband 'thought it best' to treat me like a pariah. No one asks *me*! And you… you have no right whatsoever to 'think it best.' You have no authority over me."

Alec was lashed by memories of his grandmother's tirades. She'd terrorized the family—lied, pitted one relative against another, brutally manipulated. "You are a guest in my house," he snapped. "That gives me some authority."

"To be a household tyrant?" Charlotte glared at Alec. "You believe this of me?"

Anne and Lizzy were, blessedly, too young to remember much. He'd vowed they would never experience even the echo of those screaming rants. And here was this woman he barely knew, shouting at him.

"I see." Charlotte stepped back into the hall and slammed the door behind her. The sound seemed to echo through the room, through the years. Alec felt as if it ricocheted inside his head.

"Hadn't meant to do that just now," said Jem Hanks.

"To…?"

"I prefer to have a bit of evidence before I confront the…"

"There will be no such evidence!" What had he been thinking? Had he no trust in his own ability to judge character? He'd talked with Charlotte, seen her with his sisters. He knew her to be an admirable person.

Hanks rose, clearly aware that he was no longer welcome. "Like as not you're right, sir."

"Of course I'm right!"

With a nod, Hanks took himself off.

Alec waited another moment to get himself under control. He didn't want to repeat his foolish mistake. But the pause was just too long. Charlotte was already gone.

⁕

Tears pooled in Lucy's eyes. She blinked, then blinked again to keep them from overflowing. Even so, a few fell onto the coverlet as she shoved her things into her bag. Susan had promised to see that Miss Charlotte's belongings were packed up and sent, but Lucy hadn't wanted to ask anyone else to take care of her own few possessions. In fact, she hadn't wanted anyone to see her after she heard that they were going back to that cold, hateful house. And why? She didn't know. She knew only that Miss Charlotte had slammed out the front door, mad as fire about something. She'd thrown a few words at Ethan and brought Lucy's world crashing down around her ears.

Lucy wanted to sink onto the bed and weep. It had felt so settled here. She'd stopped thinking about the wretchedness of the last year, the terrors of their days in the empty house. Now, without a word of warning, they were going back. The place waited, like the dreadful castle in fairy tales, to swallow them up forever.

It wasn't the extra work she dreaded. She liked to work. It was the loneliness and the responsibility. Of course she would always stand by Miss Charlotte, but what could she do all alone? There were so many things about her situation that she didn't understand.

This time back in a proper household had made Lucy feel younger and maybe even less able to cope. Where she was going there would be no housekeeper or cook to offer advice; there would be no Jennings to teach her useful new skills. Lucy bent her head. It was the closest she'd ever come to flat despair.

Ethan appeared in the open doorway. "I got you a cab."

Lucy turned away, not wanting him to see signs of tears.

"The fare's paid and all." He stepped into the room. "Maybe it's just a misunderstanding, and you'll be back in a day or two."

Lucy shook her head. "Miss Charlotte doesn't lose her temper very often, but when she does…" She was that stubborn with it. "Anyway, she always meant to go back. It's her house." Which she'd known very well, Lucy thought. She shouldn't have let herself get so comfortable here.

"Well, you can visit…" Ethan began.

Lucy snapped, "I'll be doing the work of a whole staff! I won't have time to turn around, let alone go visiting."

"But you'll be hiring…"

"I don't know where to find good servants in London, and neither does Miss Charlotte. If they're all like that Holcombe and the others…" To Lucy's horror, she broke down.

Somehow, Ethan was there, an arm around her shoulders. "Ah, don't now. Don't cry. I can't bear it if you cry. I'll find them for you."

Torn between pulling away and throwing herself onto his chest, Lucy looked up. She sniffed. "You?"

"Sure. I know lots of folks."

"It isn't a fashionable household like this. No chance of tips or fancy food." Lucy hated herself for the hint of whine in her voice.

"No matter." Ethan's handsome face shifted, as if a thought had occurred to him. "I'll find you some good people. People you'll like, Lucy. They'll take care of you."

"What?"

"Of the house, I mean. Take care of the house." Ethan squeezed her shoulders. "I will. I promise."

The obvious conviction in his voice surprised her. Lucy gazed up at him; he seemed determined, as if he really meant it. And he was so big and so competent. A huge bubble of relief bloomed in her chest, ready to overwhelm her. She was afraid to trust it. "You don't have to do this just because you kissed me."

He bent closer. "Yes. I do."

The world seemed to go silent around her. The contours of his lips, inches from hers, reminded Lucy of all the dizzying sensations of the kiss. She longed to lean in and taste that thrill again. The clean scent of him, the strength of his arm, made her reel. She lost herself in his steady, sincere gaze.

"The cab's waiting," James called up the stairs. "Says his horse is getting cold."

Ethan gave her shoulders a last squeeze and released her. "Don't you worry now." He picked up her bag as if it weighed nothing. Dazed, Lucy followed him down the steps. She felt even more dejected. Whatever happened, she was unlikely to see Ethan Trask again.

Twelve

CHARLOTTE HUNCHED IN THE SHABBY ARMCHAIR IN her old bedchamber, oblivious to the chill of the fireless room. She had the worst headache of her life and felt sick, but her real hurts weren't physical. Sir Alexander had sat there and let that man accuse her of murder. The doubt in his eyes when she'd asked him if he believed it... She drew up her knees and curled into an aching ball. It had raked her soul, sent her flying out of his house without a cloak, with barely enough in her pocket to pay for a cab, and nowhere to go but the place where she'd been desperately unhappy. That fit, at least, she thought.

She'd ejected the men stationed here with a fierceness that clearly startled them, and a note to Lucy to pack her things and follow. She couldn't remember if she'd told Ethan that when she fled. She'd locked the door and collapsed in this chair to... wallow. Charlotte released her knees and slowly straightened. All right. Yes, she was indulging in self-pity. Didn't she have reason enough? Wasn't she permitted a little regret? But if she'd learned one thing since leaving her childhood home it was this: feeling sorry for yourself would eat you alive, if you let it.

Charlotte stared at the ugly wallpaper and clenched her fists. How dared he believe that odious little man? She'd lived in Sir Alexander's house, talked with him, sat at dinner with him. How could he imagine...? And she'd kissed him! Charlotte rested her pounding head in her hands. Why had she kissed him?

A hint of the bubbling exhilaration of that moment came back to her. She'd been buzzing from the evening's freedom, from the taste of society and gaiety after an arid, desolate year. And then there he was—unexpected, crackling with emotion, unbearably attractive. It had seemed so natural, so necessary to fling her arms around him and pull his lips down to hers. A shiver went through her at the memory of that amazing sensation. Even now, when she despised him, she longed to feel it again.

But she wouldn't.

Charlotte raised her head. Because she would never—never—forgive Sir Alexander Wylde. Not if he crawled on his knees from his oh-so-fashionable neighborhood to her reviled one, not if he announced to the world that he was an idiot, not if he begged, hat in hand. If she saw him in the street, she would cut him dead. Not that she'd encounter him, living out here in the hinterlands, as the high-nosed *ton* saw it. But it was the principle of the thing. Yes. That was settled; nothing could be clearer. Sir Alexander Wylde was out of her life.

If only the pounding in her head... no, it wasn't the headache. Someone was knocking on the front door. Charlotte got up and moved quietly down the stairs.

"Miss Charlotte," Lucy called. "Miss Charlotte, it's me." Charlotte undid the locks, and Lucy rushed in. "Oh, Miss Charlotte, whatever happened? Why did you run off?"

Charlotte said nothing. She could not tell even Lucy about being accused of murder. She closed the front door and relocked it.

"What a to-do. Miss Anne and Miss Lizzy wanting to know why you'd gone, and Sir Alexander mean as a bear with a sore head."

"We quarreled," she replied tersely. "My things?"

"Susan promised to make sure they were all sent. I didn't want to wait, miss, and leave you here alone."

"Thank you, Lucy." The sympathy in her maid's face threatened to erode her anger, and Charlotte blinked back tears. She was very grateful for Lucy, her staunch companion through so much, but she couldn't answer the questions in her eyes right now. "We'll need to hire some staff," she said to divert her.

"We're staying then?" Lucy sounded more resigned than surprised.

"Yes. Nobody has come back to rob the place in all this time. I'm sure it's safe." She hardly cared. "We can't afford many—a cook, perhaps a housemaid, though I think it would be wiser to have a manservant."

"Yes, miss."

Her spurt of angry energy was ebbing. Her room, the armchair, solitude, beckoned. "I don't know just how…"

"E… some of the staff over at Sir Alexander's house might have some… recommendations, like. They're going to send word."

"You asked them? Lucy, you are a gem." All the better because these servants would have heard about the robbery and its aftermath; she wouldn't have to explain or, dishonestly, not mention it. It was a great relief.

Charlotte's stomach roiled, and she became more conscious of her various pains. "Do you suppose we have anything in the house for a headache?"

"I'll go and see," Lucy said.

❧

Ethan leaned over his aunt's kitchen table, a cup of tea dwarfed in his big hands. He realized he was clutching it so hard it was like to break, and he eased off. But he couldn't be rid of the urgency that'd gripped him since saying good-bye to Lucy. She'd been so scared. The fear and sadness in her eyes had shaken Ethan to the core. He wanted to hit things. He wanted the power to make the world different. He felt he would do anything—anything—to protect Lucy, to save her from being alone and afraid. He'd abandoned his post with a muttered excuse. And now, here in his aunt's home above the grocery, the need to make people listen had rendered him almost incoherent.

He faced his puzzled grandparents across the table. John and Edith Trask had been a solid anchor and a refuge all his life. When he couldn't get on with his father and couldn't go out into the forest, their cottage was his haven. Gran was a champion cook, and her home was always full of luscious things to eat. Ethan got his size and his even temperament from Grandad, who'd been head gardener at Sir Alexander's country place. He'd counted on them all his life. But this time they couldn't seem to understand.

"What's so special about this girl?" asked his Aunt Liv. She'd settled her bulk beside him, and he could hardly ask her to leave her own kitchen. She liked to tease him, though, and always found the tenderest place to poke. She clearly was not going to miss this conversation.

"She's all alone…" What could he say—that Lucy was brave, spirited, alluring as other girls had never been? When had he even decided those things himself?

"We'd like to help, but we're heading back to Derbyshire next week," Gran said. "You know how lucky we are to have our own cottage and not to be needing to work away from home. There's things that need to be done there."

"I know." Ethan stared into his tea. His grandparents had labored all their lives, and accumulated enough to lease their own patch of land. It was an admirable achievement. They deserved to be left to enjoy it. Yet he couldn't help asking them for more.

"You thinking seriously of this girl?" asked his aunt. "You en't in a position to be doing that, young Ethan."

She was right. And it made no difference at all. "It'd be temporary, like," he said. "I'll ask around, find someone else as soon as may be." But no one else would be as good, he realized. He wanted people he could trust to look after Lucy. "It's just… they need somebody right away. She's… they're all alone in that house."

"Where there's been criminals breaking in," his grandmother added.

Ethan felt mean and small. How could he ask the

two of them, who were getting on in years, after all, to expose themselves to danger? "Just the once," he answered. "And nothing since. Sir Alexander reckons there won't be another try." He *had* heard him say that, speaking to one of the men he'd set guarding the place when he'd come by for orders.

"Tom's looking after our garden at home," said Grandad. It was the first time he'd spoken since Ethan arrived. "We could spare a bit more time."

Gran met his eyes, and they shared a moment of the silent communication that forty years of marriage had brought. She shook her head. But it was resigned amusement, not a no. "Mind you do ask around, Ethan, and find someone else," was all she said. "We need to be going home."

"Yes, ma'am." Relief coursed through him, and gratitude. They'd never let him down.

Aunt Liv, now that it was decided, got into the spirit of the thing. "You could hire on Tess Hopkins to help out. She lost her position because the young gentleman at her last place wouldn't leave her alone. And her barely fifteen!" She grimaced in disgust. "There's no young men in this house?"

"No!" Ethan said.

Gran's eyebrows went up at the fierceness of his tone.

"It'd be good for Tess. Get her back on her feet, like. And she could use the training." Gran gave her a look. "I'm just saying." Aunt Liv grinned. "Nobody better to train up the young 'ens than you, Mum."

"Oh, aye, butter me up before you send me off to work." But you could tell Gran was flattered by the comment.

And so it was settled. His grandparents would make their way to the house later in the day, giving Ethan time to send word of their arrival. "Thanks," said Ethan. He couldn't help it that his voice shook. Nor that his family obviously noticed.

❧

The following morning, Charlotte told herself she was fully recovered, even though she'd slept poorly. And when she followed the tantalizing scent of bacon down to the basement kitchen, she found that, amazingly, she had a staff, as well as breakfast. A sturdy, gray-haired woman stood over the iron stove, in the midst of explaining something to the young blond girl next to her. A giant of a man rose from a chair at the kitchen table as Charlotte entered, his white hair nearly brushing the ceiling beam. Lucy smiled from the corner as if she had performed a magic trick, which she had. "This is Mr. and Mrs. Trask," she said. "And Tess Hopkins."

The latter bobbed a nervous curtsy as the Trasks nodded to her. Clearly they were a very superior sort of servant—miraculously so. They had a weight and presence that declared they knew exactly what to do and how to do it. "You are all very welcome," Charlotte said. "Thank you for coming on such short notice."

The Trasks nodded again. "Where were you wanting breakfast served, ma'am?" said Mrs. Trask. "The dining room, seemingly..."

"Yes, it is a little odd," Charlotte acknowledged. "The main floor of the house is all taken up with my... late husband's antiquities collection. Those rooms..." It seemed too much to explain. The dining table was covered with statuary. "...can't be disturbed. I don't really live... There is a room on the second floor where I used to... where I dine, and another set up as a drawing room. My bedchamber is on the third floor." What would the Trasks think of this eccentric household? They must have come from some much superior place. But neither showed any reaction.

"I showed Tess the room next to me," Lucy put in, which meant she'd returned to her former chamber on the top floor. "Mr. Trask was thinking they'd stay down here."

"Seems tight and dry," said the giant, smiling down at her. There was something very comforting about him, even beyond his size.

The basement housed the servants' parlor and another large room as well as the kitchen and store-room. High windows provided light. They could take a bed and other furnishings from an unused bedchamber. "If you're sure that is what you would like?"

"Yes, ma'am," Mrs. Trask confirmed.

"Very well. I can show you..."

"No need, ma'am. We'll take care of it. I'll send young Tess up with a breakfast tray, shall I?"

The older woman's calm competence soothed her wounded spirit. "Thank you. That would be... lovely." And it was. The food was delicious. The young housemaid was shyly pleasant. It seemed that Charlotte had nothing to worry about but the wreck of all her life's prospects.

She had finished eating and begun to goad herself to do something useful when Tess returned with the news that she had visitors. "Two young ladies, ma'am. Said they don't have no… any cards." She paused, then carefully repeated, "Miss Anne and Miss Elizabeth Wylde."

Charlotte's pulse accelerated. "Bring them up to the drawing room, please, Tess." She barely got there ahead of them.

"Charlotte, what has happened?" said Anne as she swept in.

Lizzy, behind her, set a wicker hamper by the door and rushed forward. "Why did you run away?" she said. "It took us forever to find your address. I had to rifle Alec's papers, on his desk! Ethan heard you shout at him." They both gazed at her, expectant.

Charlotte was happy to see them, but she didn't know what to say. She shook her head.

"But you must tell us, so that we can make it all right, and you can come back," Lizzy exclaimed. She plumped down on the aged sofa, bounced once, and looked at the cushions disapprovingly.

"I was always only visiting, Lizzy. And that is… over now. It's time I got my own household in order." It sounded stiff. Yet what else was there to say? "Do sit down, Anne."

"But…"

"Charlotte has her own home to think of," interrupted Anne, with a searching look that promised she hadn't really dropped the subject.

Lizzy looked mutinous, then heaved a great sigh. She looked around the room as Anne sat in the shabby armchair. "Why do you sit up here? All the best rooms are downstairs."

"Lizzy," admonished Anne.

"Well, they are."

"Your uncle's collection is housed there, and it must stay in place, according to his will. So I... established myself up here."

"It's so small."

Charlotte realized that she'd stopped really seeing the room, indeed the whole house, long ago. She'd had no power to change anything, and her opinions were always mocked. It became easier to narrow her vision down to nothing.

Her drawing room *was* small. It had been the boudoir of some eighteenth-century mistress of the house, and there was barely room for the small sofa and two armchairs. Bland china figurines cluttered the mantel; she'd never liked the faded flowery print of the curtains—blowsy and pink. Compared with the sisters' elegant home, it was plain, charmless, and neglected.

"It's very cozy," said Anne, frowning at her younger sister.

Charlotte became aware of an odd scratching sound. Were there mice, too, she wondered despairingly? But the noise seemed to be coming from the hamper in the corner. "What is...?"

Lizzy grimaced. "I can't leave Callie alone at our house."

"Callie was discovered under a cupboard in the kitchen gnawing a joint of beef," explained Anne, poker-faced. "A very costly joint of beef."

"I did *not* let her out of the schoolroom! Cook says she can walk through walls."

"You brought the cat?"

"I can't leave her there," Lizzy repeated. "Alec is going to get rid of her."

"He is only sending her down to the country, Lizzy."

"She won't like it there. She's a London cat. She won't understand about the foxes. They'll eat her!"

"I'm sorry, Lizzy," Charlotte began. And she saw the idea being born in the girl's dark blue eyes.

"If you are going to live here…"

"Yes, but I…"

"You could keep her, and I could come to visit."

"I'm sure Callie wouldn't like…"

"She'd be company for you," Lizzy continued, nodding as if vistas were opening before her inner eye. "I'm sure she would be very good. And I would come every day to feed her and play with her."

Though Charlotte was certain the cat would be anything but good, the thought of Lizzy's company was pleasant. Not that it would truly be every day, of course… This pleasing picture dissipated. Seeing the sisters, she'd almost forgotten the recent disaster. Now, it all came rushing back. "Your brother will not wish you to visit. It…"

"I don't care what he thinks! He's being an absolute pill!"

A thought occurred to Charlotte. "Does he know you're here?"

Anne evaded her eyes; Lizzy met her gaze with practiced, yet irresistible, pleading. "So, can Callie stay? Please?"

Charlotte tried, but she couldn't resist her. "Well… all right. But when you return to the country, you must take her with…"

Lizzy was already up, heading for the hamper. Belatedly, Charlotte remembered the shelves of ancient pottery, the cases of fragile artifacts, downstairs. She jumped up and closed the drawing room door just as Lizzy undid the catch.

"You will like it here," Lizzy cooed. "Charlotte is here. And I will come to see you every day." The calico cat burst out of her prison, looked wildly around, and disappeared under the sofa. A moment later, a cat sneeze testified to the dust beneath it. Lizzy fell to her knees and peered into the darkness. "Callie."

"Remember she needs to get used to a new place," said Charlotte feebly. What had she done?

Lizzy remained on the floor. The others did not immediately realize that she was weeping. When they did, Anne rose and went to her. Gently, she pulled her up and back to her chair. "Everything is horrid!" Lizzy cried. Anne gave her a handkerchief. "Alec is beastly. Frances does nothing but moan. And now Anne will be gone all the time."

"Not all the time, Lizzy. Hardly any time." In answer to Charlotte's look she added, "I am to attend a few gatherings for young people who are coming out next year. And a dancing class. My Aunt Earnton arranged it, so that I have some acquaintances."

"Oh yes, Frances mentioned that to me. A useful idea."

Lizzy snuffled. "I know I am a selfish pig. I know it is very good for you. It's just... why can't things be more like they used to?"

Charlotte ached for her. She was so familiar with the feeling that life was one change for the worse after another.

None of them noticed Callie creeping out from

under the sofa. The cat was just suddenly there, with a paw on Lizzy's knee. The girl scooped her into her lap and bent over her. Lizzy could come and see her cat whenever she liked, Charlotte decided. If her detestable brother showed up to accuse Charlotte of plotting to murder his sister or some such thing… well, she just hoped he tried it. Lizzy looked up from Callie's variegated fur. She was going to be one of those fortunate young ladies who could cry and still be beautiful, Charlotte observed. Young men were going to be mowed down in swathes when she was turned loose on them. Lizzy sniffed. She straightened and sniffed again. Charlotte could almost feel her sunny nature reasserting itself. Callie began to groom her thick, now dusty, fur. "Tell Charlotte about your beau, Anne."

"He is not…!"

"He asked her to stand up with him three times at their first dancing class. He is *smitten*."

"Lizzy!" Anne's blush was fiery. "He's just being kind, because I have lived mostly in the country and don't know anyone."

"And he's handsome," Lizzy put in. "He has 'lovely' brown eyes."

"I shall never confide in you again, wretched girl," Anne threatened.

"I wouldn't tell just anyone! Charlotte is family."

The girls' wrangling faded into the background as Charlotte struggled with a lump in her throat and an intense wish that they really were her family.

The drawing room door opened. Lizzy clutched the cat so hard she objected. "There is no need to announce me," stated a cultured voice in the hall. Callie bolted for the cave under the sofa once more.

Frances Cole walked in, immaculate in a dark blue pelisse. "I thought I might find you here," she said, looking from Anne to Lizzy sternly. "Whatever were you thinking, to go out without telling anyone, and alone? You know that is not allowed."

"We did it because Alec is beastly," replied Lizzy. "And we wanted to see Charlotte. Why should we not see Charlotte? It's not fair!" Anne merely looked guilty.

Frances ignored her excuses. "As you must be aware, you are both in trouble. You may await me downstairs."

Her eyes were steely. This was the woman who had reared four children, and done it well, thought Charlotte.

"You can look at the artifacts," Frances added, with an unexpected dash of dry humor. "It will be educational."

Lizzy put on a martyred face. It looked as if she would argue, but Anne pulled her from the room. Frances sat on the sofa. She gave no sign that she found the furnishings shabby. "Whatever happened between you and Alec? All I could gather was that there was shouting."

Charlotte couldn't bring herself to explain. What would happen to that sympathetic gaze if she revealed Jem Hanks's accusation?

Frances waited. "Of course you are not obliged to tell me. But I would like to help."

Tears clogged Charlotte's throat. She could only shake her head.

The older woman considered her for a long moment. "Very well. But if there is anything I can do to patch it up, simply ask."

"Thank you," Charlotte managed.

Frances gazed into her eyes. A world of understanding seemed to fill her dark gaze. "Oh, my dear."

"What?"

Frances started to speak, then thought better of it.

"I'm fine. I'll be fine."

Frances hesitated again, then nodded. A claw swiped from under the sofa and caught in the braided trim of her pelisse. It tugged, then let go. "Wh... Lizzy hasn't brought that dreadful cat here?"

The horror on her face brought Charlotte a smile. "I am to keep her until you go back to the country."

"You are... no, this is outrageous. Lizzy goes too far."

"It's all right." At least she hoped it was.

"Charlotte, you are not obliged to house that animal!"

"I want to..." Frances's skeptical expression stopped her. "Well, maybe not want to, but I'd like to help Lizzy."

"You're very kind."

"Lizzy, and Anne, make it easy."

Frances's smile was warm. She rose. "If you're sure. I must get them back home now. Alec will be worried."

"Of course."

"You will remember. If there is anything I can do, or that you need, you need only say so."

"Thank you." The words were heartfelt. Frances held out a hand. Charlotte clasped it briefly, and then her caller was gone.

Charlotte sat on in the empty drawing room for some minutes. Finally, she shook herself, started to rise, and noticed Callie a few feet away, staring at her from yellow eyes. Dust lingered in her fur despite her grooming. "We will dust under the sofa," she told her. "We are just getting organized, you know. We'll find you a soft spot of your own. Oh... I do hope Mrs. Trask likes cats."

Callie stared.

"I'm doing my best. It's been... rather difficult."

Callie turned her head slowly, as if scanning the room with disdain. She stepped closer to the sofa and inserted a delicate claw into the upholstery.

"No! You will *not* shred the furniture, shabby as it may be."

The cat looked at her again, and kept looking as she deliberately raked the cloth. It was so old it tore easily.

"Callie!"

The cat's yellow gaze seemed to say, "I can do as I please. I *shall* do as I please."

Instead of anger, Charlotte felt a sudden lift of expansion. *She* could do what she liked in this house now. Henry's despicable will had said nothing whatsoever about the upper floors. "This room would work better for dining," she said aloud. It was smaller than the one that now held a table. It made sense to reverse them, and she could do that. She could do what she wanted with the space that was left to her. She stood in one quick rush. She was going to go through every room and examine every item and keep only those she liked. The rest would be thrown out or relegated to the attics, starting with those mawkish figurines on the mantelshelf. There might even be a bit of money for new curtains, if she was very careful.

"People will claim I need a chaperone."

Callie, sniffing along the baseboard, ignored her.

Exactly; she would ignore them. "For what? To fight off hordes of suitors besieging a penniless widow?" The idea was ridiculous. "I'm damned if I'll have one," she said. She'd never sworn in her life, and knew very well how shocked people would be to hear the phrase on her lips. "I'm damned if I will," she added.

Callie clawed at the molding. There probably were mice.

"You have my permission to kill any rodent you encounter," she said. Then she looked, and was relieved to discover that Lizzy had left the hamper. "Here, kitty."

Thirteen

MRS. WRIGHT WALKED INTO ALEC'S STUDY WITHOUT knocking, and wringing her hands—bad signs. Alec had braced himself even before the housekeeper said, "Miss Anne and Miss Lizzy are gone."

"What? What do you mean, gone?"

"They're not in the house, and none of the staff know where they are." Mrs. Wright sounded braced for an explosion.

Alec was already halfway to the door. "Their maid…"

"Susan has not seen them since early morning. Everyone thought they were in the schoolroom together."

It was nearly eleven. Alec pushed down panic. "Perhaps they've gone for a walk in the park or…" But he knew as well as Mrs. Wright that they were forbidden to go out without informing someone, and their maid or a footman went with them.

He should have hired another governess for Lizzy; he knew that. It had just begun to feel futile. "Gather the household." He would organize a search—of the neighborhood, of the whole of London, if it came to that.

All the servants lined up in the front hall. "Where is Frances?" Alec wondered when everyone had gathered.

"She went out," Ethan informed him.

"Out where?"

"She didn't say, sir."

"Splendid." Alec started dividing the servants into pairs to be sent into the streets. He had just finished when a key turned in the lock and Anne and Lizzy walked in the front door. Frances was close behind them. They all stopped on the threshold, startled. "Where have you been?" Alec shouted.

Anne blinked; Lizzy's chin came up in an all-too-familiar way, presaging a storm about to break. Alec struggled with a choking mix of relief and fury. He'd provided enough of a spectacle for one day. Calm, he told himself; control and reason. "Thank you, everyone," he managed. "Obviously, they are home safe."

He herded them into the study and shut the door on the sea of eyes. "Would someone care to give me an explanation?"

"I went to find them," offered Frances unhelpfully.

"Find them. Where were they?" He looked from Anne to Lizzy, resisting the impulse to shout. "And what possible excuse do you have for telling no one that you were going out?"

"We went to see Charlotte," declared Lizzy. "And we didn't tell you because you have been so horridly grumpy."

"We knew you… quarreled about something," Anne added.

"And we were *not* going to be stopped," Lizzy finished.

Frances merely stood there, observing him as if he were an interesting stranger.

Conflicting feelings threatened to derail the conversation. Alec shoved them aside. "Unacceptable. In fact, I cannot imagine an acceptable reason for you to leave this house without informing someone. Since you apparently do not have the judgment to know that, you are forbidden to go out at all."

"Anne's dancing class is tomorrow," objected Lizzy.

"She should have thought of that before…"

"I made her go without telling," Lizzy interrupted.

"I am older; I should have refused," said Anne.

It was perfectly true, but Alec was only too aware of Lizzy's powers of persuasion. "Anne will go to the class with her maid, as before. However, you, Lizzy…"

His younger sister's chin jutted even further. "I'm going to see Callie. If you try to stop me I will climb out the window and run away!"

"You know you cannot go to the country just…"

"To Charlotte's. Every day. I promised."

It took Alec a moment. "You passed that hellish cat off onto…?"

"She was happy to have her. *She's* kind!"

He wanted to ask about her. But the very intensity of that desire, the fact that he had been missing her so much even in this short time, made the question impossible. "You are both confined to the schoolroom for the rest of the day."

"I'm hungry," Lizzy objected. "Are you going to *starve* us?"

Alec glared at her. "A tray will be sent up. But be warned! If you do not begin to conduct yourself with more propriety, Elizabeth, I will have to take extreme measures."

Lizzy started to answer, but Anne tugged at her arm. "Come on, Lizzy." She pulled her from the room, for which Alec was deeply grateful. He had no notion what he meant by "measures."

Frances remained, still looking at him in that odd way.

"Something has to be done about Lizzy," he told her. "She seems to have gone quite wild during Anne's illness." Frances nodded; what was wrong with the woman now? "Should it be a governess, imagining we could find one able to manage her? Should we send her off to school?" She so passionately did not wish to go. Everything was a passion play with her lately. She wouldn't listen to sense; she wouldn't compromise. He had no doubt that she would disrupt any school he chose with rebellious pranks. "Frances? Are you listening to me?"

"I'm sure you will think of something," was the calm reply. She smiled and left him there, wondering if his whole household had gone quite mad.

Alec sat at his desk and stared unseeing at the welter of papers. A cold trickle of dread pricked through him; his sister's stubbornness and wild exaggerations had begun to remind him of his grandmother's intransigence. Temperaments were inherited; he had seen as much among his own acquaintances. But surely such tendencies could be... diverted, guided into wholesome paths? How? Shouting at Lizzy was useless, yet he kept doing it. He couldn't seem to help it.

Alec rested his forehead on his hand. Frances was no help these days. The thought of going to his stately, censorious Aunt Earnton for advice made him cringe. He became conscious of a desire to ask Charlotte what to do. She'd been so helpful with both Anne and Lizzy. She would know...

The look on her face as she'd slammed out of his study came back to him, as it had a hundred times since then. He had to go see her on his own account. He'd put it off because the idea roused such regret, doubt, confusion—and because he wanted it so much.

❦

Lucy came into the kitchen, dusty from a morning's cleaning, to find a bright fire and the scent of apples. Tess Hopkins, who had come down a bit earlier, stood beside Mrs. Trask, watching her every move. "You cut the shortening into small bits, and then work it into the flour with this." Mrs. Trask showed Tess the proper tool and then vigorously demonstrated its use. "See how the dried apples have plumped up after we soaked them," she added, hands busy.

Tess's youth and lack of experience made Lucy feel mature and competent. Tess was a good girl, if shy. Unexpected happenings made her jumpy. It was a pure pleasure to see how Mrs. Trask drew her out and taught her.

Lucy got a glass of water and sat at the kitchen table to drink it. Most everything about Mrs. Trask, and her husband too, was a pure pleasure. This kitchen was a different world with them in charge—spanking clean, full of delicious smells, calm and comfortable. It was a marvel how the same room, the same walls and stove and implements, could be so altered. It was like that with the rest of the basement, too. Ethan and James had come over to move furniture down from the spare bedrooms, and Mrs. Trask had created a cozy chamber in back. Lucy wouldn't have believed you could do that with furniture from this house, but Mrs. Trask just had a gift. She did, and Miss Charlotte, too, who was doing the same upstairs. Lucy suspected she was still arranging and rearranging, even though she'd dismissed them. It was like a curse had been lifted from the place, and the Trasks were the good fairies.

The thought made her smile. Lucy deeply admired and respected the old couple. She couldn't imagine a practical problem that Mr. Trask couldn't solve. She hoped they liked her well enough, too, though she sometimes felt they watched her rather close. Strangers getting to know each other, probably.

She hadn't realized they were Ethan's grandparents right at first. The name should have told her, but she'd just been too flummoxed to think. When it sank in, she'd been amazed by his kindness in getting them to come here. And seeing him with them since, she'd begun to wonder if she was mistaken about his character. 'Course a fellow might behave one way with his family and quite another with women he fancied. More than likely too; Lucy knew that. Still...

As if summoned by her thought, Ethan came tromping down the basement stair from the back hall. "Grandad just can't resist a garden, eh?" he said. "What does he think he can do with that patch of hardpan out there?"

"Was he being careful of his back?" asked Mrs. Trask sharply.

Ethan saluted. "Following orders, ma'am; no heavy digging. I believe he's set the cat to that. She's started a fine hole by the wall. 'Course maybe that's an escape tunnel. I wouldn't put it past her."

"Scamp." She went back to crimping the edges of her pie. "And what are you doing here again? Not slacking on your work?"

"No, ma'am. Ladies have gone to my Lord Earnton's, with James in attendance, except for Miss Lizzy, who's still confined to quarters. I have a list of errands a yard long. Can't even stay till that pie's out of the oven." He grinned at her.

"This is for dinner, my lad. You keep your greedy hands out of my baking." But she smiled back.

Ethan dropped into a chair. "Lucy. Tess."

Nodding back, Lucy noticed yet again how polite Ethan was with Tess. He never flirted with her.

"If you've so little to do, you can go out and help your grandad," said Mrs. Trask. There was an odd little twist in her tone, more, and less, than regular teasing.

"He's just wandering about dreaming a garden, Gran. He doesn't want me underfoot." Ethan turned to Lucy. "Grandad pictures it all in his head beforehand—the garden. You should see the plantings at the Wylde country place. Sir Alexander says they're like a painting. The gentry come from all over to see Grandad's gardens and consult him on what they should do with their own, too. He's like to be famous."

Mrs. Trask flushed with pleasure.

"It sounds wonderful," said Lucy. "I hope I can see them one day." There was a short silence. Lucy felt as if she'd said something awkward, though she hadn't.

"Susan says hello," Ethan went on then. "Oh, and Jennings sent word that if you want to come see her on your day out, she'd be happy to continue with the training."

Lucy's chest swelled with happiness. Maybe things would come out right, after all. Who would have thought this terrible house could feel like a home, for instance? Yet it was really beginning to.

Ethan and his grandmother chatted about folk from Derbyshire. The scent of apple pie filled the air. After a while Mr. Trask came in, Callie at his heels. Amazingly, the cat curled up on the hearth and went to sleep.

The front doorbell rang. Tess started and dropped the pan she'd been scrubbing. But after a moment she straightened her apron and went to answer it. Lucy couldn't help a tremor of apprehension herself. Who would visit them here, and what good could come of it?

❧

Alec handed his card to a very young housemaid at his uncle's former residence. She left him standing in the street for several minutes. "Madame is not at home," she told him shakily when she returned.

A lifetime of good manners sizzled and went up in smoke. "Nonsense." He pushed past the girl, sending her running as if he were an invading army. After a quick look around the empty first floor, he marched upstairs. In what he remembered as the drawing room, he found a dining table and chairs. In the room opposite, he finally discovered Charlotte. She wore an apron over a shabby gown and held a filthy dust cloth.

"Why are you doing the maid's work?" he asked, then wished he'd held his tongue.

Charlotte threw down the cloth as if it were a dead rat. She clutched the apron, began pulling it off. "How dare you...?"

Heavy footsteps on the stair heralded a white-haired giant. "Everything all right, ma'am?" he said.

Alec was disoriented. He knew this man. Where had he...? "Trask? What are you doing here?"

"The missus and I work here." He looked at Charlotte. "Ma'am? Is all well?"

Alec's head spun. It appeared that his former head gardener stood ready to eject him from the house. "I thought you were retired," was all he found to say.

"It's fine, Trask, thank you," said Charlotte. When he'd gone, she added. "What do you want?"

What did he *not* want, Alec wondered? Seeing her again, lovely even in such a homely setting, had scattered his wits. He found himself transfixed by her coppery eyes, her lips which had met his so fervently... He groped for his set speech. "I came to apologize, of course. I told Hanks that he is insane and dismissed him. He took me unawares with his ridiculous..."

"And what if other people think as he did?"

"No one would..."

"You believed it. For a moment."

"I did not!"

"I saw it in your eyes." Her voice wavered, and Alec felt it like a blow to his chest. She swallowed. "Get Hanks back. Let him watch this house, examine my background, follow me through the streets if he likes. He will find nothing wrong!"

"I know that. You have to understand; my first thought is always to protect my sisters…"

"From me?"

"No, no, of course not. I admit my mistake. I am very sorry for it." Charlotte said nothing. "There are… elements of our family history that make me… overprotective, I suppose." Charlotte tossed her apron over a chair. She was looking everywhere but at him. Increasingly uncomfortable, Alec continued, "My grandparents' household, where we lived until I was six years old, was… a place of turmoil and acrimony. My sisters and brother, being younger, were spared much of the experience, and I vowed that their lives would be… peaceful."

"Peaceful," Charlotte repeated.

He could not read her tone. But… was she staring at his lips? Nonsense; she couldn't be. "Of course my father had been even more… disturbed by the disaster of his parents' 'love match.' His whole life was made a misery by them. I learned from his example. He strove always for the reasonable path. He chose a wife for her compatible background and equable disposition; they were quite contented…" He had completely lost the thread of this conversation, Alec thought. He was saying too much, and what had it to do with apologizing?

"So you don't believe in love?" Charlotte asked. Her eyes were still focused on the floor.

"Of course I do. I love my brother and sisters. Frances. I have a very high regard for my aunt and uncle Earnton."

"Ah, regard." She made the word sound crass.

This exchange had gone wildly off track; he had

to pull it back. He had come here with a specific purpose. "What you said about Hanks..."

"You may set him to watch me! I told you I don't care."

"I have no intention of doing so. But your point... your earlier point is a good one. I hadn't considered it."

Charlotte frowned at him.

"Many people are all too ready to believe... the worst. And there is no protection from slander but the truth."

"Exactly. So you must set Hanks to work again."

"But if he is not looking in the right direction— which he is not—then how can he find the truth? I think we must take a hand in the investigation."

"We?"

She'd softened, just a little. Alec was aware of a huge relief. "You must know things about my uncle that outsiders could not..."

"There is only one thing I know about Henry. He cared for nothing but his collection. His life revolved around it—the people he knew, the subjects he thought and spoke of, everything."

"Very well. This argues that what happened to him in life must be related to it. The attempted robbery points in that direction as well."

"And so?"

"I think we should..." What, Alec wondered? What should they do? When she gazed at him that way, his brain ground to a halt, and there was only one thing he could think of. "We should... ah... ah... have an expert in to value the collection. We should have done it before this. Yes, that's it."

"But what would that tell us about robbery or murder?"

"Who knows?" Alec hurried on before she could argue. "What I mean is, money is a powerful draw for many people. I'll arrange for the valuation, shall I?"

Charlotte hesitated, then nodded. He wanted to ask if she had forgiven him but didn't dare. He became aware of the fact that he was creating an excuse to see her again, and again. He should go now—leave the table while he was ahead—but he couldn't quite make himself walk out the door. "Trask is a good man." It sounded inane.

"Yes."

"I'm glad you have him here."

She nodded, and waited.

"Well, I... Oh! That wretched cat. I'll take it back, if you wish." It came out reluctant, because it was.

At last, Charlotte smiled. "Mrs. Trask loves cats. And Callie actually seems to listen to her, mostly. Mr. Trask is going to cut a little door into the back garden. Having a place outside seems to calm Callie."

"Perhaps she'll run away," suggested Alec hopefully.

"Lizzy would never forgive me. I don't think she will, though. I think she just likes a bit of freedom." She stood straighter and added, "I hope Lizzy may visit her now and then."

Alec started to tell her that Lizzy was in disgrace and would not be allowed to visit anyone for a very long time, but something in the way she carefully did not look at him changed his mind. Clearly, Charlotte wished for this, and feared it would be refused. "Of course." He won another smile with this and at last felt the atmosphere lighten.

He had to be satisfied with that small victory, however. After thanking him, Charlotte mentioned that the whole household was very busy, and he could do nothing but take his leave.

Fourteen

A FEW DAYS LATER, CHARLOTTE AWAITED HER SECOND caller in much better trim. The drawing room was now established in the larger front chamber, furnished with only those things she had chosen. She wore one of her new gowns, and her hair was carefully dressed. There was no sign of an apron, still less a dust cloth. There would be no repeat of that humiliation. Whenever she thought of the way Sir Alexander had caught her—in a horrid old gown with inches of dust around the hem, her hair all anyway, a smudge on her cheek—she cringed. It was his own fault for forcing his way in, but still…

When he'd appeared, his height and broad shoulders making the room feel much smaller, she'd been so glad to see him—which made her even more furious. She did not *wish* to care what he thought of her. That moment when he'd looked at her with alien eyes, wondering if she were a danger to his family, had hurt more than any other slight she could remember. She'd seen then how much she wanted him to find her beautiful and accomplished and desirable. That might be a vain dream, but dust and aprons certainly didn't help.

He had come to her, however. The man who could annihilate Holcombe with a slashing word had taken the trouble to call on her and apologize. Apologize! It had been so long since any man showed concern for her feelings. Henry would have sooner—she couldn't even think of what would have made him apologize to her.

Sir Alexander would be visiting again when the collection was valued, and again as they "investigated" together. Charlotte's pulse accelerated at the thought.

There'd been no mention of the kiss, of course. Yet something in his eyes had told her it was as vivid in his memory as in hers. Her recollection of the astonishing sensations that kiss had evoked had made it hard to speak. She'd been inundated by a desire to do it again. She couldn't, naturally. One kiss could be put down to overindulgence in champagne and overlooked. More would… would what? Ruin her? She had no prospects, a meager income, a marginal toehold in society. As soon as Lady Isabella Danforth tired of squiring her about—as she surely would—Charlotte would be isolated and forgotten once more.

She'd vowed to do as she liked from now on. Could she have a taste of physical passion? It was a revolutionary idea. Briefly, she lost herself in wondering what Sir Alexander would have done if she had thrown her arms around him and…

The bell pealed below, shattering her agreeable visions, and soon after Tess ushered in Lady Isabella. Charlotte hadn't expected her to come here, so far from fashionable haunts. Indeed, she'd thought Lady Isabella would drop the connection altogether. It had been a pleasant surprise to receive a note from her. The older woman settled on the sofa. "I came to urge you to accompany me to a rout party on Thursday."

Charlotte thought that she'd really come out of curiosity, to see the place and her household. But she didn't mind. "That's very kind of you."

"My dear, Edward would never forgive me if I did not bring you along."

She'd seen no evidence of special concern from Edward. Still, beggars couldn't be choosy. "I'd be delighted to go."

Lady Isabella looked around the room as if it were a savage's hut. "Should anyone ask, we shall tell them what a terrible *eccentric* Henry was. A scholar and an eccentric." Her tone made the two words synonymous. "He buried himself—and you, of course—out here in the… hinterlands. Like a, a hermit. What could you do? But now you have been… rescued." She smiled triumphantly.

Why need they tell anyone anything, Charlotte wondered? Then she saw that it was a story to tell. Lady Isabella lived on stories, most of them scurrilous. Yes, she was a gossip. But she seemed to relish the telling as much as the malice. And she could say much worse about Henry; Charlotte didn't care.

Tess brought tea, and Lady Isabella chattered, reviewing all the current *on dits* of society. When she mentioned something about her youth, Charlotte couldn't resist her curiosity. "Sir Alexander spoke of your parents the other day."

Her caller bridled. "I can imagine the kind of thing he said. Alec always despised Mama."

"He was talking of his childhood."

"He was the most priggish child. I suppose he told you she was dreadful?"

"Uh…"

"She was beautiful as an angel, you know. My father fell in love with her the moment he saw her." She laughed. "At church, if you can believe it! She was the daughter of a bishop."

Lady Isabella looked at Charlotte as if to share a great irony. Uncertain what to say, Charlotte smiled at her.

"Their parents weren't pleased. Both sides were hoping for matches that brought much more money. But there was really nothing to object to; they came from the same class and background. And they… overbore all opposition."

"Like a fairy tale," said Charlotte, very curious as to how this tale connected with Sir Alexander's very different view.

"Well, they had a lovely wedding, in the cathedral. Mama used to talk about it often." Lady Isabella shrugged. "Fairy tales don't talk about afterward, do they?"

"No." Nobody mentioned the disasters that could follow a walk down the aisle.

"They were matched in good looks." Lady Isabella glanced toward the mirror over the mantel. "It's an odd thing; none of us is nearly as handsome as our parents. The combination didn't… take. Well, in any way, really." She shrugged. "From the smallest thing to the largest, they disagreed."

Charlotte merely looked inquiring. Lady Isabella seemed launched on a flood of reminiscence, and Charlotte was too interested to stop her.

"Mama couldn't bear opposition of any kind. It was her nature; contradiction drove her wild. And society made her giddy with nerves." She made an airy gesture. "The only thing that calmed her was brandy and laudanum. Just a bit, you know, mixed together. But as time passed, it began to take more and more. I've heard that is common." Her tone was strangely dispassionate.

Charlotte felt she was hearing too much. "I didn't mean to pry, Lady Isabella. Please do not feel..."

But her guest seemed to have forgotten Charlotte's presence. "She always told me I was all she had—her only daughter, you know. I was *hers*, more than the boys. She'd call me to her rooms and tell me everything. Sometimes, she would weep and rage for hours. They had to remove all the ornaments because she threw them."

Charlotte's view of Lady Isabella Danforth was changing by the moment. "That must have been frightening."

"One learned to duck," was the odd reply. "It was like a game. We didn't have so many games." A sly smile curved her lips. "She used to send me out dressed as a boy."

"As a...?"

"There was a... fellow nearby who sold brandy. Well, I suspect he made it himself. It wasn't a place a girl could go."

"And she sent you...?" Charlotte was appalled.

"Papa kept the liquor locked up, and she couldn't really..." Belatedly, Lady Isabella seemed to sense her listener's reaction. "It doesn't matter. In the end, of course, Simon got me away."

"Simon?"

"My husband. He was a neighbor. I'd known him all my life, and one day he came to see me and said I had to get out of that house and why didn't I marry him." She gave her tinkling laugh. "I was thirty-one years old! Can you believe I said no at first?"

"I suppose it was a surprising…"

"All I could think about was how Mama would scream at me if I so much as mentioned… But Simon didn't give up. He went to Papa. I don't know what he said to him, only that Papa came and told me I was a fool if I didn't grab the chance to escape hell. He was a blunt man, Papa. It was kind of him, though, because I was the only one she listened to when her delusions overcame her. I know it was worse for him after I was gone."

Charlotte found she had tears in her eyes. "So, it was a romantic rescue."

"Oh, well." Lady Isabella gestured vaguely. "Mama had screamed at Simon in front of everyone at a country ball. Quite humiliating. I think he liked the idea of taking something away from her. He spent every cent he had on hunting, of course."

"Simon did?" confirmed Charlotte, thrown by the change in direction.

"He was hunting mad! His string of horses cost the earth. And the stables, and men to tend them. I always thought he cared more for the horses than for Edward." She said this as if it were perfectly commonplace.

"Surely he loved his son…?"

"He was glad to have an heir, naturally. His first wife died without producing one. Poor silly Simon.

He was killed forcing a water jump at sixty-five years of age, if you can believe it? He *would* not tolerate the idea that he couldn't ride neck-or-nothing any longer. At least then we were able to sell the horses and the lodge in Leicestershire and use the income for other things."

Charlotte wondered if she talked to everyone so freely, or if she considered her a member of the family and thus privy to its secrets. Did gossip fascinate her because her own life was a lurid tale?

"My sad little story," she finished with a moue, as if reading Charlotte's mind. "Everyone in town knows it. I always wanted to live in London, so it all came right in the end." Lady Isabella's look was bright and oblivious; her smile just as usual. Charlotte could do nothing but smile back. But this seemed the wrong response; her guest's expression shifted to consternation. "You haven't brought that horrid animal here?" she exclaimed.

Looking down, Charlotte saw that Callie had come into the room. The cat strolled regally between them, tail in the air. "I'm keeping her for Lizzy. She's a reformed creature…"

Effortlessly, Callie leapt onto the arm of the sofa, inches from where Lady Isabella sat. She fixed her yellow eyes on the gently waving fringes of her shawl. Lady Isabella stood as if galvanized. "So you will come to the rout party?"

"Yes, thank you. She's just being friendly, I th…"

"Splendid. Would you mind, my dear, taking a cab and meeting me there? I know I should fetch you, but it is such a long way out here."

"Of course."

"You really must move from this forsaken spot."
Lady Isabella kept an eye on Callie as she moved
toward the door. It was as if she'd forgotten that
Charlotte had no choice but to live in a neighborhood
that fashionable Londoners viewed as next to exile.
"Till Thursday then."

"It is very kind of you to ask me."

Lady Isabella waved this away. Charlotte saw her
out, bemused by the odd mixture of traits in her
personality, then returned to the drawing room.
Callie sat in the same spot, washing a front paw with a
rasping tongue. "Was that really necessary?" Charlotte
asked her. "We do not have so many callers that we
can afford to discourage them."

The cat ignored her, continuing her ablutions.

"I realize that you did not actually attack the
shawl. Though I think that might have been more
lack of opportunity than self-control. But I would
remind you that you are not allowed on the drawing
room furniture."

Callie stopped washing and gazed at her. Charlotte
could almost hear her pointing out that the room was
often empty, and no one could keep her from the
furniture if she wished to sit on it. Charlotte sighed.
She half admired Callie's attitude and half worried that
it seemed so easy to interpret. Was she going just a
bit mad? "I *won't* end up old and dotty, holding long
conversations with a houseful of cats," she said. It was
a joke, and then it wasn't. Charlotte's hands closed as
if to grasp all that life might offer.

～

Ethan stood in the pantry next to the dining room, gloved, his hands mechanically polishing silver. He finished a fish slice, put it aside, began on a soupspoon. He needed a plan—and he needed it soon. Gran was already making noises about wanting to go home. He'd have to find someone else to work at the house, or tell Lucy's mistress about the agencies. But a staff of town-bred strangers would leave him with no excuse for visiting, not to mention the way the thought filled his head with hideous visions of roguish menservants stealing Lucy's affections away from him.

Not that he possessed them, of course. Despite all his efforts, he hadn't won her over. Meanwhile, Ethan found himself constantly imagining her with him in the forester's cottage in Derbyshire. Waiting with a smile and a kiss at the end of the day. Sharing a meal, and the bed, oh yes. Perhaps, later on, a family.

This agreeable picture dissolved. To have that life, he had to ask Sir Alexander for the position, which would rouse all kinds of ruckus in his family. He didn't even want to think about that. But even supposing it didn't exist, would Lucy leave her Miss Charlotte? He didn't think so, even though she longed to leave London. And so… his thoughts circled back to the beginning, more tangled than they'd ever been in his life. He needed a plan.

"Ethan." The tone said that Sir Alexander was repeating himself.

Ethan tried to hide his start. He hadn't even heard the swinging door. "Yes, sir. Sorry, sir."

"I'm going to see Mrs. Wylde. I shall be out for some time."

"Yes, sir."

Sir Alexander started to turn away, then hesitated. "How did your grandparents end up working for her, Ethan? I thought they had left service and were living in that cottage they own."

"They was... were down here visiting my aunt, and I asked them to do it as a favor, sir. I didn't like to think of L... of the ladies all alone there."

"Ah. Good work."

Something in the way he said it made Ethan prick up his ears. Maybe he just had love on the brain, but he got a sudden notion that Sir Alexander was more than commonly interested in the welfare of Lucy's mistress.

With a nod, Sir Alexander departed, the door swinging shut behind him.

Ethan's hands stilled as he thought back over the last few weeks. Now that he considered, he could see hints all along the way. Ha. If his master and Lucy's mistress got together, Lucy would be in Derbyshire, just where he wanted her. Developments could then... develop. And without Lucy having to do anything, which was good, because getting that girl to listen was like pulling teeth. So, how could he... encourage the situation, like?

An elbow poked his ribs. "Ethan, you great lug." He looked down to find Susan standing beside him. "What's wrong with you?"

"Nothing's wrong with me."

"Come on. You're never like this."

"Like what?"

"Mooning about instead of working. Not hearing the bell."

"Did it ring?" He was horrified at the idea.

"James went." Susan peered up at him. Her eyes narrowed with delighted speculation. "Are you in love?"

Ethan almost moaned. With all the complications suddenly plaguing his life, the last thing he needed was people sticking their noses into his affairs. He'd had a lifetime of that. "Me? 'Course not! Don't be daft."

Susan continued to eye him as if he were a horse she might buy.

"Got a letter from my dad," Ethan added. It wasn't a lie; he had had a letter two days ago, full of the usual unnecessary admonitions about doing his job well.

"Oh." Susan knew all about Ethan's troubles with his father. "Is there anything...?"

"It's all right." Ethan hated deceiving a childhood friend. "Nothing new." Except a swarm of difficulties that somehow only he could resolve.

With a sympathetic pat on his arm, Susan left him, and Ethan tried to put his mind to polishing, despite its being about as useless a task as he could imagine. He liked solid results to show for his efforts, not something that would just have to be done all over again in a week or so.

❧

Charlotte's household fell into a pleasant routine. The more she saw of them, the more she liked her staff. Particularly Mrs. Trask, who somehow limited Callie's depredations to one lamb chop and a scrap of sausage. On her first visit, Lizzy was amazed. "So you secretly expected her to demolish my house?" teased Charlotte.

"Of course not!" Callie overflowed Lizzy's lap like a fur rug. Her purr was audible. "I knew she would love it here—and you." The warm look that came with this pronouncement made Charlotte's throat tighten. "I wish I could live here, too!"

"You wouldn't want to leave your sister and bro..."

"They leave me, all the time!" Lizzy pouted. "You wouldn't do that if I came to stay with you."

A world of complications buzzed in Charlotte's brain. "Well, I would have to, because of... ah... household duties and... um... errands."

"You don't want me?" Lizzy's blue eyes threatened tears.

Even putting aside all the other objections, she would be mad with boredom in a day in this small house, Charlotte thought. This was a recipe for disaster. She tried a reason that she was certain Lizzy would never have considered. "Sadly, I can't really afford visitors."

As expected, the girl looked blank.

"My household budget is so very limited, Lizzy. I'm sorry."

"You have no money?"

"You will come to see me—and Callie—very often."

Lizzy's thoughtful frown was unsettling. She made no more mention of moving households, but as she headed home, Charlotte was all too aware of the need for a plan to forestall whatever schemes were brewing in that pretty little head.

At two, Sir Alexander arrived with an expert from the British Museum. Charlotte wondered if he'd told the man—Gerald Mortensen—that Henry's collection went to the museum if the will was violated in any particular. No, she decided.

Mortensen was a thin, laconic ferret of a man. "The keys?" he said as they stood before the display cases in the front parlor.

"Oh." Charlotte hadn't thought of this. She thought as little as possible about the whole wretched collection. "Henry always kept them with him. He had a special ring of keys with just those on it. Separate from the house keys. They… they must have been stolen along with his purse." She looked at Sir Alexander.

"Wycliffe was given his effects. There was no mention of keys." He turned to Mortensen. "Can't you make some judgment just by looking?"

"I must handle objects to authenticate them," was the adamant reply.

"Ah." Sir Alexander gazed at the rows of cases. "I don't like to break the locks."

"One of my colleagues at the museum could very likely open them," said Mortensen.

"Pick the locks, you mean?" Charlotte asked, intrigued.

The man drew himself up in outrage. "His specialty is the history of locking mechanisms. He has of necessity learned to open various types of locks, as specimens don't always come with their keys. However, here…" He gestured at the room. "These are standard cases, such as we use ourselves. It is astonishing how often the keys are lost."

Never to display cases that he was in charge of, Charlotte concluded from the distaste in his tone.

"He has a master key that works in most units. Shall I write a note summoning him?" Mortensen added.

"If you would. My coachman can take it."

This was accordingly done. Mortensen then left them. He wandered through the rooms on the first floor, examining objects not in cases. He made no response when Charlotte asked if he would like tea or any other refreshment. "He is very focused on his work," she commented when he had gone out of earshot.

"Indeed, I can verify that he has no other topics of conversation whatsoever. The carriage ride from the museum was a trifle... silent."

Fortunately, his colleague arrived within half an hour and had no difficulty in opening the display cases. His skeleton key made by the manufacturer would also allow them to be relocked. She would not be able to get at the objects, Charlotte realized, but then she had no wish to.

"Any locks in the collection?" the newcomer asked Mortensen as he handed it over. Told there were not, he departed without further conversation. "This will take time," said Mortensen, clearly wishing them elsewhere.

"And so we are dismissed," Sir Alexander said to Charlotte. He looked amused.

"Definitively. Would *you* like tea or... I think there is some Madeira."

"Tea," he replied.

Charlotte gave the order, and they went up to the drawing room. She was glad for the opportunity to show him how much better it looked than at his last visit. He made no comment, however, as they sat. "Lizzy said Anne is still enjoying her dancing class?"

"She seems to be. Although not as much as Lizzy enjoys teasing her about it."

"And what is Lizzy doing now that Anne is often out?"

Sir Alexander shook his head. "Plotting devilment, I imagine." He hesitated, then added, "You've become well acquainted with my sisters. You've seen how Lizzy is. Do you think I should send her away to school? Against her wishes?"

It was just the opening Charlotte had hoped for. The subject of Lizzy had been much on her mind. "I don't think separating her from her family is right just now."

"Just now?"

"I think she's afraid."

"Afraid? Of what?" He straightened as if priming to go to her defense.

"Of Anne moving off into the wider world and leaving her alone."

"Ah." He frowned.

"If she had more to do…"

"She would at school. As well as other young women to befriend."

"But she doesn't want to go."

"Vehemently. Lizzy believes she already knows all she needs to." He shook his head. "Frances taught the girls when they were very young. Then we hired governesses, but neither my father nor I ever succeeded in finding one who really fitted the post. They were dutiful, no more. And lately, there have been none who would stay in the face of Lizzy's… antics."

"Anne has been her only real companion?"

He frowned as if he hadn't really thought about this. "There are very few young people among our neighbors in the country."

"Well, I have an idea." She'd been cudgeling her brain for ideas, afraid that Lizzy was hatching schemes to improve her fortunes.

"I would be grateful for any suggestion."

"You might do for Lizzy what you are doing for Anne. I suspect your Aunt Earnton would know how to go about it. Find some girls Lizzy's age whom your aunt approves—let her do it, in fact—and arrange for Lizzy to meet them and get to know them. Make some new friends. Then she will not feel such a need for Anne's company."

Sir Alexander stared at her. "That's brilliant. Why didn't I think of it? I shall talk to my aunt at once. Thank you!"

His look warmed Charlotte to the depths. If Tess had not come in just then with the tea tray... But she did, and Charlotte busied herself with pouring and passing a cup. The sound of something heavy being shifted downstairs brought her back to earth—murder, robbery, accusations. "Do you really think this valuation will be helpful, that we can actually find any answers?"

"We are intelligent, logical people, with resources..."

"But as you said before, what do we know of investigating crimes? I certainly know nothing." The suspicion could hang over her forever, she thought despairingly.

"It cannot be too different from examining tenants' grievances and judging among them. And we have the advantage of *knowing* you had nothing to do with it and being highly motivated to find the truth." He met her eyes.

In his steady gaze, Charlotte saw determination, and trustworthiness, and... more? The thud of her pulse nearly deafened her. What was it about this man, more than any other she'd ever met, that captured all her attention, filled her senses? She'd known what was missing from her dreadful marriage; she'd acknowledged the lack with a distant regret, and then relief. But in Sir Alexander's presence, she felt her physical isolation as an acute ache. She needed to reach out, to rekindle that blaze of connection.

The silence was growing too long, too charged. She groped for words. "I... ah... Lady Isabella very kindly asked me to attend a rout party with her tomorrow." Perhaps he would come, as he had before.

"Did she?" His voice had gone dry.

"She was telling me about her mother." Why had she said that? Sir Alexander looked understandably startled. "I'm not sure how it came up... I... we were talking of her childhood." How could she escape this topic? He'd gone thoughtful. Was he offended?

"I'm sure I did not come off well in any story of hers about our family."

Horrified, Charlotte hurried to dispel the idea that she had been gossiping about him. "We didn't talk of..."

"She would say the same of me. Perhaps with reason. But... it seemed to me, once I was of an age to notice, that Aunt Bella rather fanned the flames between my grandparents. They communicated almost solely through her, you know, and the way she... bore tales back and forth escalated rather than eased disputes, I thought." He shrugged. "So I would take anything she says with... a grain of salt at least."

"You lived with your grandparents?" Charlotte remembered he had said something like that.

"Only when I was very young. Later, we visited only at the Christmas holidays. My father could never bring himself to refuse the invitation."

"Then you can't really know, can you?" How could he conceive what it was like to be a young woman trapped in a household where she was continually terrorized and belittled? Charlotte suppressed a shiver.

He conceded the point with a stiff nod. Charlotte sipped her lukewarm tea. Once again, the silence stretched. They had wandered into a conversation much deeper than social chitchat, and Charlotte wasn't sure how to find her way out. Sir Alexander started to speak, and she leaned forward. He said nothing. She lifted her cup again. He set his down with a chink.

"Perhaps we should…"

"I wonder if…?"

They spoke at the same moment, then each paused politely—not to say desperately. Simultaneously, they each added, "Please." Charlotte had never been more grateful for the sound of footsteps on the stairs.

"I have completed my examination, provisionally." Gerald Mortensen had a small notebook in hand. "I fear it is not good news."

"Please sit down," said Charlotte. "Will you have a cup of tea?"

Mortensen waved this aside. "No, thank you." He didn't sit either. "My preliminary assessment, which I do not believe will change appreciably upon further consideration, is that this collection is chiefly forgeries. Or, to be more charitable, modern repro-ductions. Some are quite good copies. But worth very little, of course. There are one or two pieces that the museum might be interested in acquiring." He raised an eyebrow.

"My husband's will does not allow any sales," said Charlotte, tight-lipped.

"Ah." Mortensen tore one sheet from the notebook and closed it.

"So, if my uncle paid large amounts for these items…?" began Sir Alexander.

"He was duped. Sadly, there are many unscrupulous 'dealers' only too ready to cheat those who do not seek expert advice." Mortensen sniffed.

"This wouldn't make a good, small museum, then?" Charlotte said. "His collection, I mean?"

He looked at her; a charitable person might have called the gaze pitying. "If the British Museum received a lot such as this, almost all of it would be discarded." He handed the notebook page to Sir Alexander. "These are the authentic items. I have used the numbers from the displays to identify them."

"Thank you."

"I must be going," said Mortensen. With a small bow, and no further courtesies, he left the room.

"All that money thrown away." It burst from Charlotte as she struggled to take it in. From Hanks' comments, she'd expected to hear that some of Henry's purchases were unwise. But this was too much. He had taken nearly her entire inheritance and reduced it to rubbish.

"In dealings with criminals, basically. We should talk to his man of business. What was his name— Seaton? I allowed him to disappear without…"

"Hasn't Hanks already talked to everyone? What can we learn that he has not?"

"He was a danger to them. They would say as little as possible in his presence. I might pose as a collector, a source of money."

"We already know that they cheat. You think one will confess to murder?" Charlotte couldn't curb her impatience. What was the use? The money was gone, and shockingly, in this moment, she didn't much care who had killed Henry. She could have cheerfully strangled him herself.

"I don't know that Hanks saw Seaton. I will inquire. Also, he had asked to go through my uncle's room. I put him off but perhaps now…"

"It's locked, and we can't find a key." Charlotte had discovered this when rearranging the furnishings, and had not yet dealt with it. "Henry didn't carry house keys around with him. He liked being let in by a servant. But we cannot find those keys either."

"What?"

She looked away. "Henry kept his bedchamber locked." Sir Alexander stared at her, no doubt speculating.

She'd been avoiding the room as if it didn't exist, as if she could erase the past by leaving it out of her new household arrangements. "Holcombe had a key. He took the maid in when she cleaned."

"But… you did not…?"

Charlotte turned away from his gaze. "I have never set foot in Henry's room. He did not wish me to."

Sir Alexander looked stunned. "Was my uncle completely mad?"

"I often thought so!"

Sir Alexander shook his head, then frowned. Charlotte would have given a great deal to know what he was thinking. "We might break down the door," he said finally. "But I believe I would rather get the key from Holcombe."

"He will not wish to give it to you."

"Precisely." His smile was humorless.

Picturing the meeting, Charlotte found the spirit to smile back.

Fifteen

FINDING HOLCOMBE WAS SIMPLE. HAROLD WYCLIFFE had kept a record of where each former servant had gone, partly supplied by the Bow Street Runner. Paying a visit to another man's valet, as Holcombe now was, was somewhat awkward, but Alec managed it the following afternoon, meeting the man in his new master's front hall. He didn't bother with preliminaries. "I have come for the key to my uncle's bedchamber."

"Why would I have…?"

"You have it." Alec was certain he'd kept it. It was the sort of small, sneaking thing the man would do. "You may recall what I told you about taking anything that did not belong to you when you left his house. I can summon a magistrate in a matter of…"

"I forgot about the keys," Holcombe whined. A blusterer and a bully, he collapsed in the face of opposition, as Alec had expected. "I was distraught over Mr. Wylde's death."

"Give it to me." He held out a hand.

"It's put away, like…"

"Then go and get it."

Holcombe twitched and grimaced and finally disappeared up the stairs. Alec had begun to wonder what he would do if the man simply did not come back when he returned and held out a small ring of keys. He dropped it into Alec's hand. "What else did you steal?"

"Steal?" the valet squeaked. "I didn't steal…"

"Keeping these keys was a theft. What else?"

"Nothing! I swear it on my mother's life!"

The oath of an inveterate liar, Alec thought. "If I find that you've taken anything else, no matter how tiny, you will find yourself on a transport to Australia before you can…"

"Four neckcloths," Holcombe blurted. "I didn't see the harm. *She* didn't need them, and they was… were brand new." With the indignation of a liar lied to, he added, "Mr. Henry promised me he'd left me something in his will."

The venom in his voice on the word "she" extinguished any sympathy Alec might have felt.

Holcombe took a step toward the stairs. "I'll get them." He froze. "One's at the laundry."

Alec waved this aside. "Keep them." He wondered if there was anything else that Jem Hanks had not squeezed from this man.

"You're not going to let *her* go through Mr. Henry's things? He'll turn in his grave, he will, to think of that chit pawing over his…"

Alec grabbed Holcombe's shirtfront and twisted it in his fist, jerking the valet onto tiptoe. "Should you *ever* speak of Mrs. Wylde again—and I see no reason for you to do so—you will speak respectfully. Do you understand me?" He shook the man a little.

Red-faced and choking, Holcombe nodded. Alec
held him a moment longer to reinforce his point, then
thrust him away. Watching him cough and scrabble
at the ruins of his neckcloth, Alec marveled again at
the outrages his uncle had allowed, even apparently
encouraged. He'd gone far, far beyond the line. Alec
felt that old brush of fear. Did mental instability run in
his father's family, thanks to his grandmother?

Outside, Alec started to direct his carriage to
Charlotte's, bearing the key in triumph, as it were.
But it was nearly six, and he remembered that she was
going out with his Aunt Bella tonight.

Which led to another familial puzzle. Why was
his aunt taking such trouble over a young woman
with no fortune or position in society? Of course,
Charlotte was very pleasant company—much more
than pleasant. But Aunt Bella never listened to anyone
else's conversation and cared for nothing but her
own social standing. Well, and Edward, he supposed,
though signs of that were rare. He'd never known her
to do a good deed for its own sake. Did she realize
how much it annoyed him? That might explain it.

He really ought to go to this rout party. Alec had no
doubt that an invitation was among the teetering pile
of cream envelopes on the far corner of his desk. He
was considered eminently eligible by the eagle-eyed
mamas. In previous seasons, he had sometimes enjoyed
being sought after. During his first, he had gotten quite
puffed up by it, until a friend pointed out that the
attention had nothing to do with his person and everything to do with his fortune. That, and familiarity, and
his new responsibilities on his father's death, had taken

much of the savor from society for him. To idle away hours in amusement, with the way things stood in the country… Still, he could tell Charlotte about the key, set a time to visit and open the room. Yes, of course he should do that. She would be wondering.

At home, he found Lizzy hanging about in the front hall and immediately suspected mischief. "What are you doing down here?"

"Waiting for you," she said. "What have you been doing?"

"Where is Frances?"

"Working on her embroidery in the drawing room." Lizzy seemed uncharacteristically listless. "And Anne has gone to one of her dancing parties."

"Ah."

"We could play chess. I know I said it was boring, but…"

"I'm sorry, Lizzy. I'm going out this evening."

"Oh."

Lizzy's lips turned down in the expression that Alec had always thought of as a sulk. Now, he saw sadness in it as well. "I thought I might speak to Aunt Earnton and arrange for you to meet some girls your own age here in town. Rather like Anne is doing."

Lizzy considered this as if it were a trick. "Dancing classes?"

"No, not until you are older. Just, ah, tea, perhaps or… walking in the park." He had no idea what activities his aunt might find appropriate for thirteen-year-old girls. And still less what they would wish to do.

"They'd probably be horrid," Lizzy objected.

"Then you would fit right in."

She laughed and stuck out her tongue. "I… would like that… I suppose."

"Good. Now, I am going to change, and then we'll have dinner together."

"Just you and me?"

"And Frances, of course." Lizzy wrinkled her nose, and he frowned at her.

"It's just… she's gotten so… lugubrious."

"So…?"

"It's from Dr. Johnson's dictionary. It means gloomy and dismal."

"It very well may. However, it is not a term you should apply…"

"Charlotte said if you learn a new word every day, before you know it you have a prodigious vocabulary."

"Did she?" Alec was struck again at how rapidly a bond had formed between Charlotte and his sisters.

Lizzy nodded. "And you will sound very well educated without having to read a lot of tedious old books."

"Charlotte said that?"

"Well… not exactly."

"Your own conclusion?"

Lizzy nodded, giving him her dazzling smile. Then she turned to skip up the stairs, her mood seemingly lightened. Alec watched her go with a mixture of fondness and exasperation.

"I am not in the drawing room working on my embroidery, nor am I lugubrious," said a voice from the darkened reception room opposite. "I am plotting and planning."

It startled him. "Frances?"

She emerged in the archway. "I came down for

a book I left in the library. After Lizzy spoke…" She shrugged. "I didn't want to… I'll say embarrass her, though that is rather difficult to do. At any rate, bravo, Alec!"

"For…?"

"Your splendid idea. I should have thought of it myself. Amelia will be only too happy to find Lizzy some companions, I'm sure. Some lovely, calming companions. She has a stake in it, after all. She will be bringing Lizzy out in a few years and responsible for her conduct in society."

"I thought it a good plan." Alec was glad to have her confirmation.

"Well done."

"It wasn't my idea, it was C… Mrs. Wylde's," he added absently.

"Was it?" Frances took a step closer. "You have made it up with her then? Good!"

"There was nothing to make up. Just a misunderstanding."

"Ah." She eyed him. "You were calling on her then?"

"Yes. If you'll excuse me, I want to write a note to Aunt Earnton before I go out."

"Of course. What are you doing this evening?"

"Aunt Bella is taking Mrs. Wylde to a rout party, and I thought that I… that is…" It suddenly occurred to Alec that he wished to keep his motives to himself.

"I hope you have a very pleasant time." Frances gave him a sweet smile; her dark blue eyes sparkled up at him. Alec was again struck by the resemblance to Lizzy, which had somehow eluded him for thirteen years. "What are you plotting and planning?"

Her smile broadened, and she laughed. "That would be telling."

"I can be trusted," Alec suggested. He remembered Frances's inquiries about the house near Butterley. "Are you plotting escape?" he added lightly.

"I would never wish to wholly escape my family," she replied.

This did not precisely answer the question. What did she mean "wholly"? But Frances walked up the stairs without saying any more. As Alec went off to his bedchamber to change and dispatch the note to his Aunt Earnton, he thought perhaps he should call on her as well. His mother's sister was a woman of infinite resource, and he felt very much in need of her expertise.

❧

There was a sagging bench in the narrow back garden of Henry Wylde's former home. Unpainted, neglected, stuck in a corner behind a shed, it was like the rest of his place had been—awkward and comfortless. But it was hidden from the windows, and so Lucy used it as a place to hide when she wanted to cry.

She hated her need to weep. It made her feel weak and treacherous. But her resistance didn't make it go away. Every so often, the lump rose in her throat and her eyes burned; circumstances loomed like a great wave rising over her head, ready to crash down and drown her. She just had to slip away and cry it out. The tears didn't make her feel better, exactly—just less like she was going to burst into a thousand pieces. Her only comfort was that no one knew of her bouts. She couldn't have borne the mortification.

On this particular evening, she had tiptoed out after readying Miss Charlotte for her evening party and seeing her off in a cab. The others were busy in the kitchen and probably thought she was still working upstairs. She wiped her eyes with her sodden handkerchief and sniffed. But the storm wasn't over. Tears welled up again and spilled down her cheeks. Hiccupping sobs escaped her. She struggled to suppress them. Above all, she mustn't be discovered.

As if the fear had brought it, a figure loomed over her in the growing darkness. At first she thought it was Mr. Trask. She leapt to her feet, groping for an excuse.

"Lucy?"

It was Ethan. Was that better or worse than exposure to his grandfather? Worse, Lucy decided. "What are you doing here?" It came out choked and sullen. But why was he creeping about, sneaking up on people? He didn't even live here, though you wouldn't know it half the time.

"You're crying." He sounded shocked.

"I'm n-not." And then of course she was, harder than ever. She turned away. But he was blocking her escape to the house.

Ethan stood there, a great hulking lump, then he took a step forward and enfolded her in his arms.

Lucy froze. Obviously, she should shove him off and give him a blistering earful for his impudence. But the relief of those strong arms around her, the broad shoulder right there, seemingly designed to support her aching head, were so very tempting. And then his hand began to gently stroke her hair. "There now. What is it?"

Ethan held her without stiffness, without intrusion, as if there was nothing in the world he'd rather do. His hand moved softly on her hair, rhythmic and soothing.

Something broke open inside Lucy, and she let go the tears she had been trying to hold in. She didn't understand what was happening at all. All she knew was—his touch magically made the crying a true release instead of a useless storm of emotion. She couldn't resist. She gave herself up to the embrace, and leaned on him, and cried. His great, gentle hands held and comforted her. His body felt like a shield against every harm. The part of her that doubted and argued was stilled. Nothing seemed to exist but the two of them in the soft dark.

Some unmeasured time later, Lucy found herself sitting beside Ethan on the bench, his arm encircling her, her body tucked tight against him as if it had always belonged there. "Now, tell me," he said. "If anybody's hurt you, I swear I'll…"

"No. It's nothing like that. It's stupid…" Lucy's embarrassment over her weakness crept back. She had never been a weepy, clinging female, and she wasn't about to start in.

"No, it isn't," Ethan declared.

Unable to help herself, Lucy blurted it out. "I heard your grandparents talking about going home. I didn't know they were… temporary, like. I mean, if I'd 'a thought for a second. A 'course they want to go back to the country. Anyone would. It's just I'll miss them so…" Almost as much as she missed the countryside herself. She broke off, clenching her jaw. She would *not* cry anymore.

"Ah," was all Ethan said.

She couldn't see his expression in the dimness. Suddenly, she was afraid to say any more. She wriggled a little away, but his arm pulled her close again.

"I asked them to come as a favor," he said. "I couldn't stand the notion of you all alone here."

The lump came back in Lucy's throat.

"But they will be going home, it's true. They're not in service anymore, and they deserve their rest. I'll have to be looking for somebody else."

"It's not your job to find…"

"I got to take care of you, Lucy!" The force in his voice stunned her. "I… I love you. I do."

Lucy stared up at him. Though she could barely see his face, she could feel his sincerity in the hard lines of his body, the tremor in his arm around her shoulders.

Ethan spoke faster, nearly babbling. "I reckon Sir Alexander will give me the forester job. Old Elkins wants me to have it, and there's no reason he wouldn't listen to him. Can't see why Hobbs—he's the steward—would fight it. Would you marry me, Lucy, and come live in Derbyshire? There's a cottage, with a garden and all. It's a right lovely spot."

Lucy's head spun. Feelings she'd denied or ignored when she thought Ethan was only flirting broke free, like water from a burst dam. Tenderness, desire, trust, love—yes, love—flooded through her.

"Lucy?" Great hulking Ethan Trask sounded nervous as a boy. "We'd be happy there. I know we would. I'd do my utmost to make sure you had everything you wanted."

She turned under his arm, gazed up at him. The

moon was just peeking over the top edge of the garden wall, and she could make out his face now, despite the growing darkness. He looked scared, and that touched her heart as nothing else could have done. Her arms slid around his neck. Ethan bent his head and pulled her even closer. Their lips met, and the touch vibrated through Lucy's whole being, set her afire. It was like nothing she'd ever experienced. The kiss paused, and renewed, even more intense. It shook her to the very soul. She gave herself up to him and to her own desire. Ethan's hands strayed over her, leaving trails of warmth along her skin, bringing more and more of her to pulsing life. Lucy lost herself and the world in his embrace.

At long, long last, they pulled back a little. Lucy gazed up at him, open in all ways. "I'm thinking that's a yes," said Ethan, sounding as shaken as she felt.

She laughed, trembling and suffused with heat. She could stay here forever, she thought, encircled by his arms. And then reality came rushing back. "I'd have to leave Miss Charlotte here alone." Lucy's elation died. She had cared for Charlotte Rutherford since she was a child who'd just lost her mother. It was more than simple duty. There was a bond between them older than the new one with Ethan. His promise of a different life came at the cost of someone else's suffering. Lucy couldn't bear that. Life stretched out bleak before her once more.

"Maybe we could fix that," Ethan said.

"Fix... what do you mean?"

He hesitated.

"Oh, Ethan, what could we do? I'm trapped and no

mistake." She hated thinking of Miss Charlotte in that way, but the fact was, in this moment, she did. She threw herself back into his arms and huddled there. He held her.

❧

Strolling into the rout party, Alec found it like a hundred others. Musicians played unheeded in the largest reception room; in another, young women were taking it in turn to show off their musical talents, and their shapely arms, at the pianoforte. Older guests hunched over their hands in the card room; servants laid out a lavish buffet. And everywhere people talked and talked. He'd often wondered where society found the words night after night to generate this roar of conversation.

He moved through the rooms looking for Charlotte, often obliged to stop and respond to acquaintances' greetings. He barely avoided having to listen to a deb warble the latest ballad. He glimpsed Aunt Bella and her cronies interrogating some hapless fellow beside a potted palm. God help the man if he was trying to conceal a juicy bit of gossip from them. He'd begun to wonder whether Charlotte had decided not to come when he spotted her sitting with Edward and his friends. As usual, they had established a corner bastion of chairs and coaxed their own supply of champagne from the servants.

Charlotte wore a gown he hadn't seen before, of some glistening coppery stuff—silk, he thought—that echoed her eyes and hair and made her a gorgeous monotone save for a necklace of green beads. It ought to be emeralds, Alec thought; emeralds to rival the sparkle of her gaze.

He made his way slowly through the crowd, watching Charlotte laugh and sip her champagne. He'd never seen her look this carefree. The realization rankled so sharply that he stopped and took a grip on his reactions. Her smile looked so natural, the tilt of her head so relaxed. She leaned back in her chair, the lines of her body open and enticing. She'd never appeared so happy with him, never listened to him as eagerly as she seemed to one of Edward's vacuous friends. Was she shallow, after all? And why should that make him angry?

It didn't. He wasn't angry. He stepped closer.

"So she brought us all along to see for ourselves that the drawing room was haunted," one of the men was saying. "And the cloth on a small table *was* moving in and out, with an eerie buzzing sound, just as she'd said. So Tony walks over and flips up the cloth, and there's his bulldog, fast asleep underneath."

"Buster always snored like a steam engine," said another man—Tony presumably, chiming in on his cue—and was rewarded with peals of laughter.

Alec let it die down before closing the last little distance to the group. "Good evening." Edward glanced up at him. Alec was sure that he'd been aware of his arrival and ignored it.

"You all know my cousin Alec," Edward said carelessly. "Alec, I think you're acquainted with everyone."

He'd met them. He always forgot their names. He supposed that was as rude as Edward's careless greeting, but it was difficult to see it that way.

"Oh, except..." Edward gestured toward two girls who didn't look familiar.

"Mary Simmons and Susan Blake," supplied one of the women. Elliott, that was it. She was married to the plump man. The other couple was called Billings. He couldn't recall the names of the remaining two men, the storytellers. Well, one was Tony, obviously. Uninvited, Alec snagged a nearby chair and brought it to their circle. He headed for a place next to Charlotte, but Miss Simmons and Miss Blake quickly moved to make room for him between them, while Edward draped an arm across the back of Charlotte's seat, clearly refusing to yield the spot. Alec set his jaw, reined in his temper once again, and sat.

"Alec who?" said Miss Simmons, and giggled. "Edward didn't tell us your last name, the naughty boy."

"Wylde," he supplied. Here was a girl whose name his cousin couldn't recall referring to him as Edward, as if they'd known each other since childhood. It represented all he disliked about his cousin's set.

"Ooh, and are you?" breathed Miss Blake. She giggled as well.

Someone should take away her champagne for her own good, Alec thought, and then wondered if he was becoming an intolerable prig.

"Practically worthless," Charlotte said to Edward. She had to be referring to his uncle's collections.

"You don't have any champagne," observed Miss Simmons. "Tony, he has no champagne!"

Alec strained to hear what else Charlotte was saying. Edward leaned toward her and spoke too low to overhear. He became conscious of a desire to throttle his cousin.

"He'll have to snag himself a glass," said Tony. "Can't pour it down his throat." He waggled the bottle, and the two girls dissolved in giggles.

He should have told her not to tell anyone, or... the truth would discourage robbery, he supposed. And what harm could it do? The real problem was, he hated to see Charlotte in such intimate conversation with... anyone else. He burned to pull her to her feet and take her away from Edward.

This wouldn't do. He would not be ruled by irrational feelings—still less stage a spectacle for all to see. He could just imagine the turning heads, the whispers. Aunt Bella would be in the front rank; how she would love it if he made a fool of himself. Damn the girl! Why must she laugh that way, with her head thrown back, her lovely throat exposed as if for kisses? Kisses he could almost feel burning on his own...

Alec realized that the plump Mr. Elliott was speaking to him across Miss Simmons. "Believe you were at Eton with my brother," he repeated.

"Oh, ah, yes?"

"John Elliott. Cricket."

Translating this laconic statement, Alec remembered playing with his brother on the school eleven. He hadn't known him well outside the playing fields.

"Alec here was a cracking bowler," Mr. Elliott told the others. "Mainly thanks to him we trounced Harrow at Lord's three years running."

Everyone looked at him. What did one reply to that kind of statement? "Er, how is John?"

"Married, and getting fat, like me," the man laughed.

"I have never truly understood cricket," said Miss Simmons, leaning in and breathing champagne in his face. "Do explain it to me."

Alec managed to refrain from telling her that he would rather slit his throat. "Is this your first Season in London?" he replied instead. Unsurprised by her affirmative, he asked if she was enjoying it. It was like winding a clock; she ran on and on, leaving Alec free to watch Charlotte and plot a kidnapping.

Tony went for more champagne. An older woman came and extricated Miss Blake, looking as if she wanted to take her by the ear. Edward turned to speak to Mrs. Billings on his other side. Alec seized the opportunity. "Some sensible soul has opened a window. Would you care to get some air?" he asked Charlotte.

"It is hot, isn't it?"

Taking this as agreement, he stood, offered a hand, and urged her to her feet. Maintaining possession, he pulled her arm through his and navigated a path to the open French doors. "You didn't mention that you were coming tonight," she said.

"It was a spur-of-the-moment decision." He kept walking—through the doors and out onto a flagstone terrace. Other couples strolled there, taking advantage of the night air. Lanterns made pools of light in the gardens.

"Oh, it's lovely." Charlotte raised her eyes. "The moon's up." She took a deep breath. "Something in the garden smells wonderful. I'll have to ask Mr. Trask about planting some of it, now that it's May. I want lots of fragrant things like this." She breathed deeply again.

Alec felt the rise and fall of her torso against his arm. Heat brushed his skin like trailing fingers. Without thought, he pressed closer. Charlotte looked up at him and smiled.

A man could fall into those copper eyes, he thought, and never come out again. It would be easy and delicious—and dangerous. He said the first thing that came into his head. "I got the key from Holcombe. He had kept it, as we suspected."

Charlotte's smile faded. "Oh... good."

The enthusiasm had left her voice, and he cursed himself for an idiot. He could have talked about gardens or any other damned thing.

"I suppose you'll bring it by," she added tonelessly.

"I thought tomorrow," he said.

"All right."

"It would seem to me that..."

"Shall we rejoin the group?"

Alec cursed silently again. "Don't you find them rather tedious?" Irritation made his voice too sharp. He retained possession of her arm and did not move.

"No. Why would I?"

"Well..." *Because they are*, was the only reply that occurred to Alec.

"They're kind and amusing... and restful."

"I beg your pardon?"

"They never talk about anything... lowering. And they don't... require anything of me. I don't have to think about Henry or what I am going to do. They make me laugh."

Alec got the point. He was the one who reminded her of her problems, and did depress her spirits. But

Edward was just as much Henry Wylde's nephew as
he. Why didn't some of that stigma apply to him?
"Edward's set is rather fast, you know." He'd planned
to talk to her about this at some point, but not in such
a self-righteous tone.

Charlotte shrugged.

Alec knew he should stop himself, but he couldn't.
"Their company could damage your reputation. You
should take care to…"

"My reputation as a duped and penniless widow?"
she interrupted. "With no prospects or real connection to society?"

"You exaggerate…"

"Here as a result of Lady Isabella's charity?" Her
voice had grown sharp. A woman nearby turned to
gaze at them.

"I would hardly call it…"

"Am I not entitled to a bit of amusement?"
Charlotte broke in again. "I don't see why you should
begrudge me that."

"I do not!"

She tugged at his arm, forcing him to move toward
the open door—or create a scene for the avid eyes
around them. "It doesn't seem too much to ask. I
cannot see the harm in a few amusing stories, a…
respite from the problems that, yes, must be addressed."
She sounded near tears. Alec felt as if someone had
punched him in the chest. He wanted to argue that she
was being unfair, and he wanted to sweep her up and
remind her that they'd shared a kiss that was far from
being a "problem." Except that it was. He hated this
roiling mixture of emotions that tied his tongue.

They stepped through the doors, into the heat and roar of chatter. Charlotte freed her arm; he had to let her.

"I will see you tomorrow. At one, perhaps?" She gave him a stiff nod and turned to walk back to Edward's group. From across the room, Alec's cousin smiled in triumph.

Sixteen

CHARLOTTE INSERTED HER NEEDLE INTO THE LENGTH of blue velvet and pulled the thread through. They had found the cloth in a forgotten trunk in the attic, and though faded, it would make far better dining room curtains than the current flowery chintz. If she ignored the main floor, which she did as much as possible, she was more and more satisfied with the look of her house.

She glanced up and discovered Callie sitting five feet away, her tail neatly curled around her front paws. The cat had taken to appearing like a ghost wherever Charlotte was and watching her. "Good morning," Charlotte said, continuing her sewing. This was the last panel. She hoped they could hang the new curtains before Sir Alexander arrived. Let him see how well she was managing her household now.

Callie stared at the needle slipping in and out of the cloth. Her pupils expanded darkly.

"No," Charlotte told her. She stopped sewing for a moment and searched her workbasket. Finding an almost empty wooden spool, she pulled off the remaining thread and rolled it along the floor. Callie pounced, batting the spool across the carpet. Charlotte returned to her seam and her thoughts.

Sir Alexander had managed to dim the luster of the rout party last night in more ways than one. After he'd gone, Charlotte had noticed Miss Simmons's mother fetching her, and finally recognized the pattern. Unmarried girls were not left among Edward's friends for long. Clearly, it was not felt to be proper. She didn't see the objection; they didn't talk scandal or flirt outrageously. Well, there was the champagne, perhaps. With Tony continually filling one's glass, it was all too easy to overindulge. She'd been careful, the memory of last time still vivid. But otherwise, the group seemed harmless, with a refreshing lack of formality. Margaret Billings had invited her to drive in the park, and she was certainly going. Charlotte plied her needle, entertained by Callie's twitching tail and the swoop and clatter of the spool from one corner of the drawing room to the other.

How could it hurt—a bit of amusement in a life that had been devoid of it for so long? Yet she had been made to feel irresponsible. And she resented it. Aware of silence, Charlotte looked up. Callie crouched like a sphinx, the spool imprisoned between her forepaws, and stared at her. "Sir Alexander never lets you forget your duty," she said to the cat.

Callie blinked her yellow eyes slowly. Her brindled fur caught the light streaming in the window.

"It's not as if I am neglecting what needs to be done. Quite the contrary." The cat's yawn flashed small fangs.

"Precisely. It's tedious to think about one's problems all the time."

Callie batted the spool, sending it scuttling across the room. Her hindquarters waggled, and then she was up and after it.

Every creature needed to play, Charlotte thought. She smiled as Callie captured the spool and fought it to a standstill. "Edward is very charming."

The cat looked at her, spool in mouth. It would forever bear little tooth marks. "But the odd thing is…" Charlotte's hands stilled on the cloth. "There is something about Sir Alexander. When I am with him I feel more alive, somehow. Even if it is simply a more lively irritation." She smiled. "Last night, the sky, the scent of flowers; it was as if I hadn't really noticed them properly before. And I wanted to hold his arm forever."

Callie brought her prize over to Charlotte and dropped it at her feet like a gift. Her gaze was steady and penetrating.

"Capture what I want and keep it?" Charlotte asked her with another smile. "But he spoiled everything. He is always spoiling things." She resumed her sewing. "And then I was glad to get away from him. I thought it would be a relief. But… it wasn't." Charlotte sighed. "Edward, despite his very good looks, is only… entertaining. He doesn't make me feel anything in particular. Why should that be?"

"Did you call, ma'am?" Tess the housemaid stood in the doorway.

Charlotte flushed, hoping she hadn't heard very much of that. "No, I was just… talking to the cat."

Tess looked around.

Callie had disappeared. "She was just here."

"Yes, ma'am." Tess dropped a sketch of a curtsy and went out.

The cat emerged from under the sofa. "Thank you so much," said Charlotte.

~

Ethan stood outside the door of Sir Alexander's study, working up the courage to knock. To make good on his proposal to Lucy, he had to speak to him about the forester position. But the difference between dreaming and planning and actually taking a step into the future he wanted was making him sweat. What if Sir Alexander had objections that Ethan hadn't thought of? What if he already had someone else in mind for the post, or Hobbs had put a candidate forward? Hobbs planned well ahead for the estate, he knew that from his brother. He would be aware that Old Elkins was ready to go. What if he couldn't offer Lucy a life in the little cottage near the edge of the forest? What if he couldn't have it himself? He didn't know what he'd do if that happened. For years, he'd seen himself there.

Even if it all went smooth as silk, there was still his dad. Ethan didn't want to bring Lucy into the family in the midst of a feud. In his imaginings, they visited with his parents and sisters, were a welcome part of occasions filled with laughter and conversation.

He wasn't afraid of his father; that wasn't it. But he hated wrangling. More, he wanted his dad's respect for the work he chose. Could he be made to understand?

Stop havering, Ethan thought! He forced himself to knock. At a word from inside, he went in. Sir Alexander sat at his desk, but he didn't seem deep into his work. He was gazing out the windows. That was good. "I wondered if I might speak to you, sir?"

"Yes? What is it, Ethan?" He sounded distracted but not impatient. That was good, too.

"It's about..." Ethan had gone over this speech in his mind a hundred times. All of that flew out of his head the instant he opened his mouth. "It's about... about old Elkins, sir."

"Elkins?" Sir Alexander frowned. "Who is Elkins?"

"Ol... Fred Elkins, the forester, in Derbyshire."

"Oh. Yes, I recall. What about him?"

"Well, he's getting on in years, you know, and suffers from the bone ache something terrible." This was not important! Ethan rushed on, speaking faster and faster in the face of Sir Alexander's obvious puzzlement. "He's wanting to go off to Cornwall, to his daughter's place, and... take it a bit easier, like. And I was hoping to... or, I mean, I wanted to ask you about having his position, sir. My taking it over, I mean."

"You? As forester?"

He was making a hash of this, saying it all wrong. Nothing to do now, though, but soldier on. "Elkins's trained me since I was a lad. I spent just about every free minute with him, I was that interested. I know what needs to be done and how to do it, and I'd be... I believe I'd be right good at it, sir. Do a fine job for you."

Sir Alexander examined him. His surprise had given

way to serious appraisal. "I think your family had other hopes for you?"

Ethan set his jaw. "It's what I love to do. Working in the woods. It's where I belong." Here, at least, he sounded dead certain.

"Ah." Sir Alexander considered him a bit longer. "I see no problem with the request. I will have to discuss it with Hobbs."

Ethan nodded; he'd expected this. He thought the estate steward would accept him if Sir Alexander brought it up; he knew of no reason why not. Of course, with his brother Sam working right next to him in the office there, word of his request would reach his father like greased lightning. He'd have to get a letter in the same packet Sir Alexander sent home. The thought of composing it made him want to groan.

"I do recall now that Hobbs mentioned Elkins's wish to leave," Sir Alexander added. "You understand that no change could be made until we return to the country."

"Yes, sir."

Sir Alexander continued to gaze at him. "If it is what you really want, I think it will be satisfactory."

Ethan felt the grin spread over his face. He couldn't help it. "Thank you, sir!" he exclaimed. With a small bow, he left while he was ahead.

A bit later, laying the table for luncheon, Ethan's hands shook with elation and relief. He'd done it! He'd succeeded—or as well as. He'd reached out to get the life he wanted, and he hadn't been refused. More than anything, he longed to run and tell Lucy. Probably lucky he couldn't get away to do that. Best to wait until all was signed and sealed and he was sure of the cottage that would be their home.

If he could get her to Derbyshire.

James gave him a look, and Ethan realized he was standing stock still with a handful of forks. Hastily, he began setting them out.

He hadn't told Lucy about his idea of trying to bring their master and mistress together. Partly, he worried she'd object, and it was the only plan he had. Partly, he had no notion how he was going to manage it, and he didn't want a rash of unanswerable questions. She'd just disbelieve him then. He'd do it, somehow, because he had to. He'd figure out the details some other time.

For now, he just wanted to think of them married and snug in their new home. Then they wouldn't have to crouch on a rickety garden bench, fearing the sound of an opening door. Ethan lost himself in memories of their kisses, the feel of her body under his hands. He wanted her as he'd never wanted anything in his life.

"Watch it," said James.

Ethan had nearly walked right into him. With a mighty act of will, he forced himself to concentrate on the task at hand.

❦

Charlotte, Tess, and Lucy did get the curtains hung before Sir Alexander arrived. He didn't see them, however, as he went directly to the locked room at the back of the house that had been Henry's domain. Lagging behind, Charlotte heard the key turn. Even more than the main floor, she'd been ignoring Henry's bedchamber as she transformed the house. It let her pretend he'd never existed. Today, she would have to think of him again.

Of course she was curious, and acutely aware of how strange it was—never to have seen the inside of her husband's bedchamber. But facing the open door, she mainly felt the sinking sickness that had plagued her so often over the last year. Ingrained habit told her that she would be publicly humiliated if she attempted to enter that room.

Charlotte shook herself and stepped forward. It was dim inside. Sir Alexander pushed back draperies on the back window and then the side, and Charlotte gaped. It was as if she'd left her home, her country, even her time, and been transported to a distant realm.

Against the inner wall stood a small bed that looked more like a table; she recognized the Roman style from a book Henry had once shown her. A carved wooden chair occupied the near corner, a huge terracotta urn the far one. But most amazing were the murals. In faded reds and blues and yellows, on every wall and the ceiling, they showed scenes of Roman life—men in togas, vineyards and olive trees, vistas of ancient streets. Each panel was set off by painted columns and arches that mimicked the architecture of another sort of building altogether. The wooden floor had been tiled in a mosaic style showing sea creatures. The only modern element was the heavy draperies, of a red so dark as to be hardly red at all. Oddly, for all the color, the room seemed stark and cold.

"Where did he keep his things?" she wondered aloud. "There's no wardrobe or…"

"Here," said Sir Alexander.

Briefly, Charlotte was confused as to where he'd gone. Then she realized that the room was narrower than the one on the opposite side of the hall. She hadn't noticed at first because the murals confused the eye, but part of it had been walled off.

A small door, painted like the walls, led to a narrow dressing room crowded with a wardrobe, chest, and shaving stand. The space was tasteless and strictly utilitarian. There was no window.

Sir Alexander had lit candles. One drawer sagged open. "Holcombe took some neckcloths," he said.

Charlotte turned back to the Roman bedchamber. All of this must have been done before she arrived in the house. No wonder Henry had needed money. It must have been very expensive. She looked at the painted trees, the faked stonework. Here was Henry's secret life, his sanctuary, she supposed. She felt no connection, no chord of sympathy. Why set your heart on a lost time and society, long past all warmth and life?

"We should go through the clothing, check the pockets," said Sir Alexander.

Charlotte returned and opened the wardrobe. Here were Henry's coats, dark and sober, hardly less stiff than when he'd worn them; the scent of him wafted out, and she almost felt faint. She couldn't touch these garments; the idea made her ill. "I'll get Tess and the Trasks," she said. "They can take all the clothing away and examine it." She walked out before he could object and summoned her small staff.

They stared at the strange bedchamber. But the

main floor had inured them to oddity, and they were soon carrying out armloads of clothing. "If you find anything in the pockets, no matter how small or trivial, bring it back here," Sir Alexander told them.

"Are there any family members who would want his clothes?" Charlotte asked, to anchor herself back in the commonplace.

"You could offer them to Edward," was the dry response.

The thought of his elegant cousin in Henry's drab garments was ludicrous. "I don't think he... oh, you're joking."

"I was." His expression was sympathetic. "Send them off to the workhouse. Or see if the Trasks know anyone who could use them."

"That's a good idea." With the clothes gone, she felt better. "Are there papers?"

"Some, in the chest here. Correspondence my uncle didn't wish anyone else to see. He appears to have been involved with people who are willing to steal artifacts, for a price."

"Or say they had."

"I beg your pardon?"

"Well, Henry bought mostly fakes."

"Ah. A good point. Still, they are clearly unsavory characters. I'll hand these letters over to Hanks." Seeing Charlotte's expression, he added, "He's best suited to question them."

"I know. I just..." She turned away from the humiliating memory of his accusations. "I suppose he will want to come here."

Sir Alexander nodded. "I think he must."

A note was duly written and dispatched. But they did not wait to begin a thorough search, going over each piece of furniture inch by inch, including the undersides and the backs of drawers. In the end, defeated and dusty, they had only the letters and a lost collar stud from under the wardrobe. "No real help," concluded Charlotte, disappointed.

Sir Alexander didn't seem to hear. "I am very suspicious of this wall," he murmured, gazing at the partition that had been added to the room. "When a man as devious as my uncle seems to have been adds a wall, can he have resisted...?" He ran his fingers along the narrow panels that sheathed the lower half, pressing and prodding.

He was right, Charlotte thought. Henry loved his secrets. But, for one thing, he would never want to bend over them. She surveyed the top part of the wall. It seemed to be smooth plaster, painted in stripes as broad as her forearm of lighter and darker blue. She had thought the scheme strange when she first saw it, out of keeping with the utilitarian nature of the room. Was there a crack parallel to the top of the door frame? Wavering candlelight made it hard to judge. She went to the section of plaster on the right of the door and pressed along the edge of the stripe, the top of the wainscoting, the jamb. Something gave, and three feet of the stripe opened, revealing ranks of narrow shelves fitted into the thickness of the wall.

"Good for you!" said Sir Alexander. He picked up a candlestick and brought it over. They peered inside together.

A small object rested on the lowest shelf. Charlotte

took it out. The light gleamed on an oval of amber as large as her palm. A delicate insect floated within it. She heard Sir Alexander's breath catch. "That, or something exactly like it, belonged to my grandfather. It was always in his study in Derbyshire. He used it as a paperweight."

Charlotte put it back as he reached to a higher shelf. Their hands brushed in passing. He took down a china cup; gold rimmed the base and lip. "I believe this comes from his club. I've seen such settings when I lunched there with friends."

Something glittered on the top shelf. She couldn't quite see. Charlotte stretched up. "There's a fork," she said incredulously. She tilted it in the dim light, revealing a monogram.

Sir Alexander bent nearer. "That is a piece of my parents' wedding silver," he said, sounding outraged. He held the candle closer.

Charlotte replaced the fork and retrieved an enameled snuffbox. It rattled. The lid resisted her fingers, then sprang open to reveal a chunk of polished stone, brightly veined with red.

The top shelf is full of earrings," said Sir Alexander from his superior height.

"Earrings?"

"Single ones. No pairs." He reached up and retrieved them.

Charlotte gazed at the glitter of jewels in his hand. "No!"

"What?" asked Sir Alexander.

"That lapis one is mine. One of my favorites. Lucy and I looked everywhere for that earring. Last fall." They'd ransacked her room and examined every part of the house where she'd been. Charlotte had even dared to interrogate the other servants, who'd sneered at her and tried to convince her that Lucy had stolen it. And through it all, Henry had stood silently by and said nothing. Charlotte shivered. He'd gone into her room when she wasn't there, into her jewelry box. He'd fingered her things. Had he noticed that she often wore the blue earrings? Had he remembered that they'd been her mother's? Had she even told him that...?

"Do you recognize any of the others?" The evenness of his voice calmed her a little.

"No." She picked it out. "I'm taking it back." Her tone dared him to object, but he didn't. How had Henry gotten so many women's earrings? No women visited, and he... but what did she know about where he went and who he saw? "He was a thief. A sneaking thief."

"He stole from people who were important to him, somehow."

"I wasn't important to him," objected Charlotte. "Except for my money."

"My uncle was a benighted fool!"

The emotion in his voice silenced Charlotte. She became acutely aware of his shoulder brushing hers. The room seemed warmer suddenly. "Things from his father... his brother. Did he get on with your father?"

"When they were young... I don't know. Father was five years older. They were both sent to Eton, and I never heard that they didn't get along. But when my Aunt Bella started her lawsuit, my uncle said he thought she was quite right, and if she were successful, he would do the same. Father was very angry."

"This was…?"

"Almost fifteen years ago now. You must understand that my aunt and uncle received substantial legacies when my grandfather died, and more when my grandmother followed him three years later. My father did inherit the estate, but he was expected to make his income from managing it well. The liquid assets went to them, which didn't keep my aunt from accusing Father of deception, forgery, and a dozen other things," he finished bitterly.

Charlotte shifted uncomfortably. It sounded dreadful, but Lady Isabella had been so kind to her. She contented herself with saying, "Henry would do anything for money."

"Wait, there's one more here." Sir Alexander reached high again. "No, not an earring, this is…"

"My father's!" Charlotte almost wailed. She stared at the watch fob of sapphire bound with silver, her throat tightening. "My mother gave it to him the day they were married. He thought he'd lost it; it broke his heart. And I…" She'd been so impatient, so unfeeling. His memory lapses were common by then, and she'd blamed him for misplacing a precious remnant of her mother. Henry—damn him, damn him!—had visited around that time, she remembered.

All the regrets, humiliations, disappointments of the last year burst upon her in one great wave. So much lost, such… cruelty. Yes, it was cruelty. What else could you call it? A sob shook her, and the tears descended—unstoppable. They racked her chest, so intense she swayed on her feet.

Sir Alexander's arms enfolded her, drew her in,

held her close. She leaned; she let her head sink on his shoulder, and she cried. The sneers, the rages, the cold night hours when she'd blamed herself for all of it drove those tears. They poured out of her, bitter salt, and his embrace held it all. Safe, it was safe to cry, here and now. She wasn't alone. She allowed herself to give way completely for the first time since this nightmare began.

She couldn't have said how long the tears lasted. It seemed long, and yet just a little while before self-consciousness returned. The shoulder of his coat was wet. "I... I'm sorry." She tried to pull away.

"What have *you* to be sorry for?" he answered gently. Charlotte looked up, into green eyes full of compassion—and something warmer. She felt the hard muscles of his body pressed against hers. Heat vanquished the last tears. She raised a hand to his cheek, touched it softly. His eyes flared. His arms tightened. She pulled him down to her.

The kiss was like the last time, and different. The revelation of touch returned, the sheer physical joy that his lips could rouse in her. But this time, something deep within Charlotte leapt and melted. It was more than a kiss; it was being kissed by *this* man. She would never get enough—how could one get enough?—of this glory. It was everything she'd been denied; it was life itself.

She slipped her free hand under his coat—up over his chest, along his ribs. His body was an undiscovered country, a call to explore the heights of sensation. His lips drew her on, fired every inch of her. She was not going to endure an existence that lacked physical passion, Charlotte vowed. She had made mistakes, taken wrong turnings, but she was not going to miss out on something so sweet, so intoxicating.

The knocker on the front door echoed up the stairs. Footsteps padded in response. They sprang apart.

"I... ah..." Sir Alexander cleared his throat.

Charlotte was breathless.

"Most likely Hanks," he said hoarsely.

She could only nod.

"He... ah... yes. He must see these items."

"I will not give him my earring!"

"I don't see why you should." He seemed about to speak again, but the footsteps approached relentlessly. The two of them stepped back into the Roman bedroom. Charlotte longed, impossibly, to touch him again. Sir Alexander cleared his throat. "I... ah... I cannot imagine wanting to occupy this room. It's like the ancient sites one visits in Italy, empty and... lifeless."

"Yes." It was exactly what she'd felt. "No shred of comfort or vitality."

They looked at each other. Sir Alexander's green eyes seemed to hold all the vibrancy missing from the stark chamber. Charlotte was exquisitely sensitive to his height, the breadth of his shoulders, the sheer impact of his masculine presence. In this moment, he seemed the antithesis of Henry in every possible way.

Tess brought the Bow Street Runner into the room. His sharp gaze darted here and there, cataloging every detail. Charlotte's hackles rose, and she wished she hadn't consented to have him in her home. She clutched her earring.

Sir Alexander told him what they'd found. "You should 'a waited for me," was the terse reply. After that, he ignored them, going over the bedchamber and dressing room like a hound on the scent. He noted down the names in the letters and wrote careful descriptions of the items in the secret cupboard. When he came to the earrings, Charlotte stiffened. She still held her own concealed in her fist. Sir Alexander met her eyes and said nothing.

In the end, Hanks looked disappointed. "I'll pay these gent'lmen a visit," he said, tapping the pile of correspondence. "Mebbe they'll say something different from the others. A falling-out among thieves, like."

He didn't look enthusiastic. Charlotte shivered on a surge of fear and dislike. He didn't believe he was going to find anything. He still thought she was the most likely culprit.

"I wondered about Seaton," said Sir Alexander. "He seemed very eager to wash his hands of my uncle's affairs. A man of business would usually want to stay involved, gain a new client, perhaps."

Hanks nodded. "Aye, there's a fine little weasel."

"You've spoken to him?"

"Once I found him, which weren't easy. An old hand at covering his tracks, I'd say. I don't doubt that he knows these fellows." He tapped the letters again. "I wager he was paid to introduce them, and raked off a fine bit of cash from the dealings, too."

"If Henry discovered he'd been sold faked antiquities," said Charlotte, refusing to be intimidated, "he would... I can hardly explain how furious he would have been. He devoted heart and soul to his collection. He would have threatened Seaton—anyone—with exposure, disgrace, the... the full force of the law."

Hanks nodded again. He hadn't looked directly at her since he arrived. "Yes, ma'am. And Seaton and all would ha' threatened right back, to tell the world he was a fool—ignorant and easy to dupe. That they would put it about that his 'collection' was a load o' rubbish. Seems to me, from what I've learned, that Mr. Wylde wouldn't ha' cared for that overmuch. I'm thinking he would have backed down."

Charlotte remembered Henry's love of being the expert, the connoisseur. He'd sneered about fellow collectors who bought unwisely; he'd told stories of mocking them to their faces.

Hanks slipped his small notebook into a coat pocket. "Here's the matter in a nutshell. Like I told you before, it don't appear that a footpad killed Henry Wylde in the course of a robbery, accidental, I mean. But, say, someway, that is what happened." His pale eyes narrowed. "I'd be able to get word of it, see? I got ways of finding out. People don't want to be on my bad side." He rocked on his heels and gazed out the window. "Murder for hire's somethin' else, o' course. Deeper waters. Still, criminals ain't smart, mostly. I shoulda been able to hear somethin'. But I squeezed and squeezed and come up dry."

"And what is that supposed to tell us?" demanded Sir Alexander.

"That it weren't a criminal which done it. Like I said, a killin' like this looks personal."

Charlotte felt cold.

"You tell me Mr. Wylde didn't have no friends, and he didn't visit with his family…"

"My cousin Edward saw him at his club," Sir Alexander interrupted.

Hanks looked aggrieved. "You never told me that."

"Of course I did."

"Beggin' your pardon, sir, but you did not."

"Well, I am telling you now," replied Sir Alexander stiffly. Anger showed in the lines of his face.

Hanks's notebook came out again. "That toffee-nosed feller at the club didn't care to speak to me. Mebbe you could tell him that he should…?"

"This is ridiculous!" exclaimed Charlotte. "Edward did not kill Henry."

Finally, Hanks looked at her. His expression made it obvious that he thought he was gazing at the person who had somehow accomplished the deed. And that he was determined to prove his suspicions correct.

She'd forgotten this, Charlotte thought, when she was summing up her reputation in society. Not only widowed and penniless, but a suspected murderess. Indeed, she had no reputation to lose.

Seventeen

ALEC SAT AT HIS DESK WITHOUT REALLY SEEING THE piles of papers there. It was late, and the house was quiet, and he was thinking about Charlotte. He thought of little else these days, despite the many calls on his time and attention. He neglected his work; he lost the thread of conversations in memories of the enticing scent of her, the feel of her soft curves against him, her lips demanding and yielding. He wanted her more than he'd ever wanted any woman. And if that had been all… ah, if only that had been all. He could have dealt with desire. One way or another. He didn't think she would be averse; she'd given him reason enough to think quite the opposite. The image of Charlotte naked in his bed quickened his pulse.

But desire wasn't all. Charlotte—the idea of her, the reality of her presence—attracted every nuance of feeling, as the Earth's gravity drew each object down. Whatever he did or thought, she was somehow woven in. He was pulled and pulled with an inevitability he resented and mistrusted. He was *not* "falling in love." He *would* not. Alec stood and began to pace his study.

He despised the phrase and everything people seemed to mean by it. "Falling in love" brought idiotic decisions and a lifetime of regret. It seemed to make people stupid, laughably credulous. His case was quite different. He was moved by desire and… compassion perhaps, respect, warm regard. What paltry words. Damn it all to hell!

Edward, he'd meant to think about Edward. Alec returned to his desk, sat down again. He needed to talk to his cousin, and he didn't want to. He didn't like him. Had he ever liked him? Whether he had or not, when he saw him drape his arm along the back of Charlotte's chair…

Edward. As young children they'd been closer, while Alec and his family were fixed at their grandparents' home. Edward had lived nearby and often visited. Later, they'd encountered each other once a year at the Christmas holidays, after Alec's parents moved to an estate inherited by his mother down toward Leicester. They could have visited more often, but the tensions of the senior Wylde household were intolerable. And his father wasn't a man for visiting. He hadn't cared for people much, Alec thought, beyond his wife and children. It occurred to him there was some similarity to Uncle Henry in that—far less extreme, of course—really quite different. The idea was ridiculous. His father had cared about his tenants, who were nothing at all like a collection.

After their grandfather died, when Alec was nine and Edward twelve, they'd seen each other even less. On the face of it, they should have had much in common. Older parents—Alec's father had been thirty-seven when he'd set out to find a suitable bride. He'd done it for the sake of an heir to the baronetcy, but in the end, Alec thought, his parents had been contented. Or perhaps he'd just been told that his mother didn't miss London seasons, was happy with her gardens and her four children. He couldn't actually know; she'd died of complications of childbirth when he was eleven years old. Had that marriage simply been too short for unhappiness? The thought chilled him.

He did remember his mother as a warm presence, games on the lawn, reading at bedtime. But mostly, he remembered Frances, who'd come to stay right before his mother died. Frances had certainly seemed happy; that he could recall. She'd been more than kind to all of them, serene and competent until—well, until his father died. Since then, she'd gone moody and unpredictable. Had she been in love with his father, Alec wondered suddenly? He'd never imagined such a thing, not even once. As he thought of it now, he felt dizzy with memories realigning, assumptions turning on their heads. What people called love so often seemed something else entirely; yet here was a nameless, unacknowledged thing that might well have been love. What else had he failed to notice? Why was he noticing now?

He shook his head. He was thinking about Edward. Edward had also lost a parent young. His father died when he was ten, right before he went off to Harrow. Why had Aunt Bella sent him there? The Wyldes went to Eton. They would have become better acquainted at school. He shrugged. They hadn't. Then, Edward hadn't bothered with university. He'd come to London and established himself in society with the careless grace that Alec sometimes envied and sometimes despised. By the time Alec arrived, his cousin was a fixture, and only too ready to laugh at a young man's awkwardness among the *ton*.

Alec knew he was never at his best around Edward. His cousin brought out every vestige of self-doubt that was in him. He remembered a Christmas twenty years ago, when Edward had lured him into singing a song before the family. It was to have been the two of them; Alec, reluctant, definitely in the secondary role. But Edward had led him to the center of the room and then vanished. Standing in that circle of expectant adults, at a loss, had been excruciating; it still made him flush to think of his grandmother's open mockery, his father's embarrassment.

"Don't be an idiot," Alec said aloud. How had he gotten bogged down in the past? He reached for a pen and the inkwell and dashed off a note to his cousin. The visit was not a choice but a necessity. Edward would most likely refuse to see Hanks. And Charlotte's position was insupportable. He sanded the wet ink, folded the page, and addressed it. Leaving the note on the hall table for delivery in the morning, he went upstairs to bed.

⌘

Edward Danforth's rooms in Duke Street were precisely what a young man on the town would desire, Alec thought at eleven the next day. The large sitting room combined comfortable furniture and relaxed untidiness—a toasting fork on the hearth, a litter of invitations on the table, an assortment of bottles ready for a convivial evening. An open door revealed a spacious bedchamber with a dressing room beyond. There was no dust, just bachelor clutter—no females to watch over, nothing to consider but his own wishes and pleasures.

Edward lounged in a broad chair, one leg draped over the arm. "To what do I owe the honor of a visit, cuz?" It was his usual tone, implying that Alec was too serious, a touch tedious, and of course, amusing.

Alec gritted his teeth. "I came to talk to you about Uncle Henry."

"That old bore?" Edward picked up a snuffbox and turned it over in his fingers.

"He was killed," Alec pointed out.

"Well, I do know that."

"We need to discover who did it."

"We?" His cousin raised an elegant brow. "I mean, of course it's outrageous. Footpads running rampant in the streets, and so on. But it isn't really our business to deal with them."

"I disagree. I have hired a Bow Street Runner…"

"There you are then."

"He is having difficulties getting information." Alec didn't want to tell him about the accusation against Charlotte; he didn't trust his cousin not to repeat it. "That is why I wanted to ask you about Uncle Henry. You saw him often at his club?"

Edward sighed and put the snuffbox down. "We're both members. If I happened to run into him, I'd say a few words. Mama was always after me to do it. She thought he'd leave me his money. Favorite nephew and all. You know how she is about inheritances." He gave Alec an arch look, which he ignored. "It made sense, so I went along."

"So you had expectations?"

Edward shrugged. "I thought there was a chance. I was the oldest of his nephews, if not a precious Wylde, and I listened to him drone on about his blasted antiquities every now and then. Lord, how he could talk."

Somehow, Edward's manner always annoyed him. Alec was certain he knew that and did it on purpose. "Perhaps you thought it was a long wait for the legacy?"

His cousin laughed in his face. "Are you asking if I sneaked out after Uncle Henry and attacked him in the street? On the off chance he meant to leave me something? Really, Alec! I'd no idea you had such an active imagination."

Alec, watching him, could see only amusement in his face. Everything was amusing to Edward. He didn't seem to care a great deal about anything.

"It would have been a fine joke on me if I had, eh?" He shook his head. "A museum! Only Uncle Henry could imagine that anyone would want to come and see his musty old bits."

"Which turned out to be fakes, practically worthless." Alec tried to peer beneath his cousin's smooth surface, without success.

"Really? So if he had left them to me, I'd have been disappointed. Particularly if I'd killed him for them. Fortunate thing I didn't."

"Indeed."

Edward laughed again. "A fine joke on him, though. He spoke about that rubbish as if it were a king's ransom. The old fellow must be writhing in his grave." His cousin leaned back, crossed his leg over a knee. "The thing I can't believe is that he got Charlotte to marry him. Where did he find her?"

Like his mother, though not as actively, Edward gathered bits of gossip. Alec didn't want to answer, but he had no real excuse to refuse. "He corresponded with her father. They met at Bath, where her father often went for his health."

"Bath? What was Uncle Henry doing at Bath? Ah, he went there to snag Charlotte, I suppose. Can't blame him. Taking little thing. And well endowed."

Alec couldn't help stiffening. He saw Edward notice it with a sly smile.

"Dowried, I mean. She says he spent a tidy sum that was hers."

"Indeed," was all Alec could find to reply. Again.

"Pretty now that she's better dressed," Edward insinuated. "A lovely package altogether. Did you find her so when she was staying at your house?"

He used that tone to goad him. Alec knew it, and still his muscles tightened further. "Did Uncle Henry ever say anything to you that would help solve his murder?"

Edward looked at him with half-lidded eyes, like a cat who was considering whether to continue tormenting an unresponsive mouse. Finally, he shrugged. "Good God, I never listened to him, Alec. Couldn't bear it. All that tedium, and he let me charge the wine he drank to my tab. Aren't uncles supposed to treat you?"

Why had he expected anything from Edward, Alec wondered? His cousin thought only of himself.

"Although... he did say something rather odd a few months ago."

"What?"

"He offered me some advice." Edward raised his eyebrows at the absurdity of the notion. "Told me never to rely on people, no matter how long I'd known them or what the relationship might be. No one could be trusted."

"That's all?"

Edward nodded.

"Had he been talking about antiquities dealers? Perhaps he'd discovered some deception?"

Edward frowned, then shrugged again. "No idea. I told you, I couldn't listen to him for more than a minute. Had to think of something else or go mad."

Alec tried other questions, but Edward remembered nothing useful. When he began to twit Alec about turning up at parties when Charlotte was in attendance, Alec took his leave.

He returned to a house that felt rather empty. Anne was out at a dancing class, Lizzy on a visit arranged by Aunt Earnton, Frances somewhere, elsewhere. For him, there were the piles of paper on his desk and the frustration of a wasted morning.

❧

Lady Isabella had invited Charlotte to accompany her on a round of morning calls, to "extend her education" in the ways of society. Charlotte had accepted out of politeness and gratitude, and curiosity. Lady Isabella's kindness to her had been such that she would do whatever she asked. And she was interested in seeing the *haut ton* in all its aspects. However, as the morning wore away, it seemed that the visits were chiefly designed to gather and distribute bits of gossip. Stories heard at one house were retold at the next, in exchange for other tales that could be carried on to a further drawing room. She soon noticed that those who had nothing new to offer a hostess were less valued callers—the poor in social currency.

The morning might have been more interesting, she admitted to herself, if she'd been acquainted with the people involved and their histories, as everyone else seemed to be. But she wasn't. She was also a novice in the language of looks and gestures that embellished these conversations, implying much more than was said for those in the know.

They ended at Mrs. Prine's house. Squeezed between two mansions, it was even smaller than Henry's, though in a far more fashionable neighborhood. The inside was like a jewel box, each element lovely and obviously chosen with care. Charlotte complimented their hostess as they were ushered into a parlor hung with gold brocade, and Mrs. Prine looked pleased.

The two older women began to pool the gleanings of their mornings, not only exchanging tales but also dissecting them in an almost professional way. As they decided between themselves which calls they would make on the morrow, Charlotte was reminded of two generals planning a campaign. She had no doubt they would find out whatever they wanted to know.

Tea arrived, and the two turned their attention to Charlotte. "You know, my dear, you really must order a few more gowns," said Lady Isabella. "You can't be seen in the same ensemble too many times." Mrs. Prine nodded her agreement.

"I can't afford any more," Charlotte admitted, clearly shocking Mrs. Prine—whether because of her poverty or her willingness to speak of it she didn't know.

Lady Isabella waved this away like an unpleasant smell. "As to that, one must… allocate. Some small economies at home—invisible—can help you support a creditable appearance."

Mrs. Prine nodded again, and Charlotte wondered what she knew about it. Everything in her house was obviously costly. Neither of these women could have any idea of what it was like to watch every penny.

"I'm sure my modiste would be quite accommodating in extending credit," Lady Isabella added. "I can speak to her…"

"No. I will have to make do with what I have. Mrs. Trask… that is, I know a good seamstress, and we are going to see if we can alter some of my old dresses to make them more modish." This idea had emerged when she found Mrs. Trask at her fancy work, completing a dress for one of her granddaughters that might have come from the finest shop on Bond Street.

Mrs. Prine looked scandalized, far more shocked than she'd been by any gossip they shared. Briefly, Charlotte considered telling her that the seamstress was her cook, but Lady Isabella seemed annoyed, so she kept this to herself.

They left soon after, embarking on the long drive to Charlotte's neighborhood. "I was wondering about Henry," she ventured. She'd been considering this topic all morning, and now she had the opportunity.

Lady Isabella turned to her with raised brows. "Henry?"

Sir Alexander had advised her not to talk about what they'd found in Henry's rooms, but surely Henry's sister must know things about him. They'd spent the first ten years of Henry's life in the same house, and school holidays for years after that. "He wasn't very... communicative, you know. And since he died, I've been wondering... oh, why he never married before he met me." The earrings in his hidden cupboard showed that other women had figured in his life. "Was he never attached or engaged when he was young?"

"Henry?" Lady Isabella repeated.

"Young men are... susceptible. Surely when he was first presented to society, he..."

"Henry never attended a *ton* party in his life," Lady Isabella interrupted. She said it as if the idea was ludicrous. "Or any other sorts. He was such a... morose person."

"Even when he was young?"

"He wasn't."

"Wasn't...?"

"Young. He seemed fussy and old even when he was a child. At university, they say he spent all his time buried in the library. Everyone knows that young men get up to all kinds of mischief at college, but not Henry."

"And then he came down to London," Charlotte said.

"He leased that house—close to the British Museum, can you imagine?—and then bought it with his inheritance after Father died, I suppose."

"So he never mentioned anyone..."

"My dear, he didn't even tell us when he married you!" Lady Isabella looked as if her nose for gossip had been roused. "Why do you ask?"

Charlotte thought of telling her about the earrings, but Sir Alexander had been so adamant. "It's just strange, knowing so little about a man one was married to."

"Husbands are always a mystery, my dear," was the airy reply. "Now, in the much more important matter of your wardrobe…"

"I really cannot spend any more, Lady Isabella. I'm sorry. If you feel my… appearance reflects poorly on you, I would not blame you…"

She waved this aside. "If you were to sell some small things from…"

"I can't…"

"Because of Henry's *ridiculous* will, I know. But you might easily find a way around that. You must know that people from the very highest rungs of society occasionally need to… exchange items they have inherited for… cash. Which they do not want known, of course. So embarrassing. There are people who manage such transactions and would never breathe a word of the sale…"

"It isn't that. Well, it is. But I don't think such people would be interested, you see. Henry's collection is practically worthless."

"What?"

"We had a man in from the museum to evaluate it, and he said one or two pieces are authentic and worth something, but the rest is just… well, more or less clutter."

Lady Isabella seemed stunned. "But... nothing?"

"Henry spent thousands of pounds on objects that are good for nothing but paperweights." Charlotte couldn't keep the bitterness from her voice.

"Thousands of..." Lady Isabella looked devastated.

Charlotte was touched by her concern. She hadn't realized that Lady Isabella had taken her situation so to heart. She tried to lighten the mood. "The burglar would have been quite disappointed if he'd managed to steal anything."

"The... yes. Quite a joke on him." Lady Isabella recovered herself. She gave a trilling laugh. "Well, I am very sorry, my dear. I had hoped to be of some help."

"And I appreciate your kindness." The carriage pulled up, and she prepared to get down. "Thank you for a... lovely morning."

"Of course."

Charlotte used her key to enter as the carriage moved off and was startled to find Callie sitting in the front hall, tail curled around her front paws, as if waiting for her. "Hello, Callie." Two heads popped over the banister above her, and Lucy and Tess came hurrying down. "Is something wrong?"

"Well, Miss Charlotte, the cat had a... a relapse, like," replied Lucy.

"She tore a fine linen dishtowel to shreds," added Tess. "Mrs. Trask said it ain... isn't even good for rags."

They both stared accusingly at Callie, who ignored them. She was gazing so steadily at a bit of wall behind Charlotte that she had to turn and look. There was nothing visible but paneling. "That is very disappointing to hear," she told the cat. "I thought you were a… a reformed animal." She was trying not to laugh, and Lucy saw it.

"It was one of the *new* dishtowels, Miss Charlotte."

It was true that they couldn't afford to replace many household items. "Very bad. You are a bad cat."

Callie remained oblivious. Lucy sniffed.

"Mrs. Trask must have scolded her at the time," Charlotte said.

"She did, miss, but…"

"Well, we shall hope it doesn't happen again." What else did they think she could do? Charlotte was just deeply grateful that Callie had not turned her destructive attention to the "exhibits" on this floor. She started up the stairs. The two maids headed for the kitchen. The cat slipped past her and when she reached her bedchamber, Charlotte found Callie already there. "You miss Anne and Lizzy, don't you?" she said as she took off her hat. "I do, too."

❧

Lucy yawned and folded up her mending. "I'm off to bed," she said to the rest of the staff. She kept her voice casual, but Mrs. Trask gave her a glance that made Lucy nervous. No one was better than Mrs. Trask at putting two and two together. Still, Ethan had said his good-byes a good quarter hour ago.

She paused a moment outside the room, but nothing was said about her departure, so she hurried up the stairs and slipped out the back door. Ethan was waiting at what she now thought of as "their" bench. He rose as soon as she appeared, a large dark shape with open arms. Lucy could do nothing but walk into them.

Enfolded, held against him like a treasure, she couldn't keep hold of her doubts and worries. The feel of his coat against her cheek, the heady smell of him, drowned out everything else. She rested there for a needful bit of time, then raised her head and laced her arms around his neck.

The kiss enflamed every inch of her. Heat blossomed from deep in her belly and ran out to her finger ends, and then farther still, as if her soul touched his where their lips met. This couldn't be wrong. It was meant to be. Ethan's big hands slid up her sides. His thumbs grazed her breasts under the stuff gown, and Lucy heard herself groan softly. She pressed closer. One of Ethan's hands dropped to cup her body and pull her closer still. The other continued its circling, circling, until she thought he'd drive her mad with wanting him.

Abruptly, he pulled away. A wordless sound of protest escaped her.

"Ah, Lucy." He was breathing hard. So was she, Lucy noticed, and her knees seemed about to buckle under her. "We'd best stop before I do something I oughtn't." He pulled her down onto the bench, keeping hold of her hand. "Ah, Lucy," he said again.

For a brief while they simply sat there, breathing.

"I asked about the job," Ethan said finally. "It'll be all right, seemingly. The cottage and all, for us to live in."

Lucy's mood soared and then came crashing down, weighted by all the worries his touch had erased. "That's fine then… for you. Just what you wanted." He'd leave London at the end of the season, and he'd never come back.

"For us."

Tears clogged her throat. "I want to go; most all of me wants to go. Maybe I should be able to just take off... But I can't. It's stupid!"

"No, it isn't. It's the way you are." He squeezed her hand. "Look, we all know there's lots of servants who're nothing but that. They come and go, and nobody cares much except those as have to find replacements. Then there's some who're more like family. It can't be just them that thinks so, of course. That'll get you into trouble, and no mistake. But your Miss Charlotte feels the same. Anyone can tell that."

Lucy took a shaky breath. "You say that even though you want me to give notice?"

"I want you to come away and marry me and be with me all my life long. But I want you to do it freely and gladly. I want you to be happy and not regret one thing."

Lucy's tears escaped. He was just the man for her. Couldn't she marry him and never look back? Shouldn't she—and he—be happy? If she spoke to Miss Charlotte... Miss Charlotte would tell her to go and not look back. Then the Trasks would leave, and there'd be just young Tess and whatever town-bred strangers she found to take the other positions. Miss Charlotte would be unhappy—not as unhappy as she'd been this last year, maybe, but sad and alone. And she wouldn't begrudge a bit of it.

Lucy thought of herself married to Ethan, snug in her neat country cottage. She longed for it with her whole being. But to sit at the hearth knowing Miss Charlotte was here without any tie to her old happier life in Hampshire...

She'd do it, Lucy realized. She'd go. She couldn't give him up. But her heart would be sore at the way of it.

Ethan's arm had gone round her shoulders. "Don't cry, Lucy. I can't stand it. Look… I have an idea how things might all come out right."

She sniffed, looking up at him. "What do you mean?"

"I'm thinking… that is, I have a notion that Sir Alexander is… fond of Miss Charlotte. Interested in her, like."

Lucy frowned, trying to take this in.

"And maybe she likes him as well. If they was to get together…"

"Marry, you mean? Miss Charlotte's just got out of a horrible marriage. She won't be wanting another one."

"Now, who's to say that? Sir Alexander is nothing like this Henry Wylde seems to have been."

"No…"

"He's well-liked in the servants' hall and at home among the tenants. He's right good to his sisters. According to Jennings, he's a prime match as well."

"Are you selling him to me then?" asked Lucy, a thread of amusement running through her.

"Just saying he's a different kettle of fish entirely from his uncle."

"Maybe so." Lucy thoughts ran back over the last few weeks. Was Miss Charlotte sweet on Ethan's master? It might explain some oddities she'd noticed. It was possible. Then again… was she just being swayed by selfish hopes? "Even if there is some… something between them, what's it to do with us?"

"Well, we could… encourage it, like."

"How?" Before he could answer, she added, "Anyway, we've got no right to interfere."

"We wouldn't be interfering. Just helping things along."

"I don't know." As Lucy tried to state her doubts, the lamplight went off in a basement window.

"It's late," Ethan said. "They're locking up. You've got to go. You're coming with the others to my aunt's house tomorrow evening?"

Lucy had been invited to a celebration for Ethan's cousin, home on leave from the navy. The Trasks were going, of course, and she and Tess had been invited as well. "Miss Charlotte said I should, but it'll leave her all alone here."

"Just for a few hours. She could go visit Miss Anne and Miss Lizzy."

"That's a good thought. I'll tell her." Ethan stood. "I worry about you walking in the streets at this time of night."

"I know how to go, and I've got a stick," he assured her, hefting a large cudgel he'd leaned against the garden wall. He swept her up for a last kiss, and Lucy forgot everything else in the dazzle of it. Then he was gone, and Lucy was slipping through the back door just ahead of Mr. Trask locking up. At the foot of the stairs to the upper floors, she found Callie sitting like a guard dog. She edged past her, followed by the stare of two yellow eyes, thanking her lucky stars that cats couldn't talk.

Eighteen

SINCE CHARLOTTE HAD BEEN WATCHING FOR MARGARET Billings' arrival, she was able to admire the way her new acquaintance pulled up in front of the house—as if she'd handled horses all her life. She had her own lady's phaeton, and she held the reins of a beautiful chestnut pair. "You really do live quite out of the way, don't you?" she said when Charlotte emerged.

So here was another fashionable person who saw any venture outside a certain area of London as a wilderness trek. "I would have been happy to take a cab to meet…"

"Nonsense. Hop in."

Margaret's groom offered a hand up, and Charlotte climbed into the seat beside her. He swung onto the perch at the back as Margaret eased the reins, and they clattered off. Margaret looked very dashing in a long-sleeved blue gown with military frogging and a hat with a feather tilted over one eye. Charlotte was grateful for the warmth of the June morning, so that she didn't even need a shawl. To sit in this modish equipage wearing her fusty old cloak was unthinkable.

She liked this wiry, dark-haired woman and was glad to have a chance to talk to her alone. Margaret's eyes often danced with laughter, and her wit was a byword among Edward's group of friends. Now, there was this new skill. She turned and guided her horses as well as any man Charlotte had ridden with—not that there were many of those. When she said so, Margaret gave her a broad smile. "I watched my father teach my brothers and begged and begged for lessons until I wore him down." She glanced at Charlotte, eyes sparkling. "He finally admitted, just last year, that I had more natural talent than either of the boys. Not that he would ever tell *them* that."

Charlotte laughed.

"I knew William was the one for me when he promised me my own phaeton," she added of her husband, laughing too.

"How did you meet?"

"Celia and I were schoolmates. She is Richard's sister, you know. He and William and the others were all at Harrow together, and they came up to town about the same time. I tease William sometimes that I might have chosen Tony instead of him. It's not true, of course, though he offered for me."

"Doesn't that make things awkward between you?" wondered Charlotte.

"Oh no. He didn't really mean it. And I'm very glad it wasn't serious, because he drinks far too much."

Her candid ease, as well as her obvious enjoyment of life, was enviable. Charlotte risked a touchy question. "It seems girls are often... ah... removed from the group at evening parties."

Margaret didn't seem surprised or the least embarrassed. "Well, we aren't a circle for fresh-hatched debs. What's the fun of being married if you have to keep behaving like a chit just out of the schoolroom?" She turned the horses into Hyde Park. With the season in full swing, it was full of carriages, showy mounts, and beautifully dressed members of the *ton* walking the flower-bordered paths. Everybody was looking at everybody else, bowing and stopping to chat, flirting and gossiping; the grassy expanse was like a giant drawing room. She was part of a London Season, Charlotte thought. Not a central part, not a giddy, head-turning Season, but far more than she'd dreamed of just a few months ago. It seemed too good to be true.

They drove slowly along a graveled lane, stopping often as those ahead paused to converse. Margaret nodded now and then and greeted some people, but there was no opportunity to introduce Charlotte. Not that she cared; she was fascinated by the social interplay going on all around them. It was like watching a play.

They were nearly to the other side of the park when she finally recognized a face. Edward Danforth rode toward them on a spirited black horse that seemed to object to the presence of other riders. He brought his mount up beside them and tipped his hat. "Well met, fair damsels."

"Poseur," replied Margaret. "I can't believe you've brought Dancer into this melee."

"It's good training for him."

"Nonsense. It's a chance to show off your riding skills."

Edward gave them one of his dazzling smiles. "May as well let the young sprigs see how it's done."

"You'll look all nohow if he bolts and throws you."

"He has better manners than *that*." The barouche in front of them stopped suddenly and then backed a little. Margaret reacted immediately, narrowly avoiding a collision. "Bravo, Margaret," said Edward. "I believe you've come to equal my mother at the ribbons."

"Lady Isabella drives?" said Charlotte, surprised.

"Oh yes, she's a notable whip. She's even handled a team, in the country. Though she's gone off it in the last few years." The line of carriages moved forward again, and Edward stayed beside them. "You said the other night that you've never been to the opera," he said to Charlotte. "Would you care to go on Friday? With my mother and me?"

"Oh. That would be pleasant." It was a little odd that he was inviting her for Lady Isabella, but they were well acquainted by this time, after all.

"I'm sitting right here and yet not invited," commented Margaret.

"Because I am well aware that you hate the opera."

She grinned. "True. William's mother despairs that I have no ear. It all sounds like stray cats bawling in an alley to me."

"Do not be influenced by this philistine," Edward told Charlotte. "She cares more for horses than art."

"So I do," said Margaret cheerfully. "And now I am ready to turn my horses, Edward, so please get out of my way."

He bowed from the saddle and moved off. Charlotte admired the neat way Margaret maneuvered the pair around a tight corner and set them crossing the park in the opposite direction. "Quite a charmer, our Edward," Margaret commented then.

"He's very good company."

"Famous for it."

Charlotte wondered yet again why she did not find Edward more exciting. He was strikingly handsome, amusing, attentive. And yet she merely liked him—no more than that. Why should one man—with less extraordinary looks and manners—be riveting and Edward only pleasant? There was no explaining it.

Margaret shot her a sidelong glance. "Not a marrying man, of course. At least not yet."

For a moment, Charlotte was confused. "Oh, Edward? No, I shouldn't think so."

"So if anyone was hoping for an offer from that direction…?"

"Me, you mean? Of course not." She was suddenly certain, even though she had never considered the matter before, that Edward would only marry for a fortune. One larger than she had ever possessed.

"He's not nearly as great a catch as his cousin," Margaret added.

"His…?"

"Oh, come, don't be missish. Sir Alexander Wylde has been rather attentive."

"He's been kind enough to…"

"My dear, he shows up wherever you are, hovers and glowers in the best style!"

"Glowers?"

"You must have noticed the way he scowls at Edward whenever he is near you."

"I haven't… does he?" The idea sent a thrill through Charlotte.

"He certainly does." Margaret laughed. "I would say if you play your hand with any skill at all, *he* might make an offer."

Charlotte sat very still. She'd enjoyed observing the lively social scene. She'd seen how everyone gossiped. But she hadn't imagined that the obsession with others' doings would be turned on her. She'd thought of herself as invisible, a nobody. The idea of being under such scrutiny made her squirm. And yet she longed to hear more about Sir Alexander's interest in her. "It could be just politeness."

"This is my fifth London Season, my dear. I can tell the difference. Why do you think Edward is paying such…" She pressed her lips together, looking chagrined.

"What?" When Margaret just shook her head, Charlotte put the pieces together. "Edward is singling me out to annoy Sir Alexander?"

"I beg your pardon, Charlotte. I did not mean…"

"It doesn't matter." And it didn't—much. A little sting, perhaps. She hadn't imagined that Edward felt any real regard for her.

"Ah… well, as a friend, I advise you to grasp the opportunity. You don't dislike Sir Alexander?"

"No!" The fierce denial escaped her lips before she could clamp them shut. Charlotte closed her fists in her lap and looked away. She was so far from disliking him… She thought of him constantly; memories of his hands on her set her aflame. "But there is no chance of… what you mean."

"Whyever not?"

Because she was penniless, had been married to his wretched uncle, and was suspected of murdering her own husband. Because Sir Alexander meant to contract a brilliant, "suitable" marriage with no complications of love. He would never offer for her. He only held her in a way that melted her bones.

She would have given anything he asked, Charlotte acknowledged. She would have tossed propriety to the four winds. But he hadn't asked. She'd thought he hadn't been interested enough to ask, but what if she was wrong? Margaret said she was. If he cared for her as she did for him...?

"If you need someone to give him a hint," Margaret suggested. "I could play the matchmaking 'mama.'"

"No!" Margaret knew nothing of his family history, of his determination not to make a love match. Sir Alexander Wylde's wife would be suitable in all the ways Charlotte was not—prominent family, heaps of money, serene and expert in the ways of society. She could almost picture her, in all her polished, hateful glory. Most of all, she would be a woman who did not love him. That was what he intended. He had made it clear. She fell short on all counts, because... Charlotte had to swallow a rush of emotion. If she was honest with herself, she had to acknowledge that she had fallen in love with him over these weeks. Perhaps she could have gone on denying her feelings without Margaret's prodding. Now, they crashed over her like a summer squall. He was everything she wanted.

"You needn't feel shy," Margaret added. "It's done all the time. Just a little push, nothing..."

"Can we talk of something else?"

Her tone drew a frown. "Very well." Margaret's voice had gone cool. She'd offended her, Charlotte thought—this woman she'd hoped to make a friend. But that regret was overwhelmed by the turmoil in her mind. The conventional sequence of events that Margaret proposed was impossible. Yet the older woman, far more versed in the subtle signals of society, was convinced that Sir Alexander had shown a clear attraction to her. So perhaps he had been driven to those kisses they shared as strongly as she. He hadn't spoken of it directly. He was too much a gentleman. What if… what if she did?

The remainder of the drive was nearly silent. Charlotte tried to make conversation, to mend her fences with Margaret, and she made some progress. But the rhythm of easy comradeship they'd begun to develop did not resume. There was no mention of another outing when she climbed down from the phaeton and bade her good-bye.

Inside, Charlotte found Lizzy, Anne, and Frances all awaiting her in the drawing room, cozy around a tray of tea and Mrs. Trask's mouthwatering scones. Callie's variegated fur overflowed Lizzy's lap. "Lucy said you'd be back soon, so we waited," the youngest Wylde told her.

"Insisted on waiting," said Frances, with an ironic look at her youngest charge. Lizzy wrinkled her nose and concentrated on the cat.

"I'm so glad you did. Just let me take off my hat. I'll be right back." It soothed Charlotte's spirit, five minutes later, to return to them, at ease in her home as if they were family. "Georgiana says that no one goes to Ranelagh any more," Lizzy was declaring when Charlotte re-entered the drawing room. "It is utterly passé." Frances and Anne exchanged an amused glance. Charlotte already knew that "Georgiana says" had become a refrain in Lizzy's conversation since she'd begun the visits organized by her Aunt Earnton. She learned herself, during Lizzy's increasingly rare calls, not to dispute any maxim of the omniscient Georgiana, at the risk of scorn heaped upon her head by her faithful acolyte. Charlotte imagined Georgiana Harrington as one of those sturdy, horse-mad girls, with pale hair, slightly bulging blue eyes, and a nerve-scraping laugh. She had no idea if this vision was correct and no desire to find out. She'd gently discouraged all Lizzy's offers to bring her for a visit.

At last, Georgiana's latest maxims were exhausted. "Oh!" continued Lizzy, sitting up straighter and eliciting a protest from the cat. "Anne's beau has jilted her!"

"He was not my…" Anne began.

"He turned out to be nothing but a heartless flirt. He has begun standing up three times or more with a horrid freckled redhead at every dancing class."

"Lizzy!" admonished Frances.

"You should take up novel writing, because nearly every word you just spoke is pure fabrication." Her sister's tone was uncharacteristically sharp.

Lizzy showed her unrepentant dimples. "But it doesn't matter a whit, because Anne is always besieged with partners, and he is just an idiot!"

Her older sister sighed. "Promise me *again* that you do not say such things to Georgiana and the other girls. It would be disastrous to have your outrageous flights of fancy circulating in society. As if they came from me!"

"I wouldn't," Lizzy protested. But she looked away, meeting no one's eyes.

"If you have," Frances chimed in sternly, "then you must stop. Such stories really could make it much more difficult for Anne when she comes out."

Her dark blue eyes large and serious at last, Lizzy nodded.

Anne turned to Charlotte. "How are you? You have made this room look quite lovely."

She accepted the compliment with a smile, and they talked for a while of inconsequential things. Then, Anne and Lizzy went down to visit the Trasks, whom they knew well from Derbyshire, and Callie followed them. "I am glad to have a moment alone," Frances said then. "I wanted to thank you."

"Me? For what?"

"Do you remember, soon after we met, you asked me what it was that *I* wanted out of life? I must tell you, that question has been an immense help to me." She smiled at Charlotte's look of surprise. "Perhaps it sounds simple and obvious to you. But if one has never looked at things from that perspective, it can make a great difference. I have been acting on it."

Charlotte was pleased and fascinated. "How?"

Frances's smile broadened until it bore a remarkable resemblance to one of Lizzy's mischievous grins. "Don't expect heroics. But, for one thing, I have been corresponding with old friends, renewing contacts. I never fell completely out of touch with them, but I didn't write as often as I might have during these busy years. The response has been gratifying." She gave Charlotte a look from under dark lashes. "I have an invitation to spend part of the winter in Greece."

"In… that sounds… interesting."

Frances nodded. "My best friend from school is living there. Her husband is involved in some sort of diplomatic mission that is likely to take more than a year, she says. She is urging me to come."

Charlotte knew little of Greece beyond the ancients. "The country is ruled by the Turks?" she managed.

"And perfectly safe, Diana assures me. Of course I cannot go *this* winter." Frances looked at Charlotte with what seemed like speculation or assessment. Charlotte couldn't imagine what she meant by it. Frances started to speak, hesitated, then added, "But once Lizzy is older, I am determined I *shall* have an adventure of some kind, thanks to you."

The energy and determination in her voice were inspiring. Charlotte started to deny any responsibility for this change, but she *had* been thinking that one must grasp the possibilities that presented themselves in life. Frances was right. You had to dare. She turned to agree with her, and Callie streaked into the drawing room trailing a tatter of pink ribbon. Lizzy was right on her heels. "I thought it would look pretty around her neck," she explained, breathing hard. "But she doesn't seem to like it."

Since the cat was manically shredding the bit of silk in the far corner of the room, Charlotte could only concur.

❧

The piles of papers on his desk had totally lost their hold on Alec. The mood of the countryside was dire, he told himself. Events were nearing a flash point, and no one seemed able to halt the slide. But his mind continually veered back to gold-coppery hair and eyes, to a smile that made his heart turn over. He would see her this afternoon. Not so very long, though the minutes dragged like hours.

A knock on the door heralded Ethan. "A letter come by courier, sir." He handed over a thick packet. "He rode hard."

Alec slit the envelope and began to read, his mood quickly going grim. This was it, then. Time was up. Personal considerations would have to be set aside. He summoned Ethan back and rapped out a string of instructions.

Alec's mind remained burdened later that day, as he took Charlotte to call on an antiquities dealer who had refused to speak to Jem Hanks. His premises were near the shopping mecca of Bond Street, but not on it, in an area prospective sellers could visit without embarrassing encounters with friends. The address was announced by a brass plate so discreet you might take the place for a private house, or miss it altogether if you didn't know where you were going.

The man himself was slender and cool, with pale blond hair and a supercilious air. His dark coat obviously came from Weston, and his linen was impeccable. Next to Alec he looked small, almost sylphlike. "We came to talk to you about your dealing with my uncle Henry Wylde," Alec told him.

"I do not speak about my clients," was the smug reply.

His manner made Alec want to shake him. Even the man's name was pretentious—Carleton St. Cyr. "Not acceptable."

"You must understand that those who come to me depend on my discretion. If I were to speak about my business, it could cause embarrassment in many noble families. Up to the most august levels." He obviously reveled in the connection.

"But my husband did not sell to you," Charlotte said. "He bought, and we are quite aware of it."

Alec nodded; a good point. "And what he bought was not what you claimed. The items were, in fact, nearly valueless."

"I beg your…"

"How would your 'clients' feel if they heard how he'd been cheated?" Charlotte said.

The man blanched. "How dare you?"

"We asked the British Museum for a valuation of my uncle's collection, including objects you sold him." Alec showed the man receipts found in the hidden room. "They are all worthless."

St. Cyr rifled through the pages. "But that… that is impossible." He seemed truly shaken. "These so-called experts can be mistaken, you know. Or deceptive. I have seen them give low valuations so that they can buy up collections on the cheap."

"There was no question of a sale here." Alec retrieved the receipts. "And it is the British Museum we are speaking of, not some petty antiquities dealer." He used the word purposefully.

"My stock comes from impeccable sources," the man said.

"Do you actually know how to tell if items are authentic?" Charlotte wondered.

From the way his eyes shifted, Alec saw she'd scored a hit. "My services are based on mutual trust. Everyone is aware of the… origins of what I sell. They are happy to acquire beautiful things that were once owned by prominent…"

"Things which you have accepted as whatever people say they are," added Charlotte.

He drew himself up. "I deal with honorable people. To question their word would be…"

"Wise, seemingly," Alec interrupted. "So everything you sell is fakery? Puffed up by its supposed association with some impoverished aristocrat?"

"No! That is slander, sir. If you dare repeat such lies, I will take you to…"

"Then it is a coincidence that everything my uncle bought from you was valueless?"

Conflicting emotions flitted over the small man's face. There was something important he wasn't telling them, Alec was sure. "I maintain that your 'expert' was mistaken."

And that was his final word, no matter how Alec insisted or threatened. Indeed, his threats of exposure backfired, as the dealer seemed very sure he would have support from the highest levels in a lawsuit. In the end, they were forced to go without learning anything useful. He would have to come back, Alec thought, when he could, and pressure the idiot further.

"All he cares about is hobnobbing with the nobility," Charlotte said in the carriage on the way back. "He is not a merchant, he's a… toadeater."

"Clearly." Alec felt squeezed between the need to help Charlotte all he could and the necessity of dealing with the wave of unrest now cresting near his home.

"Lady Isabella mentioned him, I think. As a dealer who was completely discreet."

When Alec turned to her, she looked as if she wished she hadn't spoken.

"It was when she thought I could sell some of Henry's things," she added hurriedly, "before she found out that I can't."

"And why would you need discretion in that case?"

"Ah… that is…"

Aunt Bella had probably suggested something less straightforward. "She may have used this fellow, I suppose. I've always wondered how Danforth's estate could provide what she appears to spend."

"She's been kind to me," was the only reply.

Exactly, Alec wanted to say, and why? But he didn't because it was insulting. They pulled up in front of her house. "I wanted to tell you…" Alec began.

"You should come in," interrupted Charlotte in an odd tone. "I need to speak to you as well."

"Is something wrong?"

"Not at all. It's only—this and that."

She smiled at him, and Alec's pulse automatically accelerated. "The horses…"

"It doesn't do to keep them standing, I know. Perhaps you could send them home and get a cab later?"

Alec knew he should refuse. It was nearly six. He had a thousand things to do, preparations to make. But the whole tide of his heart pulled against that knowledge. He handed her down from the carriage and gave

Tom the coachman the order. As his equipage pulled away, Charlotte used her key instead of ringing. He followed her into the house, his thoughts a turmoil of questions and desires that must never be spoken.

Nineteen

"THEY GOT TEMPLES WITH HEATHEN STATUES TWENTY feet high," said Ethan's cousin Jack. "All gold and glittery. Some of 'em has six arms. And every morning they washes them with milk, giving them a bath in it, like."

"Go on," replied Mrs. Trask. "That'd be a pure waste of gallons of milk."

"It's true, Gran. I seen it myself, when our ship put in at Bombay. One of the fellers took us into the city to see. Anyhow, they've got plenty of milk in India 'cause it's a crime to kill a cow there."

Ethan's aunt shook an admonitory finger at her son. "Now, Jack, you've traveled and we haven't, but that doesn't mean we'll swallow any rigmarole you care to spin."

"It's true, Ma. I swear." Jack put a hand over his heart. "The Hindoos claim that cows are holy. Got 'em wandering all over the city doing as they please. You're in big trouble if you hurt one." Though he was only twenty-six, Jack had sailed to both India and the West Indies.

Ethan watched all the adults present shake their

heads in wonderment. The children, who'd marveled over Jack's tales earlier, now played a noisy game of lottery tickets in the back parlor. There was ale and a juicy roast, and Lucy sat next to him, looking relaxed and interested, as if she'd been part of the family for years and years. It was all just as he'd imagined, and Ethan's spirit expanded with warm contentment. It was hours before they had to be back at their posts. He'd sent off his letter home and not yet had an answer, so he could bask in the belief that his future would be as pleasant as this.

He moved so that his shoulder brushed Lucy's, wishing he could put an arm around her and show their connection before everyone. When she turned her head and smiled at him, he only just stopped himself from kissing her.

"I hope Miss Charlotte is all right," Lucy said.

At that moment, Ethan didn't care a whit about Lucy's mistress. All his consciousness was occupied by visions of his own happiness. But he knew better than to say anything like that. "She said she was going to visit Miss Anne and Miss Lizzy."

"She said she *might*."

"Why wouldn't she?"

There was a flurry at the door, and Tom the coachman came in. He hadn't been sure he'd be free to come. Prodded by Lucy's elbow, Ethan got up and crossed the room to speak to him. "You got the night off, after all?"

"Aye," said Tom, taking a deep draught of ale. "Ah, that's good, that is. Left the master at Mrs. Wylde's to be getting a cab for himself later on."

Lucy wouldn't like that, Ethan thought. She'd want to go on home to make sure all was well, ending the evening, as far as he was concerned, here and now. And maybe doing even worse. Wasn't it better for them if her mistress was left alone with Sir Alexander? 'Twasn't proper; that was true. People would talk scandal if they heard of it. But how were a man and a woman ever to get together if they never had a moment alone? That was a problem he understood very well, surrounded as he was by prying eyes and disapproving elders. Here was, maybe, an opportunity to further his plans of getting Lucy up to Derbyshire.

An unfamiliar ruthlessness rose in Ethan's breast. He wished no harm to Lucy's mistress; she seemed a nice enough young lady and treated Lucy well. But his own happiness, and Lucy's, mattered more to him than anything else. If there was any chance at all… "Keep your trap shut about it," said Ethan to the coachman.

Tom goggled at him. "Eh?"

"No need to tell everybody what the gentry's up to."

The coachman frowned, shrugged, and went back to his tankard. He'd open his trap eventually, Ethan knew. Someone would ask a question, and Tom would answer without thinking, and it'd come out. What would he say to Lucy then? Ethan looked at her, across the room, pretty as a picture in her blue dress and laughing. He'd think of something. For tonight, they'd just enjoy themselves.

"All's well," he said to Lucy when he sat down beside her again. It wasn't a lie. As far as he was concerned all was very well. And maybe it was getting even better, back there at Lucy's house. A man could hope so, anyhow.

❦

Charlotte sat on the edge of the armchair cushion in her drawing room, sipping a glass of Madeira. She'd gotten the wine herself, without mentioning servants. And why would they talk of servants? There was no reason to do so. Or about the fact that she and Sir Alexander were alone in her house. He would leave immediately if he discovered that, and she did not wish him to leave. She gulped her wine, and let the warmth spread from her fluttery stomach throughout her body.

Charlotte knew that what she was thinking was mad—or it would have been, to the gently reared young lady she'd been a year ago. But she wasn't that person any longer, would never be again. The year with Henry Wylde had changed her, first to an abject creature deprived of all joy, and then to a woman determined to steer her own life. Her future would *not* be all mean economies and superficial companionship. She would *not* dwindle into genteel poverty and meager, melancholy regrets. She would take what she wanted and damn the consequences. She would!

The glass trembled in her hand, and she rose to pour another draught of liquid courage. Sir Alexander Wylde had moved her as no man had ever done. He drugged her senses and roused longings so fierce she could not resist them. Not only that, she knew she could trust him. He would never betray her secrets.

The silence had grown long. "You wanted to speak to me?" said Sir Alexander. "Is something wrong?"

Charlotte stood for a moment with her back to him, then she placed the goblet on the tray with a decisive chink and went to sit beside him on the sofa. Before she could falter, or change her mind, she slid her arms around his neck and raised her lips to his. There was an instant's thrill of doubt, a stutter of hesitation, before he gathered her into his arms. Then the kiss sent fire racing along her veins. It was the same as before; his hands and mouth enthralled her, roused every inch of her to pulsing life. Here was the vital spark that had been missing from her marriage, her whole history. This intensity was worth any price.

Sir Alexander pulled her onto his lap. She tightened her arms around his neck and gave herself up to the marvels of sensation. Thoughts fled; any vestige of resistance dissolved. Everything was body—the hard muscle of his thighs supporting her, the bastion of his arms around her, the texture of his lips drawing her on into more and more heat. Charlotte felt as if her insides had gone molten. She melted against him while holding him close with all her strength.

For Alec, the rules of a lifetime were battered back and forth by a relentless tide of desire. This wasn't right; he shouldn't do this. She was a widow; she had come to him and clearly wanted him. To give in would bring scandal on a young woman he... admired. He wanted her so desperately he couldn't bear it. His hands roamed her body, frustratingly clothed; her lips burned on his. He couldn't think; he stopped trying. He crushed her to him, then surged to his feet, cradling her, and carried her down the corridor to the bedroom.

She didn't protest. She clung to him. And when they reached the door, she turned the knob and flung it open from his arms. Alec hardly noticed kicking the panels shut behind them. All his senses were riveted by the girl he held.

They tumbled onto the bed together, pressed close now all along the length of their bodies. This kiss seared, maddened. His body cried out for the touch of flesh on flesh. He drew back and shed his coat like an outworn skin. Charlotte's fingers fumbled with the row of tiny buttons down the front of her gown, awkward with eagerness, clumsy with desire. Careless of folds and fastenings, Alec rid himself of his neck-cloth and shirt and boots, scattering them heedlessly on the floor. She thrust her fingers through her hair, scattering hairpins like rain over the coverlet.

Then Charlotte sat before him in only her shift, her gold-coppery hair foaming over her shoulders, her eyes glinting in the last light of sunset that slanted through the window. Fighting his pounding heart and throbbing need, Alec forced himself to slow down. He sat beside her on the bed, nestled her close with an arm around her shoulders, and cupped one breast with his other hand. Savoring her gasp of pleasure as he teased it, as he took her mouth again. Through another long kiss, he eased them down onto the featherbed.

Her hands caressed his chest, his ribs—feather light, yet leaving trails of fire wherever they went. His own fingers found their way under the hem of her shift and delicately along the silk of her inner thigh. She moaned softly and opened to him, pushing up toward his touch. The sound she made when he obliged half maddened him. Her arms tightened around his neck, deepening their kiss beyond anything he'd ever known. He let his fingers flicker and tantalize until Charlotte's breathing became a pant in his ear.

"No," she protested when he removed his hand to free himself from his breeches, unbearably constricting. He made quick work of it, then resumed his teasing. Only when she stiffened and cried out in joyous release did he give in to his own raging desire and slip inside her.

The pleasure and relief of it was exquisite. He plunged into that glorious warmth and... through an unexpected resistance. Alec drew back; Charlotte's arms pulled him closer. Far too aroused to think, or to stop himself, he moved again. She met him eagerly. Together, they found a rhythm that mounted and built until the world blurred into ecstasy. Somewhere in the glory of it, Charlotte cried out again. And Alec heard his own voice join hers as release carried him away.

Only when the storm had passed and they lay enlaced, breathing, did Alec acknowledge what his body had discovered. She'd been a virgin. Not an experienced young widow wise in the ways of intrigue. How had he imagined she was, with all he knew of her marriage? He hadn't wanted to think of it, he admitted. He'd wanted... her. Desperately. Far too late, he wondered what the household had heard, what ruin he had brought upon her by yielding to his desires? And hers, yes, but he was the more experienced, and thus responsible, one. And what the hell was he going to do about it now?

Charlotte felt her pulse slow in tandem with his.

She pulled in a deeper breath and let it go. Every inch of her felt wonderful. There had been a flash of pain, but it was nothing compared to the tide of amazing sensations that had come before, and after. She pushed her hair back from her face and stretched sensuously. Suddenly, she was ravenous. She sat up and lit the candle by the bedside. By its light she saw him, naked in her bed, his lean muscled body sculpted by the dancing golden illumination. "Are you hungry? The servants left a cold supper in the dining room."

Sir Alexander—no, Alec; she had to think of him as Alec now—rose on one elbow and looked at her. Charlotte smiled at him and got no smile in return. "Left?" he said.

"They are all out." She started to explain about Ethan's cousin, then didn't bother. She was too contented to form the words.

"Are they?" His expression was peculiar.

"Yes, we are all alone." She ran a hand down his arm, enjoying the feel of it under her fingers.

"So you... planned... this?"

Something in his tone, his face, made Charlotte draw back. Suddenly, she felt naked and exposed. "I... no. I... took advantage of... the circumstance." She hadn't thought beyond the moment; now she was beyond it, and in uncharted territory. The way Alec was gazing at her—did he despise her for giving in to her desire? Had she become quite another sort of woman in his eyes?

"This is... I must apologize for my conduct..."

"No. You must not." Without conscious thought, Charlotte's hand reached for her shift. In an instant, everything seemed to have changed in the room. Tender intimacy had dissolved into awkwardness. She slipped on her shift. Alec rose and began to dress.

"I should go before anyone returns. There must be no gossip…"

Nothing to connect him with her; nothing to trap him, Charlotte thought. Briefly, she felt stricken. Then she remembered. She was in charge of her life. She had done what she wanted to do; there could be no whining now over consequences.

"I have no time to… to deal with…" He gazed at her, looking torn. "Charlotte, I am leaving town first thing tomorrow. I *must* travel to Derbyshire. I've had word from several sources that the countryside is about to go up like tinder. I cannot ignore this crisis."

"Oh." And what was she to say to that? She had no hold over him. He had no obligation to her. And the state of the country was undoubtedly important.

"People have reached a breaking point," Alec added, almost as if pleading for understanding. "I need to provide some help and leadership for those on my lands, and perhaps others, if they will listen. There will be no hangings if I can help it."

Sitting on her tumbled bed, barely clad in her thin linen shift, Charlotte could only nod.

"It is all arranged," he finished. "I don't know how long I will have to be away."

"I… I hope you will be careful."

Charlotte's voice quavered, and Alec wanted to take her in his arms and promise that he'd come back to her. But he didn't, because he couldn't explain even to himself what that meant, precisely. He could not make her his mistress. Every feeling revolted at the idea. She was not the sort of woman to be relegated to the demimonde. But what else could he…? His mind was a chaos of conflicting thoughts and desires. They would have to reason it out when he returned, he told himself. The state of the country was an issue larger than either of them. Still, leaving her there on the bed, gilded by candlelight and clearly tinged by sadness, was one of the hardest things he'd ever done in his life.

Twenty

CHARLOTTE DID NOT FIND THE OPERA TO HER TASTE. She'd never been particularly musical, and it seemed that even the finest singing in the country was not going to change that. It sounded to her like senseless warbling, punctuated by screeching at the top of some very powerful lungs.

Or perhaps, truthfully, she was too preoccupied to enjoy any performance just now. She could think of nothing but Alec—his touch, and the wonder of it; what he thought of her now; and what would happen between them on his return. No matter how often she reminded herself that she had done as she wished, and damned the consequences, she worried that she'd forfeited his good opinion, destroyed her connection with his family. How could she have forgotten his sisters when she made her rash decision? If he forbade them to see her again, it would be a crushing blow. And Frances Cole, whom she had come to like very much; what would that aristocratic lady think of her if she found out? A trip to Greece was one thing; Charlotte's escapade was quite, quite another.

These worries, joined with images of Alec's dangerous errand, of riots and executions, of him stepping between furious factions and being caught in the crossfire, ruined her evening.

It did not help that Lady Isabella was distant and snappish all evening, seeming more interested in the champagne with which she had liberally stocked the opera box than in the music or conversation. She kept Edward's glass constantly filled as well as her own and was disdainful when Charlotte refused a third. In fact, everything about the outing seemed pointless and irritating. The opera had scarcely begun when she was wishing she hadn't accepted the invitation.

Thankfully, the ordeal was nearly over. The carriage clattered over the cobblestones, the sound a stark contrast to the silence within. Next to her, Lady Isabella leaned back against the cushions, her eyes closed. Edward lolled across from them, his handsome face marred by a loose smile. Charlotte wished that home was not so far away.

Lady Isabella sat up suddenly and peered out the carriage window. "Edward!" Her voice seemed loud in the closed space. "Tell the driver to turn here. I'm fagged to death. I must go home."

Edward knocked on the roof and gave the instructions. Apparently, they'd been passing very near Lady Isabella's neighborhood, because before Charlotte knew it they pulled up. Edward jumped out and handed his mother down. Neither of them paid their guest the least heed.

"I can go on alone," Charlotte called through the

open carriage door. She was so weary of Edward and his mother. "It's such a distance. There's no need for…"

Lady Isabella waved a hand without turning, as if she couldn't be bothered. Edward, however, left his mother on the threshold as her front door opened and leapt back into the carriage. "Nonsense," he said. "Must escort you home." He took the place at Charlotte's side, very close, and pulled the door shut. "Aren't we very good friends?" He flung an arm around her shoulders as the vehicle started up again.

"Edward!"

"Oh, come, you're a widow, no innocent deb."

For a searing moment, Charlotte wondered if he had somehow found out about last night. But he couldn't have. Even if Alec was not the man she thought him, he would not have confided in this cousin.

"Why not have a bit of fun?" he added. "What's the harm?" Without warning, he dived forward and kissed her.

Suddenly, he was all clamping lips and roaming hands. Charlotte had a momentary awareness of how utterly different this was from Sir Alexander's embrace. Then she was pushing him away. "Don't! Stop it!"

He didn't let go. "You can do as you like, you know." The wine on his breath puffed in her face. "Take your pleasures where you find them. You even have your own house."

He seemed oddly pleased by this, and Charlotte realized he liked the idea of a *cheap* mistress. "No! Let go of me."

"Promise you I'm discreet. Very, very discreet. None discreet-er." He laughed and grappled with her.

Charlotte fought hard and finally pushed him away. She sprang up and pounded on the roof. "Stop! Stop the carriage!" The vehicle jerked as the driver slowed. Charlotte nearly fell.

"Whatsa matter with you?" Edward groped, trying to gather her into his arms; she slapped his hands away. "Anybody'd think… ah…" He pulled back a little to leer at her. "Ol' Uncle Henry never touched you, did he? I wondered where he'd found the nerve." His eyes gleamed in the dimness. "My God, a virgin widow. Little darling, you deserve to be introduced to love by a man who knows what he's doing. And I promise you I do." He lunged.

"Sir?" The driver called down.

Charlotte shoved Edward away with all her strength. His drunkenness helped her repel him. She jerked the door handle, tumbling from the carriage and nearly to the pavement. She stumbled a few steps, then found her feet. For an instant, she was disoriented. Where to go? Her home was still far away. All the houses nearby were dark. She had no choice but back the way they'd come. She picked up her skirts and began to run through the darkness toward Lady Isabella's home. She heard Edward shouting at the driver to turn the carriage around.

Fortunately, a house farther down had left links guttering from the end of some party, and she could see well enough to go at top speed, though her evening slippers were not made for cobblestone. She considered pounding on that door, but she couldn't risk it. She might find it full of men like Edward, drunk over their cards. She took advantage of the time needed to turn the carriage in the narrow street to flee.

They hadn't turned since they dropped Lady Isabella, and they hadn't been going very fast. Narrow brick house, Charlotte told herself; black lacquer door, two steps up; number fifty-three.

The torchlight faded behind her. She ran in near darkness, praying not to hit any loose cobbles. A house with lit windows came to her aid, shedding golden light on the street. Again, she thought of stopping; then she saw the number—sixty-five. She was close. Hoofbeats sounded at her back, and she ran on.

There it was, Lady Isabella's town house, with a light upstairs. Charlotte jumped up the two steps and pounded on the door. The carriage was coming closer; she could see the lamps approaching. She pounded harder. A glow moved in the fanlight above the door. "Lady Isabella!" she called. "Please open the door!"

A lock clicked back. Charlotte saw Edward leaning out of the carriage window. When the door cracked open, she pushed it with all her strength.

"Here now." A tall, dour-looking woman stumbled back as Charlotte slammed the door behind her. She recovered quickly and raised an oil lamp to illuminate her face. "You can't come in here."

Charlotte stood still, listening, afraid of a knock, of Edward's blustering intrusion. Would his mother side with him or her? But after a moment, she caught the sound of carriage wheels moving off down the street and sagged with relief.

"You can't come in," repeated the woman.

She was dressed like an upper servant, probably Lady Isabella's dresser, Charlotte thought. She would have waited up for her. "I'm sorry. I am Charlotte

Wylde, a... a friend of Lady Isabella's. Perhaps she has mentioned me? It was rather... an emergency." She quailed at explaining exactly what kind.

"I don't care," the woman said with surprising rudeness. "You have to leave."

Charlotte was suddenly exhausted. She had to sit down. "If you would send someone for a cab, I will go. But right now, I need..." She tried to walk around the woman, who stepped sideways to block her. "I'm sorry to be a bother," she added with some annoyance. What was wrong with this woman? "I must sit for a moment." Evading another sidestep, Charlotte moved to a dark archway and found herself facing a totally empty room. Puzzled, she stepped across the front hall and discovered another—bare floor and walls, no furniture, nothing but some ornate draperies blocking the view from outside.

"What are you doing here?" Lady Isabella stood on the stair landing, her hair down, wearing a lacy nightdress and wrapper.

"You have no furniture." The words escaped Charlotte before she could stop them. It was just so odd.

Lady Isabella looked past her to the servant. Some silent communication passed between them.

"I beg your pardon for intruding this way, I was..." How did you explain to someone that her son had behaved like a blackguard? Charlotte felt a hand close around her upper arm.

"You look worn out," said Lady Isabella. "Come upstairs and tell me what's wrong."

"Oh, no thank you, I only need a cab..."

"Nonsense."

The dour servant urged Charlotte up the steps. She was unexpectedly strong, and Charlotte couldn't shake her off. Above, the corridor was bare, and they passed two empty rooms before entering a luxurious bedchamber. The gown Lady Isabella had been wearing at the opera lay on the bed.

"Do sit down. Perhaps some of the hot milk, Martha?"

Charlotte was pushed into an armchair by the fire. "No... really... I just want to go home." The servant went to a tray on the bedside table.

"Where is Edward?"

Charlotte turned to Lady Isabella. "He... he had too much champagne, I think. And..."

"Forgot himself? Oh, dear." She gestured, and the servant handed Charlotte a glass of warm milk.

"I don't want..."

"My dear, it will do you good. Please, this is all my fault. Have your milk, and then we will get you home." Mistress and servant gazed at her, clearly not intending to move until she complied. It was all extraordinarily odd, but all Charlotte could think of was her own bedchamber, with Lucy waiting to help her to bed. The idea almost made her weep. She drained the glass. "Send someone out to find a cab, Martha." Lady Isabella smiled. "It may take a little while. You just rest."

The dour woman went out. Charlotte put her head back and passionately wished herself elsewhere. Why did Lady Isabella live in an unfurnished house? It made no sense, although it reminded her of... she couldn't remember. She was so tired. The evening had been a strain, and last night had been... glorious but complicated. She was so worried about… so many things. And then Edward and the run through the dark streets. Her eyes closed. She opened them. It would be impolite to… The world wavered and faded to black.

❧

"You lied to me," Lucy said. Her voice broke; she couldn't help it. She wanted to be angry, but it near broke her heart to think Ethan had slipped something past her, knowing full well she wouldn't like it a bit. Here she was, as worried as she'd ever been in her life, and the one she ought to be able to turn to had gone sneaky.

"I didn't lie," Ethan began.

"You did the same thing as." With all the coming and going between the two households, it had been certain that Lucy would learn Tom the coachman had left Sir Alexander at their house, alone with her mistress. Miss Charlotte had been acting right odd ever since then, too, though she denied it. Lucy couldn't forgive Ethan for hiding the information from her. She'd been avoiding him. But this morning, anxiety had propelled her into a cab to Sir Alexander's home. It was the Trasks' day out, and she hadn't known where else to turn. She'd hoped for Mrs. Wright, or even Cook; they'd have good sensible advice. But of course, her luck was out. Ethan had been the first person she saw, even though she'd come in the back door rather than knocking at the front. He'd swept her off to the empty study before she could argue. "I can't trust you," she added, desolation on top of fear.

"You can, Lucy. I swear on my life that you can." Ethan put his hands on her shoulders. "Tell me what's wrong!"

Lucy let out a sigh and slumped in his grasp. "Miss Charlotte didn't come home from the opera last night. I'm afraid she's lying dead in the street somewhere. Like *him*." Lucy could no longer hold back her tears. Ethan enfolded her, and it felt too good to resist. "Your grandparents had already gone out when I looked in her bedchamber. I was lettin' her sleep in, see, 'cause she told me yesterday not to wait up. And then it was just Tess and me, and Tess wringing her hands and having the vapors. I didn't know what to…"

"There must be a reason. Who'd she go with then, Lucy? It'll be all right."

"L-lady Isabella." Lucy found her head resting on his shoulder. It felt like home, even though he was a lying viper.

"Maybe she spent the night with her then."

Lucy straightened, sniffed. Reluctantly, she stepped away from him. "Why would she do that?"

"Well… it was late… and… if Lady Isabella took ill or some such and needed help… and it's a good drive out to your place."

"Miss Charlotte would have sent word if she'd done anything like that."

"'Course she would. But if everyone was asleep, see, when they got there…."

Lucy tried to believe him, then shook her head. "What about this morning then? You're saying all Lady Isabella's servants are still abed? And no one to bring a message?" Lucy's fears rushed back. "Miss Charlotte wouldn't worry us like this. She never would. Something's wrong!"

The study door, not quite shut, moved on its hinges. Lizzy Wylde peered around the panels, face brimming with curiosity. "I thought I heard voices." She came into the room. "Hullo, Lucy. Is Charlotte here so early?" The girl looked from Lucy to Ethan, speculation dawning in her eyes.

Lucy swallowed, wishing she could scrub the signs of tears from her cheeks, and dropped a small curtsy, "Miss Lizzy." She didn't know what else to say. She'd seen enough of the youngest Wylde sister to be wary of setting her loose on a problem, even if she'd been of an age to help.

Lizzy looked from Ethan to Lucy. "*Is* Charlotte here?"

"N-no, miss. I was just… I came to…"

"Ethan has not gotten you 'in trouble,' has he?" Her glance from one to the other of them was bright as a wren's. It was clear she had no idea what the phrase actually meant.

Ethan went stiff as a board, his eyes big and glassy with horror. Lucy might have giggled if she hadn't been so worried. "No, miss… uh… nothing like that. I came because I'm worried about Miss Charlotte."

"Is she ill? What's wrong?"

"More a mix-up, like," blurted Ethan. "I'll go over to Lady Isabella's and inquire, shall I?"

"Oh, if you could…"

"Inquire about what?" Lizzy asked. "Tell me what has happened!"

Lucy wasn't sure what to do. She didn't think

Miss Charlotte would want the girl brought into it—whatever it was.

"Lucy?" called a quavering voice from the hall. "Are you here?"

"Tess?" Lucy rushed out to find the young housemaid, white and scared-looking, hovering near the swinging door to the back premises.

"I took a cab on my own," Tess said. "It cost all the money I had, but you said to if there was any news…"

"Miss Charlotte came home." Lucy's flood of relief was immediately crushed when Tess shook her head.

"No, a boy came and left this." Tess held out a piece of paper.

Lucy almost ripped it from her hand. She unfolded it and read the few lines scrawled there. "Gone to the country? On 'the spur of the moment.' What does that mean? It doesn't make any sense."

Lizzy took the note and read it, Ethan looking over her shoulder to follow along.

"Miss Charlotte wouldn't go out of town without me," Lucy declared.

"Maybe if she was…" Ethan began.

"Or her clothes and all her things," Lucy interrupted impatiently. "She wouldn't."

"It's not her writing," Lizzy said.

Startled, Lucy stepped over to peer at the note again. The girl was right; it didn't look anything like Miss Charlotte's hand. She should have noticed that.

"It is Aunt Bella's notepaper. I've seen that before. But I don't know her handwriting." Lizzy's eyes grew large and excited. "Perhaps she was forced to write it. Perhaps they've both been kidnapped by brigands!"

"I can still go to Lady Isabella's and inquire," Ethan put in carefully. "Her staff might have more news."

Lizzy nodded. "You should. Because whatever Charlotte might like, Aunt Bella would *never* leave London in the middle of the Season. She would *have* to be kidnapped to do so."

With this tacit permission, Ethan departed. Lucy spent an uncomfortable half hour forcing down the cup of tea that Miss Lizzy pressed on her. Tess didn't even manage that; she sat in a chair twisting her hands together and looking terrified. When Lucy suggested consulting Mrs. Wright, Miss Lizzy refused. She didn't seem eager to see the housekeeper.

At long last, Ethan slipped back into the study. "The place is empty," he told them, looking puzzled.

"Aunt Bella is gone, you mean," Lizzy replied.

"Everyone's gone. Every*thing's* gone."

"What do you mean?" Lucy was confused.

"When nobody answered the bell, I slipped around to the back of the house." He avoided their eyes, and Lucy suspected he'd gone over a wall. Which didn't bother her one bit. "I looked in a few windows. There's no furniture in the place."

"No..." Lizzy frowned. "That's... you must be mistaken."

Ethan shook his head. "No, miss. Begging your pardon, but I checked all the rooms on the ground floor. They're empty."

There was a short charged silence. "You're saying that Aunt Bella has moved out of her house? But she... she wouldn't. Not in June anyway. She... I've heard Frances say that she *lives* for the London season.

It is everything to her." Lizzy looked at the message again. "This is exceedingly odd."

"If Lady Isabella went to the country, it'd be Derbyshire," said Ethan carefully. "That's where her estate is."

Tension had been building in Lucy. "I have to go after Miss Charlotte," she declared. She had no idea how she could manage that, but she didn't see what else to do.

Lizzy's dark blue eyes sparkled again. "Like a rescue? Perhaps they really have been kidnapped, and all Aunt Bella's things stolen, too. Do you think the criminals will demand ransom? I'll come with you!"

"No, I'll go," Ethan said. "I know Derbyshire like the back of my hand."

"I want to come!" Lizzy's face got the mulish look that meant trouble.

"Well, you can't, Miss Lizzy, and that's that." Ethan's tone brooked no argument, thought Lucy admiringly.

Lizzy scowled. Lucy waited for the explosion. Then, amazingly, she sighed. "I suppose Frances would kick up a tremendous fuss. And Anne." She pressed her lips together. "But I so want to help."

"Maybe you could say that you sent me down to the country. So I don't just disappear, like." Ethan's face showed that he knew the flaws of this idea.

"I'm not allowed…" Lizzy paused, then smiled evilly. "Of course I will. Frances is always saying I do outrageous things. What's one more? You must swear, though, to tell me *everything* when you return." Lucy started to protest, but fortunately, Miss Lizzy didn't wait for a promise. "You will need money. I... I believe post chaises are awfully expensive, though."

"I'll take the stage, miss. And I have a bit of savings..."

"So do I," put in Lucy.

"No, no. I'll get it. I know where Anne... that is, it's not a problem." Lizzy turned and ran from the room.

Lucy looked at Ethan. She was grateful, and frightened, and despite their recent disagreement, she loved him with all her heart. "I'm going with you," she said.

Tess gasped. "It's days to Derbyshire. That wouldn't be proper!"

"I won't sit in the house wringing my hands and waiting!" She glared at Ethan as if he'd been the one protesting. "It's no use saying I should."

Ethan simply held her gaze. The love and tenderness and respect Lucy saw there made tears come to her eyes once again.

Twenty-one

WHEN CHARLOTTE WOKE SHE WAS MOVING, AND IT made her feel sick. She had a dreadful headache; her mouth was dry and foul. But worst was the confusion. She was looking at a square green blur. She blinked, squinted. It was a carriage window, with countryside reeling past. Her stomach protested, and she clenched her jaw. What was going on? She couldn't think straight.

"She's come 'round," someone said.

Charlotte turned her head; even that small movement made her dizzy. She was curled sideways in a carriage seat, and Lady Isabella's dour servant sat opposite.

"Stupid girl."

Charlotte turned a bit farther. Lady Isabella sat beside her, dressed for traveling. "What... what is happening?"

"We are going into the country, at the height of the Season," Lady Isabella replied petulantly. "And it is all your fault."

Charlotte reviewed the words twice, but they still made no sense.

"*And* I had to pay for a post chaise. Do you have any idea how much that costs?"

She knew the answer to this. "No."

"Stupid girl," said Lady Isabella again.

Charlotte tried to straighten on the seat and discovered that her wrists were bound together with many loops of twine. She held them up before her, astonished.

"It's no use screaming. We told the driver and postboys that you're mad and have to be restrained or you will hurt yourself. And that you might be quite noisy when you woke." Lady Isabella said this as if it were the most natural thing in the world.

She must be dreaming, Charlotte concluded. "This is a nightmare."

She didn't realize she'd spoken aloud until Lady Isabella sniffed. "The nightmare is that idiot St. Cyr mewling to me about your snooping and how he was going to have to reveal that I provided some of the things Henry bought or his reputation would be ruined. Reputation! He's nothing but a jumped-up tradesman. What sort of reputation can he have?"

"You provided…?" Her mind still refused to work properly. "Why would you…?"

"For a portion of the price, of course. You really *are* wretchedly stupid."

None of this seemed real. "But where did you find ancient Roman…?"

Lady Isabella gave a ladylike snort. "Ancient! I had them made by an acquaintance of Edward's. Not all young artists find poverty to their taste, you know. Henry was such a fool; it worked perfectly. And if you had not brought in that museum… person, we might have sold them all over again. But you haven't the least spark of enterprise, have you? And then what must you do but force your way into my house and see... It is no one's fault but your own that I had to remove you."

"Remove...?" Charlotte stared at her bound hands. "I will be missed. Someone... people will come after me."

"I sent a note to your house saying we had a notion to visit the country," was the smug reply.

"Visit...? Without any luggage or...? Are you insane?" Charlotte leaned toward the window. "Help!"

The dour servant reached across and grasped her upper arm so hard it made her gasp. "We should give her more of the laudanum, ma'am."

"Yes, yes, very well. This is so tedious."

Martha had a grip of iron. Charlotte fought her, but she was still dizzy and weak. In the end, she was held immobilized, her nostrils pinched shut until she was forced to open her mouth. Lady Isabella tipped a small bottle into it with scant regard for dosage, and Martha clamped an arm around her jaw until she swallowed.

"There." Lady Isabella replaced the cork and tucked the bottle into her reticule. "Neatly done. Martha took care of my mother, you know." She spoke conversationally, as if Charlotte might be interested in this information.

~❦~

Time dropped away. Charlotte barely woke when they stopped for the night at an inn. The next time she was really conscious, they were driving again. Her mouth was dry as dust, and the headache was excruciating. "Where are we going?" she managed to croak.

"My country place," Lady Isabella replied. "What

people will think of me—leaving town in June—I do not know. But you are as inconsiderate as the rest. No one thinks of *me*."

Charlotte struggled to gather her wits, to remember the conversation the last time she was conscious. "You sold all your furniture to… that dealer?" She couldn't recall the man's name at the moment.

"Not all at once. Or all to him." She seemed to find it a tiresome question. "And St. Cyr gave me much less than it was worth!"

"But… why?"

Lady Isabella glared at her. "It costs the earth to live decently in London. Clothes, servants, a box at the opera, a carriage and horses. Well, I am reduced to a hired coach now, of course. Edward must have an allowance out of the revenues from the estate; he has a position to keep up. Only think how humiliating for both of us if he could not have a fine string of hunters or a good address for his rooms?"

"Edward was involved…?"

"As if he would be so helpful! No, it is always left to me to find a way to keep things going. Everyone has simply expected it. My parents, Simon, Edward. No one else lifts a finger. When I think how Edward complained about saying a few words to Henry when he saw him at the club."

"It's all about money," Charlotte said. She felt like the stupid girl Lady Isabella had called her. Her mind just wouldn't work.

"Naturally I thought Henry would leave his fortune to Edward. And well he knew it! I had no idea he'd married. I cannot keep track of *everything*!" She blew out an exasperated breath. "Henry was always a sneak. And malicious? That ridiculous will. I should have remembered how devious he'd always been and provided a will myself. That was a mistake. I admit it."

A horrible realization was rising in Charlotte. "Did you kill Henry?" she whispered.

Lady Isabella tittered. "He was so shocked when I walked up to him in men's clothing. I don't suppose he even noticed that Mama had made me wear them. He never noticed anything but himself. It was simple to hit him the first time."

"My lady," admonished Martha.

Her mistress ignored her. "Edward had told me that it is very dangerous for boxers to be hit just here." She put a hand to her temple.

"You shouldn't say any more, ma'am," Martha advised.

But Lady Isabella didn't seem to hear. "I had to strike him several times to make sure he was dead, of course. But I'd found a spot that was dark and hidden. Then, it was all for nothing. A museum—the idiot!" She turned to glare at Charlotte. "And now, on top of everything, you!"

"It's time for her dose, ma'am." Martha leaned forward and caught Lady Isabella's eye. She held it for a long moment.

"Is it? Oh, very well."

Charlotte barely struggled this time. She was too shocked.

Another inn went by in a blur. When Charlotte came to consciousness in the post chaise for the third time, she felt beyond horrible. Her muscles ached; her head pounded; her stomach twisted; her throat and wrists were rasped raw. She didn't want to open her eyes and reveal that she was awake, but she was desperate. "Is there any water?" She could barely croak.

"We have a flask of tea," Lady Isabella replied, as brightly as if they were on the way to a picnic. "Give her some, Martha."

She thirstily drank two cups held for her by Martha, then slowly ate some bread and cheese she was offered. As the day passed, even with the rocking of the carriage, she began to feel slightly better. If only they would stop giving her the drug, she might be able to think what to do. From something Lady Isabella said to Martha, she gathered the journey would end later that day. Suddenly, she remembered something. "We're going to Derbyshire?"

Lady Isabella raised her eyebrows. "Yes."

"You live near your parents' old house." Now Sir Alexander's, and he was in Derbyshire! If she could get away and find him... Noticing Martha's eyes on her, Charlotte kept her face blank.

"Oh, yes," Lady Isabella replied. "All my life, I was the one who was there, called on for any emergency, complained to... you cannot conceive the continual complaints. And still my father left me next to nothing! What did my brothers ever do for him? James simply... disappeared as soon as he was able. And Henry! He cared nothing for my parents, or indeed for anyone but himself."

There, Charlotte had to agree. "A liar and a thief," she murmured.

Lady Isabella frowned at her. "What?"

She hadn't meant to speak aloud. She was so very disoriented and tired. But what did it matter? "Henry had a whole hoard of things hidden away. We just found them a few days ago."

"What sort of things?" was the sharp reply.

"A snuffbox, earrings, my father's…"

"Earrings?" Lady Isabella loomed over her. "A large teardrop pearl? An emerald with a diamond setting? Ruby clusters?"

"I'm not sure about all those. I saw a pearl."

"Damn Henry!" Lady Isabella clenched her fists, and for a moment Charlotte feared she'd hit her. "Those were my mother's jewels. They… came to me."

Her tone made Charlotte suspect that they had not come in the ordinary course of legacy.

"It's been years since I lost those earrings. Well, I didn't lose them, did I? Now we see." She gave Martha a burning look. "How did Henry…? Christmas! He must have taken them when he was up for the holidays, before Papa died. If only I'd known they were there the night I went in, I could have…"

"It was you? The robbery?"

"I had his keys," Lady Isabella said impatiently. "If Henry could be fooled by the objects Phelps produced, why not others? Then there was no house key, and I made a noise, and you began to shout. You, again!" She turned to glare at Charlotte. "You will give those earrings back to me!"

She made it sound as if Charlotte had stolen them. Under the circumstances, however, this seemed the least of her worries. She simply nodded.

"I sold the mates for a pittance, because what can

one do with one earring? And now I shall have to do the same with the others. It is not fair!"

She was so fierce that an idea penetrated Charlotte's confusion. "We could go back and fetch them."

Briefly, it seemed that Lady Isabella might do exactly that. Then Martha leaned forward and put a hand on her arm. "No, of course not. I will get them... later."

"What are you going to do with me?" Charlotte couldn't help but ask. She received no answer, and she began to suspect that Lady Isabella had no idea. But whether that was good news or bad in this insane situation, she didn't know.

It was nearly dark by the time they pulled up before a sizable country house. Charlotte got only glimpses of the brick façade and a few pieces of sheeted furniture as Martha hustled her inside and up two sets of stairs. The place *felt* empty, however. The ancient housekeeper who'd hobbled out to meet them was obviously surprised by the visit.

Martha took her to an unused maid's room, barely lit by one tiny window under the eaves, empty but for a sagging bed. She pushed her down on the iron bedstead, which creaked under her weight.

"Please," Charlotte said as the woman turned away. "You must see that this is mad. You cannot keep me here."

With an uneasy look, Martha simply left her in the growing dark. The lock that clicked behind her sounded sturdy. But she did not give Charlotte any more laudanum, and for that at least she was thankful. She began to tear at the twine on her wrists with her teeth.

✎

Battered by the endless rocking and bouncing of the stagecoach, Ethan and Lucy stumbled into the inn and found a small table in the corner of the common room. It was low-ceilinged, smoky, and crowded; the coach had been jam-packed, too, and poorly sprung. If he was worn out, how must Lucy be feeling, Ethan wondered? The long hours crammed in with other passengers, nosy ones and rude ones, had been hard enough for him. He was big, and he had a thick skin. Lucy was more delicate, and eaten up with worry as well. He'd shielded her as much as he could by sitting between her and the rest, but there was only so much he could do. He looked her over, saw the dark circles under her blue eyes. You couldn't sleep on the stage, not unless you were half dead already, which they weren't, quite yet.

The barmaid plopped down plates of stew and mugs of ale. Ethan paid with what he feared was pilfered coin. He hoped Miss Anne wouldn't mind, in the end.

"Somethin's got to be done," railed a drunken voice from the other side of the room. A man in a much-patched coat banged his tankard on the tabletop. "Twice-damned gover'ment wants to let us starve, I say take what we need, any way we can, and let 'em shove that down their fat gullets."

There was a growl of agreement from other tables, and Ethan was torn between further worry about Lucy's safety and a reluctant understanding. Just yesterday, he might have disapproved of the outburst. But he'd seen a thing or two since then.

The farther north they went, the worse it got.

They saw ragged people trudging along the side of the road with their meager belongings piled in hand carts. Skinny children with hopeless eyes followed as they could, the youngest riding atop the carts. Evicted, one of the passengers had explained, for not being able to meet their rents, there being no work or no decent wage to be earned. Some of the villages they passed through had an abandoned air, like the war had been here in England rather than foreign parts. In one of them, children had flocked 'round the stagecoach when it slowed, hands out, begging. Begging! Beggars were creatures of the city, to Ethan's mind, created by the filthy, crowded conditions there. It had shocked him for sure to see them out here, and made his beloved countryside seem an alien place.

He'd known that times were bad. He'd read the letters from home, listened to James rant about news in the papers. But that wasn't the same as seeing it, not by a long shot. He knew Lucy felt the same; he'd seen it in her face as they traveled. And not a blessed thing he could do about it.

Now, she sat slumped across from him in the loud, smoky room, every line of her showing how tired she was. "Eat your dinner," Ethan urged. "You need to keep your strength up." To set an example, he took a bite of stew. It was passable, not like the swill at the last stop.

"What'll we do when we're there?" Lucy asked wearily, and not for the first time.

Ethan didn't mind repeating himself. "We'll go to Sir Alexander's place first. It's nearest where the stage stops. They all know me there, o' course, and they'll lend me a horse. I'll ride over to Lady Isabella's house. It's not far. And then we shall see."

"What if she's not there? What if we made a...?"

"The note said the country. Has to be her house. Where else would it be?"

Lucy's lip trembled. "Oh, Ethan, what if something bad's happened to Miss Charlotte?"

"Now why would it? No need to think that." Though how could you help it, Ethan thought, with the way things had been going.

"What else am I to think?" Lucy pushed her stew around the plate.

"Eat," Ethan urged her again. He spooned down his own portion. "And quit worrying. I'll take care of this," he assured her.

"How? We don't even know what it is..."

"However I can. However I have to. I'd do anything for you, Lucy." The flash of fear in her face touched him. He longed to sweep her into his arms, and for far more than comfort.

"You mustn't... you must take care. If there's danger... you don't think Miss Lizzy could have been right, do you? About kidnappers?"

He shook his head. "Don't see how. Doesn't make sense."

Lucy extended a hand across the table. Ethan took it and held it in his much larger one. His heart swelled within him, and he smiled at her. What better could a man ask than to help and protect those he loved? Yes, he'd like to take her upstairs to bed, and so he would someday. For now, her trust in him was almost as gratifying. "Don't you worry, Lucy," he said again.

"We'll make it right." The smile she gave him in return, tears glittering in her pretty blue eyes, made Ethan feel he could do anything.

Twenty-two

ALEC WYLDE WAS AS TIRED AS HE HAD EVER BEEN IN his life. He'd had little sleep since the journey up from London, and what he had managed was fitful, plagued either by dreams of fire and disaster or by vivid visions of Charlotte warm and eager in his arms. Whenever he thought of her, which was constantly despite the troubles he was trying to resolve, he regretted leaving her so soon after their time together. He should have... he didn't know what he should have done, and that was the crux of the problem.

Failure seemed to be his lot just now. He rode the countryside trying to calm the people, to save them from their own justifiable anger. If they turned to violence, they'd be hunted down and hanged; that he knew. This government had proved it again and again. On his own lands, they listened, but of course they had received some assistance. Beyond its boundaries he was met with sullenness or fury or—worst—a broken recitation of rightful grievances. He had no remedy for these and no answer for the stares of hungry children and their desperate parents.

This morning he was headed for the main southern road; rumor suggested that a group of men intended to set up a barricade there, to disrupt travel in that direction. Nothing was more likely to attract the army and result in arrests and the kind of executions they'd seen in Nottingham not so long ago. He would try to reason with them, dredge his exhausted brain for some argument that would move them. But he wasn't optimistic. Some of these men believed the government would make changes if they were forced, and they didn't want to hear the contrary. Well, he wished it himself, though he couldn't have that faith. Some were so angry they simply required an outlet, to stave off despair. A few just enjoyed making mischief. But all of them risked their lives, unless he could convince them to disband.

He rode his largest hunter to look impressive, searching up and down the road until he came upon them. Then he spoke for nearly an hour, summoning all the eloquence he possessed. Finally, combining threats of what the government would do and promises of aid, he managed to persuade them to remove the carts they had used to block the highway. He was watching them hitch up their horses, hoping they were not simply moving to a different part of the road, when he noticed a post chaise approaching from the south.

He urged his horse along the highway, fearing that some of the rowdier men might decide to stop it. And indeed the group paused to watch as the carriage swept closer. Alec planted himself in the middle of the road so that it had to slow. People must be warned that it was a very bad time to travel in Derbyshire. A man leaned out of the vehicle's window. Alec was astonished to recognize his cousin Edward. "Alec!"

"What are you doing here?" Edward never left town at the height of the Season. For a moment, Alec wondered if he might have come to help his tenants. Then he let that ridiculous thought go.

"Let me pass!"

Edward looked as if he'd slept in his clothes. He was tousled and unshaven. Alec had never seen him less than perfectly groomed since he left school, which meant that something was very wrong. "What's happened?"

"I must get home. Let me pass!" Despite his commands, the driver pulled up. It was that or run Alec down.

"I doubt you can get through. Haven't you heard what's happening? The countryside is in an uproar. Roads blocked, men gathering to protest…"

"They would not dare stop me!"

"That is exactly what they would do, Edward. Why do you think they are setting up barricades?" Alec indicated the carts that were still partly blocking the way.

His cousin seemed at a loss. He ran a hand through his hair, mussing it further. "Blast it. Damn both of them to hell."

"Who? What are you doing here? What has happened?"

"Get in," his cousin snapped.

"Why…?"

"Tie your horse to the back and get in! I can't be shouting private business across a highway."

He was so agitated that Alec decided to comply. But when he'd climbed into the chaise and faced his cousin, he demanded, "What the devil is this about?"

"There's something… wrong with my mother."

"She's ill?" What was he doing up here, in that case?

Edward tapped his fists on his thighs, vibrating with tension. He seemed reluctant to speak, and yet at his wits' end. "She seems to have brought Charlotte here," he blurted finally. "And I don't know what she means to do with her."

"Do…?" Alec wondered if his cousin had had some sort of brainstorm.

The admission appeared to have broken a barrier, and words tumbled out of Edward now. "We'd been to the opera, the three of us. On the way home, Charlotte and I had… a disagreement. My fault entirely. I was… not myself."

Most likely drunk, Alec thought, his blood burning at the idea of this "disagreement." What had Edward done?

"I woke late the next day and had to spend a bit of time… recovering. I felt vile, if you must know. It was afternoon by the time I made that hellish long drive out to Charlotte's house to apologize. Then, when I got there, I found the place all at sixes and sevens. They'd received a note saying that my mother was taking Charlotte on a visit to the country. Charlotte hadn't come home the night before, hadn't summoned her maid. No warning, nothing packed, an impulse, the note said."

"In the middle of the Season? Aunt Bella would never…"

Edward waved him to silence. "You needn't tell me. I went over to her house. I have a key. And I found it empty."

"They'd left already?" It made no sense.

"No, Alec, I mean *empty*. Only my mother's bedchamber and one servant's room upstairs had furnishings. A few bits in the kitchen."

"I don't understand."

"The rest of the place was bare walls and floor-boards," Edward almost shouted, as if volume would get his point across.

"But… that's…"

"Unbelievable? Inexplicable? I have used those terms and more on this damnable journey."

Alec tried to remember the last time he had been inside his aunt's house. It was years ago. He began to feel cold despite the warmth of the June afternoon. "I still don't understand what you think is happening."

Edward stared at him out of bloodshot eyes. "I don't *know* what is happening. I *suspect* that Mama has been selling her things to support her… style of living." He rubbed his face with both hands. "I've wondered how she managed to dress as she does and keep a carriage. I didn't really pay attention. Why should I?"

"Edward!" He got his cousin's attention. He wanted to shake him. "What has this to do with Charlotte?"

"Don't you see? She must have gone into Mama's house when she… She must have seen the empty rooms. Mama would never forgive her for the humiliation."

When she what, Alec wanted to ask? Should he take the time to choke out of Edward just what he had done? Not now. "All right, she will never forgive her. Why in God's name would that lead her to come to the country?"

Edward gritted his teeth. "Will you listen to me? Nothing matters more to my mother than her place in society. It's what she lives for. She's... a bit... fanatical on the subject. And now I find that she's sold everything she owns to maintain her position." He put his head in his hands. "I've heard her telling people she had painters in, and then it was workmen moving a wall. Who listens to such things? But I realized as I traveled that she has been making excuses to keep people out of her house for a very long time. The idea that her shift was discovered, that it might be revealed to the *ton*, would make her frantic. I don't know what she might do to protect... well, she has already gone far beyond the bounds... Oh, hell! I followed as soon as I could. From what I could discover on the road, I am a day or more behind them."

The only part of this that he cared about hit Alec like a roundhouse blow. "You think she would harm Charlotte! Over such a triviality?"

"I have been trying to *tell* you that it is not a triviality to her! You have never understood Mama, never considered what she was made to endure..."

"Endure?" Alec's brain filled with jumbled visions—his aunt in a fury, Charlotte threatened. "You think Aunt Bella has gone... has become like Grandmama?" Alec saw a screaming rictus of a face, shattering glass, paroxysms of hysteria.

His cousin blanched and looked away. "No! Of course not. There have been one or two occasions... but it is not the same... Martha knows what to do."

"Martha? The same Martha who took care of...?"

"Yes! Why not? Mama has known her since she was a child. They... handled a great many crises together." Edward scowled, then pounded on the roof of the chaise. "Devil take it, I have to get home!"

Alec opened the carriage door and stepped down. "I shall ride across the fields to your house. It's the only way to get there quickly. Can I get it through your head that the countryside is practically in arms? The army is on the way to suppress what amounts to a popular uprising. The roads are dangerous."

"I'll take one of the post horses and come with you."

"Without a saddle or bridle? Over the walls and hedges?"

Edward leaned out and grasped his arm. "Give me your horse then."

"No." Alec pulled free and walked away.

"It's my mother!" Edward jumped down and pursued him.

"Who is threatening to harm Charlotte!" If anything had happened to her... Alec's blood burned in his veins. Edward caught his arm again. They grappled in the road, heedless of interested eyes from the carriage and the dismantled barricade. Alec twisted, jerked free, and landed a solid blow to Edward's midsection. His cousin folded, huffing for breath. Alec ripped his horse's reins from the back of the chaise and mounted.

Edward gazed up at him, still gasping. "Alec. Please."

Alec didn't remember ever hearing that word from his cousin. Edward's anguished expression reached him, though he had no intention of giving him what he wanted. "Up ahead, take the left fork. Go through

Tarne. You have a better chance that way. But I warn you, men are out on the roads, in the villages, and they are angry. They are not stopping to listen to excuses." He wheeled his horse and headed for a gate that led into the fields.

∼∽∼

Sometime in the endless night, Charlotte had freed her wrists, gnawing like a trapped animal at the layers of twine and tugging at them until her wrists were raw. Unbound, she'd felt her way around the dusty floor and, thankfully, found a chamber pot shoved all the way back under the rickety bed. She still felt weak and disoriented, but it was a huge relief to be untied and away from Lady Isabella.

She watched dawn lighten the small window, far too small to be any use for escape, even if she hadn't been at the top of the house. The door was sturdy, the walls solid. Without tools, she had no chance of breaking through them. The sparse contents of the room offered no weapon. She had no resources but her wits, and they were far from sharp. She still fought the muzziness of the drug and the fatigue of the forced journey.

When the lock clicked, she braced for a fight about her bonds, but Martha merely frowned at her wrists. She'd brought a glass of water, which Charlotte wanted so desperately she nearly cried. But when Martha stood by waiting for her to drink it, she knew it was dosed. "What are you going to do to me?" she asked, holding the glass.

Martha merely waited, leaning against the closed door.

"People know where I am. They will come here

looking for me." And so they would, eventually. How long might it take? "What Lady Isabella has done will be exposed," she tried. "This is not some trivial matter. How can she imagine...?"

There was a cry outside, and the clatter of something large falling. Martha looked toward the window. With a lightning twist of her wrist, Charlotte dumped the contents of the glass into the straw mattress, then put it to her lips as if drinking. She got one tantalizing wisp of moisture on her dry lips, enough to make her thirst even stronger. When Martha turned back to her, she lowered the empty glass. "There will be real trouble if you do not let me go," she said to distract her further. Perhaps she imagined it, but she thought Martha looked uneasy. She only took the glass and left, however, locking the door behind her.

Charlotte waited until her footsteps died away, then tried the door. It felt as impregnable as ever. But they thought now that she was drugged; that was one small advantage.

The day wore on. Charlotte was alternately frantic and exhausted. She longed to collapse into sleep, yet she had to remain alert for any opportunity to break free.

It was late afternoon before one arrived, in the person of the old housekeeper with a tray of food. She looked surprised, and alarmed, to see her awake. "Feeling better, miss?"

Charlotte took the tray from her, set it on the bed, grabbed the old woman's shoulders, and forced her down beside it. She snatched the key from her trembling hand. "Perhaps they have told you I'm mad. That is a lie. I have been kidnapped, and all of you are going to be held accountable for it." And so much else, Charlotte thought. But that was not to be mentioned here and now.

The old woman stared up at her with wide, frightened eyes.

"If you keep silent when I'm gone, I will tell the magistrates that you had no hand in my abduction."

The housekeeper shrank away from her, nodding.

Charlotte didn't know if this was agreement or simple fear, but she couldn't afford to wait, and she wasn't willing to hurt the old woman. She locked her in the room with no guarantee that she wouldn't start shouting at any moment and moved as quickly as she dared along the bare corridor.

She found the back stairs and crept down to the kitchen, fortunately empty. A short corridor led through the scullery and out into the yard. The conflicting needs to hurry and to be careful were almost unbearable, and Charlotte's heart pounded as she stopped to listen. She didn't know who else might be here—stablemen, farm laborers? But if there were horses… She raced across to the stables and found them empty. Disappointed, she took the time to dip handfuls of water from the horse trough and drink, then slipped into some shrubbery behind the building and worked her way around the house. She wasn't able to run for very long; her body hadn't recovered from the drugged journey. She needed transport, and direction to Sir Alexander's house. Luckily, Lady Isabella didn't appear to have a staff of servants to search for her. Martha was formidable, but she was just one person.

At the end of the drive, she had to decide which

way to turn. She debated briefly, afraid her choice would be just the wrong one, and eventually chose to go back the way they'd come. At least that led to the London road, at some point. She couldn't recall the whole of the route.

The day was waning. Charlotte slipped along the side of the country lane, ready to hide if she heard anyone approaching. Seeing her walking in her now filthy evening dress and slippers, her hair crushed by days in a chaise, people might easily believe she was mad. She didn't want to risk any encounter so close to Lady Isabella's home. But for a long while, she saw no one; the countryside was curiously empty.

The sun approached the horizon. Shadows slanted across the rutted lane. What would she do once it was full dark, Charlotte wondered? The June night wouldn't be too cold. She could spend the night in a field, she supposed—but it was a daunting prospect.

She heard the rattle of cart wheels approaching, then the clop of hooves. For a moment, she froze. This could be rescue, or servants of Lady Isabella's returning to the house. She must have more than one old woman taking care of the place. If they'd been given the story of her madness... She couldn't think. Her head felt as if it had been stuffed with cotton wool. If she asked for help, surely... She remembered the sullen faces and hostile eyes of countrymen they'd passed on the road. Sir Alexander had said Derbyshire was on the edge of violence. She couldn't risk it.

Charlotte plunged off the hard-packed ruts and into the fringe of weedy growth beside the lane. There was a clump of small trees not too far away. She ran. If she could just reach… her foot caught in the hem of her gown, and she went down with a thump that sounded like a thunderclap in her ears. Heart pounding, she curled small among the weeds and held her breath. The hoofbeats came closer; the rattle of the cart seemed almost on top of her. And then it passed and went on along the lane, back the way she had come.

Charlotte lay there, waiting for her pulse to slow, her hands to stop trembling. Then she stumbled up and began walking once again.

❧

"Can't we go any faster?" Lucy asked. The old cart Ethan had borrowed from Sir Alexander's stables seemed to crawl along the lane. It was nearly dark, another day passing, and they hadn't done a thing but wear themselves out traveling.

"I'd be going faster if I'd ridden," he complained.

"And how would you take Miss Charlotte away if you was on horseback?" Lucy countered. "Throw her across your saddle like some lunatic in an old tale?" He had no reply to that, because she was right.

"You should have stayed at the house," Ethan grumbled instead. "I don't like the feel of the countryside. Tempers are up. Something's in the wind."

"I wasn't going to be left there amongst a lot of strangers." And if Ethan couldn't see why, he was no better than a numbskull, Lucy thought. It had been bad enough walking up to that grand estate smudged and rumpled from the long journey, having traveled for days alone with him. How was she going to explain that kind of scandalous goings-on, if she was left there, when the housemaids and all started eyeing her and whispering? She couldn't tell them about Miss Charlotte; she'd never betray her mistress by gossiping about her. So what was she to say? And all the while knowing that Ethan's family was part of the staff, and people who'd known him all his life. She might get on the wrong side of his father—or worse, his mother. And then how could she live right next to them if they were married? Couldn't he see that she mustn't be plopped down there like a parcel with no explanation? It was clear as clear, but not to him seemingly.

Gates loomed in the growing darkness. "This is it," said Ethan. He turned the cart and headed down the drive.

Lucy clenched her hands in her lap. She imagined a grand butler ordering them from the door, or a high-nosed housekeeper having them thrown out of the house by a group of hulking footmen. Ethan was big, but he was just one man. And she didn't want him hurt. But they had to find Miss Charlotte. Her stomach churned with nerves.

They drove right up to the place. Strangely, the building was dark except for one lighted window on the second floor. Ethan directed the horse around to the back premises and pulled up near the stables. "We'll have to leave her standing," he muttered as they climbed down. He looped the reins over a post.

The back door wasn't locked. Nobody locked their doors in the country. They slipped inside a dark corridor. "Have you been here before?" Lucy whispered.

"No. The family don't visit here much."

They groped their way to the kitchen. It was

spooky how empty the house felt. Ethan circled the room and found an oil lamp, which he lit after another hunt. Aided by its wavering light, they walked quietly up the stairs. "Where is everybody?" Lucy whispered.

"Reckon they closed the house when they went up to London. There ought to be some servants, though. It's right odd."

It was more than that, Lucy thought. Her anxiety grew.

In the upper corridor they followed the light to the room she'd seen from outside. Its door was half open. Ethan hesitated briefly, then pushed it wide and stepped in. Lucy followed right on his heels.

From a huge four-poster bed, Lady Isabella shrieked like a train whistle. A big woman standing right next to her whirled and faced them. "Who are you? What are you doing in this house?"

"We've come for Mrs. Wylde," Ethan said. His voice didn't shake at all, Lucy thought admiringly.

"I don't know what you're…" the big woman began.

"We know you've got her," Lucy interrupted. "We had the note. And we didn't believe it for a minute!"

"Get them away from me! Get them away from me!" cried Lady Isabella. She brushed at her arms as if flicking dust from her nightdress.

"You are trespassing," her servant tried.

"You'd best send for a magistrate then," Ethan answered. "Because we're going to keep right on doing it." He stepped farther into the room. Lucy liked how he loomed over them.

"Martha!" Lady Isabella sounded fretful now. "Why are these *people* in my bedchamber? Can't you understand the simplest order? Am I always to be disregarded and harassed?"

A look of resignation, or maybe defeat, settled on the woman's sharp features. "Come with me, then," she said.

She led them out of the room, Lady Isabella's cries of "Martha!" echoing behind them, and up to the top floor of the house. There by the light of the oil lamp, she unlocked an unpainted door and threw it open. "Take her and welcome," she said. "I can't stand this any longer."

Lucy hurried forward. Ethan waited by the door, making sure she'd have no chance to slam it on them, and held the lamp high. Its light fell on a mean little room with a shabby bedstead. A wizened woman lay curled upon it, drowsing. "What's this supposed to be then?" demanded Ethan.

The old woman sat up, then cowered back as Martha strode in. "What the... where's the girl?"

The crone crouched even lower. "She said she'd bring the law down on us. I'm not being taken by the law, I'm not! I haven't done nothing."

"She should have been sleeping," Martha muttered. "How did she...?"

"Where did she go?" Lucy asked.

"How'd I know?" the old woman replied. "She locked me in here and went off."

"You old fool," said Martha.

"I ain't such a fool as you, getting yourself into trouble for the likes of..." Martha raised a hand, and the ancient woman fell silent.

Ethan turned away. "Come on. She must be walking."

"In the dark?"

"We'll find her." He hesitated, then turned back to address Martha. "You keep any horses?" At the sullen shake of her head, he added, "You'd best hope the young lady is all right. Because if she ain't…"

Lucy clutched his arm as pictures of various disasters crowded her mind. "Let's go!"

❧

Charlotte crouched in deep shadow by the wall of a stone cottage. Up ahead, the flickering orange light of torches outlined the buildings of a village. The sight had been hopeful at first; she'd expected to find someone she could ask for aid and had hurried on. But then she'd heard the shouting, and the low growl of male voices in response, and slipped into hiding. She peered carefully around the corner of the cottage. At least fifty men milled about the village center. Some of them carried long pikes; others held the torches that threw warm light on angry faces and shaken fists. Charlotte leaned against the stone wall in exhaustion. It seemed she'd left Lady Isabella's prison only to fall into the midst of a riot.

One man stood on a step or box, head and shoulders above the others, a black silhouette against the flames. He brandished a gun as he spoke, his voice raised to carry. "Men of Derbyshire, how long are we going to watch our children cry with hunger? Or our wives weep with fear?"

There were more growls of agreement, but one voice shouted, "Who're you to stand up there above us, Jeremiah Brandeth?"

The speaker turned in the direction of the questioner.

"Not above you, brother. I'm just like you, a stocking knitter who can't find work because of the damned machines, with a wife and two children to keep. I'm willing to work. Are you?"

This brought a much stronger roar of approval. Pikes were waved in the air.

"We want our rightful work and a chance to do it, that's all. And this government ought to know it. We'll march down to Nottingham, we will, and show 'em they need to listen to their own people."

There were mutters in response to this proposal. Charlotte heard some reluctance, mentions of the army riding men down. She remembered that Alec had deplored the brutality in the suppression of protests in Nottinghamshire not long ago.

"We'll stop in at the ironworks down Butterley way," the speaker added. "There's weapons there for the taking. Let anybody try to stop us, we'll give him a taste of this." He waved the gun over his head. "And there's bread and beef and ale waiting in Nottingham. Cash money, too, for any man who comes. We'll take over the damned army barracks. The whole country is ready to rise and join us. There's sixteen thousand just waiting to march on to Newark!"

Another man began pounding on the door of a house behind the speaker. "Open up, Mary Hepworth!" he shouted. "Every house is required by the revolutionary committee to provide a man and a gun."

"Get away with you!" screeched a female voice from within. "Criminals! You're a disgrace to Derbyshire."

Someone threw a stone and broke a window in the house. The man on the box continued to wave his gun, and all at once it fired through the shattered glass. Charlotte couldn't tell if he'd aimed, or if it had simply gone off in his hand. But a cry rang out from within the house, followed by the female voice shouting, "You devil, you've killed Bill!"

Some of the men in the crowd fell back, murmuring. A good portion looked as if they might leave at this development. A few at the edges did fade into the darkness. "Stand where you are," cried the shooter. "I'll shoot any man who turns tail now. By God, I will."

Horrified, Charlotte shrank into the deepest shadow. She hadn't expected it would come to this, not murderous violence. She turned and fled silently back the way she had come.

Twenty-three

ALEC HAD RIDDEN DESPERATELY CROSS-COUNTRY toward his aunt's house. Fortunately, his hunter was used to rough footing and tricky jumps. Nonetheless, it was well after dark by the time he reached his goal, clattering into the stable yard with no effort at concealment. He left his horse and raced through the empty scullery and kitchen. He had taken to carrying a small lantern, as well as a pistol, in his saddlebag, because so often lately his rides extended into darkness, and the lantern had fitfully lit his way through the last miles. Now, on the main floor, it illuminated only sheeted furniture. Had Edward been mistaken? Had they not come here, after all? Apprehension pounded in his veins as he climbed the stairs and thrust open door after door along the dark corridor. Finally he discovered his aunt in a bedchamber near the end of the hall. She huddled in a chair with two servants bent over her. "Where is Charlotte?" he demanded.

The three women shrank back. Aunt Bella, pale and tired-looking, put a hand to her throat. "Ch-charlotte. What do you mean?" She made an effort to straighten.

Her hands were visibly shaking. "She is in London. Is she not? I mean I suppose she is, though I have no way of telling…"

"I know you brought her here, Aunt. Edward told me."

"Edward?" her voice quavered on the name.

"He called at her house, discovered the message you'd sent, and went looking for her at your place. He has a key, you know." He held her eyes. "To your curiously empty house." It was a calculated cruelty, but he was nearly mad with worry. Fear for Charlotte overrode every other feeling. "Take me to her. And if you have harmed her in any way, I swear I will…"

"I don't know what you're…" Aunt Bella began through trembling lips. But she couldn't complete the sentence. Her face slowly sagged as the full weight of what he'd said sank in.

"She's gone," interposed the taller servant. When she spoke, Alec recognized her as the woman who'd cared for his grandmother in her later years. "She was here, but she ran away. We don't know where she is now."

"Out? Tonight? Alone?" The servant nodded. "Do you know what's happening out there? Do you have any idea of the mood of the countryside?"

The older servant began wringing her hands. "I didn't know nothing about it. I didn't have nothing to do with it. I told them others…"

Alec spoke through clenched teeth. "If anything happens to Charlotte Wylde, you are to blame. And you may be sure that you will be brought to book. Which way did she go?"

The tall servant stepped forward, interposing herself between Alec and her mistress. He suddenly remembered her name—Martha. "We don't know. My lady has not been well, you understand. She is in a delicate state…"

Alec gazed past her with contempt. "A 'delicate state' like my grandmother's? I believe such states are self-induced. And if you think that is an excuse for this… outrage, you are dead wrong." The three women simply stared at him, frightened, lost, blank. There was no help here, and no time. Alec turned on his heel and went back to his horse.

With the lantern to supplement the tiny sliver of moon, he rode to the end of the drive. Where would she go? One way led to the small village of South Wingfield; the other through a long stretch of agricultural land. Charlotte wouldn't know that, of course. Which way would she have chosen? Surely she would stay on the roads, not attempt to walk cross-country. Alec peered in one direction, the other. How could he possibly find a lone woman in all this countryside? What if she'd fallen, been hurt? His heart seemed to turn over in his chest, and his mouth went dry at the thought. His pulse thundered against the sounds of the night.

Then and there, Alec realized he could not endure a world without Charlotte in it. If she was lost then… so was he. His doubts and denials flamed to ash. He could reject the words "falling in love" as much as he liked. She was meant to be his, and he hers, for all their lives.

Charlotte stumbled along the dark lane, ruts and bumps continually jarring her knees and threatening a fall. The sounds of the riot had faded behind her. She was somewhere beyond exhaustion now. It was all she could do to lift one foot, then another, totter a step, hold her balance, repeat. Once the anxiety roused by the milling, angry men had faded a little, her consciousness had contracted to a muddled blur. Thus, the cart loomed up out of the darkness ahead without warning. She hadn't even heard the sound of hooves.

The person sitting beside the driver stood and raised a lantern, directing its beam right at Charlotte. It was a woman, which was a bit of a comfort. She put a hand up to shield her face.

"Miss Charlotte?"

She couldn't believe her ears. Could the remains of the drug they'd given her be causing delusions?

"Miss Charlotte, it is you!"

"Lucy? What are you…? How did you…?"

"Ethan and me came to find you."

The driver had already stopped the cart and jumped down. "Let me help you in, miss," he said.

"Ethan?" Charlotte was too tired and too relieved to question this miracle. She staggered over to the cart and let him help her up, squeezing onto the seat next to her maid. "I have never been so glad to see anyone in my life."

"You're all right?" Lucy touched her shoulder worriedly.

"Now I am." Or, almost. "There's trouble in the village up ahead. Men with pikes and a gun."

"What?" exclaimed Ethan.

Charlotte tried to collect her wits. "The leader shot someone in one of the houses. They're headed for Nottingham to protest the lack of work."

"Nottingham. That's this road. We've got to get off it." Ethan hesitated, frowning, then slapped the reins. "This way's still closest," he muttered to himself. "South Wingfield, South Wingfield, who do I know...? Close the lantern, Lucy." ▬▬

Lucy did as he said. Charlotte saw the glimmer of firelight behind a building ahead. She hadn't gotten very far from the village. Ethan pulled up, stopping near a stone wall that did nothing to hide them.

The murmuring roar of the mob reached them. There were more shouts. It sounded like men arguing with each other. "On to Butterley," a voice shouted.

"That's the leader," Charlotte said.

"Got to get out of sight," said Ethan, again as if he were talking to himself. The leader's voice repeated the command, sounding closer. Then Charlotte heard many footsteps, marching. "Right. The Finlays," Ethan muttered. He slapped the reins and moved forward, turned the cart into a narrow lane between two houses, and then into a yard behind the closest one.

It was only just in time. The head of the mob came into view on the road they'd just left. "Don't move," whispered Ethan.

They sat still as statues while the marchers passed. Charlotte's pulse beat in her throat. It seemed an eternity before the road was clear. "Get down, quiet like, and go to the back door," murmured Ethan then. Charlotte and Lucy obeyed, scurrying to the house. Ethan tied up the horse, then joined then. He knocked lightly on the door. "Mrs. Finlay?" he said softly. "Sarah Finlay?"

There was no response. They all looked over their shoulders, fearing stragglers.

"Mrs. Finlay," he repeated to the blank panels. "It's Ethan Trask."

There was a long moment's silence, then the door opened. Only a hint of light showed. A figure loomed in the dim illumination and raised a club to strike.

❧

The patter of hurrying footsteps brought Alec a moment's wild hope. "Who's that? Charlotte?" The sound stopped. Alec raised the lantern and shone it into the lane. "Who's there? Show yourself."

A burly fellow dressed like a laborer stepped slowly forward, holding his hands up to prove their emptiness.

"Who are you? What are you doing here?"

"I'm on my way home, sir," the man answered, responding to Alec's accent and commanding tone.

"Home from where at this hour?"

"I was just… out. Visiting, like."

"Did you see a young woman anywhere along this road?"

"A woman? No, sir. I ain't seen nobody since I left the…" His deep voice trembled and died away.

"What's wrong? Is there some trouble?" What if Charlotte had run into another of the countrymen's barricades? "I need you to tell me if there is. I am Alec Wylde. My land is nearby."

The man's head bobbed nervously. "Heerd tell of you, sir. A fine gentl'man, they say."

"I've been doing my best to help the people here-abouts. Tell me what is happening."

"I was… I didn't mean nothing…" The big man shuddered, and his shoulders slumped. "They killed someone dead in South Wingfield, sir. I wouldn't stay with them after that."

"Who did?" Alec's heart contracted painfully. "Who was killed?"

"I dunno, sir. Someone in a house. What I do know is they'll swing for it. And I ain't going to the gallows for somethin' I had no part of. I didn't sign on for killing."

Charlotte would not have been in a village house, Alec told himself. "Who are 'they'?"

"Men from the village and the countryside, sir. They've marched off to storm the Butterley iron-works or some such. Then on to Nottingham. Jere… someone told them they'd get beef and ale and weapons—money even—down there."

"They'll get soldiers and the noose," replied Alec harshly. All his work and talk had gone for nothing then.

"'Speck you're right. That's why I left them when they turned off a little way back. I'm headed home, fast as I can go." The big man shifted uneasily in the lantern light. "Will you tell the magistrate and all that I didn't go with the others, and I didn't hold with what they done back there, if they come to ask?"

Alec surveyed his anxious round face. "I will. What is your name?"

"Standish, sir. Bob Standish. Live up toward Wheatcroft."

"Very well, Bob."

"Thank you, sir."

"You'd best get back home."

The man nodded and hurried past Alec's horse and into the darkness beyond. He would know the country well enough to reach home in the night.

Alec sat still another moment. Clearly, it was his duty to go to South Wingfield and see about this shooting. If Charlotte had fled the other way... if he'd been certain of that, he would have consigned his duty to perdition. But he wasn't. She might as easily have gone toward the village—and encountered the mob. His blood ran cold at the idea.

Flicking the reins of his tired mount, he got moving.

～

"Ethan?" said the looming black figure. "Ah, I'm crazed to open the door, I am."

"Yes, ma'am. Ethan Trask, from over at Sir Alexander's place? I've been here with my ma, years ago."

"What in the Lord's name are you doing out tonight? You weren't mixed up with that gang of...?"

"No, ma'am. Trying to stay away from the troubles." Ethan took the lantern from Lucy and opened it a hair, so that dim light fell over them. "Got ladies with me. It's... it's quite a tale."

The club was lowered, and the figure stepped back. Charlotte saw that it was a broom held by a stocky village woman. Her face remained in shadow. The broom handle dropped farther. "Did those idiots hurt you?"

"No, we're all right." The noise of the mob had receded down the road. Ethan opened the lantern farther, and the woman looked them over. Charlotte couldn't imagine what she thought of her dirty, bedraggled evening dress and disintegrating slippers, of her snarled hair. "Come inside." She turned; they followed her into a neat cottage, a fire burning low in the stone hearth.

"I'll just see to the horse first." Ethan went out as their hostess lit a lamp. Wooden chairs stood on either side of the fireplace, and an iron pot hung over the coals. To one side of the room was a table piled with embroidery and fancywork, which no doubt represented her livelihood.

The village woman put her broom aside and turned, hands on hips. Her face was ruddy, with crinkles around the eyes that suggested she smiled more often than not. She wore a neat plain gown and white cap and might have been fifty.

"Do you mind if I sit down?" Charlotte didn't think her legs would hold her any longer. She dropped into a chair without permission, then put her face in her hands. Lucy came over and rested a hand on her shoulder. The three women were still until Ethan came back, closed and barred the door. "All right," said the village woman then, "whatever are you doing outside in the dark on this night of all nights?"

"It was in the nature of an emergency, ma'am," replied Ethan.

"That I can believe."

Charlotte raised her head. "I don't even know where I am."

"This be South Wingfield, miss—a law-abiding village until this night."

"Those men…"

"Say fools, rather." The woman sighed. "Though God knows they've been driven to it." She shook her head. "No one will listen to them now."

"We're on the way to Sir Alexander's house," said Ethan. "But I reckon we can't go until it's light."

She nodded. "There'll be soldiers out as well. And they won't be asking your business before they wade in." She sighed and rubbed a hand over her forehead. "I fear they'll all be hanged. And my nephew's gone with them. He wouldn't be told, knows it all at seventeen. Ah, Lord save them." She walked over and sat heavily in the other chair.

She looked so tired and worried that Charlotte's own problems receded. "Sir Alexander would help him," she said, having no doubt, with all he had told her, that it was true.

The woman's gaze was penetrating. "He does try; I've heard that." Her hostess's eyes ran over her gown again. "Excuse me, miss, but what are you doing here?"

Charlotte hesitated, not knowing what to say. Even now, she was reluctant to expose Lady Isabella to a stranger. Ethan and Lucy deferred to her for an answer.

The woman waited a moment, then leaned over the hearth. "Well, it's none of my affair. And maybe I don't even want to know. You're welcome to rest here. And in the morning you can be on your way." She took a ladle from a hook and stirred the iron pot. "Are you hungry? I've some soup."

At the tantalizing odor stirred up, Charlotte's stomach growled loudly. She hadn't eaten in… she couldn't remember when she'd last eaten.

The woman laughed. "Seems so." She took a pottery mug from the mantel and ladled a thick broth into it. When she handed it over, Charlotte sagged with relief. Aching all over from her forced journey, her mind still less than sharp, she was in desperate need of a safe haven. She took the soup with grateful hands that shook only a little. "Thank you." Slowly, she sipped. There was chicken and barley and carrots; it tasted heavenly.

"This is Mrs. Finlay," Ethan said as she served the others. "Ma'am, this is Lucy, and… Miss Charlotte." The woman nodded. Lucy dropped a small curtsy. Then, for a while, there was silence as the three of them drank their soup. The peace of the place started to spread through Charlotte, and her eyelids drooped. She swayed in the hard chair and wondered if she might ask to lie down.

The door rattled, then boomed under a pounding fist. Charlotte jerked and spilled the last of her soup on her knee. Ethan leapt to stand before the panels.

"Aunt Sarah! Open up!"

Their hostess sprang to her feet and quickly unbarred the door. A young man, barely more than a boy, stumbled through and pushed it closed behind him. Panting as if he'd been running, with a bloody scrape on his cheek, he slumped against it. He looked exhausted and afraid, and a razor-sharp scythe dangled from one of his hands. "Jim!" Sarah Finlay cried. "What's happened to you?"

"We got down to Butterley all right," he said. "But there weren't nothing at the ironworks but the factory agent and some constables. Only a few men, but nobody dared face them down. Just like always, them as is on top stays there. Nothing's changed. The rest headed for Ripley, but I'd had enough. I ran back cross-country and nearly broke a leg in the dark."

"You did right," said his aunt.

He looked up and noticed the others. The scythe came up. "Who's that?"

"Just some folks getting away from all these… troubles." Mrs. Finlay had taken up a damp cloth; gently, she swabbed his face.

"You let them in?" He squinted at Charlotte, taking in all the details of her bedraggled state, then examined Ethan, who topped him by a good six inches.

"Of course I did, Jim."

"That one's quality. Why should we lift a finger to help quality when they live high off our sweat?"

"That's not the way I see it." His aunt finished cleaning off his cheek. "Not so bad. Just a scratch," she decided.

The sound of hoofbeats approached outside. Jim's eyes widened, and in an instant he was across the room, one arm around Charlotte's neck, the tip of the scythe at her throat. "Make a sound, and I swear I'll cut you," he whispered. Ethan took a step, and the boy glared at him. "I'll do it!"

"Jim!"

"Quiet," he hissed to his aunt. "If soldiers followed me from Butterley I'm for the gallows and no mistake."

Sarah Finlay wrung her hands, distressed, uncertain. "You'll not hurt anyone in my house," she whispered.

Slowly, the hoofbeats passed by and faded. When all had been silent for several minutes, Jim's grip relaxed.

The scythe fell away. Ethan lunged and twisted it from the lad's grasp. "We'll have no more talk of cutting," he said grimly. "You sit over there in the corner and keep still."

Lucy ran to Charlotte, exclaiming over a few drops of blood shining red at her throat. "I'm all right," Charlotte said. It was no more than half a lie.

❧

Alec rode slowly on through the darkness. South Wingfield had been quiet, buttoned up tight, and he hadn't wanted to knock on any doors, alarming people for no cause. The action had clearly passed on south, beyond his reach at the moment. He slumped in the saddle, rubbed tired eyes, and regretted this side excursion. The momentum of these endless days had carried him out of his way, when all he cared about now was Charlotte. He knew he could ride the roads and fields all night and never find her, but to give up was unthinkable. He would travel in expanding circles in the tangle of lanes surrounding around the Danforth house, and when day came he would continue. He would never stop until she was safe—and in his arms.

Twenty-four

THROUGH THE SLANT OF EARLY MORNING LIGHT, THE cart rattled along a narrow lane. The June day was cool, the sky a transparent blue; birdsong filled the hedges. There was no sign, in this serene landscape, of the previous night's troubles, except that the roads were empty. Ethan held the reins; Lucy sat between him and Charlotte, the three of them squeezed close on the narrow seat. Awkwardness had descended upon them with the new day—the barrier between servant and master recalled—and they traveled mostly in silence.

"How far is it?" asked Charlotte after a while.

"Matter of half an hour or so," Ethan replied.

She nodded thanks for the information and fell back to wondering what Alec would say when she showed up at his country home. He could not blame her when he heard what had happened. But after what had passed between them, he might not welcome her either. She had argued briefly for going to the stage-coach stop instead and had hit a surprising stubbornness in Ethan that first annoyed, then impressed her.

She could see that he was right. Lucy was exhausted. She was exhausted. They had slept very little during the remainder of last night, and they needed rest before making the long journey back to London. But was Alec's house the place for that? And what other choice had she? She had no money for an inn, or a stagecoach ticket, for that matter.

They turned from the lane onto a larger road, and the horse moved a bit faster. At least she no longer wore her ruined evening dress or looked as if she'd been dragged backward through a hedgerow. Lucy had been clever enough to pack her a fresh gown, and she and Ethan had carried their luggage along with them in the cart. The thought of showing up at Alec's home the way she'd looked last night... well, it was unthinkable. She would have *walked* back to town rather than do that.

With a clatter of hooves and wheels, a post chaise rounded the curve ahead of them. Ethan pulled over as far as he could to let the grander equipage pass. It had nearly done so when a man's voice called, "Stop!" Edward Danforth's head showed at the carriage window, moving past them as the driver reined in his team.

"What are you doing here?" said Charlotte and Edward at the same moment.

"I came after you, damn it," added Edward. "Unnecessarily, I see."

They eyed each other. Edward's hair stood up in tufts, and his finely tailored coat was crushed and wrinkled. He looked wildly irritated, and as if he had slept in the chaise. "Are you all right?" he said.

Charlotte nodded. There was either nothing to say, or too much.

"My... mother?"

"I left her at your house."

"Did you?" Edward surveyed her warily. He started to speak, hesitated, then said, "I've been driving in circles around the damned countryside all night trying to get there. Up one lane, down another. Can't go this way, there's trouble; can't go that way, there's soldiers. Can't see to drive, have to stop by the roadside until it's light, for God's sake. Maddening."

"We all have our difficulties," replied Charlotte drily.

"Ah... yes. I am sorry." Edward looked away.

For his drunken advances? For not noticing his mother's unbalanced state? Charlotte decided it didn't matter. "You will have to do something about her..."

"I know!" The thought seemed to anger as much as oppress him. "I am on my way to do so."

"There is more... involved than you know." She couldn't tell him everything she had discovered here on the public highway, even if she could order her thoughts clearly enough.

Edward looked wary, then defeated. "Is there? How... delightful. I suppose I shall have to hear every sordid detail."

Charlotte simply nodded, holding his eyes in a long look.

"That bad, is it? Where are you going... Alec's?" She nodded again. "Then I shall have the... I can't say pleasure of seeing you there. But I will call." His jaw hardened. He turned to the driver of the chaise. "Move on!"

The post chaise edged past them and speeded up. Ethan slapped the reins, and their own horse leaned into the traces. None of them spoke. Lady Isabella's actions and fate were not matters they could comfortably discuss.

◆

Morning found Alec frustrated, anxious, and forced to admit the futility of his search. He was tired out; more importantly, his horse was exhausted. He could not drive it any harder. Simply getting home would be as much as the animal could manage. And they would have to go slowly, at that. Once there, he could call out his entire staff to comb the countryside for Charlotte. He could alert his neighbors. God knows what he would tell them, but he'd think of something. She had to be found. His heart contracted again at thoughts of what might have happened to her. He would do what he had to do. There had been plenty of wild stories out of his house in his grandparents' day, he thought with a grimace. He'd vowed there would never be more. But he saw no other choice.

◆

The first person Ethan saw when he drove the cart into the stable yard of the Wylde estate was his father. He stood in the middle of the cobbled space, arms akimbo, tall and scowling. It needed only this, Ethan thought. After the grueling journey and the uncomfortable night, now he was in for a tongue-lashing right in front of Lucy, along with the usual smirking stablemen he'd known since he was a lad.

He straightened on the cart seat. He wasn't going to stand for it. The time had come; he'd avoided it for too long.

He pulled up and threw the reins to one of the grooms. Jumping down, he helped first Lucy, then her mistress to the ground. "Hello, Dad," he said.

"What the devil do you think you're...?"

"This is Mrs. Charlotte Wylde." As he had known it would, the presence of gentry cut his father off. "And Miss Lucy Bowman." Lucy deserved just as much respect, in his eyes. "They're tired out and need to rest."

He watched his father throttle back his temper. His mother had told him what a long fight it had been for Dad to be able to control his quick anger. He admired that, when he wasn't wondering why he seemed to benefit so little from the effort. "Best take them inside then," the older man said. "But see you come right back and speak to me."

Ethan nodded and turned away, only to be faced with a new dilemma. By rights, Miss Charlotte should go to the front door, but... to perdition with the proprieties. The back door was right here, not around the house a hundred feet away. He guided the two women inside and along the corridor toward the front entry. Hobbs the steward would be in charge, with most of the senior staff in London for the Season, but he wasn't about to go to his offices, with his brother Sam sitting there and goggling at him and reporting it all to Dad. If he could find Sally Thorpe... they were friends; she'd help. As a senior housemaid, she could... But his luck had plumb run out. Alice Ramsay came bustling out of the kitchen after them. "Ethan Trask, what are you doing here?" she demanded. "You're supposed to be in London with the family. And who's this, then? Why are you trailing two females, uninvited, into the house?"

Alice got above herself at the least excuse. She imagined she was assistant housekeeper, when everyone knew she was just another parlor maid. "This is Mrs. Charlotte Wylde," he replied, playing his strongest card. "Relative of Sir Alexander's... come for..." For an instant his mind went blank. "Come for a visit," he finished.

Alice had an unerring instinct for a weak excuse. "A visit? With Mrs. Cole and the girls in town? Nobody visits at this time of the year."

Why didn't Miss Charlotte say something, Ethan wondered desperately? Alice would hear quality in her voice and pipe down. But she just stood there looking mortified. Lucy was flushed and staring at the floor. He couldn't bear it. "We can't leave Mrs. Wylde standing this way. Fetch some tea to the morning room, Alice."

"Don't you be giving me orders, Ethan Trask. I've half a mind to send for your mother." A small scared sound came from Lucy.

"Just go and tell Sir Alexander we're here!" He didn't want his mother brought into this just now, before he had a chance to explain some things. "He'll tell you all's well."

"Well, I can't, can I?" Alice gave him a triumphant smile. "He's been gone all night, no one knows where. Everyone's that worried, with hooligans roaming the countryside and him out trying to stop trouble, and maybe getting shot dead for his pains."

This time the sound came from Miss Charlotte. Ethan began to feel unfairly harassed. He hadn't planned beyond this point. Here was Lucy's mistress rescued. He was supposed to be a hero in Lucy's eyes, and instead he was standing in a hallway being mocked by Alice Ramsay. He'd never liked her, by God. "Come along," he said, and herded his charges on to the morning room. He sat them there, ignoring the nervous looks they gave him, and strode back to the kitchen, Alice trailing him like a foxhound on the scent. "Tea and some... scones or something to the morning room," he told a kitchen maid.

"You've no right..." began Alice.

"Relative of Sir Alexander's," he interrupted. "He'll be right glad to see her when he gets back." He fled before anyone could argue—only to bump into his father outside the kitchen door.

"There you are." He grasped Ethan's arm and urged him outside again. "You will tell me what's going on, my lad. I can't believe you deserted your post..."

"No, no, the family sent me up here." Miss Lizzy would back him up, Ethan was sure. But would it make any difference, her being a child?

"Sent you for what? You're not making any sense. And who is this Mrs. Charlotte Wylde? I don't know of any family by that name."

"She's Mr. Henry Wylde's widow."

"Oh, that one?" As always, gossip had passed from the servants in town to those in the country. It went faster than the mail, it seemed sometimes. "*She's* not what I expected. But what's she doing here?" He frowned. "And... they said you came rushing in yesterday, with *one* young woman, near to stole a cart..."

"I *borrowed* it. It's back safe and sound, isn't it? And Greylock, too?"

"Went haring off somewhere," his father continued as if he hadn't spoken, "out all night, and now you're back with *two* females and not a word of explanation for any of it."

Ethan slumped with fatigue and uncertainty. Lucy wouldn't want him telling tales about her mistress. And his dad never listened to him anyway. What was he supposed to say? "There's been some... trouble... with Lady Isabella. I... I reckon Sir Alexander will clear it up when he gets back."

"Huh." His father eyed him. "She's always been good at trouble."

He paused, and Ethan dared to hope he could escape for now. He wanted to find his mother, explain as best he could, and enlist her help. She'd know what to do about Lucy.

"What's this nonsense about you taking old Elkins's place?"

His hopes came crashing down. Of course this talk had to come when he was worn out and worried. But this was his dream. He had to fight for it. "I'm going to. We'll... I'll be moving into his cottage as soon as he goes. It's all settled with Sir Alexander." Ethan had gotten the final word on this from the steward soon after he asked for the post.

"And this is what you mean to do with your life?" burst from his father.

"Yes, sir, it is. I'm determined on it. It's what I've wanted since I was a lad."

His father glared at him. Ethan stood straighter and met his eyes, steady and determined though his throat was dry. After what seemed an endless time, the older man blew out a harsh breath. "Seems you're certain about it."

"I am. Never more certain about anything." With an effort, Ethan kept his gaze resolute.

"Well, then." The fire in his father's eyes slowly banked. "That's pretty much all I ever wanted to hear from you. Some kind of purpose. Some fight for what you want."

Ethan couldn't believe it. "You... it's all right then?"

"It was your fecklessness drove me distracted, son. If you've found the work you want to do, that you *care* about doing, then I'm glad for it."

Weak with relief, he went to find his mother.

❧

Lucy sat on the silken armchair and clenched her folded hands in her lap. It was just as she'd feared it would be all along. The staff peering at them and wondering how they came to be arriving with Ethan on their own, and no proper explanation to give them—because there wasn't one. She'd have liked to blame Ethan for bumbling his words. But what was he to say? *She* couldn't think of a lie that covered the circumstances. And anyway, she didn't want to be the cause of him lying to his family and friends.

She'd done something wildly improper, traveling alone with him all this way. She'd felt she had to do it,

that she couldn't bear to wait in London not knowing
what had become of her mistress. She wasn't sorry!
Well, she was, but… they'd found Miss Charlotte. All
right, maybe Ethan could have done that on his own.
Or maybe not. She'd picked the direction they turned
right before they came upon her. He said it made sense
to go the other way. They'd have missed her then, left
her to the mercy of those men with pikes. Who knows
what they might have done to her? It would have been
worse for Miss Charlotte to be in this house alone
amongst strangers, too. Only now Lucy had to face the
consequences. Ethan's mother was somewhere about;
he might bring her through the door at any moment.
The idea made her cringe.

Lucy wasn't used to disapproval. All her life she'd
worked hard, tried to learn all she could, gotten
along with most folks—well, not that wretched lot in
his house, but most others. And here she was about
to meet the one person whose respect she'd most
like to have—if the future Ethan had promised came
to be, that is—and she was afraid to look her in the
eye. Was she the sort of woman who'd understand
Lucy's choice? Ethan's father was stiff-necked and
particular, by all accounts. Wouldn't his mother be
the same? Lucy had worried they'd look down on
her as a mere farm laborer's daughter; she'd never
imagined they'd have cause to doubt her personal
respectability. How could Ethan have left her to face
this all alone? Where had he gone? And what was
he telling people? Surely he wouldn't mention their
attachment without speaking to her first? Only he
might. And then wouldn't the other servants stare?

What if… oh… what if his mother marched right in to object, when she hadn't said a word to Miss Charlotte about Ethan?

The morning room door opened, and Lucy's heart went to her throat. She stood quickly. But it was only a maid with a tray of tea things. She set it down in front of Miss Charlotte and gave her a kind smile. "Nice cup of tea for you, ma'am."

"Thank you." Miss Charlotte didn't sound like herself. Lucy looked at her and realized that she was at the end of her rope—drooping and silent and… sad somehow. That was strange.

"Is there anything else I can get you?" asked the maid.

Lucy stepped forward. She'd gotten so wrapped up in her own concerns, she wasn't doing what she'd come to do—take care of her mistress. That was her job and her right; the fact gave her courage. "Miss Charlotte's worn out," she said. It wasn't anyone's business why. "She needs to lie down someplace private."

The maid turned to her. She was curious; that was clear. But she seemed friendly, too. "Of course. I'll take you up to one of the guest rooms, shall I?"

Lucy nodded firmly. "I'll bring the tray."

"I can get…"

Lucy simply picked it up and waited. The maid led them out and down the hall to the front stairs—thankfully empty—then up to a pleasant bedchamber overlooking a walled garden. Lucy set the tea on a table by one of the wide windows.

"There you are. If you need anything, just ring. My name's Sally."

"Thank you," said Lucy and her mistress at the

same time. Sally gave them a last broad smile before closing the door behind her.

Miss Charlotte let out a long sigh. "Thank you, Lucy," she said. "I was… it is good to be away from everyone."

With tasks to do, Lucy's confidence returned. "Let's just take off your gown, Miss Charlotte, so it won't be crumpled. And then you can lie down in that bed and have a cup of tea, if you like, and maybe sleep awhile. I know you didn't get much sleep last night."

"No. I don't know if I will be able to…"

"Well, why not see?" She should have asked for her luggage to be brought up, Lucy thought. She'd been in too much of a hurry to get rid of the housemaid. She'd have to ring for it—later.

She bustled about, getting Miss Charlotte into bed. When she was settled there, her eyelids soon began to droop, and shortly she was asleep.

Lucy sat on a chaise by the second window. She had nowhere else to go. She looked out over the masses of flowers and trimmed shrubs in the garden. That would be Mr. Trask's work, she realized; another sign of Ethan's connection with this place. This was his home; he didn't feel alien and uncertain here, and he'd obviously abandoned her for his family and friends. But at least no one would enter this room without knocking. She'd have some warning. Lulled by Miss Charlotte's even breathing, she put her feet up on the chaise and lay back. In a very short time, Lucy was asleep as well. Silence descended on the room.

Twenty-five

WHEN ALEC PLODDED INTO THE STABLE YARD TWO hours later, he had no energy left. His thoughts were centered on food and sleep and a wash. He knew he had to rally to organize the search for Charlotte, and he would. That came first, no matter what. But his eyes felt gritty with lack of sleep, and his body ached from many hours in the saddle.

He blinked. The paved yard between the stables and the back door seemed remarkably crowded. Two maidservants were arguing with each other, one shaking a finger in the other's face. A pair of grinning grooms egged them on, and to the other side hovered… Ethan? Alec blinked again, wondering if his eyesight was failing from fatigue. It couldn't be Ethan. Ethan was in London. But it was him. The shorter, angrier maid turned, saw him, and bustled over like a hen chasing a beetle. Ethan hurried after her. "Thank heaven you're back, sir. There's been such doings here! Very irregular, as I told Ethan more than once."

Alec couldn't remember her name. He knew it, of course. But he was so tired.

"He had no right to be putting females in bedchambers and ordering tea made and I don't know what all, for all the world like he was in charge…"

Ethan stepped in front of her. "I knew you'd want…"

She popped out from behind him. "Don't you be pushing me aside, you great lug!"

"Ethan, what are you doing here?" Alec didn't speak loudly, but the yard went silent at the sound of his voice.

"I came up after Mrs. Wylde, sir."

"Cha…?" Alec shook his head to clear it.

"There was a note… only it didn't make any sense, and then I went to Lady Isabella's house and saw… It seemed like there was something wrong. So Lu… that is… I took the stage up to see if I could help. She's upstairs resting now."

"Wait, who is…?"

"Mrs. Wylde, sir."

"Cha… Mrs. Wylde is here?" Alec couldn't take it in. "Upstairs, here?"

"Yes, sir. She was worn out. We… I… took the liberty of having her put in a bedchamber."

"But…" All his searching, and she hadn't even needed him. She'd somehow come safe to his home on her own. "She's all right?"

"Yes, sir. Just tired, like I said." Ethan glanced around the yard, and Alec became aware of the circle of curious eyes. This discussion should be taken elsewhere.

But he couldn't help asking again, "You're sure?"

At his footman's confident nod, Alec finally released the tension he'd been holding through the night.

Slowly, his fear drained away. She was safe; it rang in his head like a refrain. Charlotte was all right.

Slowly, stiffly, he dismounted. "See to Blaze, Robin," he told a groom who hurried over, handing off his horse's reins. "He's been ridden too hard. See he gets plenty of oats, and a rest."

"Yes, sir." He led the horse away.

Alec wanted to see Charlotte, to be certain she really was all right. But Ethan had said she was resting. That was good. Rest was a very good idea. Very good. A few hours of sleep and he would be able to think, to wonder how she'd made it here from Aunt Bella's, and all that had occurred. For now... Alec headed inside. "Thank you, Ethan. Well done." The maid beside Ethan sniffed. Alec couldn't imagine why. "I've been up all night. I'm going to follow Mrs. Wylde's example." She was here, in a room in his house. In a daze, Alec sought out his own.

Ethan watched him go, wishing he could find a feather mattress and drop onto it himself. But his problems weren't over, not by a long shot. His mother was off visiting his sister, and wouldn't be back till tomorrow. He couldn't tell anyone about Lucy and their plans until he spoke to her. She'd skin him alive, in the first place, and anyway he needed her help in smoothing things over. He could tell her the whole story. There was no one on earth more trust-worthy. She'd understand why they'd traveled up here together, and she'd take his word that nothing wrong had gone on. As if he would! She'd like Lucy, too. He was certain about that. But she couldn't like her till she met her, and in the meantime there were cats like

Alice Ramsay making remarks and asking awkward questions. She'd shut her trap when Ethan's mother spoke to her! Till then, he had to stay alert and make sure nobody bad-mouthed Lucy, or Miss Charlotte for that matter. Sleep would have to wait.

❧

Charlotte woke in a strange bedchamber. It was a lovely room, hung with flowered chintz in soft yellows and blues. The scent of flowers drifted in through the open window. Lucy lay asleep on a chaise beneath it. The light outside slanted golden; it must be late in the day. All was quiet. She felt more rested, if not completely back to normal. She was in Sir Alexander's house, she remembered, safe.

She relaxed into the comfortable bed and sorted through jumbled memories. Her brain was finally clear of the confusion brought on by the drug given her, and she reviewed all that had happened in the last few days. Lady Isabella really had confessed to Henry's murder and the robbery attempt; that had not been a dream or delusion. She'd confessed without a trace of guilt. Charlotte still found it incredible. Clearly, Lady Isabella's mind was unbalanced. Somehow, she had concealed this, living in that sad, empty house, subsisting on gossip about other people's misfortunes. Why had no one noticed? Why hadn't her own son noticed?

Edward—he had gone to her. What would he do? And was it to be left up to him? Didn't she have an obligation to notify the authorities?

She could clear her name, an eager inner voice pointed out. The Bow Street Runner's hateful accusation would be proven wrong once and for all. She could have the pleasure of throwing his mistake back in his ferrety face and forcing him to apologize. She enjoyed that idea for a few minutes.

But her brief satisfaction would come at what cost? A murder trial in the family would bring scandal crashing down on all of them. Her own pitiable history with Henry would be dragged into a public courtroom and rehashed for all to hear. More than that, the gossip would spill over onto Alec and Anne and Lizzy and Frances. Perhaps *she* had no social position to protect, but it would wreck Anne's debut. Edward would be followed by whispers wherever he went; how he would detest that! She had a notion that trials went on for months; the *ton* would relish every twist and turn. She could see it so vividly—gentle Anne walking into a glittering ballroom and hearing murmurs fall silent, facing a sea of hard, avid eyes. Charlotte shivered and drew the coverlet higher. She couldn't let that happen.

No one but Alec knew the Runner had accused her. As far as the world was concerned, Henry Wylde had been killed by footpads. It was old news now, mostly forgotten, and no one had cared very much in the first place, Henry being Henry. Perhaps Lady Isabella's crimes could be kept secret, though of course something must be done about her... The main thing was—Alec must know the truth. That was all she really cared about, Charlotte realized. She had to forever erase that excruciating moment when he had looked at her with pained suspicion.

Charlotte clutched the bedclothes closer. Alec. She was in his home, but she didn't feel welcome. They'd been greeted with such reluctance. The servants would be gossiping about it even now. Why had she arrived unheralded in an old farm cart? Where was her luggage? Why was she visiting when all the ladies were away? That in itself was... say unorthodox, to be charitable. What would Alec say when he returned and found her here? When he heard the news she had to give him? Their first encounter since he'd held her in his arms would be fraught with complications. More complications. As if there were not enough already. Charlotte had a craven impulse to flee. Perhaps she and Lucy could sneak out to the stagecoach stop and...

A knock on the door brought Lucy upright. She blinked blearily, then jumped up at a second knock and opened the door. Two maids stood outside, the friendly one who had brought them upstairs, and the one who had made such a fuss about their arrival. The latter gazed avidly into the room. "We've brought your things," said the first cheerily. She carried a small valise. "And some hot water." The other maid had the can. "I'm to tell you dinner's in an hour."

"Has Sir Alexander returned?" Charlotte asked.

"Yes, ma'am." They deposited their burdens. "Is there anything else you need?"

"No," said Lucy. "That'll do fine. Thank you, Sally."

They left. Lucy rubbed her eyes and then bustled about opening the case and pouring hot water into the washbasin. "A good thing we took off your dress," she said. "It's not a bit crumpled. Too bad it's a morning gown, but that can't be helped. We've got your brushes and all, so that's all right."

Lucy's gown was sadly crushed from her nap on the chaise, Charlotte noticed. Her presence was such a comfort in this house. "I haven't thanked you properly, Lucy, for coming after me. I'm sorry. I believe the drug they gave me was still having an effect."

"No need for thanks." Lucy seemed subdued.

"Of course there is. You and Ethan…"

"Nothing improper went on, while we wa… were traveling!"

"I never imagined it did."

Lucy muttered something under her breath.

"Has anyone reproached you?" Charlotte's temper flared. "Just tell me and I will speak to…"

"No, no, nothing like that, miss."

"Believe me, I will see to it that they don't." Lucy gave her a smile but didn't look convinced. And indeed Charlotte understood that she could do little about servants' gossip.

"There's no need to worry," said Lucy, as if she spoke to herself as well as Charlotte. "I expect we'll be going back to London as soon as may be?"

"I was just thinking the same. But I believe stage-coaches generally leave in the early morning."

Lucy nodded. She gestured with the towel she was holding. "Best get ready for dinner, then." Her blue eyes were somehow bereft. Charlotte didn't understand it, but she felt the same melancholy in herself. She and Lucy had been together so long. She was a friend more than a servant, and yet… there seemed no way to voice the feelings that they clearly shared. "What would I do without you, Lucy?"

The words made the maid stiffen. Why?

"No worry about that," Lucy replied. "I'm right here. Come and wash before the water goes cold."

∽

Dinner in the "small" dining parlor was stilted. With servers continually in and out, bringing dishes and removing them, waiting just behind a swinging door to fulfill any requests, there was no opportunity for private talk. Charlotte, nearly bursting with the news she had to give Alec, struggled to find topics of conversation. She was also terribly aware of how odd it was for her to be dining alone with him, to be visiting him alone. She felt watched, and judged, and thoroughly uncomfortable. And Alec seemed a different man from the one who had left her bedchamber just a few days ago, much more like the distant gentleman she'd first met on the day of Henry's death. "What... do you have any news of the men who were marching to Nottingham?" she asked him.

"How do you know about that?" was the sharp reply.

"I... heard... about it." She couldn't tell him— here—that she'd been crouched in the darkness as they whipped themselves up to set off.

He closed his lips on another question. "A courier came by with news this afternoon, since I am one of the local magistrates. They marched on through Ripley, gathering more men, willing or not so willing in some cases. Toward Codnor and Langley Mill—you won't know these places, of course—they woke up several innkeepers demanding beer and bread and cheese. The beer made things worse, I'm sure. It was raining hard by then, and I'd wager a good few slipped away home.

Twenty Light Dragoons caught the remainder at Giltbrook, and they scattered under the charge. About forty men were captured. Not the leaders, they think, but those will be taken soon enough. The government won't rest until they are. Lord Sidmouth has a network of agents who will ferret them out."

Sidmouth was the Home Secretary, Charlotte remembered. "What will happen to them?" she wondered.

"Transportation to Australia for some. The leaders will surely be hanged." He said it with a weary finality.

"If that man…" Charlotte could almost remember the name shouted out. "If they hadn't fired on the house in the village…" Alec was scowling at her; she had forgotten again that he didn't know she'd been there.

"They killed a servant in Mary Hepworth's house in South Wingfield," he agreed after a short silence. "But even if they hadn't, the punishments would be the same. 'Armed insurrection' will not be tolerated."

"Insurrection?"

"That's what it is being called—that and high treason. Some of the leaders had formed 'revolutionary committees' and sketched out plans for a general uprising. These are not words any government can easily tolerate. The impulse may have come from unemployment and privation, but…" Alec threw his napkin on the table. "Have you finished eating?"

She had been moving the last bites around with her fork. She shouldn't waste food when people were starving, Charlotte thought. But she didn't want it. "Yes."

He rose. "Then perhaps we can go into the library and discuss… the family business that brought you here."

"Yes," she said again. Nervous now that the moment had finally come, Charlotte followed him out of the room.

❧

Ethan had no duties, as he was unexpectedly home, and neither did Lucy while her mistress was at dinner. So he shouldn't have had much difficulty spiriting her out of the house into the long golden June evening. Lucy herself was the problem. She stubbornly ignored his signals, sticking by Sally Thorpe in the servants' parlor as if they'd been friends all their lives. He finally had to resort to outright asking if she'd like to see the rose garden. "Grandad would be that glad to know you'd seen it."

"You know Ethan's grandad?" Alice Ramsay was quick to ask.

"And my grandmother, too," Ethan put in. "They're great friends."

"Really? How'd that come about?" Alice looked from Ethan to Lucy speculatively.

"All right." At last Lucy stood, though she didn't look happy. "I'll... I'd be glad to see Mr. Trask's gardens."

Ethan pulled her out and away before Alice could stick her nose in any further. He walked her fast down one path, and through a gate, and brought them out among swaths of heavy, sweet-smelling blooms.

"Oh," Lucy said.

"Right pretty, eh?" He looked out over the clusters of rose bushes spreading around them. A flood of reds and pinks and whites, climbing over an arbor and spilling along a stone wall, so many it was dizzying. The perfume was better than a hundred fancy shops. "You like roses, I remember." Lucy turned to him. "It was one of the first things you told me. White roses in the moonlight."

"Don't try to get around me when I'm mad at you, Ethan Trask!"

"Mad? Why?"

"You know very well why."

If that wasn't just like a female, claiming you knew what was in their heads when you had no blessed idea. And no warning. "I do not. We rescued Miss Charlotte, like we came to do, and…"

"And you just dropped me in it here, with everybody staring and making up Lord knows what stories. What your family must think of me! Not that I've met any of them, properly." She took a step away from him and stared down at a deep red rose.

He couldn't pretend not to understand what she meant, not with that dratted Alice snooping and sniping for all she was worth. "I've wanted to introduce you, official like. As soon as my mother gets back from visiting tomorrow, I'll tell her we're getting married. Best to tell her first. Well, I have to, Lucy. But she's a wonder, she is. She'll make it all right…"

"You'll what! I never said I'd marry you, Ethan Trask."

"You…" Hadn't she? Ethan distinctly remembered… what? Hadn't she said…? It was all settled. They were *here,* and he'd got the position, with the cottage and all. And it was okay with his dad, against all the odds. As soon as the family was back from town, they'd marry and move in. He'd seen it all in his mind, clear as clear.

"There's the matter of your lying to me. You're forgetting that, seemingly."

"Lucy! I didn't lie. I might not have told you…"

"That's the same as a lie!" She glared at him with those devastating blue eyes. "You think you can 'forget' to tell me things you don't want me to know whenever it suits you?"

"I won't do it again."

"How would I know whether you did?"

He was getting annoyed now. Why did she have to make things difficult? "Because I told you I won't, Lucy. I promise. You can trust my word."

"Oh, what does it matter?" Tears trembled in Lucy's eyes. "I can't leave Miss Charlotte, after all that's happened to her. She needs me more than ever."

"I thought you weren't going to let that stop…"

"And everybody here thinking I'm no better than I should be. How could I come to live among them? They'd always be whispering. I couldn't *bear* that."

"Nobody thinks…"

"It's no good, Ethan! It's not going to work. Just take your new job and your cottage and everything you always wanted and… be happy!" Lucy turned and fled from him. He chased her into the house, but under all the curious eyes waiting there he couldn't follow her up to Miss Charlotte's bedchamber and pound on the door like he wanted to. Thwarted, furious, Ethan strode back outside to sulk.

❧

At last, at long, long last, Alec had Charlotte to himself. When the library door closed behind them, it was all he could do not to sweep her into his arms and crush her to him. All the details of their last time together flooded him—the feel of her skin, her lips, the soft sounds she'd made when he touched her just... His body responded so strongly to the memory that when her lips parted to speak he nearly groaned.

"I have to tell you about Lady Isabella," she said.

Longing to consign his aunt to perdition, Alec offered her a chair and took one himself.

"You will find this hard to believe, I know, but she was the one who..."

Maddeningly, there was a knock at the door. One of the footmen looked in. "Mr. Edward Danforth is here, Sir Alexander. He says it's very important that he see you."

"Damned right it's important." Edward pushed in past the servant. "All right, man, you may go. No, wait, bring me some sandwiches. I'm perishing from hunger."

The footman looked to Sir Alexander for permission, got an exasperated nod, and left.

Edward stalked in and dropped onto the sofa. "Have you got any brandy? There's nothing at... at *my* house, and by God I need some."

Could he throw his cousin out, Alec wondered? Just take him by the collar and the seat of his fine tailored breeches and... No. He went over to the sideboard and poured them both stiff brandies. "Charlotte?" She shook her head.

Edward drank deep and let out a sigh. "I've gotten most of it out of Martha," he said heavily. "I think so anyway. But I wanted to hear your story. I can't trust her not to have distorted things to her own advantage."

Charlotte nodded. "I've had to sort through my memories to be sure. They gave me something..."

"Laudanum," supplied Edward. In answer to Alec's horrified look, he added, "Yes, just as Martha used to give Grandmama. Mixed in wine or milk. It is what she knows." His tone was dry as dust. "Keeps her charge quiet when she gets... hysterical. I blame the drug for much of what occurred."

"And what is that?" Alec hated the feeling of being on the outside of knowledge that Charlotte and Edward obviously shared.

"I'm clear now on what I heard," Charlotte continued. She swallowed. "Lady Isabella killed Henry."

"What?" He couldn't have heard correctly, Alec thought. But Edward was nodding. "How could she possibly...?"

"She was the thief at my house, too. She had Henry's cabinet keys and thought to take something to sell."

"But..." Alec's mind whirled. He grasped at the tatters of reason. "Begin at the beginning and tell me everything that happened, in order."

And so she did, talking for half an hour, with one interruption for the arrival of sandwiches and the occasional interjection from Edward. Alec listened with mounting horror, particularly when Charlotte revealed the danger she'd been in, but also at the revelation of more mental disturbance in his family. Aunt Bella's aberration was far worse than his grandmother's. *She* had sniped and railed and thrown china;

she'd been devious and selfish, though he could remember, too, flashes of gaiety that captivated a small child. Aunt Bella had gone so far beyond that line it was mind-boggling.

When Charlotte finished, there was a long silence in the library.

Edward went over to refill his glass. When he offered the decanter to Alec, he snatched it away and sloshed brandy into his own. Charlotte had glossed over her reason for fleeing the carriage after the opera, but the gap was easy enough to fill. Alec wondered if punching his cousin in the face would relieve his feelings. Possibly. But it wouldn't solve the far larger problem of Aunt Bella. He drank, then topped up his glass once again. The three of them stared at each other. "And so it was all about money?" Alec said at last.

"Money to keep up her social position," Charlotte corrected. "Lady Isabella sold all her own things…"

"*My* things," Edward interrupted gloomily.

She nodded. "To buy the latest fashions and keep a carriage and… everything. And when they were gone, she formed the scheme of producing 'antiquities' for Henry to buy. But then, that wasn't enough. So she thought to get Henry's legacy for Edward."

His cousin winced, drained his second brandy.

"Why didn't you notice how much she was spending?" Alec asked him.

"I can't keep track of everything."

"You don't know the revenues from your own estate?" Alec's contempt leaked into the words.

"Of course I do! I just… I needed an income

myself." He shrugged defensively. "I thought Mama practiced economies…"

"Aunt Bella?"

"Well, she didn't want me asking, did she? She threw a fit if I tried to discover anything about her expenditures. I hate brangling." He reached for the decanter again, and Alec gave it to him. "Was I supposed to question the word of my own mother?"

"Apparently, that would have been wise."

"Oh, it's easy for you with *your* income and your damned…"

"What is to be done?" asked Charlotte in a crisp voice that cut through the incipient quarrel.

There was another uncomfortable silence.

"I know she deserves…" began Edward. "I know strong measures must be taken, but she is my mother. I can't send her to the gallows, for God's sake."

"She is a murderer!" Alec pointed out.

"I know! But if it all comes out, the scandal wouldn't stop with her."

"Your difficulties seem to be of your own…"

"I'm mostly worried about Anne," said Charlotte. Startled, Alec turned to her. "Her come-out would be a disaster if Lady Isabella were publicly accused and tried."

She paused, and Alec saw the whole dreadful picture as her words sank in.

"There's Lizzy and Frances, too. It would be awful for them. And not fair; they haven't done anything wrong."

"The Earntons," added Edward in a frightened murmur. "My God, Amelia Earnton would skin me alive."

Alec couldn't argue with that. "We must do something. Aunt Bella cannot be left to... to go on as she has been."

"No. I've been thinking of little else, you may believe. And I have a... proposal." Edward drank from his glass. "You have some kind of place up in Scotland, don't you, Alec?"

"A lodge near Inverness," he agreed.

"I was thinking we could send Mama up there, with suitable... helpers. *Not* Martha."

Alec considered the idea.

"I know it belongs to you, and she is my mother. Perhaps you think I should keep her here at my house..."

"No!" He did not want the newly revealed Aunt Bella for a neighbor. "I've never used the place. Grandfather bought it thinking he would hunt there, I believe."

"Or get away from Grandmama," Edward offered, some of his customary humor surfacing.

"It's rather rustic, I understand." He couldn't imagine Aunt Bella in such a place. But did that really matter? No.

"Right at this moment, I don't care," was his cousin's reply. "The farther it's buried in the hinterlands, the better."

Alec nodded. "Very well. We... you must find some trustworthy... staff."

"And that fellow St. Cyr will have to be squared away," answered Edward.

"I shall leave it all to you." Now that the matter was settled, Alec wanted Edward out of the way more than he had ever wanted anything in his life. "Can we end this now? It's late and we are all tired." Charlotte looked exhausted.

"Yes, all right." Edward rose, stumbled on the edge of a carpet, and sank back down into the sofa cushions. "Can I have a bed for the night, Alec? I'm half soused, and anyway I don't want to go back. She's sent all the servants off on 'holiday' except Martha and some ghastly old crone."

Trapped, Alec went to ring the bell.

"I'm going to bed," said Charlotte, standing.

Alec almost protested aloud. He had to talk to her.

"I'll make arrangements to return to London in the morning," she added.

"No!" The others looked at him, startled. Alec nearly cursed aloud. There was nothing he could say with Edward lolling so annoyingly on his library sofa. They were still staring at him. "I... I would be happy to... do that for you."

With one wide-eyed look at him, Charlotte slipped away. Why had he said *that*? Damn, damn, damn.

"Trouble in that quarter, cuz?" his cousin smirked.

Alec spoke through clenched teeth. "If you start in on me now, Edward, you will be very, very sorry."

For once in his life, Edward shut his mouth.

Alec stood by the bellpull, all that he had heard tonight churning in his brain. Without meaning to, he spoke the question aloud. "Do you ever worry that there is some... thread of instability running through our family? A temperamental imbalance? Our grand-mother, and now your mother..."

"Hogwash!" Edward sat up straight and scowled

at him. "Instability? My father was as stable as a clod of earth. Yours was dull as ditchwater. I didn't know your mother well, but if she was anything like her sister Earnton…!" He shivered. "My mother lived under Grandmama's thumb for the first thirty years of her life. You have never made any allowances for that."

"I know it was difficult for…"

"Difficult! She was terrorized from earliest childhood. This does not excuse what she has done, of course, but in my mind it goes some way toward explaining it. That and Martha's 'medicines.' We're not under some… curse, Alec. My God, you're as steady as your parents. More! And whatever you may think of me, at bottom I'm quite… level-headed."

The footman arrived, and Alec gave the order for a room to be prepared. When Edward had gone, he stayed, contemplating the idea that the parent he'd modeled his life around could be seen as dull as ditchwater.

❧

He didn't want her here, Charlotte thought as she walked toward her bedchamber. He wanted her gone, had offered to speed her on her way. He'd scarcely looked at her as they talked. He was regretting their time together in her bed. He saw her as a mistake. Everything was horrible. Tears burned in her throat; she choked them back and entered her room to find her maid sitting on the chaise with reddened eyes. She jumped up as if stung. "Lucy, have you been crying?"

"No, miss! My eyes is just tired, that's all. From… from everything."

"It has been a bit too much, hasn't it?"

Lucy merely nodded.

"We need to go back to London, to our own place." The idea wasn't comforting, not in the least.

"I asked about the stagecoach to London," replied Lucy dully. "It goes through the village near here at eight in the morning."

"Oh. Good. We shall be on... Ah, I have no money. I shall have to ask Sir Alexander..." The idea revolted her.

"I have some. Enough." Lucy hadn't told Ethan she'd brought her savings, as she'd been certain he'd make a fuss about it—the great lug. She'd known it would come in handy.

"You think of everything, Lucy. Of course I will pay you back as soon as we are... home again." The word didn't sound right. But that house in London was her home, and would be from now on, with no Lady Isabella to invite her to society outings. Edward wouldn't want to see her, any more than Alec; she would forever be a reminder of his mother's disgrace.

"Yes, miss."

They gazed at each other with identical bereft expressions, then simultaneously looked away.

～

Alec sat on in the empty library, brooding. There was nothing else to call it, but he was too keyed up for sleep, too worn out for anything else. He'd sent all the servants to bed; the candles were burning down; and still he sat, thinking about Charlotte. She filled his mind and all his senses. When he'd held her in his arms in the dimness of her bedchamber, had his hands on her skin, his lips on hers, it had been all a man could want in this world. When he'd thought her in danger, perhaps injured or lost, he'd realized he couldn't live without her. That moment, at least, had been sharp and certain; he would have done anything to get her back. Then, he hadn't been needed to save her. That rankled, though it shouldn't, he supposed. Listening to her tell the story of what his aunt had done, he'd resented his absence from the tale. He had, he admitted, though it was petty and ridiculous. He'd wished... yes, that was it. He'd wished to show her that some member of his family could act... virtuously, for *her* rather than themselves. Instead, Charlotte had had a frightening demonstration of the legacy of... not instability perhaps, but... unhappiness handed down the generations of Wyldes. *Another* demonstration, he amended; she'd already had a strong dose from his reprehensible Uncle Henry. How could she wish to form a closer connection with such a family? For that was what he wanted, Alec realized. He wanted her as his wife. Nothing less, and no other woman, would do.

He rose and paced the Turkish carpet. She'd come to his arms so ardently, back in London, surely she wanted the same? Or had, before Aunt Bella drugged her and threatened her. She'd joined their conference here in the library as if she belonged, without recrimination. And she'd sworn she would never be called "Mrs. Wylde" again. Alec rubbed his forehead as if that could order his whirling thoughts.

Charlotte wanted to go back to town. He couldn't

bear to let her go, and yet... perhaps that might be
best? She could go, and he would see her later there
and tell her...? Coward, said a mocking inner voice.

Though he knew it was a mistake, Alec went over
and poured another brandy. The drink made his head
even fuzzier, which was good... and bad. One more,
and he might not be able to think at all. No, that was a
bad idea. Feeling slightly ill, he decided to step out for
a breath of air. He'd check on Blaze. Poor old Blaze.
A fine mount, he'd pushed him too hard, and all for
naught. Nobody had needed him. Nobody at all.

The stables were dark and quiet, pleasant with the
familiar smells of hay and manure. Clumsily, Alec lit
a lantern and carried it along the aisle toward Blaze's
stall. His pulse jumped when a dark figure rose from a
stack of hay bales "Who's that?" He raised the lantern
high to show the man's face. "Ethan?"

"Yes, sir," came the heavy answer.

"What are you doing out here at this hour?"

"Nothing, sir. Just... thinking, like." His luck was
right out tonight, Ethan thought. He'd been sure no
one would look for him here, it being his father's
domain and everyone knowing their history. Now,
unbelievably, here was the master himself, and he was
in trouble. He held the evidence behind his back, and
of course the thrice-damned bottle clinked on a
button on his coat. Now he was for it. First Lucy; and
maybe he would lose everything else, too.

"What have you got there?"

Half blinded by the lantern light, Ethan just gave
up. "It's a... a bottle of rum my cousin Jack brought
me, from Ja... Jam... someplace in the Indies." Not

wanting to ask in the kitchen for a drink, and be told no anyhow, he'd fetched the bottle from his attic room. First time he'd even opened the cursed thing! He'd wanted just one quiet drink. All right, maybe he'd had two. But he wasn't drunk, and he wasn't on the job, anyway. Not that that'd matter if Sir Alexander chose to object. Ethan saw his dreams keeling over like a felled tree.

Alec's heart had slowed down again. He lowered the lantern. "Jamaican rum, eh? Can I try a taste?"

Startled, and almost hopeful, Ethan drew the dark bottle from behind him. "O' course, sir." He wiped the mouth on his sleeve and held it out.

Alec set the lantern carefully on the dirt floor, well away from the hay. He took the rum and tilted down a healthy swallow. Raw fire lit his throat and roiled in his already uncertain stomach. "Ah, that's... hah... that's done it." He had to sit. He moved to the stack of bales next to his footman and hit it with a thump. The stable wheeled about him for a moment. "Oh, Lord." Definitely an error of judgment.

Ethan watched the master slump on the hay and wondered what to do. Should he call someone to help get him to bed? He didn't want to be caught here with the bottle. Sir Alexander thrust it at him. "You'd better take this." Ethan took it. "Sit, sit," he added. Uneasily, Ethan sank down beside him. This was a wonder, and no mistake, side by side with the master on a hay bale, and him deeper in his cups than Ethan could ever remember. "What were you out here thinking about?" he asked.

Why had he said that? Why had he been such a

fool as to come out here in the first place? He tried to think of a safe answer, but his brain didn't seem to be working. The unvarnished truth popped out of his mouth. "Love."

"You too? Is it contagious?"

Ethan kept his mouth shut this time. He didn't want to be asked about Lucy.

"Do you believe in love then, Ethan? Do you believe one can marry for love and not face disaster?" Alec heard himself slur a word or two and found he couldn't care.

Had he learned about him and Lucy somehow? But no, he couldn't have. "I've seen it in my own parents, sir. They're right happy together, after thirty years."

"Are they? And how do they manage that?"

"Well…" He didn't know what to say. He'd never considered the matter. They just were. "I… I reckon they respect each other, sir." The thoughts came to him as he voiced them, surprising him, from some unsuspected store of experience. "And they… it seems to me they like each other as well as loving. Uh, friendly, I mean. They're not much alike, maybe, but… at bottom they… they agree on really important things."

"Hah." This sounded rather sensible, not the airy-fairy nonsense people often talked about love.

Ethan, heart in his mouth, his own happiness in the balance, dared everything. "Was… were you thinking of Miss Charlotte, sir?"

"Miss…? Ah, her maid still calls her that, doesn't she? It's rather endearing." There was a word he never used, observed some distant part of Alec—the part that kept informing him he was drunk and should get himself inside and to bed. He continued to ignore it. "I was thinking of her. Yes. Do you remember my grandparents at all, Ethan?"

He blinked at this change of subject. "No, sir. Not really. I've heard… that is…"

"I can imagine. They were a love match, you know. And it went very bad."

"Well, my mum says…" Ethan lost his nerve for a moment. Would Sir Alexander reprimand him—or worse, his mother—for gossiping about the family? All the servants did, of course.

"Yes? Tell me what she said."

He didn't sound angry. "Well… Mum says it never was a love match, just some kind of… of brainstorm. Seeing as how they only knew each other a matter of weeks and never… endured anything together." Ethan had always admired the way his mother could speak so clearly and get to the heart of a matter. There was no one whose opinions he valued more. "Mum says a real love match is when you've seen how the other person acts when things are tough, like. And even if maybe you don't agree with them about… whatever it was, you understand, and you still feel certain how you feel." That last hadn't come out quite right. Ethan realized that the master was staring at him, openmouthed. He closed his own.

Silence enveloped the stable. Ethan shifted nervously. He'd forgotten his place in a big way. His mother would have boxed his ears if she'd heard all that. And he didn't know if it had been helpful, or just bone stupid.

After what seemed forever, Sir Alexander spoke. "It seems a night for home truths."

"I beg your pardon, sir?"

"Nothing. It appears she's a very wise woman, your mother."

Limp with relief, Ethan nodded. "She is that."

Sir Alexander leaned back against the pile of hay bales. He began muttering to himself, almost as if he was having a conversation with someone unseen. Ethan grew uneasy. He could do no more; he'd dared as far as he was able. "I should fetch somebody to help you inside." The master was too big a man to handle by himself in this state.

"No, no, I don't want that. I've sent everyone to bed. I'll just rest here a bit longer. You can go if you like."

As if he'd leave him here alone in the stables; Ethan leaned back as well, waiting. Minutes passed. The master stopped muttering. Gradually, Ethan realized that he'd fallen asleep. Now, what should he do? He'd been told not to wake anybody, and he was that worn out himself he couldn't hardly keep his eyes open. In fact... In another moment, Ethan was sleeping, too.

Twenty-six

NEITHER CHARLOTTE NOR LUCY SLEPT WELL. LUCY hadn't had the heart to go to the servants' quarters and face the curiosity of that Alice, and the others. She'd taken the chaise once again. It was broad and comfortable, but she tossed and turned nonetheless. The first light of dawn was pinking the sky, and the birds were just beginning to sing, when they rose and dressed. Lucy packed the small valise. "Stableboys rise very early, I believe," Miss Charlotte said. "We will go out and find someone to drive us to the stagecoach stop." Lucy didn't think they'd be about quite so early as this, but she didn't argue. It was best that they go. She'd come for Miss Charlotte, and she'd gotten her, and that was the end of the matter. Ethan... what if he'd spoken to his mother already? What if she was just waiting for morning to come and give Lucy the once-over and tell her she wasn't near good enough for her precious son? Maybe she wasn't... wouldn't, but... she just hadn't thought it through, Lucy admitted. She'd dreamed of coming to Derbyshire with Ethan, of settling here as his wife. She hadn't considered the sort of introduction this impulsive journey would provide. Could be she was making too much of it, as Ethan seemed to believe. She understood now, though, just how much she valued the respect she'd earned in other households.

"Lucy?" Miss Charlotte was standing by the door.

"Yes, miss. I'm ready."

They crept out like housebreakers into the cool fresh air of a June morning. Lucy breathed deep. They'd be back in the smelly city all too soon. Walking quietly, they went into the stables. As Lucy had feared, there was no one about, no sound but the soft stamps of horses' hooves in their stalls. Except… there was something… not… snoring?

They rounded a stack of hay bales and came upon two large men sprawled untidily over them, sound asleep. There was a dark brown bottle on the dirt floor, alongside a lantern.

"Alec!" said Miss Charlotte.

"Ethan!" said Lucy at the same moment.

With a snort and a jerk, Ethan woke. He peered at them, bleary eyed, then sprang to his feet. His knee knocked into Sir Alexander's on the way up, and he opened his eyes, too. Right away he closed them again, as if the light hurt him. Lucy couldn't take it in. How could footman and master be lying out here like two tosspots after a rowdy night? It was unheard of; it was… unseemly.

Sir Alexander opened his eyes again. "Oh my God, you really are there, aren't you?"

"We are not phantoms of a drink-addled brain," replied Miss Charlotte sharply.

Sir Alexander threw up a hand. "Not so loud, if you please."

Ethan stood there like he'd been stuffed. Well, what could he say, after all, the great lug? "And when I think how you told me off for a few glasses of champagne!" Miss Charlotte didn't lower her voice the least bit.

Sir Alexander winced. "What?"

"What in the world are you doing out...? No. I don't care. All I require is someone to drive me to the stagecoach stop." She turned and looked around as if expecting a stableboy to have shown up. The same idea seemed to occur to the two men. Ethan looked anxious. Sir Alexander sat straighter, pale and pained. "You can't go," he said. "I must speak to you."

"I am going, and you are obviously in no state for conversation."

"I forbid you to go."

"You... what?"

He'd made a mistake there, Lucy thought. That was no way to get 'round Miss Charlotte, never had been since she was a little girl. Her eyes had taken on that sparkle that meant she was mad as fire.

Sir Alexander struggled to his feet. He seemed steady once he got there. "You can't go," he said again. "Please... Ch..."

"You cannot stop me! You... you... drunkard!"

Oh, now she'd made him angry. Lucy could see it in his face. It was true that wasn't quite fair. She'd never heard that he drank much. She looked to Ethan, but he wasn't going to be any help. He was watching the stable door like the wrath of God might come roaring in any minute.

"I can tell my staff not to transport you," said Sir Alexander through gritted teeth.

"How dare you? I will walk!" Yes, Miss Charlotte was right furious now.

"I will have you fetched back," he snapped. "Carried, if necessary."

"You wouldn't…"

"This is not the moment to test what I would do, believe me. And please don't shout." Miss Charlotte clenched her fists at her sides and glared at him. Lucy heard stirrings above, where the stableboys slept.

"We… we should go in," said Ethan. He was nearly as pale as his master.

"An excellent idea. We should *all* go in, take a little time to… freshen up, and then…"

Miss Charlotte whirled in a flurry of skirts and started marching back to the house. Lucy could do nothing but follow her. As she went, she heard Sir Alexander say, "Ethan, get someone to bring water and headache powders to my room, at once."

An hour or so later, Ethan showed up at the door of Miss Charlotte's bedchamber, which was improper, but Lucy was beyond caring by this time. Her mistress had sat fuming and muttering the whole time, and now she headed for the library with murder in her eye. It was all going from bad to worse.

"Come on," said Ethan.

"Where?"

"Never mind, just come."

"I don't want to see anybody…"

"You won't be seeing anyone but me." Ethan practically dragged Lucy from the bedchamber, down the still mostly empty halls, and out to the rose garden. It was the best place he could think of; the sweet scents and rich color might soften her up. Also, no one was likely to be in this part of the garden so early in the morning.

"What are you doing? Let go of me, Ethan Trask!"

But she hadn't said it until they'd made it to the roses, which he took as a good sign.

"And what on earth were you doing in the stables, drinking with Sir Alexander?"

"That was odd," he admitted.

"Odd?" She glared at him out of those clear blue eyes he always got lost in.

"I'd gone off by myself, because you'd been so harsh with me, Lucy."

She snorted.

"And I was having one drink to… console myself, like." He responded to her expression. "It was just… well, all right, two drinks, Lucy. But no more than that, I swear." When her face remained stony, he added, "Do I seem like I had too much?"

Lucy eyed him. He wasn't pale anymore, like he had been in the stables. He looked like he always did, tall and handsome and nigh irresistible and… heaven help her.

Ethan nodded. "And the master comes in, soused already."

"Ethan!"

"Well, he was. And then he had some of the rum Cousin Jack brought me and then he orders me not to fetch anyone to take him in. I couldn't just leave him there!"

Lucy could see this.

"And I was that tired, I fell asleep. But that's not what I wanted to tell you." This was the moment. Ethan was stepping into unknown territory once again, and even more nervous than last night, if that was possible. "The thing is, Lucy, Sir Alexander's in love with Miss Charlotte."

"What?"

"He told me so."

"Told *you*? Whyever would he tell you?"

"Well, he wasn't himself, was he? I'd bet anything he's offering for her in the library right now." Before she could recover from this surprise, Ethan grabbed her hand and sank to one knee. "It makes everything right, don't you see? Oh, Lucy, you will marry me, won't you? I don't see how I can live without you, and that's a fact."

She gazed down at him. His deep, dark eyes were utterly sincere. She felt like she could read his soul in them. His hand was strong and sure on hers. "You won't be telling me any more lies?"

"Never!"

All the complications that'd been plaguing her seemed to fly away. Whatever people here thought of her, whatever was happening in the library, she didn't think she could live without him either. "Yes. Yes, I will."

Ethan surged to his feet and swept her into his arms. For the very first time, this place felt like home.

❧

Charlotte sailed into the library on a wave of anger. Yet through it ran a thread of hope that she couldn't suppress, even though she despised herself for it. He didn't want her to go. He'd threatened extreme measures—outrageous, insulting measures—to keep her here. She wasn't an unwelcome intruder in his house. Not that that meant he could order her about. "How dare you summon me as if I were your servant?" she demanded when the door had closed behind her.

"I didn't. I merely invited you to my library for an important conversation."

He looked almost back to his usual self—handsome and magnetic, and smug and incredibly irritating. Charlotte crossed her arms and raised her chin. "Yes?"

"Will you sit down?"

"No." He raised his brows as if she were being stupidly unreasonable. She hated it when he did that! "Then we will stand. Charlotte…"

He said her name in the way that made her breath catch, and then he said nothing more. He was looking at her as he had that night in her bed, a look to melt bones. Why didn't he go on? "Yes?" she said, her voice a bit unsteady.

"When I thought that something might have happened to you, that I might have lost you… I realized…"

Charlotte had begun to tremble. This man who always had so much to say seemed suddenly stricken with a maddening inability to talk.

"That I can't ever lose you. You must marry me." She blinked. "Must?"

"I meant…"

"You are to command, and I am to obey. Is that it?" So much of her cried—yes! But was this the way she was to be asked? Or, more like, not asked.

"I didn't say it properly…"

"Say what, precisely?" If he could do no better than this… Charlotte nearly burst into tears from the turmoil within her.

He strode over and grasped her arms. "Say that I love you with all my heart. And I want you to be my wife more than I've ever wanted anything."

The tension went out of her on a long sigh. Her heart pounded with joy and relief. "I thought you had vowed never to make a love match?"

"The devil with what I said. I was an idiot."

"You can be, but… yes. I am so in love with you, and yes."

He pulled her into a kiss that drowned out everything but the feel of his hands on her, the taste of his lips, the glorious knowledge that this and so much more was her future. It was an endless time before they separated, and then only to sit close together on the sofa, his arm warm on her shoulders.

A thought suddenly occurred to Charlotte. "Oh."

"What?"

"Mrs. Wylde. I never wanted to hear that name again."

"Well, you will be Lady Charlotte Wylde. Entirely different."

"Umm." She smiled impishly at him. "I suppose it's all right then." She raised her lips again, and he took them.

Twenty-seven

JULY WAS A LOVELY MONTH FOR WEDDINGS IN Derbyshire. The stone church near Sir Alexander Wylde's estate was draped with pink climbing roses, the air saturated with their scent. All through the adjoining village, flowers bloomed and bees were busy.

On a sunny day near the end of the month, there were two ceremonies scheduled, and all of Sir Alexander's staff had been given the entire day off. Hired help from the village would put the finishing touches on a feast that had occupied many hands for many hours, and serve it through the day's continuous celebration.

Early that morning, Lucy Bowman sat before a dressing table mirror, enjoying the expert ministrations of Jennings herself. And if that wasn't enough to intimidate, on top of wedding nerves, a knock on the door brought Ethan's mother into the room. Jennings patted her shoulders and said, "You'll do." As she went out, Lucy wanted to beg her not to leave. She was not yet at ease with her soon-to-be mother-in-law. Though any awkwardness over her traveling with Ethan had been smoothed over, she remained in awe of this self-assured woman with Ethan's dark hair and deep eyes. Her smile was kind, though. "I came to be sure you know how welcome you are to our family," she said.

"You don't know me very well," Lucy couldn't stop herself from pointing out.

"I know my son, and I've never seen him so... steady in himself. It's a delight and no mistake."

"I mean to be a good wife to him. To make him happy."

"My dear, you already have." The smile that came with this reply made Lucy's heart swell with joy.

❧

Ethan Trask, who'd been dressed and ready for an hour, fidgeted about the family home, unable to light anywhere. "Nervous?" asked his brother Sam, who would be standing up with him at the altar. He looked amused.

Ethan nodded. "Not about the big thing. Lucy's what I want, no doubts there. I just want to make it through the service properly, you know? I don't want to flub the words and spoil it for her."

"You won't."

"I hope not. You're the one always puts every foot right, Sam. Not me."

"Seems to me that's a thing of the past, brother."

Ethan met his eyes and saw the conviction there. "Really?" It meant a lot hearing this from Sam.

"It's what I think. Dad, too."

"He said that?"

Sam gave him a nod, and a wide grin.

Ethan grinned back at him. "Cor!"

~

Jennings had moved on to Charlotte's luxurious bedchamber and was dressing her hair when Frances Cole looked in. "May I watch Jennings do her customary superb job?"

"Of course." Charlotte was very glad to see her. This was a time when she particularly felt the lack of family, and Frances was almost like family for her. They sat companionably together while the dresser worked her magic. When she had finished and gone, Frances said, "What is it?"

"Am I so transparent?" Charlotte tried to laugh. "It's just... marriage. My history with it isn't... good. I don't really think I'm making a mistake, but..."

"Does it feel the same as the other time?"

"No! Of course not. Nothing like."

"And Alec is nothing like Henry."

"I know. I know. I'm just being silly."

"It's not silly. Nerves are natural before taking a big step in the world. I've felt it."

"About your trip to Greece this winter?"

"Yes. But you have to dare to take what you want, don't you?"

"Yes," said Charlotte, her mood lightening. "Yes!"

"You and Alec had all those adventures without me. I mean to have some of my own—a bit less... strenuous, of course."

"I should hope so. I'm finished with adventures myself."

"Oh, I wouldn't be so sure of that. Lizzy is all yours now."

"Ah." They laughed together.

❧

Down the corridor, Alec had answered a summons from his Aunt Earnton, who had surprised him by making the trip up from London for this day. "I hope you know what you're doing, Alec."

"I do." He smiled, in high spirits. "I'll be saying that later, won't I? I definitely do."

"It's not a good match. It's not even a decent match."

"Nevertheless, it is the match for me."

"This is not what I expected from you, of all people. You've always been so sensible."

"I have, haven't I?" He smiled at her perplexity. "Don't worry, Aunt, you'll come to like her."

"Oh, like her. I do like her. She's a charming girl. But…"

"It's going to be fine, you'll see." He dropped a kiss on his staid aunt's cheek, clearly startling her.

After a moment, she smiled. "Perhaps it will, after all."

❧

Later that morning Lucy Bowman walked down the aisle on her father's arm, aglow in a gown of white muslin sprigged with blue that matched her eyes. Ethan Trask awaited her at the altar, unable to suppress a grin at the lovely sight she presented.

The second ceremony was somewhat grander, though no more joyful. The groom's sisters looked ravishing, and more than delighted, in rose pink gowns.

And though the youngest, Lizzy, carried an oddly large basket instead of flowers, which was distinctly heard to meow during a pause in the music, no one minded. As they watched Sir Alexander Wylde and Charlotte Rutherford Wylde exchange their vows, onlookers smiled and nodded to each other and said in satisfied whispers, "You know, it's a love match."

Checkmate, My Lord

by Tracey Devlyn

The stakes are high, the players in position…

Catherine Ashcroft leads a quiet life caring for her precocious seven-year-old daughter, until a late-night visitor delivers a startling ultimatum. She will match wits with the enigmatic Earl of Somerton, and it's not just her heart that's in danger.

Let the games begin…

Spymaster Sebastian Danvers, Earl of Somerton, is famous for his cunning. Few can outwit him and even fewer dare challenge him—until now. After returning to his country estate, his no-nonsense neighbor turns her seductive wiles on him—but why would a respectable widow like Catherine risk scandal for a few passionate nights in his bed?

Praise for *A Lady's Revenge:*

"Devlyn makes a unique mark on the genre with her powerful prose and gripping theme."—RT Book Reviews, *4 Stars*

"Devlyn reveals the darkness of the spy game and entices readers with a talented and determined heroine."—Publishers Weekly

For more Tracey Devlyn, visit:

www.sourcebooks.com

Lady Eve's Indiscretion

by Grace Burrowes

—— ❦ ——

Lady Eve's got the perfect plan

Pretty, petite Evie Windham has been more indiscreet than her parents, the Duke and Duchess of Moreland, suspect. Fearing that a wedding night would reveal her past, she's running out of excuses to dodge adoring swains. Lucas Denning, the newly titled Marquis of Deene, has reasons of his own for avoiding marriage. So Evie and Deene strike a deal, each agreeing to be the other's decoy. At this rate matrimony could be avoided indefinitely... until the two are caught in a steamy kiss that no one was supposed to see.

—— ❦ ——

Praise for bestselling author Grace Burrowes:

"Delicious... Burrowes delivers red-hot chemistry with a masterful mix of playfulness and sensuality."
—Publisher's Weekly *Starred Review*

"Captivating... Historical romance at its finest and rife with mystery and intrigue."
—Romance Fiction *on* Suite 101

For more Grace Burrowes, visit:
www.sourcebooks.com

When You Give a Duke a Diamond

by Shana Galen

❧

He had a perfectly orderly life…

William, the sixth Duke of Pelham, enjoys his punctual, securely structured life. Orderly and predictable—that's the way he likes it. But he's in the public eye, and the scandal sheets will make up anything to sell papers. When the gossips link him to Juliette, one of the most beautiful and celebrated courtesans in London, chaos doesn't begin to describe what happens next…

Until she came along…

Juliette is nicknamed the Duchess of Dalliance, and has the cream of the nobility at her beck and call. It's seriously disruptive to have the duke who's the biggest catch on the Marriage Mart scaring her other suitors away. Then she discovers William's darkest secret and decides what he needs in his life is the kind of excitement only she can provide…

❧

For more Shana Galen, visit:

www.sourcebooks.com

About the Author

Once Again a Bride is a brand-new Regency romance from bestselling author Jane Ashford. Jane discovered Georgette Heyer in junior high school and was captivated by the glittering world and witty language of Regency England. That delight led her to study English literature and travel widely in Britain and Europe. Her historical and contemporary romances have been published in Sweden, Italy, England, Denmark, France, Russia, Latvia, and Spain, as well as the United States. Jane has been nominated for a Career Achievement Award by *RT Book Reviews*. Born in Ohio, Jane currently lives in Boston.